Navel of the Sea

Elizabeth McKague

Savant Books and Publications
Honolulu, HI, USA
2019

Published in the USA by Savant Books and Publications
2630 Kapiolani Blvd #1601
Honolulu, HI 96826
http://www.savantbooksandpublications.com

Printed in the USA

Edited by Sabrina Favors
Cover Image by Justine Lucas-McKague
Cover by Daniel S. Janik

13 digit ISBN/EAN: 9780999463314

First Edition: January 2019
Library of Congress Control Number: 2018965188

Dedication

To Romain and Justine, and in memory of my father.

Acknowledgements

Special thanks to Kenneth Wilkes, Charles Palau, Duncan McNaughton and Jean Tosto.

I

Gozo, Italy

Present

An invisible breath killed the flickering flame.

"Claude? Claude!" cried Marianne. "My candle went out!"

A tall, lean man of sixty years slowly got out of his chair and casually crossed the threshold from his study into hers. Her voice rang out in frustration rather than fear.

She listened to the floorboards whine beneath his slippers. The sea outside was whistling. A ginger moon rose above a patch of night clouds sending a faint shaft of eerie light through the open window beside her desk, dividing the darkness.

Claude struck a match and lit the candle. "You know, my dear, that if you used your laptop like everyone else on the planet…"

"Go on. I'm not done yet." Marianne cut him off as she picked up her pen and frantically resumed scribbling across the top sheet of a stack of loose paper.

"You could write in the dark, like I do," he finished.

"That's not writing, that's typing. And it's bad for your eyes."

He leaned forward and kissed her cheek.

"Go on!" Her hand fluttered.

"Well." Claude stood erect in the moonlight. His head of thick white hair seemed to glow. "I think we should take advantage of this power outage."

"How so?" Marianne's pen boomeranged from left to right and back again across the candlelit blank space of the page like a bat in the dusk.

"We could take a blanket down to the beach."

"The beach, at this hour? It'll be filled with bonfires and teeny boppers."

"Exactly."

Marianne took off her eyeglasses and set down her pen. "You're a crazy fucker, old man."

Claude watched her smile. She was a cranky old bitch, but for all these years, she hadn't forgotten how to smile. It was her 'kiss me' smile. So he did and they set their work aside for the rest of the evening.

The next morning, the refrigerator was humming and the coffee maker crackling, its alarm set to 7 a.m., as always. The couple ate their perfect toast and took their vitamins in silence.

"Are you finished with your section?" she asked.

"Four, three, no—two more pages."

"Is it good?"

"Of course it's good!"

"Are you sure?"

"No, but I'm sure you'll tell me if it's not."

"Oh, I'm sure it's good."

"Are you?"

Marianne batted her eyelashes playfully but didn't smile.

Claude crinkled his eyebrows. "How?"

"Because mine is good, very good. Terrific actually."

"Hmm," he growled. "Who's going in to town today?"

"Obviously, since you're *finished*…"

"Almost." He left the little, round, walnut kitchen table and went upstairs. When he came back down, dressed smartly in a peach-colored linen shirt, black shorts and tan leather sandals, Marianne had the kitchen tidy and was already seated at her desk, the pen in her hand flying like a comet across the flat, blank universe before her. She was still in her sleeveless white nightgown. God bless her! Claude snickered to himself. She still had the figure of a girl.

"Don't forget the post!" she called out.

He stopped in the open doorway. "Love, that is the point now, isn't it?"

"Yes. Right." She turned to him for a second, fear, not frustration this time in her dimming old eyes, then turned back to her work. "We need tomatoes, bread, cheese—get the kind you like, I don't care, but you know I prefer goat's milk. Oh, I don't care."

Claude walked out the open front door but turned back and stood in the foyer cautiously for a moment. "What if it's not there?"

2

"The goat cheese?"

"No, the postcard."

He watched the tussles of her long hair, the burgundy dye faded on certain strands to brown and salt and pepper, shake furiously. "Then it's not there," she snapped.

Claude stepped out onto the whitewashed stone porch. "Another scorcher today, I imagine!" he called back, knowing she wouldn't reply. "Obsession," he muttered to himself. He hopped on his bicycle and made a mental note of remembering to water the bougainvillea draping the posts to the porch, and the roses out back and the ferns on the lawn.

He could not deny that the postcards had taken over their lives since they arrived on the island. Marianne decided they should go and live in "the navel of the sea," as Homer vaguely located the island of Ogygia. According to Euhemerus and Callimachus back in B.C., and convincingly confirmed by Ernle Bradford, who sailed Odysseus' route in 1964, the navel of the sea was in geographical actuality the second largest of the Maltese islands, Gozo. In honor of its mythical origins, Claude named the villa they'd purchased two years ago, *Calypso*. After all, it's what they both wanted at the time, to go into hiding together and write for the remainder of their well-lived lives.

He peddled faster, swerving around a harem of plump, stupid chickens aimlessly conglomerating in the center of the narrow dirt road. There was no reason, he thought, to die. Yet none to stay alive either, except to love his wife. But she…now, she lived for the postcards! No, no, that is inaccurate. She lived for the book and the book could not be written without the postcards. Claude had stopped wondering where the hell they came from or whether or not they were even real; whether or not he wasn't dead already and Gozo, the villa, the bougainvillea and the gorgeous Mediterranean Sea were some kind of heaven or purgatory. Even the occasional three minutes when he stuck his dick in her, and whatever else was left of pleasurable physical sensations in this simple existence—a juicy plum, a glass of scotch on the rocks, the shade of the cypress trees in an arc above him as he rode toward town—real? And so, like his wife, he'd come to believe that the only true reality was the postcards and the pages that had to be written after receiving each one. "A wager against death itself." He laughed out loud. "A damn bargain with eternity. Huh!"

The town of Xaghra was twelve kilometers from their home on the sea. He could've taken the Fiat, but desired a leisurely ride, desired time (real or not), just

3

time. For Marianne, time didn't exist outside of the book. Obsessed! Claude's mind rambled on as the bicycle wheels bubbled over the cobblestones to the village. Like the woman in that French story who falls in love with a house plant, wouldn't leave its side, became pale and wan and then one night while she is sleeping, the plant grows and grows, twisting its vines all around her and strangles her until she dies.

He locked the bike on a rack before the pink wall of the post office and went shopping in the village. "Yes, my dear wife, it appears you are preoccupied with writing and I, old Claude Renoir, am preoccupied with death."

When he returned to the Villa Calypso just past noon, he told her this thought.

She replied, "So, what's the difference?"

"Maybe there isn't one."

Her honey brown eyes, set deeper with age into their shaded sockets, yet still as alert as ever, widened as she watched him open the canvas sack he'd carried on his back.

Out of it, he took a very fine bottle of Delicata Gran Cavalier syrah wine, a jar of olives, a freshly baked loaf of *panbrioche salato*, six ripe tomatoes still on the vine, a huge cake of *caprino* goat cheese and several small balls of *gbejna*, the local sheep's milk cheese he liked so much, and set them on the kitchen counter.

"And?" Marianne picked up the tomatoes and smelled them sensually.

"No mail. Sorry."

She set the tomatoes down on the counter top so swiftly and harshly he was sure they would burst. His wife's face flushed as she sighed, "I'm going in on Monday. You obviously didn't do it properly."

"Stop it. Right now," Claude said calmly, thinking that if she continued they'd end up getting into the whole English woman marrying a French man ordeal.

"Actually, I'm driving back in today." She peered out the little kitchen window as if she could see not only the village that was a few miles away, but also every shop and street up close through the view.

"It's Saturday. The post closes at one," Claude almost whispered.

"Then I'll just make it, won't I?" She grabbed the car keys from the little porcelain dish by the front door, always open, and rushed out.

When she returned, Claude was watering the yard. She walked past him in a flurry, a whirlpool, a goddamn tornado, too flustered even to be upset by the spray of the hose soaking her wet.

No postcard.

The afternoon passed with the two of them working quietly in their separate studies. At six, Marianne made an early supper and they opened the wine on the veranda at the back of the villa, overlooking the sea.

"Tomorrow is Sunday." Her weary voice was blushed by the sound of the close, constant waves.

"So, we'll take a break. Drive up to the cliffs…"

"Oh, for Christ's sake! How long does it take a postcard to reach the navel of the sea from another bloody century?"

Claude scratched the back of his head. "I'm thinking a Renaissance gig."

"No, no, the Byzantine era, or perhaps something around the time of the burning library in Alexandria. Now, that would be exciting!"

"The Neolithic period."

"Oh, that would be something, to write a love story from the mind of an ape."

"The end of the reign of Louis the Sixteenth."

"Please! Not the French Revolution. It's far too complicated."

"The Vikings."

Marianne shook her head and sipped the blood red wine. "You know, what I'd prefer is some obscure, medieval German village. The dark ages, yes, that would do."

Claude pondered the seascape then turned back to her and blurted out, "San Francisco in 1967."

"What a joke that would be, huh? You were sixteen and I was eight, *man*!"

They burst out laughing. The sun was setting and the violet twilight brought forth a coolness rising up off the deserted shore that they savored silently together for some time.

"So, are you finished yet?" Marianne stood, gathering the dinner plates.

"One more page."

"I meant with the tomatoes."

She'd sliced them and mixed them with olive oil and fresh basil torn from their own little garden. The dish was so delicious, neither dared to finish it.

"Save them, I'll eat them for breakfast," he told her, wanting her.

And she knew that, so she kissed him.

5

Elizabeth McKague

II

La Belle Epoque
Paris, 1890

Solange wanted a lover, a real lover. Desperately, she needed a lover. It was requisite to her profession, her fine appearance, 40 years of age, and her life in Paris. An actress without a lover became fodder for gossip in the Faubourg salons. Granted, after each performance, the men lined up at her dressing room door backstage, top hats held before their waistcoats and bouquets of roses thrust forward in shaking, lavender leather gloved hands. But so far, none of them had the kind of genuineness she knew she needed from a man. A man she could, with all her heart, truly love.

"You must receive some of them," her manager shouted. "Where do you think your fame comes from anyway, luck?" he mocked.

"I'm a good actress, Theodore."

"Bah! Talent has nothing to do with this business. This is *Le fin de siècle*, madame, the end of the century: actress equals mistress and this is the Theatre des Varieties, not the opera. You are Solange Debruier, not Marguerite Bresil and certainly not Sarah Bernhardt."

She spun around in her pink satin robe to glare at him, the kerchief in her hand stained with lipstick and rouge.

Theodore sighed. "How beautiful you are, plain like that, like someone from the Bible."

Solange threw the kerchief at him. "You are a cruel man and I detest you with all my heart. Now…let them in. A journalist or a banker or someone of that sort to further my career, but no dandies! All day rehearsing and three hours on stage and still you keep me working."

Theodore kissed her auburn hair. "There, there, my treasure. You'll thank me when your rent is due for that posh little flat you cherish on the Quai de Conti." Theo stabbed a bottle of champagne into an ice bucket and, with bloodhound anticipation, opened the door.

The actress cringed and assumed her second role for the evening, taking flowers in her satin robe with her wavy hair down from eleven until midnight. After that, she'd change into her sleeveless blue cuirass dress if she had accepted an invitation to Café Flore in St. Germain des Pres, her white cotton batiste dress if off to a party on the Champs Elysses, her black lace gown for a late supper at Laperouse on the Quai des Grand Augustins, or if offered a luxurious dinner at Closerie de Lilas in Montparnasse, she'd put on her magenta bustle dress with the bateau neck line and fish tail train. One place or another, it was all the same to her where she went, because even though surrounded by admirers, she would be alone with nothing save her longing for a genuine lover.

A short, bald, fat man entered her dressing room. He had a face like an onion and a nose like potato. Solange accepted his bouquet of yellow roses and pretended to be amused. Next, in came a tall man, thin as a knife with waxy hair black as Le Seine at midnight, and coal eyes set so widely apart it was as if one lived on the left bank and the other on the right. He carried a single red rose. His name was Jean-Pierre, the type of generic name she abhorred, and his sharp, angular gestures as he tried to contain himself from groping her behind caused the actress to feign a headache and furtively beg Theo to throw him out.

"What was that all about?" her manager growled. "Jean-Pierre is one of the top journalists for *La Figaro*!"

"Didn't you see? He was preparing to carve me up like a Christmas roast."

Theo poured her a glass of champagne. "Alright, alright, calm down. One more, eh? Oh and here..." He handed her a card. "The owner of the Delaville restaurant has reserved a table for you."

Solange sipped the bubbly wine. "Really? Oh, how scrumptious! Very well, last one. I suppose we should get another paper man in here."

A strikingly handsome young man of medium height with soft blond curls in a frame around his face of gentle features came in. He was impeccably and fashionably dressed but in clothes that showed a great effort to hide severe wear. His ungloved hands, thin and delicate almost like a girl's, were empty.

"Uh, the flowers, Monsieur?" Theo whispered into his ear.

"I forgot them."

Theo gasped.

The man sat in a chair opposite Solange's make-up table, crossed his legs and spoke while staring directly into the actress's sapphire blue eyes. "Actually, I had two dozen red roses, but I gave them away, one by one, spontaneously, out of charity."

Solange laughed and held out her hand. The young man kissed it. Theo advanced but she shooed him off. Her visitor took out an inkwell, pen and book. "So, how long have you been an actress?"

"Twenty four years. One for each abandoned rose." Solange blushed and sipped from her glass. "Would you like some champagne?"

"Yes. Thank you. And where did you grow up?"

"In the south, the Languedoc region."

"And where was your first appearance on a stage?"

"The Cabaret Voltaire. But my dear, these questions have already been asked and answered a thousand times. Every journal knows my story already. You must be new to the field?"

"Oh, it's not my field. I'm not a reporter." The handsome fellow set down his writing tools. "I'm just curious."

"But why?" the manager barked. "You must be working for that scoundrel over at the Theatre Imperial du Chatelet!"

"Calm, calm, Monsieur." The young man nodded at Solange as he now returned the glass of champagne she had offered him. "I am not a spy and neither am I here for the reasons that bring these other gentleman into that long hallway outside your door. I am a lover of the dramatic arts, a playwright taking liberties. Excuse me." He stood ready to take his leave.

"Wait!" Solange rose, tightening the ribbon around the waist of her pink robe.

"Would you give me the pleasure of joining me for dinner tonight at the restaurant Delaville?"

His lips quivered. "The…on the Boulevard de Bonne Nouvelle?"

"Yes. At midnight."

The playwright bowed, accepting.

He was waiting at the bar when the actress paraded through the frosted glass double doors at a quarter past twelve. She wore her sleeveless blue gown as its cut allowed for a respectable amount of cleavage and her fiery hair was done up to show the radiant complexion of her middle-aged beauty. All heads turned as she entered the restaurant. Theodore miserably let go of her bare arm as she

9

stepped over to the bar to greet her new friend.

"I've yet to learn your name," she said.

"Abélard."

"Like the twelfth century priest?"

"Yes, but thankfully not so unfortunate."

She laughed shyly, familiar with the story of Peter Abelard's punishment for falling in love with Heloise.

Theo interrupted the dreamy eyed artists. "Our table is ready."

Abélard hesitated and Solange understood why. "Come, I've invited you."

Embarrassed, the playwright drank little wine and ate like a bird. Yet the conversation between Solange and her new young admirer flowed without a pause, and she found herself enticed as if by a spell by his candid wit and natural charm whilst Theo sat stuffing his face and sulking until two in the morning.

"I've had a lovely time," Solange told the playwright as he waited with her for a cab on the street outside. The warm June air had become brisk and he placed his well-worn tailcoat over her shoulders. For ten minutes they waited in silence, lost in the close proximity of their warm bodies standing on the sidewalk, side by side. Her cab arrived.

"Please do come to the theatre again tomorrow night." Solange returned his coat. The same look of anxiety crossed his demeanor and she again guessed the cause of his hesitancy. "I'll leave a guest pass at the box office!" she called out as the horses trotted off, carrying her charismatic profile in the carriage window away.

Abélard did not show up the following evening. Solange didn't believe it at first but Theo brought his unclaimed ticket backstage to prove it to her. The actress felt so humiliated that she refused an invitation to dine at the Count de Malreaux's mansion on the Boulevard de Courcelles, yet at the last minute, coaxed by her rapacious manager, changed her mind and appeared in black lace, adorned.

For a month there was no sign of the mysterious, attractive playwright, but he did not leave her mind. At times she found herself worrying almost to the point of illness. "What if he's starving or homeless? What if that very night we met he was stabbed by a thief or run down by a four-horse carriage?" Her infatuation with young Abelard consumed her spirit fire and she had no reservations about expressing her emotions in all their intensity.

The other actresses at the Theatre Varieties consistently consoled her, and

Theo did his utmost to keep her physical and mental condition at balance so she could finish the season without a tragic breakdown, for he saw that dark well of artistic insecurity filling up inside her. At one moment she was so melancholy that he felt that if he could, he would weep for her. Then in an hour she'd become as amiable and delightful as ever, only to transform from the prodigal princess into a wicked witch, demanding of everyone and everything around her. Her mood swings would have been intolerable for Theo, yet the irony was that she began to entertain her admirers without moaning one bit.

Her dressing room was crammed with vases of flowers and cigar-smoking journalists past midnight and afterwards she was off to The Arcades, cafés and restaurants along the boulevards where she'd stay, entertaining gentlemen and dilettantes alike until dawn. Theo also noticed that Solange had become more fond of wine than ever before, and in the first rays of daylight, as he put her into a cabriolet to get back to her lovely flat on the Quai de Conti, her hair would be completely undone and her gown so disheveled it sometimes appeared to have been put on right side wrong.

Still, Theo was amazed, as was her audience, for each evening from eight until half past ten, Solange would get on stage and give a performance like never before, often equal to if not better than the infamous Madame Bernhardt.

It was the last night of the season. The curtain closed upon a mirrored city of applause so brilliant it was as if all of Paris had given Solange Debruier a standing ovation from the thousand-fold chandelier lit windows lining that sleeping dragon, Le Seine. Alas, the dragon awoke that night, and from its depths brought forth the missing playwright.

"He's here," Theo told her as she removed her make-up with a cream. "He's at the end of the line."

Solange slapped on her silk robe and let down her hair. "So, bring him to the front!"

He entered her dressing room with a sad, obviously discounted bouquet of wilting pink tulips.

"Why, they're lovely." Solange brought the flowers to her lips then held them to her chest, rather than immediately passing the bouquet to Theo without a second glance or thought, as was her way. "So is that why you've kept yourself away, to save 50 centimes to buy me flowers?" She laughed, sipping champagne.

"Actually…"

"Oh, Abélard!" Now that he stood before her, the disquiets and qualms of

11

the past month disappeared. She would have knelt at his feet if her manager were not in the room.

"I did save to buy you flowers but that's not why I didn't come sooner," he said.

She sat and laid the tulips on her lap. They matched the hue of her robe precisely. "Tell me."

He hesitated to answer. His smart brown eyes rolled toward the corner where Theodore stood, blatantly eavesdropping.

Solange saw such gravity and compassion in the young man's countenance that she begged Theo to go out of the room and announce to the line-up that she was too exhausted to admit further visitors or accept invitations.

"But it's your final night! You have sixteen parties waiting for you!"

Solange was adamant. When the two were finally alone in the room, she said to Abélard, "Come to my apartment in an hour. Here is the address."

Solange escaped the mob of disappointed fans by exiting the theatre through an underground passage that opened out two blocks away onto the Rue Drouot. She disappeared alone, leaving Theo to deal with the irate crowd.

When she stepped out of a landau at the gate to her residence, he was standing right there beneath a street lamp, his brow and blond locks damp from running through two arrondissements and across Le Pont Neuf to get there. Solange unlocked the iron-gate and he followed her through a courtyard smelling heavily of hyacinth, up a dark stairwell and through a long corridor. The embers of a fire, which her maid had kept alive for her return, gave off the only light when they entered the front room of her apartment. She lit a lantern and he added wood to the fire then maneuvered the logs perfectly with an iron poker until the hearth was ablaze.

She relaxed in a wing-backed, velvet, pearl chair and he sat across from her on the divan, upholstered with embroidery of vines.

"I'd ring for refreshments but I don't want to wake my maid," she explained.

He waved it off. "The reason I didn't come to you sooner is because I was working night and day, but not for money." Abélard leaned forward and opened the same worn tailcoat that had covered her shoulders one month before and pulled out a manuscript. "Here, I've written you a play."

The actress read the title page and scanned the list of characters. "May I read it?"

"Now?" It was nearly half past one in the morning.

"Why not. Do you mind?"

"Not at all. In fact, I'm flattered."

"My young friend, I am the one who is flattered." Solange rose, saying she would prepare coffee herself, but he offered to go into the kitchen and do so. She settled back and turned the page.

By three in the morning, Solange was immersed in Act III, Scene V, and the playwright was fast asleep, slouching on the divan. She put down the manuscript only to stretch his fine frame out properly and cover him with a quilt, then read on and on.

At the brink of daybreak, the poet woke to see the actress seated across from him in her wing-backed chair, her cheeks wet with tears. He sat up and rubbed his eyes. "Madame, what is wrong?"

She smiled. "Nothing. It's beautiful, absolutely remarkable. I don't think I've ever read anything as exciting and touching in my entire career." She bit her lower lip, gazing into his tired eyes. "You're a genius."

He tried to thank her but was speechless.

Solange rose. "Oh, I am exhausted."

He stood as well. "Yes, I shall leave."

"Leave? Oh, no, please don't leave." She held out her hand. He took it and she led him into her bedroom. He turned his face away as she took off her dress and crawled into her luxurious bed in her undergarments. "Come, you should get some proper sleep now."

The playwright was about to decline as politely as possible but lost his courage upon seeing her fiery red hair spread out on the soft downy pillows and the outline of her figure beneath the freshly laundered linen sheets. He removed his jacket, vest and worn leather boots and lay beside her. She stretched her arm across his chest. "That's nice, isn't it? We'll just hold each other and sleep." She closed her eyes. He lay awake beside her for only several minutes more, listening to the pretty coos of a morning dove perched on the rail of her balcony, then they both fell into a deep slumber.

They woke at noon with arms entwined. Their fresh eyes met and the poet kissed her. Soft at first but the passion and longing quickly grew. He undressed her eagerly, touching her breasts and bottom. She skillfully tore off his clothes and stroked her slender fingers across the few hairs on his chest. His hands caressed her whole body and decided to dwell in the precious flesh between her thighs. She grasped his thin hips. They kissed and kissed and Abélard, mounting the actress, let her guide him inside her, so lavish their lips and taut his limbs, and perfect her curves.

Solange screamed in ecstasy and the poet let out a rough, compelling sigh of release and pleasure.

The maid knocked on the bedroom door. "Madame, are you alright?"

Solange laughed. "I'm fine, Elise, absolutely wonderful! Please darling, make us a grand breakfast for two."

She wrapped her pink robe around her and gave him an extra robe made of green silk. The sleeves came only to below his elbows and his muscular calves spindled out from the hem that reached just below his knees.

Solange teased him happily. "You look like a leprechaun."

"A French leprechaun!" He laughed.

They drank coffee at a small table in her bedroom, set before the tall window that opened out onto a narrow balcony lined with pots of red geraniums. The sky over the Seine was a somber gray, like a fuzzy old cat. They ate with great appetites then Elise ran a full bath for the two of them where they spent an hour gazing into each other's eyes, their naked bodies pulsing in the steamy, deep water, scented with jasmine.

Abélard made love to her again and again. They slept, sent Elise to buy pâtes and oysters, drank champagne with lunch and Bordeaux with diner, fucked and laughed and talked endlessly for three whole days about *La Petite Armoire*, a new play by Abélard Philippe Tesson, starring Solange Debruier.

At dawn on the fourth morning on the Quai de Conti, Abélard kissed Solange's brow as she half-woke to the cooing dove. He was fully dressed and his tailcoat was buttoned.

"Where are you going?" Her eyelashes fluttered.

"Home."

She sat up, pouting. "Where is it that you live, my love?"

"Rue de Mezieres, in the Sixth."

"Why that's a deplorable district."

The poet shrugged. "We starving artists stick together."

"Bosh! I suppose you have a single room with a coal burning stove, a mattress stuffed with straw, one chair, one table and a leaky roof."

"I do. But it's not that bad. It's the life I'm used to."

She tugged at the lapel of his jacket. "And this, I assume, is the extent of your wardrobe?"

"They are fine clothes."

"Fine but threadbare." She sat up and rang for Elise to serve coffee and croissants.

"I really must be getting back now," he stated sternly.

"Back to what? A crust of bread and an oily faced old landlady? No, no. You are moving in with me."

"In here?"

"Of course, unless you prefer a loft in Montmartre or a second floor flat facing the Parc Monceau. We could move if you like, but I have become rather fond of my balcony."

"Solange..."

"Abélard."

"You are too kind. All of this has happened so suddenly. I must continue to write and work. I must try to find a producer who is willing to stage my play."

"Well, we know all that, don't we? And all will be so much easier if you sleep in a real bed and have at least two decent meals a day."

Elise came in and set the *petit déjeuner* on the small table by the window. Solange put on her robe and poured the coffee. "So, after breakfast we'll go to the Place de Clichy and get you fitted for a new suit. The tailors there are the most fashionable..."

"Solange..."

"Then after a stroll through the Tuileries, we can lunch at Le Procope. It's where all the famous artists gather and darling, you've yet to taste their truffles! After that we'll take your play to Theo and have him line up appointments for you. I was thinking when I read it that the Montparnasse Theatre would be quite suitable, but of course, the Odeon would be ideal." She held a cup out to him.

"Solange, please." He refused the coffee. "I must leave. Listen, the past three days and nights have been like a dream for me, you must know that my dear, dear lady. But I am sensitive and I need a few days of solitude to make sense of it all in my soul. I'm sure you can understand."

"A few days, is that all?"

He kissed the actress on the cheek. "I'll try to return by Saturday."

"Try?" She sulked. "Very well, but not here. Meet me at Le Procope on Saturday at eight o'clock. That way, if you don't come, I can drown my sorrows in company."

On Saturday evening, Solange waited alone for her lover at a table set right inside the entrance to the café. By nine o'clock, Theo joined her. By ten, five tables had been pushed together and she was surrounded by reputable critics, actors, painters and writers, including Emile Zola and Victorien Sardou. By eleven, empty and half-empty bottles of wine towered above the plates of remaining fois gras and caviar that were mapping out the surface of the tabletops, and everyone was lit up by the carefree ambiance of the company. All but Solange, who sat with her eyes upon the door, waiting.

By midnight she was tired, drunk and depressed. Theo brought her home and although she hoped with every nerve in her body that her poet would be standing there beneath the lamppost, he was not.

On Sunday, she dressed in black velvet and hailed a barouche to the Rue de Mezieres.

"Are you sure you have the correct address, Madame?" asked the driver, knowing it was one of the most sordid streets in Paris.

"Yes. Drive on, please."

She got out and stepped in a mud puddle. A blind beggar was at her feet, banging on his empty tin cup with a spoon. She let a few copper coins fall from her hand and watched him grow silent as they rattled in the tin. She lifted her skirt and knocked at the first filthy tenement house. A putrid-smelling man in soiled shirtsleeves answered, salivating. He didn't know a Monsieur Tesson. Neither did the emaciated sculptor next door, nor the withered old concierge at the hotel across the street. The lovesick heroine dragged herself from door to door far into the afternoon, until her knuckles were red from knocking and her ankles sore from skipping over puddles and skirting around the mangled arms and legs of bums, rotting clumps of garbage at the edge of gutters, or plop in the center of the lane, horse dung.

Finally, she noticed a young woman dressed in a neat blue frock, with her hair done up properly and wearing clean white gloves, come out of a building across from one of the neighborhood's seedy cafés.

Solange approached her. "Excuse me. Mademoiselle, I'm looking for someone who resides in this district, a Monsieur Tesson. Do you know him?"

The young girl was quite startled, whether because of the playwright's name or the actress's opulent attire, Solange couldn't tell.

"Abélard? You want Abélard?"

"Oh, yes, I do, very much in fact, with incredible desire, want Abélard."

Her spirits lifting, Solange burst into laughter.

This frightened the girl and she began to move quickly away.

"Please, wait, my dear. I am fatigued from my search. Tell me, do you know him?"

The girl hesitated. "Can we go in there?" She pointed to the cruddy café across the way.

"Oh, yes, let's. I'll buy you a tea."

"And a sandwich?"

"A sandwich and a tea. Shall we?"

Her name was Clotilde. She was Abélard's sweetheart.

"We have not spoken to each other for the past week, except on one occasion. We used to dine at this café together every Sunday and share a glass of the house wine. I've been waiting for him to propose to me."

"Propose!" Solange was not a good actress in that moment.

"I am a virgin, Madame. I am poor, but I have my scruples."

"Of course you do."

"I live with my mother. She has the consumption, the poor dear. I work as a seamstress by day and as a cashier for the lottery at night. For six months, Abélard and I have only had the afternoon on Sundays to meet and be together..." Clotilde burst into tears. Her sandwich was served. The desperate creature wiped her eyes, took off her gloves and ate ravenously.

"He is...fond of you, then?" Solange, her natural pride and ambition returning, boldly asked.

"I thought so, I truly did. But I was a fool. I believed he respected me. You see, he disappeared for three days and when he returned, I met him in the street and he...he wanted to, he asked me to..." She burst into tears again and nearly choked on her last bite of soggy ham.

"Shh. Shh." Solange put her soft hand over the coarse skin of Clotilde's as the younger woman wept.

A drunkard in the street outside was shouting obscenities and at the same moment, the bartender of the café simultaneously dropped a teakettle and cursed wildly. The few decrepit men at the bar began to roar over their drafts of beer and for a moment, Solange thought she might faint because of the depravity of the scene.

When all had settled, the actress asked, "And you haven't seen him since?"

"No. His room is empty. I've knocked a hundred times. His landlady told me he's gone to Languedoc-Roussilon to visit his sister."

"Where in the Languedoc?"

"Goudargues. He spoke of her once, Antoinette is her name."

"Antoinette Tesson, in Goudargues..." Solange's mind reeled. The dismal light in the café lifted and she saw a summer's day, apple trees, haystacks and golden fields. Antoinette used to be her best friend. They'd hold hands and sing as they walked along the sleepy country roads in the still of the heat or gossip about neighboring farmers' sons as their bare legs dangled off of rocks into the cool stream, pick cherries and boysenberries to make jam in the Tesson family's kitchen, play with the new litter of kittens just born in the barn, giggle and dance and pretend that they were great actresses, using the door to the coal cellar on the ground in the backyard for a stage. And all the while, they had a shadow. Antoinette's little brother, ten years younger, following them everywhere, watching them with glee.

He'd applaud at their made-up plays, make a mess with the berries in the kitchen, and wade out into the stream, trying to catch tadpoles with his hands. Solange, an only child, adored the boy. He was like a pet to the two teenage girls. When Solange was sixteen, her father, who had raised her alone, passed away and she was sent to Paris to live with a cantankerous old aunt. Solange wanted the world and was overwhelmed by the metropolis. She was young, beautiful and brave. She made friends in the cafés and began to dance and sing in small cabarets. Theo discovered her a few years later and made her a star. Her rise to fame, the radiance of Paris, all that hard work and especially changing her birth name from Lebruie to Debruier had obliterated her memories of childhood. After her Papa died, what was there to look back upon?

And now, in that miserable pub on the Rue de Mezieres, it all came back to her; the sunshine and the meadows, blue checkered tablecloths and white cotton frocks, the kittens, the cellar door, her dear friend Antoinette and that darling little rascal of a brother, named Abélard Tesson.

"Madame, Madame!" Both the bartender and Clotilde were calling to her. She came back to the present moment. The check needed to be paid.

Solange walked with Clotilde to the Place St. Sulpice at the edge of that lamentable district where she waited to flag down a cab.

Before Clotilde walked on to the seamstress shop, she asked, "Why are you looking for him anyway?"

Solange smiled at the girl, took out her purse and placed a gold Napoleon in her white-gloved hand. "That is for your mother's health. Now, take care."

They kissed each other's cheeks, Clotilde's wet once again with tears.

That night, Solange found Theo with Sardou at Le Procope. She asked to speak with him in private and told him all that had happened, about the play, the lovemaking and the haystacks.

He was reluctant at first about her intended voyage as rehearsals for the next season began in two weeks, yet finally gave in and promised to bring her the following morning to the Embarcadere des Batignolles to catch a train.

Solange's memories of the Languedoc flooded through every moment that disappeared all the way from the Gare St. Lazare to her final destination in the Provinces. Madame Tesson, Antoinette and Abélard's mother, remembered Solange and greeted her affectionately. The actress was thankful, yet dare not tell the old farm lady that she had fallen in love with her son. Antoinette had married the local notary and moved into the quaint little village close by. Solange knocked on the door of a tall stone townhouse in Gourdagues with trepidation. She had no excuse for not writing to her dear friend for twenty-four years, and to show up now because of cruel love…it was outlandish indeed!

Abélard himself answered the door and she fell with a faint in his arms. The journey, and even more so the memories, had worn her out. He brought her inside and laid her on the sofa in the salon. Antoinette used smelling salts to bring her to consciousness. Solange sat up in shock and put her fingers through her mussed up hair. She was speechless.

Abélard consoled her. "It's okay. I have told my sister everything. I came here…as I said, I needed time to make sense of it all. You see, on that fourth morning, I looked at you while you were sleeping and my love, you looked sixteen! And I realized who you were. I remembered it all and grew frightened. And I ran, like a child, I ran."

"And now, is there sense to this, to us?" Solange pleaded.

"All I know is that I love you," he said very softly, shyly.

Solange wept tears of pain and joy. "*Moi aussi, mon amour, moi aussi!*"

"I think it's beautiful," said Antoinette. "Like a fairy story."

"But what about Clotilde?" Solange asked, admitting, "I met her when I was searching for you."

He was surprised. "You really have gone searching for me, my darling, haven't you? To be honest, she was not more than a friend, a ray of light in that depressing street, and I'm ashamed to have continued to see her, even when I became aware that she believed there was more."

Reassured, she threw herself into his arms and they kissed passionately.

They took a hotel room and stayed in Goudargues for one more week, taking long walks along the canal or in the forests of Valbonne in the late morning, sipping lemonade under the green awnings of lazy cafés in the late afternoons and in the evenings, dining with Antoinette and her reasonably cheerful husband in their townhouse, or visiting Madame Tesson on the farm for a delicious country meal. The serenity and slow-moving hours in that golden region of France was perfect for the freshly awakened passion that kept the actress and the playwright inseparable.

On the day before they were to board a train back to Paris, Solange, more out of curiosity than jealousy, for at her age she understood too well the needs of vigorous young men, confronted Abélard about a particular thing Clotilde had said.

"It's true," he confessed. "But it was not out of sheer desire that I asked her to sleep with me. As I said, she had a different idea about our relationship in her mind and although I didn't want to hurt her by telling her I'd been with you, nor cowardly abandon or ignore her, I couldn't find the words or actions to break it off with her, for she is so simple, so pure. Perhaps it was a cruel thing to do but I knew that if I were to give her the impression, which is obviously true, that I'm not the saint she thought me to be, that I was 'insincere,' well...I'd hoped it would make it easier for her to forget me."

"I can see your strategy, but I'm not sure it worked completely. She was very upset when we talked. Perhaps when you gather your things from Rue de Mezieres, you might try to speak with her my dear, for although she's rather high-strung, she really seems to be a nice girl."

"Gather my things?"

"Well, you don't think I could let you return to that wretched district. And I dare not imagine the longing I should suffer if I were to spend a single night in my bed without you."

He smiled and kissed her. "My things can fit in my pocket, Solange: a notebook, an ink bottle and a quill."

They were both ecstatic to return to their love nest on the Quai de Conti and for the following week resumed their luxurious, wanton Parisian ways. Solange took him to Monsieur Labac on the Avenue Trudaine where he was fitted for two suits of the latest fashion in the finest fabrics available, which he'd wear in the evenings when the couple went out to take a box at the Opera or the Comédie Française, before dining at a reserved table amidst the opulence of Le Grand Vefour on the Rue de Beaujolais, or amongst the elite at the restaurant Corcellet. In the mornings, he wore nothing, for they'd stay in bed until noon, tossing about while Elise was sent to Les Halles to purchase delicacies such as quail pâte in Malaga wine, *boulette d'avesnes*, *chouquettes* and of course a bottle of Duval-Leroy Grand Cru champagne. In the late afternoons, they'd stroll amongst the flowers and the statues on the wide paths of the Tuileries, follow the houseboats along the river then cross the Pont St. Michel to gaze at Notre Dame, or go shopping on the Rue de Rivoli. Solange bought him silk kerchiefs, leather bound notebooks, expensive pens, a Swiss pocket watch on a gold chain and cigars, which, after offered one by a fellow at a café in the Latin Quarter, he'd taken a liking to.

Infatuated with the teenage redhead dancing on the cellar door in the blurry memories of his early childhood who had grown into this elegant, exciting woman now clinging on his arm, Abélard allowed Solange's extravagances but not without expressing his own inner feelings of guilt.

"I don't need another cravat," he told her one day in a shop on the Rue de Rivoli.

"But this one is red; you don't have a red one yet."

"And I don't need one, either. I don't need any of this, Solange. It's starting to feel…oppressive."

She looked to the ground, insulted. He kissed her. "Listen, I love *you*, not the silks or the chocolates or tonight's amazing box seat to *Carmen*."

"I thought you liked Georges Bizet."

"He's a wonderful composer. Darling, I know you mean well, but your generosity overwhelms me. You must remember where I was living just three weeks ago: leaky roof, leaky boots, a hard-boiled egg for lunch and a wedge of cheese for dinner."

"But how could you have been happy that way?"

"Happiness was not at issue. I cared only for my work, and after I met you that first night in your dressing room, I cared only to write you a fabulous play."

"Which you did!"

"Yet…it sits upon your nightstand."

Solange took his arm as they left the shop. "Ah! That's what's bothering you. Oh, don't worry about that, with my connections you'll have it staged in no time. And when it becomes a smash hit, and Abélard Philippe Tesson is more famous than Molière, you can be the one to pay for the champagne!"

Abélard put his hands in his pockets, absently searching for the hole in his old trousers that he used to pinch when he was tense, until he remembered he was wearing the brand new black wool slacks she had bought for him the day before yesterday.

On Monday morning, when Solange left their powdery blue bedroom on the Quai de Conti to attend the first reading of a new play for the upcoming season, an unanticipated sense of extreme relief settled his beating heart. Alone, at last! He bathed, shaved, dressed in his old, worn tailcoat and went out gloveless and without a scarf. He carried ten newly printed copies of *La Petite Armoire* tucked under his arm, repressing the humiliation that the typesetting had been paid for by Solange. He went to the smaller theaters about town, determined to have his play produced without his lover's connections or interference. It was a matter of pride but also of proving himself worthy solely upon the merit of his work. Alas, because he was nobody, an interview with producers or directors was not granted, but he was able to charm the pretty secretaries and leave copies of the manuscript in managerial offices for a possible review.

At six o'clock, with the last printed text rolled up in his hand, on his way to a new experimental venue near La Sorbonne, he ran into his old friend Balthazar, a painter who lived on the first floor of his old tenement building on the Rue de Mezieres. They were very happy to see each other and Balthazar invited the playwright back to his studio to share the few sausages, baguette and the cheap bottle of Cotes du Rhône he was carrying with him. Tired from being on his feet all day, Abélard accepted and felt restored in the painter's raw studio at the bare wooden table with the simple meal. He told him about Solange and the lifestyle he'd been leading, the sensual sex-crazed mornings, the dove on the balcony overlooking the Quai, the silk cravats, restaurants and box seats, yet without bragging in any way. But Balthazar noticed that his friend seemed melancholy.

Balthazar furrowed his black, bushy eyebrows. "Do you love her?"

"I do, immensely. Yet her enthusiasm is exhausting!"

The painter laughed. "Then I suppose it's true what they say about actresses!"

Abélard had to laugh also. "I do love her. I guess I should stop complaining and try to get used to it all."

His friend sneered. "Why, of course I do see your point. Ah! The moral dilemma involved in choosing between *une tarte de pommes* or *une gâteau chocolat* after the *boeuf bourguignon*."

Abélard sat quietly for a moment, staring beyond the single flames of two candles at the half-finished canvases on easels in the shadowy corners of the studio. "She spoils me and the irony is that here I am, returning her generosity by whining like a brat."

The painter, a big, burly fellow with a thick black beard, sighed, perceptive and honest as a child. "She's older than you?"

"By ten years."

"You are her pet, my boy, her little kitten. I'm sure she adores you but her embellishment and nurturing instincts are smothering your masculinity."

The playwright finished his glass of wine. The bottle was empty, the thin sausages eaten. He sat up gracefully and puffed out his chest. "Listen, Zahar, I've got twenty francs in my pocket. Let's go out for a real dinner, shall we?"

The painter's eye lit up, then immediately dimmed like the teardrop shaped, flickering candle flame before him. "We shall, my friend. But first I must show you something."

He rose with the candle in his hand and his friend followed. Before the light came even close to the canvas, Abélard recognized the model in the painting of a woman reclining on her side upon a red velvet cloth, completely nude. It was Clotilde.

"Zahar!" the poet gasped. "But how…she is…so virtuous."

"Was so virtuous." The artist shrugged. "Your last request affected her. She's become, well, let's say, more agreeable." He paused as his friend gazed at the beautiful, youthful, white limbs, belly and breast in the painting. "Antoine, too," he added.

"The sculptor?"

Balthazar nodded.

"And?"

"No, I haven't slept with her. She has been coming here to pose the past few Sundays and I pay her two francs an hour."

"And Antoine?"

"I don't know. Maybe. You know how he has 'a way' with women."

"I've ruined her!" cried Abélard.

"Nonsense. I swear, out of all of us, you writers certainly are the most self-centered. Don't give yourself such importance, my friend. Clotilde's mother

23

died a fortnight ago. Somehow she'd received 100 francs in a Napoleon coin around the same time, so she quit her night job and is trying to set up her own drapery shop. I believe it was her mother's death and not the fanatical religious devotion she had to *you* that freed her."

"Freed her." Abélard repeated the phrase. Questions of morality, liberty, masculinity and the nature of the female spirit began to dance on the stage in his mind like characters in a traveling medieval play. He burst out laughing, slapped the Herculean painter on the back and whisked him off to Le Procope, where they sat at a small table across the room from a celebrating group of painters including Edouard Vuillard, Pierre Bonnard and Armand Guillaumin, who had just won 100 francs in the lottery.

At eight o'clock, Solange whirled through the door on Theo's arm in a new, sea green dress and went straight to the animated circle of artists. Although the playwright saw her instantly, he didn't move and continued to discuss the age of Impressionism with his dark friend.

After twenty minutes, she saw her lover and dashed across the narrow room. "Why darling, you're here!"

"I am."

"You must join us. I've been waiting for a moment like this. Come, I'll introduce you to everyone."

The starving artists did not resist, and the established party welcomed their presence with genuine mirth. By ten o'clock, Balthazar's ideas about chiaroscuro had Vuillard in awe and Abélard's vision of a symbolist stage set design had Bonnard leaning forward with his elbows on the table. The enlightened bunch remained lively past midnight. Solange was in her element and Theo, picking at his plate of lobster, felt like a distant God.

Toward the end of the night, Abélard departed with Solange, leaving Balthazar in the other artists' company. The lovers walked the deserted, early morning streets to the Quai de Conti in silence, an exhausted, pleasing silence as soft as the dark blue sky sleeping on the moonlit, gray slate rooftops.

The comfortable silence remained until the next morning, when Solange asked him, "What will you do today?" as she dressed for rehearsal.

"Same thing I did yesterday, visit the theaters with copies of my play."

"But darling, there's no need. Theo has already spoken to Francois Daudet. Oh, in last night's excitement, I forgot to tell you. He's willing to stage your play at the Menilmontant!"

"The theatre on the Rue Boyer?"

"Yes. Isn't it wonderful?"

"But has Monsieur Daudet even read it?"

"Not yet. Thank you for reminding me. I must bring him a copy this afternoon."

"How can he agree to direct it if…Listen, Solange, I'll bring the copy."

"As you like. Just make sure he knows I've sent you." She twisted her long, wavy, blood orange hair atop her head and pinned it up with Japanese combs. "I was thinking that tonight we might dine at the café Zephyr in Montmartre or would you prefer Le…" She stopped, seeing his expression past her own image in the mirror. "Darling, what is wrong?"

Her lover sighed as he came up behind her and kissed her neck. "Nothing. Everything is perfect. The café Zephyr is fine."

"Good." She placed two 20-franc notes on the little table by the window where they'd shared so many intimate breakfasts. "Here, you can hire a *barouche* and pick me up at seven." Then she kissed him and left the flat in a state of exhilaration.

He left shortly afterwards and returned to all the theaters he'd visited the day before. Out of nine, seven had reviewed his work, or claimed that they had, and rejected him. The other two said they would know by Friday. He went to the Rue Boyer and walked up and down the street before the grand theatre Menilmontant for nearly an hour, torturing himself with confusion between his desire for recognition as a dramatist and the humiliation of having his play staged, not because of its own merit, but because Francois Daudet obviously owed Solange a favor. What that favor was in return for, he could not bear to imagine.

At last he turned the corner and, without knowing where he was going, ran for several blocks, his blond curls flowing behind his ears and the returned manuscripts flapping at his side in his angry, quickly moving arms. He soon found himself on the grounds of the Cimetiere du Pere Lachaise and took refuge for several hours strolling amongst the cool, stony graves. At five o'clock, he took an omnibus to Theatre Bravade, the experimental venue he'd missed yesterday. The pretty secretary asked him to have a seat and returned, to his amazement, saying, "Monsieur Ropellier will see you now."

Abélard gave the seemingly earnest and open-minded director a verbal outline of *Le Petite Armoire*, and answered a few questions about his present situation in Paris and own modest background. The playwright avoided mentioning his relationship with Solange and gave Balthazar's address on the Rue Mezieres as his own. He felt uneasy about bending the truth a bit, but it was far better than getting his play produced because of a favor. Monsieur Ropellier expressed interest and told Abélard to check back in on Friday.

With his spirits uplifted, he walked to Rue Bonaparte planning to hire a *barouche* and meet his lover for a romantic dinner. Yet when the bells of St. Sulpice rang out six times he realized that the meeting with Ropellier hadn't lasted as long as he'd believed. With time to spare, he took an outside table at a Brasserie and ordered a bière. At that hour the square, bustling with people, was entertaining enough and he ceased to think of work or love, content to sip the bitter ale and simply watch. His eyes locked upon the dainty figure of a young woman in a dark blue dress and white gloves. As she moved closer he saw her face, like a porcelain doll's. It was Clotilde. He started to turn his chair to face the other direction but it was too late, for there she stood before his little table, blushing with spunk.

"Bonsoir Abélard."

"Bonsoir Clotilde."

They stared at each other with unease for what seemed to him to be moments lasting far beyond the imagined length of his interview at the Theatre Bravade.

"May I join you?" she finally spoke.

"Of course, please." He called the waiter. She ordered the same as he was having.

"You drink beer now?" He was somewhat appalled.

"The champagne here isn't very good."

His brow wrinkled and he leaned forward. "What has happened to you, Clotilde?"

"I'm changed."

"I can see that." He downed his beer and annoyed the waiter by ordering another as the second drink was brought to the table.

"You've changed too."

"Have I? How so?"

She sipped the froth at the top of the glass. "You look sad."

"Was I so happy before?"

"I don't know if you were happy but you certainly weren't sad."

He changed the subject. "I saw Balthazar's painting."

"He's a fine painter."

"I've yet to see Antoine's sculpture."

"It's far from finished."

"Really? How long until…"

"Weeks, months, maybe years."

He nodded. "I see. And does he make you happy, Antoine?"

She drank with thirst. "Well, he doesn't make me glum."

The bells of St. Sulpice chimed seven times. "I must be off." He stood.

"But you've just ordered."

"I'm late." He threw some coins on the table. "Take care of yourself, Clotilde."

She immediately gathered up the change into a neat little pile with the palm of her hand. "Oh, don't you worry, I will."

"I do worry. Don't think otherwise. I did care about you." He saw a cab approaching and waved it down. "I never meant to insult you."

She looked the other way and he hurried off.

Solange climbed into the hired cab when it pulled up before the Theatre Varieties. "Montmartre!" she called to the driver then turned to her lover. "It's nearly half past seven, and what is this single horse contraption? Where's the barouche and what, *what* are you wearing?"

He'd forgotten that he had gone out that morning in his old, tattered suit and in the afternoon's progression, failed to return to the flat to change.

"Agh!" She called to the driver once more, "No. First we must stop on the Quai de Conti, number three-twenty-one, please."

"I'm sorry," was all he could say.

"Sorry! What has happened?"

"Nothing. I forgot to change and I was running late, so…"

"Running late from what? The only thing you had to do today was go to the Menilmontant Theatre and hand over a few pages."

"A few pages. That's all it is to you, a few pages?" he shook the rejected manuscripts violently in his bare hands.

"Alright. Enough." Solange sighed as the driver stopped before the iron gate. "I'll wait here. The cab will have to do, but be quick, we have a reservation for eight o'clock."

Abélard rubbed the slight beard that he had decided to start growing on his chin. "I don't need to change."

"But of course you do!"

"I'm not even hungry."

"Well, I'm famished."

"Then go on without me."

"By myself? To dine?"

"Pick up Theo or…or…Francois Daudet!" He jumped out of the cab and Solange, outraged, watched him pass the iron gate, turn down the Rue Dauphine and disappear into a mist rising from the river.

"The Theatre Menilmontant!" she called to the driver, who quickly pulled away.

Abélard hopped on an omnibus and went to Balthazar's. The painter was just on his way out. "To a party at Antoine's," he said. "Come along. But I think Clotilde might be there."

"I'm sure she will be. I spoke with her in the Place St. Sulpice just an hour ago. It appears the seamstress and the sculpture have become quite a pair."

"So, best to them!" Balthazar grabbed a bottle of cheap wine from a shelf by the door. "Shall we?"

"Yes, but leave that here." Abélard took out his wallet. The forty francs Solange had left him earlier were still folded inside it. "We're going to make this a party that the Rue Mezieres shall remember!"

The two men went into a fromagerie and bought enormous rounds of camembert, brie and chèvre then stopped in a boulangerie and ordered a dozen fresh baquettes, bought four roasted chickens at a boucherie, fresh pears from a fruit stall and as many bottles of wine and champagne that they could carry. The sculptor was amazed when he opened the door and saw his friends loaded down with satchels. The painters, Richard and Luis, poets Michel and Jean-Jacques, the novelist Stephanie, musicians Roland and Paul, and besides Clotilde, several other attractive girls, mostly artists or students, were mingling about amongst the giant, half-chiseled statues and blocks of marble towering in the high-roofed studio. All were so surprised by the sudden abundance of food and drink that they cleared Antoine's tools off of a long wooden worktable and covered it with a clean white drop cloth. The girls ran outside and picked flowers from a little park then returned to light every candle from Antoine's cupboard and decorate the table for their feast. The happy company ate and drank. The boys flirted with the girls and after the banquet, Roland played his violin, Paul played his flute, and the party danced, sang, improvised plays and kept the wine flowing until daybreak.

One girl, a student at the University of Paris, whose eyes had intermittently been batting at the playwright throughout the entire three hours they were at table, approached him when the music started and he asked her to dance. Yet however much he wanted to and however young and quite sexy she truly was, he could not find it in his heart to desire her the way she led on that she wanted him to. As the night progressed, most of the men and women at the party were pairing off, but Abélard remained on his own. He directed the silly skits, composed poems with Michel, whose arms were around a pretty actress, and by four in the morning had picked up Roland's violin, although he could not play worth a sous. He got drunk and had fun, much more fun than he'd ever had with Solange, sitting at the best table in a posh restaurant or even conversing with the famous artists of her Le Procope entourage. Yet deep down, he could feel that she was missing.

The painter and the playwright wavered, their arms around each other's shoulders as the soft gray-violet light, that specialty of Parisian mornings, lit their way back to Balthazar's studio. And as he lay on the red velvet drape his friend had laid out for him on the floor, Abélard closed his eyes and heard Solange sighing, those sweet sighs of ecstasy that were in essence a product of his creation. Those sighs of hers, in a voice so pure in emotion, so talented and sincere, sighs that would never reach an audience other than his ears, for they belonged only to the two of them as lovers. Her sighs, a reflection of his own private, secret whisper.

Balthazar was boiling water for coffee when Abélard woke at noon. The playwright jumped to his feet. "Did you know that there is something higher than art?"

The black-beard laughed. "Oh, this is going to be good."

"I shall never be able to write a play that comes near to the truth and beauty of her embrace."

"Do you want coffee first then or are you going to take off now to run down the Rue Bonaparte?"

Abélard smiled at his friend then ran and ran all the way to the Quai.

Elise smiled also with an expression of great relief when she let him through the door. He rushed to the bedroom and found his lover sobbing in her silky blue bed.

He kissed away her tears and sorrows, until she forgave him and they made love.

Solange ran her fingers through his hair. "I don't have to go to rehearsal today. I only have three lines in the second act," she told him.

"And three hundred in the third!" He kissed her belly.

"Yes, I suppose Musset's plays are rather unsymmetrical that way."

They laughed, spoke of poetry; of the hazy view of the river from her balcony; of his determination to succeed without her philanthropy, of the effort she would make to refrain from buying silk cravats and of their passion that they felt would never end. That evening, Solange sent Elise out to find fresh fish for a bouillabaisse and they kissed and touched and fucked all through the night until they finally fell asleep, entwined at daybreak to the dove's blue note song.

III

Gozo, Italy

Present

The bells of the Citadella St. Joseph, the crumbling, ancient provincial chapel down the road, rang at 10 a.m.

Claude and Marianne looked out in the direction of the bells from the two wicker chairs on the front porch. It was the only spot outside at that time of the morning that provided any shade. He was reading her sections of the first story and she was reading his.

"What do you think?" Marianne asked in between the tolls echoing on the air.

Claude glanced again at the sentence he had just read. "Not sure yet. I'm only on the second page."

"You need new glasses, I keep telling you." She shifted in her chair and went back to reading. She was wearing a poppy-colored peasant blouse that didn't suit her, made her look like a pumpkin.

The peal of the rusty, medieval bells sailed past their modest villa toward the sea. "You never go to mass anymore," Claude said, somewhat aggressively.

"Mass!"

"You were devout when we met."

"I was never devout. I went to church to pray for a husband, and then you came along."

"You mean you never believed in God?"

Her eyes remained lowered onto the manuscript in her lap. "Oh, Christ, Claude, I don't know."

"That's funny."

"Why?"

"For all these years, I thought you believed in God."

Marianne looked at him in the soft shadow of the rooftop. "What is this about, Renoir?"

"I told you yesterday...death. When a man becomes preoccupied with death, he begins to question his methods."

"Whose methods? Yours or God's?"

"Both."

"So my husband the atheist decides to believe in God because he's realized he is eventually going to die. Good for you. May you be carried to the pearly gates upon the wings of angels. Can we work now, please?"

They read and edited for another half hour. Several inches of shade had already slipped away.

"This part about running through two arrondissements, it's impossible." Claude's voice broke through the buzz of the cicadas.

"But the actress lives on the Quai de Conti and the theater is in the nineteenth."

"It's inaccurate, Marianne."

"You didn't run?"

He shook his head. "I hopped on to the back of a courier wagon."

"Then why were you dripping with sweat when I found you at the gate?"

"I ran across the bridge as fast I could. I was a horny little devil, I dashed... swish!"

"Oh. Should I change it?"

"Maybe not. It's more romantic this way."

"What if he steals a horse or something chivalrous like that?"

"Leave it, love. I'll steal a horse when and if we 'get' The Age of Chivalry."

"*Mais mon amour, vous êtes un brave chevalier histoire que je vous écris.*"

"*Et vous êtes mon princesse dans une tour.*"

"Yeah, right." She scowled. "And besides the running, dashing...?"

"Overly dramatic and unrealistic as hell, but they *are* people in the theater, so it works. Yes, it's good."

"Yours, too."

"Shall we drive to the cliffs?"

Marianne sighed. "I suppose so. It is Sunday, there's nothing else to do."

"We could fool around."

She smiled her 'kiss me' smile.

Just then they heard the purring sound of a motor and wheels driving up the lonely road to Villa Calypso. A young man in his late twenties, his chest bare above a pair of Hawaiian surfing shorts, whizzed up their driveway on a Vespa scooter. He jumped off and approached the porch.

"Hey, hi there. So, I'm renting the villa next door. Anyway, I went into Xaghra yesterday to get my mail, and the clerk gave me this by mistake." He held out an envelope. "Our boxes are right next to each other."

Claude took the envelope and looked at his wife, fearing she might fly into a rage, but to his surprise she was completely calm, her deep eyes transfixed upon the young man's physique.

"Pagolo's villa? I didn't know he was renting it out." Marianne smiled a different smile that Claude didn't recognize. It was wide and friendly but somewhat sinister and in that poppy blouse, he thought that now she looked like a jack-o-lantern.

"Just for the month of July." The young man posed, as if out of habit, his hand rested on a cocked hip. His long hair swung to one side in a sudden, soft breeze. "He had to go to Naples. Family matters, I think."

"His mother's dying," Claude added.

"You didn't tell me that," Marianne scoffed.

"I didn't think you'd care."

"Of course I…"

"Well, I'm gonna take off. Nice to meet you." The postcard deliverer took his phone out of his pocket, made a face, then put it back.

"Oh, yes. But thank you for this, thank you so much. You've no idea how important this is, how much it means to us." Marianne sort of jiggled about on her toes and her boobs bounced beneath that ridiculous orange tent.

Claude cleared his throat and turned back to the surfer. "Are you American?"

"From California, my wife and I. I'm here for the surf and she's here for the culture. Well," he said with a shrug, "You know how it is."

"Oh, I do. I certainly do," said Claude, ironically.

"New neighbors. What a delight." Marianne stretched out her wrist and introduced herself and her husband. Her wedding ring so tarnished, Claude noticed.

"I'm Dave." The tan surfer with the sculpted torso straddled his shiny white scooter. "Have a good one!"

The Renoirs watched him drive off.

Claude frowned. "Have a good one what?"

"You know, a good day, a good time. It's an American saying."

Claude put his arm around her waist, hidden there beneath that awful billowing blouse. "Have a good fuck, that's what I thought he meant."

She slapped his still considerably firm behind and ran into the house, faster than Abélard on Le Pont Neuf to open the envelope. They always arrived the same way, in a generic white envelope with an abstruse international stamp and of course, no return address.

Claude entered her study eating the leftover tomatoes straight out of a Tupperware container with a fork. "Mmm. Much better the next day, if that's even possible."

"You're right."

"Yeah? So we'll refrigerate them overnight next time."

"It's the Renaissance."

"No shit!"

"Florence. 1492."

"Hmm, the dawn of Machiavelli. Too bad the Medici's have fled, corrupt as they were, Lorenzo seemed pretty cool." Claude held a fork full out to her. "Really, you have to try this."

She waved him off and sighed. "I don't know, Clues. That period? And it's so overdone." Clues was her pet name for him. Neither of them remembered how it came about.

"But it's us," he said. "Our story, yet to be told."

"I suppose. I'm just afraid of clichés."

"Let me guess, I'm a painter."

"Nope. I am."

"I'm a fucking priest?"

"You're a model. An artist's model."

"Am I gay?"

"No, you're just a beautiful boy who's a little hard up."

"Weren't we going to fuck?"

Marianne looked at the postcard. "I have anxiety about this, Clues, I'm not sure I like it. Can't we send it back, exchange it for a time and place less... overdone?"

34

"I'm in. What's the return address?"

"You're a clown."

"Listen, let's drive to the cliffs. It will calm you down."

"No, 'Pietro', we'll do the cliffs second."

Claude then thanked the heavens, for his wife took off that absurd, Fauvist orange blouse. "*Pietro*, seriously? What about Paulo or Roberto or Michelangelo? Antonio...I like that one. Antonio."

"You were just Abélard. You can't have a name beginning with the same letter twice in a row. What about David?"

"Giocomo!" He set the empty plastic container down on her desk next to the postcard. He put his arms around his shirtless wife, leaned her against the desk and kissed her with fierce passion, true passion. Yet at the same time, he worried he was just masking his fear of death.

Afterwards, she changed into a cool, white linen tunic and grabbed the car keys from the little tray by the door. "This time, I'm going to drive."

On Monday, Marianne was still in turmoil about "the Renaissance gig." She spent the morning walking on the beach. A few surfers were riding the waves. Ideas confused by memories rushed upon the surface of her mind then receded like the tide. It would not become clear until the writing began. The last story had been easy, whipping forward like a stormy night, slashing down page after page like rain against a windowpane. But this time she was procrastinating. She needed something more than the signal of the postcard. With *Le Belle Epoque*, the vital and eternal realm of language flooded forth from her pen as if she was transcribing into verbal cries the music of waves, but this time she needed more.

One of the surfers paddled in and crossed her path with his board at his side. It was the American, Dave.

Marianne looked at his broad, bronze shoulders, hairless chest, tight abdomen and muscular thighs as he stepped out of the sea, his floral printed swimsuit clinging wet around his groin. *My God*! she thought. There it is, the personification of male youth and beauty and my model for Giocomo, or Pietro, or...

Dave was not physically different from the Italian surfers that followed him out of the water, a few of them no doubt more handsome, lithe and svelte, and of course she'd seen many young, half naked men before, but there was something about the American that for the first time in a long time awakened her libido.

"Hey," he said.

"Good morning. How's the water?"

"Awesome."

"How are things over at Pagolo's villa?"

"Cool."

"And your wife?"

"Great."

Marianne estimated that her newfound muse had a rather limited vocabulary, yet his vigor had already penetrated her curiosity, so she invited him and his wife to the Villa Calypso for dinner that evening.

"Rad." He shook drops of salt water from his shoulder-length dark hair.

"Pardon?"

"Like…that's radical."

"Three words, wow," Marianne murmured.

Dave titled his head and stuck his finger in one ear. "What?"

"I suppose it is rather radical, but we'll have a good time and a fine meal. You see, it will be nice for my husband to have some company."

"Right. Sure. Cool."

He can't even compose a complete sentence, she thought. How delicious! Clues was going to have a ball.

"So, around seven?"

Dave smiled. "Right on. Later."

Marianne ran, or rather trotted, back home, grabbed the car keys from inside the open door and drove into Xaghra without even entering the house. Claude glanced up from his desk to watch her pull out of the driveway as if she were a criminal making a get-away then peacefully went back to his typing.

He met her in the kitchen when she returned with two sacks of groceries and six bottles of wine. She kissed him smartly on the lips, to his surprise. "Hello love. Be a dear and pick me a few oranges from outside, will you?"

"What's up?"

She laughed. "You sound like *him*."

"Who?"

"The American."

"What American?"

"Dave."

Claude's eyes narrowed. He ripped off the end of a fresh loaf of ciabatta and bit into it.

"Don't ruin it!"

"Ruin what?" He looked at all the food she was setting out on the counter. "Are you having a party?"

"Yes, I'm having a party and I'm making *your* tomatoes with basil in olive oil, steamed mussels, fettuccini Alfredo with asparagus and fresh rosemary, and sangria. Oranges, please. Dave will be coming over with his wife."

"Who's Dave?"

"The American!"

"Oh, I get it, the Pagolo's villa guy."

"Finally. Now, some oranges would be nice; they're here at seven."

Claude went outside, single words followed by full stops reeling through his mind. Sangria. Death. Oranges. Florence. Marble. Asparagus. Death. Rosemary. Dave. Americans. Mussels. Lorenzo, Paolo, Pietro, Alessandro. No A's. *La Morte*. Zaccaria. Z's, Z's from here on in.

He set the oranges on the wooden chopping block. "Call me at 6:30," he said, and went back into his study.

At 6:30, Marianne stood in the doorway to his study wearing a close-fitting purplish-brown dress hemmed just below the midpoint of her thighs, with spaghetti straps holding up her sagging breasts. "Half an hour. Call to change."

"Change, yes, I think I will." Claude went to his bookcase and pulled out a volume of Voltaire's *Candide*, retrieved a bottle of scotch and poured himself a short glass.

"Really, we have company coming." She shook her head. "Black shorts and sandals?"

"It's Gozo, and they're from California."

"But I've made such a lovely dinner and decorated the table on the veranda. Claude, can't we show our guests a bit of elegance?"

Claude sipped his scotch. His white t-shirt had gray tones and although the man was trim, by no means did it hide his 60-year-old belly. "I know what this is about."

"At least put on a clean shirt."

"You're avoiding the story."

"Opposite. Completely. I'm walking around the story so I can see it properly first, that's all."

"Hmm." He set down his glass of scotch. "The green one?"

"Light green."

"Why darling, that shirt always makes you horny!"

"I'm already horny, I'm always horny."

"Sarcasm will get you nowhere." Claude raised one white, bushy eyebrow.

She shooed him out of his study and watched him climb the stairs to their bedroom, filled with admiration and genuine love for that dawdling, brilliant old man who needed to be her husband.

Ten minutes after seven, the American arrived with his wife clinging to his back on the Vespa.

Dave introduced her. "Jos."

"Short for Josie?" Claude asked.

"Jocelyn," she answered.

"Of course." He shook the girl's hand. She was petite, cute and somewhat reserved. He could tell by her eyes that she was smart and wondered what she was doing with an airhead like Dave, but there was only one possible answer. Marianne was smarter than Claude when they married and at the time he thanked the God he didn't believe in for his manly physiognomy.

"It's nice to meet you, Mr. Renoir." Her black hair was cut very short and sort of spiked out around her china doll-like face. She wore a cadmium yellow, strapless summer dress. Claude thought she looked like a sunflower. Tonight, in her puce-colored dress, Marianne looked like an iris. Dave was wearing a black, v-neck t-shirt, white slacks and flip-flops. He looked like a daisy. Claude himself was just a plant, a generic green plant with black roots, a weed. Good, he thought. I get to play the weed.

The young couple followed Mr. Renoir through the mosaic-tiled foyer, through the living room and into the kitchen. Jos was introduced to Marianne and handed her a bottle of Pinot Grigio.

"Perfect! We'll have it with dinner, but first let's go out onto the terrace. It's such a lovely evening."

The four of them passed through the two studios whose walls were lined with bookcases filled with messily stacked books.

"You're writers?" Jos asked.

"He is. I'm not," was Marianne's reply.

"She's lying. It's the other way around, actually," Claude asserted.

"I never lie." His wife turned with her back to the ocean as they all stepped out onto the pretty deck, covered with a trellis of subdued violet wisteria.

"It's true." Claude sighed. "She tells the truth, always, anywhere, at any time, at all costs."

"Sangria?" Marianne dipped a glass ladle into a large punch bowl and filled four tall glasses.

"You have a spectacular view." Jos smiled.

"Ours is shit," Dave added.

"It's not so bad," Jos said quietly, embarrassed by her husband's careless language.

"Well, Pagolo will never cut down his cypress trees. It's bad luck. Italian superstition," Claude warned.

"Killer sangria!" Dave held up his glass.

"*Salute.*" Claude offered and they all toasted.

"Look!" Dave pointed at the sea. "A dolphin."

They moved to the edge of the terrace and Marianne leaned over the balustrade, standing so close to Dave that if he turned his head towards her, he'd be able to see down her cleavage. But why would he want to do that? Claude thought. She's a fifty-two-year-old iris and he's a fresh daisy.

"So what do you two do for a living?" Claude asked, keeping his eyes on the dolphin.

"I teach Freshman English, but really, I'm a writer, too," Jos answered.

"Too? No such thing. One is a pianist. Two are pianists. Separate yet together, forever, you know, one big happy family."

She sipped her drink. "And what a happy bunch we are!"

Ah, she is smart, he thought, and sexy, but not in a genuine, gifted way like Sophia Loren or Juliet Binoche. Not sexy in the innate, *I can't help it* kind of way, but simply because she's been sucking on that moron's gigantic knob for the past five years of her life. Otherwise, she was plain as a candlestick and she probably taught those asinine bores from the Beat Generation.

"Do you do poetry?" he asked.

"I've written a few poems."

Jos finished her sangria and went back to the punch bowl. Claude followed her, leaving Marianne hanging half off the balustrade besides *Handsome.*

"No, I mean, when you teach."

"I wish! They won't let me."

"Who won't?"

"The administration. I'm not even allowed to teach fiction anymore to first year students. My old syllabus contained all the classic must-reads: Joyce, Hemingway, Fitzgerald, Kafka…but now there's this new bullshit curriculum. I have to teach non-fiction only to aid in the instruction of essay composition. Well, that's America for you. English majors aren't even allowed to study literature until their sophomore year. It's ludicrous! Once I gave my students an assignment based on a single poem by Keats and the chairwoman tore me apart."

"Were you fired?"

"Worse, I was guillotined."

"'One can say I am going to be guillotined, he or she will be guillotined, he or she has been guillotined, but it is impossible to say, I have been guillotined,' It's a quote from Stendhal."

Jos burst into laughter, her pale cheeks rosier than before. Finally, the smart, cute chick with the hunky husband had relaxed. This is going to be fun, thought Claude. Now let's get back to playing the iris and the weed.

Jos took a pack of cigarettes from her little handbag. "Do you mind?"

"Go ahead. May I…?" He pulled a flap of matches from his pocket and lit it for her in the sudden gust of a short-lived wind.

"Wow. You're good with a match," she said, and they laughed.

Marianne swerved by the punch bowl. "Darling, come help me with the first course."

Claude followed his wife across the threshold of the terrace.

"I see you're acting clever with the pretty girl."

"Me? I'm not clever. You're the writer remember, I'm just the housewife. What the hell did you put into that sangria anyway?"

"Same thing I put into the fettuccini and the tomatoes, love."

"Okay, alright. Walk around it, walk around it all you like, I don't care."

She handed him a large bowl of steamed mussels and took the plate of tomatoes & basil in her own hands. "Let's just have a nice night. I think they're rather charming, in a curious sort of way."

"She's charm incarnate. He's a cartoon."

They sat at the table. The sunset was an orchestra.

For a moment, the conversation about Gozo halted and they all stared out to the sea.

"Dragons in the sky," Dave murmured.

"I forgot what you said that it is that you do, David?" Marianne asked in an affectionate way.

"Surf, paint, play guitar, write sonnets…stuff like that."

"He's a real Renaissance man." Jos squeezed his knee under the table.

Marianne smiled at Claude then rose to bring in the main course.

"And that pays well?" Claude sneered.

"Oh, you meant like for a living…yeah, I own an organic farm in Mendocino."

"I don't think they know what that means, honey," Jos, tipsy and continually sipping at the sangria, slurred.

"Right. I grow pot, weed, ganja, you know, *marijuana*." He pronounced the word as if he were explaining a complicated phrase to a toddler. "Yeah. I got ten acres." He bobbed his head up and down like a popped up jack-in-the-box.

"You don't like mussels?" Marianne asked Jos, who had only served herself a small helping of tomatoes.

"She's vegan." Dave sucked the juice from a mussel shell and licked his fingers. "I keep telling you, doll, you're missin' out. These are delicious!"

"Oh, I should have asked." Marianne then served the fettuccini, yet Jos just gave herself another serving of the salad.

"There's no meat in the alfredo," Marianne said.

Dave shook his head and pronounced, "*Vegan*," the same way he had, *marijuana*. "No dairy."

"And I'm also gluten free," Jos added.

"So you live on nuts and berries?"

"Pretty much."

"Like a deer," Marianne commented.

"Or like Shelley," Claude said.

Jos finished her sangria. "I'd asked Dave to mention it, but seems like he forgot."

Claude smiled at the teacher as he uncorked the wine she'd brought and filled the four crystal glasses that were set upon the table. The two men ate ravenously and complimented the chef as the conversation swayed from the landscapes and traditions in the Maltese islands to those of Northern California. Marianne was pleased her dinner party got on so well.

The Renoirs stood on the front porch beneath their moonlit bougainvillea, waving good-bye to their guests as Jos tried three times before she could get herself onto the back of Dave's scooter.

"She's completely sloshed," Claude said, still waving.

"What do you expect after two slices of tomato and half a bowl of punch?"

The Vespa headed down the dirt road.

"Well, we probably won't be seeing them again." Claude put his arm around his wife.

"Nonsense. Dave is giving me a surfing lesson tomorrow."

"Ah, so you've decided to paddle around it now."

"Baby, I'm gonna fly!"

They woke in the morning to the sound of rain spattering on the terra cotta tiled roof. Marianne reached out to touch her husband but he got out of bed and went sleepily into the kitchen, unaware.

Marianne ate her dry toast and swallowed her vitamins. Claude took his coffee cup and the leftover fettuccini out of the refrigerator and disappeared into his study.

She appeared in the doorway in an hour. "What are you doing?"

"Writing."

"About what?"

"*About what*. For God's sake woman, get to work."

"But I'm going surfing today, remember?"

"It's pouring out."

"Maybe it'll clear up."

"Look!" He waved at the window streaming with rain. "It's a goddamn deluge, my dear."

She sighed. The phone rang. She went into the living room and answered then returned to sulk in his doorway. "That was Dave."

"Yeah?"

"The lesson is off, because of the rain."

"Uh, huh."

She moved into his study and pretended to read the titles of books in his bookcase, although she knew his library like she knew his body. He ignored her and continued typing. In a sudden frenzy, she began pulling the books from the shelves and piling them on the floor.

"What the hell?" He turned in his chair.

"I'm going to organize this for you, alphabetical order or by category, which do you prefer?"

"Jesus, Marianne."

"You've been using the Lord's name in vain quite a bit lately, do you know that?"

"So, maybe I'm mad at him."

"Because you're not dead yet?" She held up a heavy book. "How on earth can you have the *Paradisio* all the way over here when the *Inferno* and *Purgatorio* are all the way over there?"

"Get out."

"What?"

"Get out of my room. This is my room and I don't want you in here right now."

She slid down to the floor with her back to the bookcase and folded her knees to her chest. She hugged them and stared at the windowpane being beaten by fast rain.

Claude took a deep breath and watched her for a while but did not go to her, just watched.

After several minutes she whispered, "Matteo."

"Are you sure?"

"Yes. His name is Matteo."

Claude turned back to his computer and typed a few lines then leaned back to read them. His chair creaked.

Marianne stood. "I think I'll make a salad for lunch. Endive, apples and gorgonzola."

"Sound good." He held his coffee cup out in the air. "Would you mind bringing me some more coffee, my dear?"

She swiped the cup from his hand. "And her name…"

"Yes?"

"Is Concetta."

Elizabeth McKague

IV

The Painter's Model
Firenze, Italy, 1492

Concetta would not, under any circumstances, for any reason under the sun, be forced by anyone to cut off her long, wavy, autumn blond hair. After Botticelli's last exhibition, boys in the street began to whisper, "Venus on the half shell" behind her back.

She stood before the announcement posted outside of the Florentina Studiorum Univeritas, unable to take her eyes off it as the dome of Santa Maria del Fiore, looming over the square, turned golden then pink in the setting sun.

She had to get the position. She was without a doubt, gifted beyond any other young painter in Florence. Only two months ago, Leonardo Da Vinci himself had stopped before a stall she'd set up in the market place to sell her paintings, signed with a male's name, *Concetto Gambiani*.

"Who is this Gambiani, do you know him?" Da Vinci asked her.

"A relative," she nervously blurted out.

"Is he in Florence?"

"Feisole."

The Master picked up one of her works and examined it carefully. "Genius! I must meet this fellow. Do you know his address?"

Concetta stuttered and in her excitement told the wrong lie. "He was in Fiesole but now he is traveling, we don't know where he's gone. Perhaps as far as Africa."

Da Vinci nodded and gave her twenty florins for the painting. "Pity. I could've shown him how to stretch his canvas without buckling the corners. I'll take this one. Good day, Signorina."

A shade began to cover the Piazza di S. Maria in Campo. Two boys shoved in front of her to look at the poster, then dashed off. It read:

Master Mariotto Albertinelli is accepting applications for one new apprentice. Interviews will take place on Saturday, January 5th, from 8 until 5 at 39 Via della Studio. Portfolios must include two landscapes, one cityscape, two portraits, one biblical scene, four still life studies and one nude.

When Concetta returned home, her parents and three younger brothers had just sat down to dinner.

"There you are." Her mother rose to get her daughter a place setting.

Concetta was in fact starving but confidentially, yet falsely, complained to her mother of menstrual cramps and was excused from the table to spend the evening alone in her attic room. She climbed the three flights of stairs, closed her door behind her, took off all her clothes and stood before an easel where she placed an imperfectly stretched canvas.

With a fire blazing in the hearth behind her lighting up the room and the black night outside, her image was reflected in the glass of her tall bedroom window. Her family's house was on the Lungarno Corsini and her window faced the dark space above the width of the Arno. The distance between her house and those across the river was great enough that if anyone were to gaze across the river from that height they would see nothing but a bright yellow blaze filling a tall, remote rectangle of glass across the way. Concetta sharpened her charcoal and began to sketch her own nude body.

Little did she know that on the opposite side of the Arno, directly across from her attic room on the Lungarno Guicciardini, a young man named Matteo, who had spent many hours posing for the untrustworthy painter Biagi, had just received his work's wages in the form of a telescope. For the past hour he'd been pointing it at the stars. At one point he lowered it and focused it on a couple arguing in the street below, then on a fisherman gliding his boat toward the river's shore in the glow of a lantern. Next he focused on the jolly crowd seated at outside tables beneath the awning of a restaurant and spent an entertaining amount of minutes watching thieves adroitly pickpocket tourists. He set the telescope down, poured himself a glass of wine and sprinkled his pipe with the miniscule amount of opium Biagi had also given him for his services that day.

Posing in the stance of a disc thrower, half-freezing in a cold stone tower without a stitch on from dawn until dusk before a room filled with men, one third eager for artistic perfection, the other third for Matteo's young ass and the remaining third eager for both, is far more difficult than one might imagine. Besides his gorgeous appearance, Matteo was an excellent model because he knew how to do nothing for long periods of time. This did not mean that he was idle or simple at all, for while his body did nothing but look good, his imagination was racing with dreams and desires the whole while. He made up stories for himself, placed himself on battlefields with a mighty sword, on a ship sailing the sea to far off lands, or in the yard of a Medici palace, a courtier adorned in silk, casually gallivanting about with courtesans of his choice, or in the meadows of Tavarnuzze on a summer's day, chasing rabbits as he used to in his idyllic childhood.

"Matteo, keep your left leg straight!" Biagi would order, and alas, the dreams would slip away, but only for a second, and soon enough he'd return into the arms of some fair maiden wandering about in his mind.

He drank the small glass of wine and puffed on the pipe, then lifted the telescope and pointed it in a direct line across the river.

Wow, he thought, that must be some strong stuff.

He set the telescope down, drank and smoked some more, then focused the lens upon the same scene in the amber glow of the same window he was surprised to find a moment ago.

A woman was standing there behind the glass pane, completely naked and utterly beautiful, still as a statue, although his telescope told him she was quite real. She's posing, he realized, for he knew the job well, but for whom?

"It's for you," a voice called out behind him.

He put the telescope in a dresser drawer and turned to see Pietro, the lad who recently moved into the apartment below, walk through the door with a message in his hand. "I thought it was for me, but it's for you."

Matteo read it. "What chance!" he said happily. "Finally, a real job. Mariotto Albertinelli wants me next week. I do hope he'll pay in coins."

"They rarely pay in coins, if they end up paying at all!" Pietro grumbled, "I got a parrot in a cage today, an ugly parrot that won't shut up. *Michelangelo, Michelangelo....*" Pietro squawked, raising his voice in an awful high pitch. "The bird is driving me crazy! I'm going to the market tomorrow to try and sell the damn thing. What did you get?"

Matteo dare not show him the telescope. He lifted up the bottle of wine and the pipe, and invited the boy in, thinking, after all, they were comrades in arms, and legs, and torsos.

Concetta's parents were very supportive of her art and let her leave her shift at the family bakery early each day so she could return to her attic room and complete her portfolio. By Friday night of the New Year, all her pieces were perfected and she let herself fall into a deep, peaceful, nine-hour sleep. She woke the next morning to the crowing cock in a neighbor's yard and filled the basin in the bathroom, but on second thought decided not to wash because boys were dirty creatures and she needed her complexion to appear not so soft. She took ashes from the hearth and rubbed them in half circles below her eyes, trying to dim their natural, feminine glow. She put on black stockings, brown knickers, a white camicia and brown leather boots with long pointed toes, all borrowed according to her size from separate brothers. Then she wound up her hair into a tight knot atop her head and put on the wig of coarse, chestnut-colored hair that curled just below her ears. Finally, she crowned her costume with a felt béret she'd also bought at the wig shop, as they'd become quite fashionable lately amongst the male students.

With the portfolio under her arm, she walked along the wintry green river and turned onto the Via Por Santa Maria to stop into her parents' bakery for a moment out of the prickly, icy air. She was delighted when her father stepped up to the counter saying, "And what can I get for you this morning, my fine young lad?"

Her mother came out of the kitchen carrying a tray of rolls fresh from the oven. "Fool! It's Concetta."

Her father laughed. "My, my. Well, you'll have the wool pulled over their eyes today, my girl. Good luck!"

She embraced her parents and grabbed a warm roll.

Even though she arrived an hour early, a long line was already expanding around the block. The doors of the famous Albertinelli studio swung open at eight that morning. Two apprentices with stoical faces and superior attitudes took the portfolios inside, giving grave doubts to many of the one hundred boys wearing fingerless knitted gloves, who had been shivering in the line since daybreak. Each applicant received a tiny slip of paper upon which a number was written accompanied by the words:

Twenty portfolios will be accepted for further consideration. Interviews begin at noon. If your number is not called out at that time, you may pick up your work from the back door of the studio.

Such a cold, formal reception put a sulk upon every young artist's lowered chin. With four hours to wait, the applicants found themselves amiss. Many had traveled from the countryside and outer villages of Tuscany, and these boys set off in pairs to explore the spectacular city. Those who were locals either returned to their homes or escorted each other into a café for breakfast. The others, their hearts leaping, could do nothing but sit on the cold, sun-stroked stone steps of the Duomo and try to amuse themselves by tearing off bits of bread from the lunches their mothers had packed for them to toss at pigeons.

Concetta, whose heart she believed was fluttering the most, sat on the steps for a while but upon feeling that the other boys were eyeing her somewhat suspiciously, jumped up and crossed the Piazza di San Giovanni to follow the Via Roma to the Piazza della Repubblica where she decided to lose herself for the next three hours in the chaotic squall of the marketplace.

At first she thought she might have made a mistake, for many of the bakery's customers who had known her since she was born were shopping or selling wares. She pulled her béret forward to shade her eyes and kept her face down. She became so nervous that soon enough she accidentally bumped right into Signora Salducci, one of her mother's closet friends, knocking the good woman's basket of apples and pears to the ground.

"*Scusi, scusi.*"

Concetta dropped to her knees to gather the fruit and when the signora replied, "What a nice young man you are. Your parents must be very proud," the disguised artist regained confidence and let herself delight in the movement and colors of the busy market, where fires burning in metal bins gave off heat, scented by a post-Christmas pine wood smell.

On Saturdays, the Piazza della Repubblica hosted the largest market in Tuscany. Anything you could imagine was on display and being bargained for: fabrics, perfumes, tools, pots, pans, musical instruments, furniture, meat, cheese, produce, livestock in cages, barrels of beer, bottles of wine, books, maps, board games, costumes, masks and exotic plants from distant foreign lands. Concetta stopped before a table selling horsehair paintbrushes and picked up one after another to test their strokes in the palm of her hand.

"Michelangelo is coming! Michelangelo is coming!" A very high, shrill, annoying voice rang out over the busy square.

Concetta turned round to see two boys parading through the throng. One of them was holding a parrot in a cage above his head.

Concetta laughed out loud.

The boys stopped before her.

"30 florins," the taller, handsome one, whose arms were empty, solicited her.

"For a silly bird?" she mocked.

"20 florins!" the shorter one begged.

Concetta shook her head and passed on to the next stall selling mechanical clocks, which all showed the same hour, eleven-thirty.

She quickly barged through the market and reached the Via della Studio just as the double doors were being opened. The two resigned representatives stepped out and one of them announced, "When your number is called out, line up here to my right. Interviews with the Master will begin immediately, in numerical order."

The second assistant then read from a sheet of paper in his hand, "Twenty-one, forty-seven, five, twelve, sixty-nine, ninety-two…"

At once the boys that were gathered in the street before the studio all started to whisper, either cursing to themselves or congratulating each other. The whispers fastidiously became a great hissing sea and the final numbers were difficult to hear.

"thirty-six, twenty-eight, fifty, eighty-three…"

Eighty-three. That was her number. Concetta searched the pockets of her first brother's jacket, then the knickers belonging to her youngest brother. How could she have lost the ticket? 83—that *was* her number. She must have gotten pickpocketed at the market, for her small notebook and pencil, along with half of the roll she'd saved from the bakery were also missing.

The boys who had been selected pushed and shoved their way forward to take their place along the facade of the building while the less fortunate ones sadly turned the corner to retrieve their portfolios from the back door.

Nineteen boys stood ready on the right arm of the stoic facilitator, who, after checking all their tickets, yelled out once more, "Eighty-three! Eighty-three!"

Concetta rushed forward.

"I'm eighty-three, but I seem to have lost my ticket."

He said nothing and began to rearrange the line in numerical order. She was second to last.

Once again, the contestants found themselves with hours of waiting and formed groups to fool around in the high afternoon sunshine, or dawdle about, or play kick ball in the street, whilst the solitary boys sat on the studio steps to read books or take out their sketch pads and charcoal.

Concetta wished to sketch yet she had no materials. So she sat, satisfied to daydream. At one point she noticed that a boy sitting on the step above her was drawing her. She smiled at him, thinking he was rather charming, then remembered that she was supposed to be a boy. So act like one, she told herself and went to him. "Can you believe it? I was pickpocketed at the market earlier. They stole my sketchbook and pencils." She put out her hand. "I'm eighty-three."

"Ninety-two." He shook her hand then tore a few pages from his pad and loaned her a pencil. "Here you go. We have plenty of time to waste."

"Thanks." Concetta returned to her spot on the steps, but instead of sketching the statue of winged Mercury in the Piazza del Capitolo, which she'd done many times before, she faced 92 and started to draw him. He laughed and they spent the next few hours learning every detail of each other's appearance.

Well, after Papa and Signora Salducci, if I can fool an artist, too, she mused.

Her number was called out at four o'clock.

"Signore, the Master will see you now."

Concetta followed the assistant into an enormous studio and was struck with awe by the recognizable smells of turpentine and oils, the many easels and canvases, palettes splattered with an assortment of colorful paints, baskets stacked with brushes, yards of fabrics in long rolls, odd props, ladders, tools, and especially a heavenly glass triangle raising out of the ceiling, through which poured a triple beam of glistening late afternoon light.

A tall, well-dressed, good-looking gentleman in his early thirties was pacing before a long wooden table where her paintings lay exposed. He pointed a finger at her biblical piece and read the signature in the bottom right corner. "Tell me, *Concetto Gambiani*, why is it that you chose this particular scene? It is a very odd choice, almost every student I've had does 'The Annunciation'."

Concetta shrugged, and, feeling baffled, decided it best to simply tell the truth and explained, "I have three brothers Master, who I used as models. I wished to capture the folds of their long robes as if illuminated by the miraculous light of the North Star, so I pinned old tablecloths to their shoulders and placed a candelabra atop the tallest cupboard in our kitchen."

"And the headdresses?"

"I made paper hats in the shapes of some oriental crowns I once saw at the market."

He looked at the painting once more and a wise smile lifted the corners of his moustache. "Quite clever, Concetto. And the portraits, I see you've used the technique of *sfumato* to obscure the sharp edges of light and shadow."

"Yes, sir. I followed the advice of Da Vinci who is known to have said, 'When you do a portrait, do it in dull weather or when evening falls'."

Mariotto's smile widened even more.

"This landscape here is rather beautiful, red poppies growing in a golden field under a deep blue sky."

"Yes, Signore Albertinelli, I wanted to use the three purest colors to represent the purity of nature: ultramarine, gold and vermillion."

"And your cityscape, a daring perspective, looking up at the Pont Vecchio from what appears to be the midst of the Arno."

"I paid a fisherman to take me out in his boat one day."

Finally, the Master let out a gruff yet very merry laugh.

"Well, your craftsmanship certainly shows in this still life of green apples. I feel as if I want to reach right in and take a bite!" He placed his large hand, curled around an invisible apple to his mouth and snapped his teeth. "And this one of dying lilacs shows you have a dark side."

"I believe that painting is just that, as Da Vinci says, 'an effort to create synergy between the dark and the light'."

Mariotto then held up the painting she'd done of herself in the window and stared at it silently for quite a while. "But this, this piece is remarkable. It is the jewel in your crown. The stark intimacy and delicacy of the flesh tones, the illumination of the figure rendered by an impeccable skill of chiaroscuro, and the final touch of a taffeta veil over her face...for a boy your age, why, it's outstanding."

Concetta tried not to blush but couldn't help it and lowered her head.

"Come now! Don't be embarrassed. You're a lucky fellow to have a lover who is willing to pose for you in such a sensual, natural way."

"I don't have a lover, sir," she whispered.

"Then good, for you must devote yourself to your art, and we all know how women take up too much energy and time. But whoever this whore is in your painting, don't let her slip away. She is a fine model with a very fine frame."

Concetta's face was crimson by now and it took all her strength to suppress a tear.

Mariotto walked to the other side of the table and slapped her on the back. "Oh, come along now, I'm having a bit of fun. Artists are complicated monsters yet we do need our pleasures." He put his heavy arm around her shoulder and led her to a desk where he unlocked a drawer and pulled out a contract.

"I've one interview left, yet I'm already clear about who I want to be my new apprentice." He dipped a quill in the inkwell and slid the paper across the desk. "Sign here."

The scroll was very long and filled with paragraphs in a fine script. "I'd like to read it first, Signore Albertinelli."

"Be my guest! Not only talented but smart as well. We're going to do just fine, you and I."

The contract was filled mostly with rules of conduct, a work schedule of eight in the morning to six in the evening, Monday through Saturday, and legal notations against forgery. The last paragraph stated her wages, a mere 20 florins a week. She suddenly felt a bit dizzy as she'd eaten nothing but half a roll that morning and the quill in her fingers hovered at the bottom of the page.

"Is there a problem? Okay, twenty-five florins."

Concetta's rational mind was suddenly overcome with more emotions than there were olive trees in Italy. She signed, bowed, and copied the Master, who spat into the palm of his hand, and offered him the firmest grip she could muster up.

When she walked down the steps of the studio, her expression was so bewildered as she passed by the less fortunate number 92, that his own heart beat with hope and expectation.

Her dreams had come true but the reality of faking her sex from dawn until dusk, six days a week had her head spinning.

That evening back home on the Lungarno Corsini, her mother's tears glistened on the brioche she brought to the dinner table.

"Mama, it's not a prison. I'll be home every night and all day Sunday."

"My dear," her father's soft voice broke in to console his wife, "God gave our daughter a gift. It would be a sin to keep her in the bakery for the rest of her life."

"Papa's right," the eldest of her brothers asserted.

"We didn't wear tablecloths for nothing!" Her middle brother laughed.

"Perhaps I can become a painter, too," her sweet little brother chimed in.

"Stop, stop!" Her mother dried her eyes. "These are tears of joy. Concetta, I am so, so, so very proud of you!"

When she arrived at the studio on Monday morning she was put to work right away. Alessandro, the less impassive of the Master's top two assistants, gave her a crate of raw eggs and she spent two hours extracting the yolks for making tempera. The boys were required to mix paints, set up easels, build wooden frames and stretch canvases, which, as Da Vinci had mentioned and Albertinelli noticed, was not Concetta's *forte*.

By late morning, it was time to create the setting for the model who would be coming in that afternoon. A tall marble column was carried into the studio by several of the stronger boys while others gathered miscellaneous props such as a broken vase, a live mulberry bush in a pot, and several feather-tipped arrows that had to be arranged as if they'd fallen to the ground. Concetta was consigned to hang two long velvet drapes, one red and one blue, on either side of the column. She did so and meticulously altered the folds and flow of the material to give them a rich depth in the light that poured through the sunroof of the studio. Mariotto was impressed. The group broke for lunch at noon and when they returned an hour later, the Master was binding a young, nearly naked man to the column with ropes. The subject was St. Sebastian.

"Is that too tight?" Mariotto asked the model.

"Perhaps a little looser," he answered.

The Master then attempted to alter the folds of the model's loincloth, yet was unhappy with his design. "Concetto!" he called out. "Come here. You did such a fine job with those drapes, here, see if you can't make his loincloth reflect the light."

Concetta approached the man strapped to the column and with shaking hands, gently began to manage the folds of the thin white cloth that was sloppily covering his privates.

"No, no, no." Mariotto growled and tore the cloth completely off the boy then shoved it in Concetta's hands. "You must start over. Now hurry up or we'll lose the afternoon light."

She froze, but only for a second. After all, she did grow up with three brothers. It wasn't like she'd never seen one before. So again, with great care and aesthetic gentleness, she wrapped the cloth beautifully about the model's groin.

"Perfect!" cried the Master. "Now, get to work."

They sketched for the rest of the day. The model, whose name she learned was Matteo, took only two short breaks. Concetta immersed herself in her work. She drew each line with such precision and naturalness it was as if she were actually running her fingers through his dark curly hair, tracing the masculine structure of his jaw line, his chin and neck with her fingertips, touching his broad shoulders, hard, strong arms, proud chest, tight abdomen and narrow hips; caressing the soft, semi-transparent cloth covering his genitals, grasping the adamantine muscles of his thighs and balancing her own tenderness with the sturdiness of his calves and bare feet. Although she didn't draw his hands, they were present in her sketch of his pose, for the tension could be felt in the rest of his body from having them tied together behind the marble column pressing against his back.

She drew his face last: the cleft in his chin, the shadow beneath his cheek bones, his humble nose as if she were so close she could feel his breath, his lips as if she had kissed them and his eyes like mirrors of her own. She captured the pain and compassion in his expression completely, carried away by genuine sympathy for this martyr who was not St. Sebastian, but Matteo, a jolly boy trying to sell his friend's parrot whom she had met in the market last Saturday, now tied to a column for five hours in a temperamental artist's studio.

At times, their eyes met and she knew he was watching her. Surely a boy like that wouldn't remember me, she thought.

Yet he did, not from the market, but from the concentrated half hour he spent several nights ago, looking at every inch of a beautiful girl standing naked in her window through his telescope.

As the bells of the Duomo rang out at six o'clock, the model was released from the column. He rubbed his wrists and put on his clothes.

Mariotto paraded through the studio examining the work of his apprentices, harshly criticizing each boy's piece with no reservations at all. When he stopped at Concetta's sketch, he stood there for some minutes, disappearing into her drawing, then moved on without making a single comment. Matteo had watched this exchange and went directly to Concetta's easel.

"That's me," he said softly, also drowning in her picture like Narcissus in the pool.

"Well, you are the model," she said, faking a rough, low voice.

"No, I mean, that's truly me. All day long while I've been tied to *that* monstrosity," he said with a wave toward the marble column, "you've been releasing me into this work of pure beauty."

She bowed her head, not wanting him to see her blush.

He gathered himself together and chummily shoved his shoulder against hers. "Damn boy, you'll make a great painter someday!"

Concetta smiled. "Thanks."

A few of the apprentices who were heading out the door called to Matteo. He nodded at them then turned back to Concetta. "We're going to The Dragon. Why don't you join us?"

"The Dragon?"

"A tavern near the Ponte Vecchio."

"Oh no, I can't. I must return to my family."

"Alright. Well, another night perhaps."

"Sure."

Matteo returned to the studio once more that week. The subsequent afternoons were spent priming their canvases and sketching the props of the set. They began painting the following Monday. Albertinelli thought it curious that Concetta chose to use a vermillion glaze over her burnt sienna underpainting, as the other boys followed the traditional use of successive glazes of beech wood or tar-based browns, yet he said nothing.

Matteo modeled on Wednesday and Friday and held the same schedule until the end of January. Each time he was in the studio, his eyes would meet Concetta's and they'd exchange glances filled with infatuation, yearning and embellishment. He would often speak with her at the end of each session and continued to ask her out to The Dragon, yet she always refused. She worked very hard and although she did enjoy her time at the studio, even the mornings filled with busy chores, she needn't smear ashes beneath her eyes anymore for she developed natural dark circles. Her devotion to her painting of St. Sebastian was something she'd never felt before. It consumed her with a spiritual fire and cooled her with freshness, like stepping into a great bath of lapis lazuli blue water. And yet there was more, more, more. There was Matteo. She was falling in love with him.

For the entire month she played her part well and although she didn't participate in the sort of camaraderie that the others had with one another, she was amiable enough, accomplished all of her duties and most importantly, had them all in reverence of her astonishing talent and craft. Perhaps she was quiet and appeared to be somewhat of a loner, but they thought, such are the signs of genius, and so did not pester her to partake in their brotherly small talk, games or adventures.

Finally, on the last Wednesday modeling in Albertinelli's studio, Matteo asked her out again and she accepted. They met with the usual boys who frequented The Dragon and Concetta drank wine with them. After several bottles had been emptied and the moon was high above the Arno, Matteo stretched out his arms to either side, placing one around the shoulders of his comrade Pietro, who had joined them, and the other around Concetta, who was seated there right next to him.

"My two best friends!" He laughed tipsily. "I love you both...so much." He shook the shoulders of Pietro and suddenly turned and kissed Concetta's cheek.

She pulled away and stood. "I've had fun, but I must be going."

Matteo stood and searched his pockets, intending to pay for his share of the bill. "Blast! I left my wallet at the studio."

Concetta took a portion of her wages from her pocket and threw some coins on the table.

"No, no. I can't let you do that," he protested.

"It's nothing."

"Ah, it's everything, if we are going to be true friends I must pay you back right away. You know how it is with men when money is lent."

She nodded, unsure of what he meant. Her brothers stole from each other all the time, then argued and called in their mother or sister to play judge. Sweet little Marco, the youngest, usually got shafted. A wave of love for her brothers flowed over her and she realized she was drunk.

"Right," she gurgled in an exaggeratedly deep voice. "So, let's go get your wallet."

They walked in silence in the bright, watery light of a waxing moon.

Matteo stopped on the steps of the studio and slid his fingers into the mouth of a lion's head carved on the building's façade to retrieve the key.

"I've never been in the studio at night before," said Concetta, suddenly excited and in a daring mood. At Matteo's side, she felt so brave.

She followed him in. The indulgent moonlight pouring through the small glass triangle in the roof cast a delicate, eerie glow upon all the easels and canvases, the gigantic marble column and her majestically hanging drapes.

"Ah, here it is." Matteo picked up his wallet from the modeling stage. Just then they heard footsteps and Matteo pulled Concetta down as he ducked behind the column. Mariotto walked into the studio, a goblet in his hand and a black satin robe hanging loosely about his large frame. Then the sound of laughter as Alessandro danced into the room, naked, and flung himself at the Master who took the not-so-stoic-after-all apprentice in his arms and began to fondle him without discretion.

Matteo squeezed Concetta's hand and they quietly crept toward the front door, dashed down the steps and onto the street. They looked into each other's eyes for half a second, exchanging the same intensity and aching that each felt from a distance on those days when she'd look up from her easel to see him gazing at her with his hands tied behind the column.

Drowning in the submissive moonlight, as if Narcissus' pool were for two, they walked side-by-side to the river and parted at the Ponte Vecchio without speaking.

Matteo returned to his top floor apartment on the south bank of the river and as he had done each night for the past month, sat in the dark with his telescope to watch a beautiful young woman in a night dress with long, wavy, gossamer golden hair walk into her attic room, climb into her bed and blow out the flame of a candlestick. But tonight, the small doubts he still harbored about her identity were completely dispelled. For in the candlelight of that same attic window, he saw Concetto appear, take off a wig, then the boots, stockings, knickers, vest and shirt, and become the girl he fell in love with one month ago. She put on her nightgown and brushed her long, wavy hair, then, as if making a wish, blew out the flame.

The episode in the moonlit studio did not change her impression of Albertinelli in the least. She remained obedient and extremely grateful to him for seeing her talent amongst ninety-nine applicants. Mariotto had also shown her unusual courtesy throughout the first weeks of her apprenticeship. Although there were times, when he was in one of his moods, that he screamed at her because of a misplaced bottle of linseed oil, a missing sponge or improperly cleaned brush, just as he would and so often did to the other boys, his tone when berating Concetta was subtly less offensive. She sensed that perhaps he saw her, as was in fact the case, as being rather a solitaire, and thus less resilient to violent confrontations, as well as being both physically and emotionally frailer than the others in his studio.

That Thursday afternoon they worked on the details of the objects in their paintings, knowing that tomorrow was the model's last day and the last chance they'd have to render the flesh of St. Sebastian.

He came in at half past noon on Friday. Mariotto bound him to his post then broke the tips of four arrows and glued one over his heart, two below his ribs and one to his inner thigh.

"Agh! Agh!" Matteo cried out, pretending that the arrows were actually piercing him, making the group laugh.

Again, the Master called Concetta to the stage and handed her a palette dabbed with dark red paint. "He's bleeding now," was all he said.

She took up her brush and painted red drips on the model's skin at the points where the arrows had been glued to him. She had to kneel to paint the blood trickling down the inside of his muscular thigh.

Matteo felt his entire being tingle with each stroke of her brush. He glanced down at her kneeling at his feet and was overcome with desire.

Concetta returned to her easel and the group painted in silence for two intense hours.

"Blast!" Mariotto suddenly yelled. "We're out of black! How can we be out of black at a time like this? Paulo, you didn't mix enough paint this morning. And of all colors, black!" He raged on and on, torturing Paulo, then said, "Concetta, you're almost finished and the rest of us need the light while we have it. Go down to the storeroom in the basement and bring up a jar of black pigment." He handed her a key and the moment she left the studio, Matteo requested a short break.

"Yes, of course," the Master grunted.

The model put on a red robe and sat at the base of the column to eat an orange. After ten minutes, Mariotto growled, "What is taking him so long? We'll lose the light. Matteo, go down into the basement and see what the hell he is doing."

"Who?" Matteo, thinking of the girl beneath the boy's clothes, asked sincerely.

"Who? Concetto, that's who!"

"Oh, yes, right."

She had tripped on the uneven stone steps to the storeroom. When she fell, it all came crashing down; St. Sebastian pierced with arrows, the ridiculous wig and stupid hoax, the endless work and exhaustion, all that she'd been repressing to the others and herself because the world would not accept her gift unless she was a boy. Her very soul seemed to bleed with the love she felt in her heart, the ache she felt in her true sex for Matteo and the predicament she'd put herself into, a battle for recognition in art, and passion, that either way would end up a fiction. She sat on the bottom stone step and let it out, sobbing and weeping with all her might. The might of a female.

Matteo, in bare feet, nimbly climbed down the tricky stairs. She did not see or hear him approaching until he was nearly in front of her. She quickly wiped away her tears but he was standing there before she had time to rise.

"Are you alright?"

She jumped up, swallowed her agony and feigned a deep voice. "I tripped."

He grabbed her, suddenly burning with desire, leaned her back against the damp cellar wall and kissed her deeply. She knew not where she was, only that she was trapped in the arms of the man she loved. She kissed him sweetly. Although he wanted to, he dare not touch her breasts, fearing that if she discovered his knowledge of her true identity she might flee. So he grabbed her ass and squeezed, his tongue in her mouth, his chest pressing so close to hers. She ran her fingers over the contour of his shoulders, torso, hips and thighs as she'd done mentally that first day she drew him. They could not part from each other's lips. At one point, her hand brushed against his penis. He was aroused, jutting out like a rock in the Lurgurian Sea along the coastline.

"Go ahead," he whispered. "Touch me."

Concetta remembered where she was and who she was supposed to be. He thinks I'm a boy, she surmised. I'll be found out.

She pushed him off of her, took the jar of black pigment from a shelf and ran, oblivious to the pain in her ankle for the pain in her heart was so much greater, up the stairwell.

Matteo leaned against the musty basement wall where one moment ago she had felt his lust for her. He tilted his head back, looked at the dark overtones of a rotting, wooden beamed heaven and sighed.

"At last!" Mariotto snatched the jar of pigment from her hands and gave it to Paulo. "Black paint, now, now!" He then turned to his star pupil. "What has happened? Why are you limping?"

"Am I limping? It's nothing, Master. I tripped in the stairwell."

"Very well, back to work. Everybody back to work!"

Matteo returned to his bondage post and Concetta suffered, standing on her legs with her left ankle swollen to the size of a grapefruit, for two more hours. Yet she let her imagination ride her technique and when the bells of the Santa Maria del Fiore rang out at six o'clock, her St. Sebastian was complete and looked so alive she thought she could hear him breathe.

Matteo was waiting for her in the street outside 39 Via della Studio when she came out, dragging one leg behind the other.

"You're hurt," he said.

"I'm fine." Her rough voice gave way to her real one.

"Come, put your arm around me. I'll walk you home."

Desperately in pain, she agreed.

Her mother came to the door as they entered the house. "Concetta! What has happened?"

The painter's eyes widened and her mother corrected herself, "I mean, Concetto, my son, Concetto."

Matteo ignored the charade. "Your daughter has been injured, Signora."

"My daughter?"

"Yes, your daughter. Whom I love with all my heart."

Concetta's eyes met his, the same way they had throughout the first month of the New Year, with the same longing, the same need for recognition. But now he realized, as well did she that it was not for recognition of her talent but for her very being, her life as a woman.

"*Tante grazie*," her mother told Matteo, then called out to her eldest son to run and fetch the doctor.

"May I come by tomorrow," the model asked, "to check on her?"

Signora Gambiani consented and closed the door on his enlightened brow.

The doctor ordered her to stay off her feet for a week. "Not only has she sprained her ankle, but she is exhausted. If she continues on she will become feverish."

Matteo came the next day as he'd promised after informing Master Albertinelli of Concetta's condition and was shown up to her attic room. He sat at her bedside and took her hand in his own. "Concetta, my love."

She unwillingly removed her hand, for she loved him too, but his confession had come too suddenly and she felt confused. "When you kissed me yesterday, I thought you were…I thought you believed me to be a boy."

He laughed quietly. "I'm not that way. I've known who you are all along."

"And the others at the studio?"

"Oh, they're convinced that you are Concetto, an odd, eccentric kind of boy genius. Believe me, I'm the only one who knows the truth."

"But why, how?"

He told her the whole story, beginning with Biagi's telescope.

She blushed deeply.

"Don't be embarrassed, after all I've stood before *you* naked as Adam for an entire month!"

She smiled.

He took her hand again and looked into her moist eyes, "I want to kiss you."

Every day Matteo crossed the Ponte S. Trinita and spent hours in Concetta's room. Albertinelli had paid him well in coins and he brought her flowers, chocolates, a leather bound sketchbook, silk ribbons for her Venus-like hair, a delicate silver chain and a printed volume of Pico della Mirandolo's *On the Dignity of Man.*

She appreciated everything, ate the chocolates, painted the flowers, wound the ribbons into her long locks of hair, wore the chain around her wrist and became engrossed in the book of philosophy that by the week's end she'd read from cover to cover.

When he arrived at her family's tall house on the Holy Day, he found her on her feet, setting the table in the dining room for the Sunday feast. He took her in his arms and although he said happily, "You're better, I'm so glad," she could tell something was wrong.

"Matteo what is it? Do they know? I return to the studio tomorrow."

"No, no. That's all good."

"Then what is it?"

He took a letter from his pocket and gave it to her. She read:

Dear my faithful Matteo,

The great and honorable Andrea Mantegna visited my studio this week. He was struck numb by Concetto's painting and has commissioned you to model for his own painting of St. Sebastian. He expects you to model in his studio in Venice for four months and will pay you 1,000 florins. I've enclosed Mantegna's advance payment of 150 florins. You must hire a horse and ride out at once.

Congratulazioni!

Mariotto Albertinelli

The parchment floated to the floor from her hands. "Four months?"

"One thousand florins, my love. Then I shall return and..." he knelt at her feet, "...we can get married."

She took his hand and pulled him up. "Married?"

He took a ring with a miniscule sapphire sparkling in its center from his pocket. "Will you, Concetta Gambiani, be my wife?"

"Yes."

They embraced and kissed fervently. Mrs. Gambiani came into the dining room, "Oh Matteo, will you stay and have dinner with us?"

"Yes, Signora, I'd love to."

"Concetta, come help me in the kitchen for a moment, please?"

Concetta began to follow her mother but Matteo held her back. "Come with me to my apartment tonight after dinner. Find a way to sneak out; I'll wait for you in the street."

She gazed at him, remembering their encounter in Albertinelli's basement. "It's impossible, my room is too high to sneak out of and I couldn't chance going downstairs while everyone's asleep, they might hear me."

Matteo thought for a moment. "Then say your ankle hurts again, that you must sleep on the sofa so you can rest for your return to the studio tomorrow."

She kissed him again, quickly, but did not promise anything.

He waited on the Lungarno Corsini, ready to pace and daydream until midnight if he had to, and was surprised to see her come out of her house at nine.

"That was fast." He smiled.

"My parents are bakers, they sleep and wake early."

They crossed the bridge, climbed to his attic loft and were instantly naked in his bed, tossing and turning and kissing and burning with passion for the rest of the night.

Matteo walked her back across the Ponte S. Trinita before her parents woke at five the next morning, then returned to his place to pack a small bag and leave Pietro 100 florins to pay his share of the rent. He hired a horse and rode out of the Florence gates at the crack of dawn.

Concetta put on the wig and her brothers' clothes and returned to the studio.

Mariotto and the others greeted her warmly and she was put on egg duty again. Their next subject was going to be *The Last Dance of Salome*. The Master took Concetta aside that morning and said, "Your little prostitute would make an ideal model for our upcoming project."

"I haven't seen her lately."

"Hmm. Well, perhaps you should look for her. I could give you a bonus if she agrees to pose for us, and if you do in fact find her, you could take a second bonus for yourself!"

"Yes, sir."

On Tuesday, Mariotto came to her as she was separating out the egg whites, "Well?" he whispered.

"No luck. It seems she's left town."

"Yes, she probably went off to Rome. It's where they all go eventually, thinking they'll make it big doing cardinals, but what often happens is that they are found dead in the streets. Oh well." He slapped Concetta's back. "There's plenty more where that came from, eh?"

"Yes, Master."

When they were ready to begin sketching, a radiant woman with long dark hair came in to pose as Salome. Concetta's pencil moved with the usual alacrity and skill, yet she felt detached from the subject and her vision lacked the passion she'd had for St. Sebastian. Matteo was in Venice tied to Mantegna's marble column, and she experienced a tremendous sense of alienation and hatred for her disguise. The radiant model was expressive of such proud femininity that Concetta realized she was jealous. And like the other artists, she was irked by the model's behavior for she was very demanding, took frequent breaks, complained about everything and was unable to stop wiggling her fingers and toes, delighted by the tiny bells Mariotto had placed on them.

Alas, the apprentices endured and did their work.

Matteo's first letter arrived and then, a letter came every other day. The month passed by as they both worked all day and poured their hearts out to each other at night with their quills sailing in a small circle of candlelight.

He told her that Andrea Mantegna had a temperament equal to Albertinelli. "Yet with riches attached, so it's worse!"

She wrote to him about how the new model was a disaster and confessed her lie about the whore, to which he replied, "He's right though. They do die in Rome." And then he requested, "Send me a sketch, my love, of you. The way you were in the window."

She did so, but this time the figure was not wearing a veil. She wrote, "Send me a drawing of you as well. Look in Mantegna's wastebasket. Like Mariotto, I'm sure in moments of frustration he often throws excellent sketches away."

He sent her a fine picture, followed by packages of silks, spices, dyes and scrolls of the finest paper, writing, "The market place in Venice is loaded with merchandise directly from the orient."

She sent him a tin of butter cookies she made with her mother on Sunday and wrote, "My love, your gifts and words mean everything to me, I live for them, but they are not you. Three more months! What shall I do?"

"Paint," he replied. "Paint and know that I will marry you."

Between the passionate yearning for Matteo that consumed her soul and the assiduous hours at the studio, Concetta paid no attention to the fact that she did not bleed on her regular day in February. When she took the sacrament at mass on St. Valentine's Day and heard the words, "The blood of Christ," she guessed the reason.

That evening she told her mother.

"You must leave the studio."

"Never."

"What if Matteo…?"

"He returns at the end of May." She held out her hand with the engagement ring on her finger, which she always put on the minute she got home and turned back into a girl. "Remember mother, we are to be married."

"I do trust Matteo, but this is preposterous! You must leave the studio before you begin to show."

"I won't do it, mother. It's my work, my calling. I'll just say that you're feeding me too well and I've gotten fat!"

Mrs. Gambiani threw her hands, covered in flour, up in the air, and the white flakes fell around mother and daughter like snow. She sighed. "We mustn't tell your father about this until you are wed."

"Yes, of course, Mother."

"Oh, Concetta, what a mess you've gotten into!"

Concetta went to her attic room and composed a thoroughly concentrated letter to Matteo.

With Salome's Last Dance completed, the apprentices spent the first part of March cleaning and organizing Albertinelli's grand studio and working on individual pieces of their choice.

At the end of the month, Mariotto announced that the group would be taking a trip across the Arno to visit the studio of Francesco Granacci, "To see something highly educational and profoundly unforgettable."

The group arrived on the Via de Bardi, and one of Granacci's assistants, stoical as Alessandro, let them in. Immediately, many of the boys pulled out their kerchiefs and placed them over their mouths and noses, for the smells of turpentine and oils they were so accustomed to were plagued by a stench so putrid that Concetta gagged behind the cloth she held to her face. Before them, laid upon a long table, was the corpse of a naked, bloated old man. The body was swollen and its skin was of a grayish-blue hue.

"Glad you could make it." Francesco shook Albertinelli's hand. "We've dragged him from the river. Now gather round, pupils." He then took a scalpel, sliced into the dead man's stomach and began pulling out the bloody entrails while speaking. "As painters, we must learn to see the human body from the inside as well as the out..."

Concetta felt it coming and ran outside the front door, turned a corner and vomited in the street. She dare not return to witness the autopsy and although miles from home, had no choice but to walk in that direction. She followed the south side of the riverbank and by early afternoon found herself on the Lungarno Guicciardini, crossing before Matteo's apartment building. Her stomach was in turmoil and she felt faint, so sat on the front steps to rest. The cerulean sky was streaked with rumpled sheets of random clouds. White, hints of yellow and gray, that's how she'd paint them. Perhaps her mother was right, she should leave the studio, go into confinement in her attic room and take care of her pregnancy. I could paint the clouds each day, she thought, capture the changing sky above my lover's loft across the river. And I'd send him the paintings to let him know how much the beautiful city of Fiorenza misses him. She began to weep.

Just then Pietro came out of the front door of the building. "Concetto!" he said with surprise. "Have you come for Matteo? He's in Venezia."

Again, she was forced to wipe the tears from her eyes and speak in low tones. "Is he?" She stood. "Well if you write to him, tell him I stopped by. Good day."

Pietro grabbed her arm gently before she went on her way. "You don't have to pretend with me, Concetta."

"What are you talking about?"

"He told me everything. I suppose he needed a friend to confide in. He also asked me to care for you during his absence, but I was not sure how to approach you."

She wept again and let herself be, just be.

Pietro put his arm around her. "Come, I'll walk you home. Matteo will be glad to hear of this happy accident."

As they crossed the Ponte S. Trinita, she asked him to go to Albertinelli's and tell him that "Concetto apologizes for running out of Granacci's studio but that he had become suddenly ill, not because of the dissection but...what should I say?"

"That you drank too much wine the night before."

"Good. Yes. And tell him I'll be back to work in the morning."

"You know, Matteo would want you to do what is best for the baby."

"And that is exactly what I shall do. He, you and everyone must trust me."

Throughout the month of April, Concetta had to put down her work several times during the mornings to rush into the bathroom and vomit. When they painted in the afternoons, she kept a tin of crisp wafers next to her easel that her mother had baked for her to ease the nausea. She explained to Mariotto that she'd developed a temporary stomach condition and that she could no longer spend her mornings cracking eggs. He assigned her to stretch canvases, but her corners buckled, so then he made Alessandro, who usually spent his hours before noon lounging in the Master's grand bedroom, reluctantly come downstairs to show the gifted apprentice how to fix the corners properly.

April's subject was portraiture. Mariotto would drag in old women, street orphans, barmaids, butchers and vagrants, anyone willing to pose for a few florins. Then one day a handsome, finely dressed man appeared in the studio and shook Albertinelli's hand.

"You've been recommended by a friend of mine. I'm Cesare Borgia, in Florence from Rome for a fortnight and thought I'd have my portrait painted."

"Of course, Your Excellency." Mariotto blushed, knowing of the Pope's son's reputation and stunned by the man's courtesy, fine appearance and obvious wealth. "I shall dismiss my students and prime my canvas at once."

Cesare looked around at the amazed group of boys. "No, no. Let's have some fun. All of your students will paint me and then I shall choose the best one. A contest, no? And the winner gets..." He took a large purse from his pocket and weighed its coins in the palm of his hand. "One hundred florins."

Mariotto dragged a large red velvet chair into the shaft of light coming through the glass pyramid in the ceiling. "Come, Your Grace, sit here."

This time, Concetta found no difficulty immersing herself in the painting. She was intrigued by a seemingly secret, sinister nature hidden beneath Cesare Borgia's attractive features, and the elegance and pride with which he held himself appeared somewhat enigmatic, as if he were capable of both deep love and extreme violence at once. She remembered Matteo in her attic room one day as they discussed the book of philosophy he had given her, saying, "There are two things in life that one can never be objective about: *violence* and *love*."

So she painted Cesare without a trace of objectivity but with a completely subjective eye.

He chose her piece. "Concetto Gambiani...where is he?"

"Here, Your Grace." Mariotto shoved Concetta forward from the huddle of nervous boys.

"You are a fine artist, young man," said Signore Borgia as he placed 100 gold florins in her hand.

Concetta bowed and smiled for the first time since Matteo left for Venice. That evening she came downstairs to the family dinner with her golden locks flowing, a pretty white dress billowing around her figure and the fairy-sized sapphire sparkling on her finger.

"I see our Concetta is looking forward to her fiancé's return," her father said, passing her the deep dish of lasagna.

"I am, Papa." She placed a large helping on her plate.

"Ah, but my dear, if you want to look nice for your future husband, I wouldn't eat like your eldest brother!"

All around the table laughed.

"I'm celebrating tonight, Papa." And she told him about Cesare Borgia's portrait.

"Then you should have some wine."

He lifted the bottle but her mother pulled down his arm. "Let her eat first, then maybe a few drops of wine."

In Venice, Matteo thought of Concetta always. While strapped to Mantegna's pole by day, his dreams and mental wanderings took place in Florence. But at night he came alive to physically explore the environs of the stimulating, opulent and rather decadent, watery new world.

On his very first day in the studio, he befriended a charming apprentice named Stephano, a Venetian native who insisted on showing the Florentine model the splendors of the most dynamic port of the western seas. They rode gondolas through the lagoons, joined outdoor festivals in the piazzas and crashed parties held in palaces so dazzling and lavish that Matteo imagined he was in heaven. Enraptured by the flux of strange new scents, sounds, fashions, and the faces of Byzantine and Levantine foreigners enhanced the lustrous flair of the city and Matteo, with his wages in his pocket, let himself drown in the effulgence and luxury that composed Italy's glorious "City of Light."

When he received Concetta's letter telling him of her condition, he was so proud that he confided the news to Stephano. "Therefore, I won't be going out with you so often anymore, for I think it best to save my earnings for my child."

Stephano, poor as any artist, thought quickly and replied, "But Matteo, the minute you get back to Fiorenza you'll be married and tied down to one woman for the rest of your life. Why not live it up while you have the chance, eh? You'll probably never see Venice again and your fiancé is far away. Why not take advantage of your last days as a free man?"

Although part of him completely agreed with Stephano's logic, the other part, in love with Concetta, had to refuse the proposal.

So, the handsome model became a bit of a recluse throughout the month of March. After climbing down from the column and exercising his stiff limbs, he'd retire to the room he rented on the Calle di Ridotto, located on the top floor where one window framed a view of the vast variety of Eastern ships pulling into the harbor of the Bacino di San Marco, and beyond, the sparkling, wintry blue belt of the Adriatic Sea. There, with a small desk set before the window, he'd spend his evenings writing letters to his love, savoring memories of the night before he left, and proclaiming to her promises of a happy future as man and wife.

What could Stephano have meant? he wondered. *Tied down…last chance at freedom*…I'm tied down right now to a stupid marble pillar! And when I return to my love and my child, I shall be rich and free!

So he pursued this train of reasoning until the icy season began to mellow and the stormy sea became calmer. His senses once again seemed to open up to alternative possibilities. The springtime air took over his longings for Concetta in Florence like the song of the sirens while he was tied to Mantegna's mast by day, and filled the one eye in his lonely top floor room with a new point of view, as his quill lay dormant upon his little writing table at night.

On the first of April, Matteo went to Stephano as the apprentices were leaving the studio. "The Master has given me an extra payment for today."

"As well he should! I saw how that last arrow hadn't been dulled properly, but I must say, it was a treat to paint real blood running down your thigh."

"Thanks." Matteo laughed as he took his green cloak from a hook by the door, "Listen, I feel like going out tonight."

"Ah! So you've finally seen the light!"

"I suppose."

"Then come with me, my friend, and let us revel in adventure!"

They took a gondola down the Grand Canal and ordered an extravagant meal at a waterfront restaurant. Afterwards, they hired another gondola to take them to a tavern on the Campo della Carita where they sat on a terrace overlooking the Ponte dell Acccademia. At midnight they strolled through the narrow passageways and crossed the arched bridges until they came to a wealthy neighborhood where mansions loomed, lining the lagoon.

"There." Stephano pointed to a villa with its windows all lit up. "It's a masquerade."

"But we don't have masks."

"Give me some coins."

"What?"

"Do you want to go in or not?"

Matteo, drunk, gave him the money.

In several minutes, Stephano returned to the fountain where Matteo sat waiting, mildly stirring up regrets and misgivings, and longing to touch Concetta's golden hair.

"Here we are!" Stephano handed him a mask of a lion's face and held the other one to his own face, the head of a cobra. "I bought them off of two fat merchants on their way out. Those pigs go to these things early, fill themselves with hors d'ouvres and leave when they realized they'd just eaten 100 cheese balls stuffed with garlic!"

Matteo had to laugh as he held the mask to his handsome face. "Very well, let's go in."

He'd never seen the interior of such a palace before, nor such an abundance of food and drink and never, ever, such an array of attractive, elegantly dressed courtesans.

Stephano immediately disappeared into the sea of masked dancers. Matteo stood, un-strapped, with his back to a marble column, watching all the beautiful girls twirl about behind their bewitching masks. Every so often, a pair of flirtatious eyes would meet his and the dancer's lush red lips would part as if to whisper.

The past enduring weeks of thirsting for Concetta pulsed throughout his limbs, as he stood poised. A waiter passed by with a tray of fluted glasses filled with sparkling wine. He took one and drank. When he looked up, a young woman in a sapphire blue gown that sparkled like the ring he gave his love, was standing before him. Her long, blond hair flowed over her shoulders in waves and her mysterious dark eyes covered him with a clandestine proposition that he recognized instantly as the inescapable, profound sensation of lust.

"Hello," she said to him. "I haven't seen you in my father's palace before."

He felt trapped and thought, I really must try to stay away from marble columns.

Matteo sipped more wine. "I've come from Firenze."

"Oh, I adore Firenze! It's so...artistic, yet humble."

He finished his glass of wine and immediately she took it from his hand and her fingers brushed against his. "Shall we get you another?" She raised her bare arm in the air and like magic a waiter appeared with a fully stocked tray from which she took two glasses. "So, what brings you to Venice?"

"I was sent for by Andrea Mantegna."

"Are you a painter?"

He drank, although his mood was already clouded. "A model."

"My name is Nicola."

"Matteo."

She lowered her mask, shaped like white wings, and he lowered his.

Her face was very pretty indeed but he could see right away that it did not possess the genuine kind of beauty that comes from spirited passion, and she lacked the pure glow that he adored in the face of his bride to be. This girl's charm came from comfort, ease, wealth and her expensive, sparkling blue gown.

Of course when Matteo removed his mask, Nicola saw that she had guessed correctly, he was by far the finest boy at the ball. "Well, I certainly can see why the Masters would want to paint you."

He lowered his eyes and drank more.

"Come," she smiled, "Let me show you our palace. We also have a lovely garden that has become the home of three wild owls."

Matteo searched the masquerade for Stephano but did not see any cobras, so agreed.

In the garden, Nicola pretended to trip over uneven stones in the pathway and he gallantly saved her from a fall. She was in his arms, as Concetta in Mariotto's basement.

The rich girl was in heat and would not take no for an answer. But he was no better. The wine and his desire quickly overtook his rationale.

She led him to her bedroom where he woke at dawn, naked beside her. He dressed quickly and fled. The palace was enormous and he flew through many endless hallways, climbed up and down several flights of marble stairs and ran into an assortment of ambivalent butlers, maids and menservants before he found his way to the grand door that opened out onto the Riva del Ferno, where he crossed the Ponte di Rialto in the stark, yellow morning light, far too brilliant for his deep, dark eyes, of a new day.

On the first of May, Albertinelli's apprentices were told without an explanation to dismantle their easels and stack them in a corner. Next, Alessandro, unusually present at that hour, called forth the strongest boys to move several wooden worktables into the large studio through the back door. Mariotto instructed the not so strong boys to place new tools upon the tables; strangely shaped wooden spoons and crescents, knives, spools of wire, sponges, water buckets and at last, heavy lumps of clay.

Everyone was excited, as most of the young painters had never sculpted before. They spent the afternoon, "allowed to make anything you want, a goblet, a candlestick, a mask or monument, I don't care. You need to get used to the new materials."

Many of the boys made plates and bowls as gifts for their mothers. Concetta began kneading the clay, as she had so often done with flour and yeast when making bread in the bakery. The texture of the soft, red earth felt somehow familiar. She placed a small mound on her worktable and began to mold the clay into different shapes without any preconceived ideas, not really thinking, just making. At one point her experiment seemed to resemble a rabbit so she made it into one. Next she made a cat, then a turtle, a dove and finally, two fine horses with Arabian hooves. Toys for my child, she said to herself.

Mariotto walked about the studio at the end of the day. "Plates and bowls," he mumbled. "A candlestick, a goblet, and more plates and bowls."

Sighing reflectively, he stopped at Concetta's table and said in a whisper, "Dear boy, you never cease to amaze me." He then turned to the group and announced, "For the next few weeks we will be changing from two dimensions to three dimensions."

Concetta looked down for a moment and thought, just like my belly.

Concetta's pregnancy was undeniably beginning to show. She gave her second brother his linen camicia back and traded her eldest brother a clay goblet she'd made for one of his linen shirts. She gave her youngest brother his knickers back and traded with her second eldest brother, a saucer for his knickers, then gave her youngest brother the clay rabbit, out of tenderness.

The sculpture diversion ended the last week of May and they returned to painting boring still life studies of apples, grapes and pears. One more week and Matteo would return! His letters remained consistent except for an occasional delay and then the following letter would be an apology for having been unable to find a messenger. The promises and pictures he'd paint of their love with his words, sometimes poetic and idealized, other times humble and simple, kept her breathing, and the second heart beat, half his within her, living strong.

The boys in the studio noticed the healthy glow on her face and the larger clothes unsuccessfully covering her middle. One day, she heard Paulo and Antonio whispering behind her. "Look, our genius is becoming a porker!"

Alessandro was passing by and added, "I've noticed, too. It's not becoming on a young boy that age."

Salvatore, working nearby harshly commented, "I've never seen a fat artist in my life. Aren't we all supposed to be starving?"

Paulo laughed quietly. "He must have spent Cesare Borgia's 100 florins on a roasted pig!"

Antonio hissed, "If I had won the contest, I would have taken all of you out to The Dragon for food and drink."

"And spend your last twenty florins on a whore," Alessandro teased. "Now back to work!"

The boys continued to gossip, "So he thinks he's the Master now, eh?" they said of Alessandro.

Concetta turned round, unable to control her anger, "That's because he shares the Master's bed."

The boys were surprised, not at the news, for it was general knowledge, but that 'the genius' had actually talked to them.

She went back to her painting.

After some minutes, Paulo whispered to Antonio, "It speaks!"

She whipped her head around once more, so violently that her wig slipped slightly. "I heard that!"

Concetta walked home feeling disparaged and confused.

As she was helping her mother wash the dishes that evening, she said, "It's time, mother."

"What? You have five months to go yet!"

"No, I mean it's time to tell the truth…at the studio."

Her mother put down the dishrag and sat at the kitchen table, watching her daughter at the sink. It was a big baby already. After all, that handsome Matteo was six feet tall.

"You don't have to tell them," Signora Gambiani said.

"But I must, I can't go on like this…I just can't!"

"Don't tell them, Concetta, *show* them."

"What?"

"Go in tomorrow as you are now, with your hair down, in your white dress showing your lovely round belly, with the sapphire on your finger and work,

work as you always do."

"They'll laugh."

"No, they won't."

In the morning, she filled the washbasin, put on her white dress and a blue baker's apron so as not to stain it with paint, brushed out her long golden hair and even tied in the pretty ribbons Matteo had given her. She knew it would be impossible to expose the truth during the morning chores, so she left her house at noon and headed toward the Via della Studio. Something seemed different in the springtime air that day. As she came closer to the Ponte Vecchio she saw black smoke blowing in vast clouds toward the river. When she turned onto the Via Por Santa Maria Calimala, she was suddenly stuck in a frantic, fast moving crowd.

"What is happening?" she asked someone.

"They're being hanged and burned!" the man answered and shoved his way forward.

"Who? Where?" Concetta called out and received several answers at once:

"Three Dominican friars."

Ashes were floating in the smoky breeze. All of Florence had gathered to witness the spectacle and in every direction, the ends of the streets leading into the Piazza were packed with people trying to get a glimpse of the gruesome event, like mud caked on the tips of the spokes of a wheel near its axel.

Concetta had no interest in the scene—her own concerns more pressing—and finally made it through the crowd and turned down the Via de Lamberti, continuing her way to the studio. The doors were locked. As she expected, they had all put down their work to witness the frightening execution. She remembered the key Matteo had once used, opened the doors and replaced it in the lion's stone mouth. She entered the empty studio and went to her easel, the ribbons in her hair sprinkled with ash, her white dress smudged with smoke, and began to paint.

In half an hour or so, she heard the door lock turning. It would be Mariotto and the boys, returning in awe of the horror.

But this is my day, she thought, her brush carefully glossing over the umbra under painting with a vermillion glaze. She did not look up, yet also did not hear the expected stampede of ranting boys piling in through the doors. Two feet were moving toward her, it would be Mariotto. She took a deep breath, lifted her face and saw…her love!

Her brush fell to the ground, its wooden tip scratching the glaze. Matteo took her in his arms. He kissed the ribbons in her hair, her forehead, cheeks, lips, neck, shoulders, breasts and belly. Her hands grasped his shoulders, stroked his dark locks, his back, bottom and sturdy, strong thighs.

"Alright! Alright, enough now!" The Master's brazen voice echoed in the studio as he marched in followed by his students who were more animated than usual by the morning's public event.

Then complete silence.

"Matteo?" Mariotto approached his star model.

"Hello, Master. I've come back a week early."

"I can see that. Well, you couldn't have picked a better day! But why are you here and who is this woman?"

Concetta left her lover's embrace, her belly protruding.

"Ah, so you've come to show me your wife. Looks like you had some fun in Venice, eh?"

The apprentices all laughed and the Master barked, "Enough already! Back to work! Back to work!"

Matteo looked at Concetta, obviously having no idea about her plan and forgetting the whole fiasco of her situation in the studio the minute he saw her. He opened his mouth to speak but Concetta stepped forward.

"I am to be his wife, Master, but I am not from Venezia."

"Oh?"

"I'm from Fiorenza."

"Well, that's good. We don't want to lose our Matteo to the 'City of Light'. I prefer the 'city of ash' myself." Mariotto chuckled at his own sarcasm.

The boys laughed again.

"To work!" the Master shouted.

"Then he doesn't know…?" Matteo whispered to Concetta.

"Know what?" Mariotto moved the table set with pears and grapes at an angle to catch the smoky light drifting through the skylight.

"I am Concetto." Concetta spoke so quietly that the Master did not completely hear her.

"Concetto. Where is he today by the way? Does anybody know?"

The boys, afraid to make a peep, mumbled under their moustaches.

"Matteo, you're his friend. Have you seen him since you've been back?"

"Yes, Master. He is right here."

Mariotto looked around the studio. "Where?"

Matteo put his arm around Concetta. "Here. But he is a she and her name is Concetta. She is carrying my child and is soon to be my wife."

"Hah, hah!" Mariotto laughed, a rare thing. "What are you two playing at? Haven't we all had enough for one day?"

"I am thus, sir," Concetta said. "I pretended to be a boy so I could get into your studio and learn from your venerable greatness, Master. I must paint, you see, it's what I love and what I do…"

"Oh, Matteo, take your lovely bride and be off now, this is no time for jokes. We have work to do here." Mariotto moved closer to the couple and stood beside them before Concetta's easel, staring at her canvas. "A vermillion glaze."

"As always, Master."

He took her chin in his hand and examined her face. "Can it be true?"

She took up her brush. "Give me to the end of the day and I'll show you."

Albertinelli threw his arms up in the air. "Very well. To work, to work, everyone!"

Matteo kissed her good-bye and promised to return at six to escort her home. When he did walk through the studio doors that evening, he saw Mariotto talking quietly with his bride. Then, astonishingly, Master and pupil hugged each other and Concetta met her fiancé, smiling.

"And Matteo…" Mariotto called after them. "We'll be doing The Crucifixion of Christ this summer, are you up for it?"

Matteo laughed. "Nail me to the cross! *Cosa certa,* Master!"

The painter and the model were married the very next day and Concetta moved into his loft across the river.

She continued to paint until she began her seventh month of pregnancy and then, as the doctor ordered, retired to rest for the upcoming birth. Albertinelli promised that she could return to the studio when the baby was weaned. Word traveled fast that Fiorenza itself had given birth to a phenomenal female painter named Concetta Gambiani. Albertinelli gained a fine reputation for discovering the artist and made many new friends as his studio was soon visited by Filippino Lippi, Andrea Del Sarto, Raffaello Sanzio, Pietro Perugino, and even the great Michelangelo di Lodovico Simoni who were all curious to see the works of this gifted girl. When Sandro Botticelli stopped in and peered at the first nude she had painted in her own bedroom window, he said, "Same hair as my Venus. Genius!"

And, at last, the prodigious Leonardo Da Vinci came by, examined Concetta's paintings carefully and sighed. "She finally learned to do the corners right."

Matteo got up on the cross every day and climbed down at night, excited to return home to his loving wife. Concetta sewed baby clothes, wove blankets and felt serene and happy turning his bachelor's attic into a clean, pretty, pleasant home. Their love grew each day and they knew it was eternal.

On 3 September 1493 at eight o'clock in the evening, Concetta keeled over in dire pain. Matteo was out of the door before she could even call after him, "Fetch my mother!"

He sent Pietro upstairs to care for his wife, then flew across the Ponte S. Trinita and returned with Signora Gambiani and a midwife in half an hour. At dawn, a healthy baby girl was born and they named her Artemisia.

V

Gozo, Italy

Present

"I saw lover boy in town." Claude set the groceries on the kitchen counter. "He was at the barber shop getting his hair cut."

"Who? What are you talking about?"

"Your lover, the American."

"Oh, that's been over for days. I got my eye on the barber now."

Claude laughed, for Xaghra's one barber was seventy years old, bald, and fat.

"Where's the arugula?" She emptied the canvas bag.

"Right here." He picked up a bunch of fresh spinach tied with coarse, pink string.

"That's it. We're getting you new glasses. We'll take the ferry to Malta tomorrow."

"Good idea. Hell, let's spend the night, two nights." He went into his study and opened his laptop. "Melliecha, St. Julian's or Marsascala? The Hilton or the Corinthia Palace Resort & Spa? Oh...how about this one...five stars..."

She came up to his desk and looked at the pretty pictures of exotic pools, seductive lounges and luxurious rooms with breezy, seaside views. "No."

He flipped the page on the screen to further alluring pictures. "This one."

"We don't have the money."

"Yes, we do."

"But there's no need. It's irrational."

He spun round in his chair. "Darling, we've spent the past six months isolated on a hill top in Gozo, of all places, writing stories based on random postcards that arrive from only God knows who, and you think taking a little holiday at our age is…"

"Irrational. If anything, we could send the money to the boys."

"The boys are fine, more than fine, and you know that." He looked her in the eyes then took his credit card out of his wallet. "I'm booking this one."

"Please don't, Clues."

"C'mon, babes!"

"No, I mean," she paused and changed the page on the screen. "I like the Hotel Pheonicia. If we're going to do it, let's do it all the way, bright lights, big city and go to Valletta."

Claude typed in his credit card number. "Ah, well. There goes the last right toe of *The Woman in the Bath*."

The other four toes, foot, ankle, calf, knee and thigh of her right leg paid for the villa, the splash of water on the tiled floor paid for the Fiat and they counted on her fingernails for their daily expenses. The hand and lower portion of her left arm sent their eldest son, Esmond, to Oxford to study law and their second born boy, Etienne, to La Sorbonne where he had recently wrote, to Claude's dismay, to say that he had decided to major in philosophy.

Auguste Renoir was Claude's great, great uncle. Claude inherited one painting of a bathing woman just four years ago when his cousin, Renoir's great grandson, passed away. Claude and Marianne were established in Paris, living in the same apartment above Claude's bookshop for twenty-nine years. Since the boys had grown and were ready to lead their own lives, the couple felt it was time to make a change. Marianne had written several novels that were minor successes and Claude had spent twenty years writing one great novel that received outstanding praise from France's most credible critics, yet hardly sold a hundred copies.

"People never see brilliance until it's a thing of the past," Marianne had said to console him. "Fuck 'em all, Clues, *I* know you're a genius."

So, to ease his bruised ego, he'd sold the painting, sent his kids off to school and promised his wife he'd take her away.

Claude left the Malta Accommodations page to check his email as Marianne still stood peering over his shoulder.

"Which should we read first?" he asked her. There were two new messages, one from Esmond and the other from Lautremont, their literary agent.

"Don't be stupid."

He opened Esmond's:

Passed my exams! Top tenth percentile. Be proud.
Love,
me.

Claude returned to the inbox.

"Wait, I want to respond!"

"You'll write him a novella. Use your own laptop." He clicked on Lautremont's message: Gallimard publishers liked the proposal. I need sample chapters to negotiate an advance. Send asap. Best, L.

She nudged him in his chair with her hip. "So, that's that. You should do a final edit before you send him what we've got."

Claude clicked on the Word icon. "Yes, ma'am!"

Marianne went into her study to write to her son. After an hour writing, she peeked into Claude's room and said, "I told him you'd transfer a hundred euros into his account to congratulate him."

"Mm hm."

"How's it going?"

"Sucks."

"What do you mean?"

"The whole thing. It's rubbish!"

"Okay. Alright. Lautremont can wait. Let's take our mini-break and look at it fresh when we return."

"I should have never sold the painting. We should have stayed in Paris. Why did we even come here? Postcards from the past…it's absurd! Why are we even writing?"

Marianne hadn't seen him in such a state for a long while. She felt worried for a moment but then told herself that his crankiness was probably a delayed reaction from seeing the American surfer get a haircut.

"C'mon, Clues." She went to his chair and rubbed his shoulders. "I love you. Let's take our break, okay? Everything will be fine."

He nodded and sighed.

She kissed the top of his white haired head then went to the window and stood staring out at the sea darkening in the coming of night. She stayed there for a long time.

"What are you looking at?" Claude stopped typing and rose from his chair to join her.

"The faeries."

"What faeries?"

"Right there. Can't you see them dancing?"

"Sweetheart, those are fireflies."

"Well, to me, they're faeries. When I was a child, my family always spent the summer vacationing in Tenby, Pembrokeshire. Oh, it was truly a picturesque little town, Clues, like something out of a fairytale and I made myself believe that fireflies were faeries."

"*Made* yourself believe?"

"I can make myself believe anything, you know that."

Claude grumbled and went outside to be alone in the tranquil night. He thought about *The Woman in the Bath*, which made him feel sad and closer than ever to the meaning, or worse, non-meaning, of death.

VI

The White Cat
Galway County, Medieval Ireland, 1234

Seven and a half-year-old Elan Fidhne O'Halloran walked along the rocky embankment covered with moss that followed the Corrib River from the gates of Galway to the Loch Lurgain Bay. One legend said it was built by the Gaelic Lords of Connemara to mark their Tuath from the tribal kingdoms of the O'Flathertys, and another said it was built by leprechauns to ward off river phantoms.

Elan leaned over the ancient wall and watched three baby otters swirling about in the limey green water. A branch of hawthorn grew out of the rocky wall just there and in that instant on a cloudy Friday afternoon, he learned which legend to believe, for it was a well-known fact that leprechauns used hawthorn flowers as keys. One little otter peeked its head out of the surface of the water and, wiggling its whiskers, whispered, "Shh."

Elan put his finger to his pink lips and winked at the creature, knowing, as all of nature knew, that truth is a secret to be shared by the few.

He walked on and reached the small harbor of the bay near twilight. He sat on the docks and watched the fishing boats unload their heavy nets filled with shoals of salmon, pike, and brown trout. Elan, a tall and confident, yet delicate-looking boy, found comfort in the rugged, long-haired fishermen with their burly physiques, creases at the corners of their eyes from days on the water under the sun, and around their mouths from laughter-filled nights at the pub.

The cached sun began to sink and the overcast sky grew dim.

"Young O'Halloran!" Corcoran O'Maolin called out as he stepped on to the shore. "Now I don't want to hear tomorrow 'bout how your Pa gave you a whipping when you got home past dark. Get yerself on, boy, and luck be with you crossing the bog...and beware of the banshees!"

Elan smiled and ran off. His Papa would never whip him, the old fellow rarely even noticed the child's existence, but his mother might grow a wee bit concerned if he were late for supper. Besides his parents and O'Maolin the fisherman, everyone else in Contae na Gaillimhe believed he was strange and many thought him to be possessed by daemons. He was a normal, happy baby but didn't speak at all until the age of five, when he suddenly began to form full sentences, expressing ideas so advanced and using words far too complicated for the locals' vocabulary. The townspeople began to spread gossip about him being a changeling and the farmers marked their lands with wooden crosses, fearing the child was a bastard of the devil. His mother, weary after giving birth twelve times, pretended not to see or hear the insults and his father, a retired, half-blind sailor seemingly close to death, cared only for his blood pudding and his pipe. Elan's brothers and sisters, that is, those who hadn't died in the crib or had by now grown up and married or moved away, sided with the other children of Galway for fear of losing their playmates. Hence, he was left alone, at peace with the magic of the callows grasslands, the woodlands and the lake.

That night when he returned to the low, greywacke stone cottage where he often slept alone on the floor in front of the hearth instead of squeezing between his two older brothers on a crude bed the size of a ladder, an unfamiliar priest was at the family table, eating cabbage stew from Elan's little bowl. His mother's tired eyes were wet and his grim old father lit his pipe and nodded at the boy. "Kiss your mother good-bye now, son."

Elan, bewildered, did so and was taken out of the only shelter he ever knew and traveled with the priest to a monastery on Inis Meain of the Aran Isles. There, the priest, named Father Braonain, whose mission, it turned out, was to drive the daemons from Elan's scrawny little being, locked the poor child in a cell for three weeks and fed him nothing but soda bread and roasted cloves of garlic.

In his isolation, Elan spent his time gazing out of the cell's one small window at how the cloud formations changed during the day and how the stars made particular patterns at night. To ease his lonesomeness, he began to converse with the quite eloquent spiders, rather chatty mice and meticulous ants that shared his room, and also with the graceful robins and melancholy sparrows that frequently came to rest upon the ledge of the windowsill.

They told him many things about the universe and he learned a great deal, yet his new friends also reminded him that, "the truth is a secret known only by the few."

The one time Father Braonain entered the child's dark, damp cell, he gave the boy a book entitled, The Holy Bible. Elan read this book all the way through, not because he liked the stories but because he found it to be an amusing contrast to the philosophies of the robins and spiders.

Alas, after twenty-one days of what some might refer to as absolute hell, but for Elan, at seven and a half years old, seemed to be more like the purgatory described in the book, he was released by a somber monk who led him to a grand room with a dark wooden desk, heavy red drapes and a sofa so downy, that the minute Father Braonain allowed the boy to sit down, he fell fast asleep.

When he woke, the priest dangled a carrot before his eyes and began to ask him many banal questions about many mundane things. The swinging of the carrot and his hunger made him dizzy and for those several, horrible hours as the dusky light pouring into the nicely furnished room played with a myriad of wily spirits, Elan kept his wisdom secret and answered Father Braonain by laconically quoting the many passages he'd memorized from that strange yet entertaining book he'd been given.

Finally, a servant came in with a candle and Elan was given the carrot to eat.

Braonain patted the boy on the head. "There, there, little bunny. You've done well."

The next morning, after a healthy crust of soda bread, the priest walked Elan out to the road and put him on the back of a wagon carrying sacks of grain. The wagon drove to the coast of Inis Meain and there, the boy was put on a sailboat. He was thrilled to be going home! But the boat passed right through Galway Bay without stopping at the harbor. Elan's wide eyes searched desperately for a sight of his tall friend O'Maolin, but the evening hour was early and all the bearded men were still out fishing. The boat continued northward up the Lough Corrib. It was a cloudless day and the lake sparkled. Elan leaned over the edge to watch the rings spread out behind the prow on the surface of the water. A few fish jumped up and said, "Hello."

"Hello," said Elan Fidhne O'Halloran.

The friendly school of trout continued jumping about and told him the story about Caislean na Circe, the noble castle up ahead that filled the greater part of a small island. They told him how it was built by a witch who left a magic hen to look after it, and told its residents that as long as the hen was cared for, no harm would come to their castle, themselves or their land. Alas, soon enough, severe storms arrived for a fortnight and the people in the castle had no way to go to the mainland to replenish their food supply. So, they roasted the hen and ate it. The very next day, in the shining sun, an army of Norman knights laid siege to Caislean na Circe and threw its hen-eating residents into the lake.

"Who lives there now?" asked Elan.

"A queen."

"Is she evil?"

"No, she is sad. They call her Tristina Agnette."

"What of the king?"

"He is dead."

"Ah, so that's why she's sad. She must be lonely."

"Possibly," said the school of trout. "But hey, we're just fish. We don't get sad and lonely!"

"Then I envy you," Elan called out as they swam away.

The boat finally laid anchor on the shores of Lake Corrib near the village of An Fhairche. A man was waiting there on a small sandy beach wearing a long, white habit beneath a black scapular with a cowl pulled over his head, and a wooden cross hanging around his neck on a chain. He took Elan by the hand, a cold, icy hand, and said, "You are to come with me, young O'Halloran."

Elan, utterly lost by now, asked bravely, "But who are you and where are you taking me?"

"My name is Ruane O'Keane and I am a Cistercian monk. I am taking you to live in our abbey where you will learn to obey the orders of St. Benedictine. Father Braonain sent me a letter explaining your special gifts." The monk squatted down to look Elan in the face. "Yet if you are to be useful, such gifts must be tamed."

The boy shivered from the sight of Ruane O'Keane's wan, hollow-cheeked face beneath the black hood. He wished to run but his belly felt sunk into its own emptiness and he hadn't the strength.

They crossed the windy beach and were soon in the village where several men were roasting a boar on a spit and women were emptying baskets of vegetables onto a long table laid out for some kind of grand feast. Elan's eyes grew wide and he felt he would faint. Ruane O'Keane noticed the boy's hand slipping from his grip and kindly asked a red-cheeked woman if she'd be so kind, under the gaze of our Lord, to give the child a repast of apples and cheese.

Revived, Elan was able to make the long journey on foot, past the village and through a dense forest to an isolated meadow where the foreboding, dilapidated, stony old abbey stood. He was greeted somberly by a group of monks and O'Keane showed him to a room in the tower, a small cell that contained a bed where a straw mattress was covered by two wool blankets. There was even a real pillow stuffed with feathers! The child slept for twelve hours. When he woke, he ate fried eggs at a table in the kitchen, was given his lessons in Latin, shown how to pray in the chapel and sent to work with the other monks on their small farm. And so, the days went on and on without change.

Life in the abbey was not so bad. He liked learning Latin, didn't mind prayer and talked to the goats and chickens in the farmyard. But the thing that made it almost magical was the abbey's library. Each night when the monks retired to their cells, Elan snuck out of his tower room with a hand full of candles he'd made himself and visited the library to search for strange, dusty manuscripts that the monks, serene and numb, had long ago decided they had no use for.

The Occitan lyric poetry of Guilhen de Peiticus, Bernart de Ventadorn, Girat de Bornelh and especially Chrétien de Troyes enlightened him far more than the Song of Solomon and he became obsessed with the stories of Roland, Perceval, Tristan, Lancelot and of course King Arthur and his knights of the round table. The tales taught him about manhood, courage, might and chivalry, but most importantly, something that the monks never could, about romance, women and love.

Ruane O'Keane had apparently forgotten about Elan's so-called "gifts," and the other monks kept to themselves. And so, alone his with imagination, life evolved thus for ten fleeting years.

Then one exceedingly stormy night, as the ferocious winds howled through the cracked walls of the crumbling abbey, and the stained glass windows rattling in their lead frames were struck with thousands of hail stones whipped from the sling shots of an army of the macabre goblins who lived in the hills, a stranger appeared.

Most of the monks had retired to their cells, but Elan, excited by the electricity of the storm, had taken his books into the kitchen to sit before the warmth and light of the great hearth.

He turned his pages to the words of the valiant Arnaut Daniel:
"Yet in spite of the ills I suffer,
I shall not desist from loving...

...I am Arnaut who gathers the wind
And hunts the hare with the ox
And swims against the incoming tide."

Oh, how he longed to travel and see the world, to be brave and meet a girl! Alas, his peasant parents, who had long since forgotten him, were ever poor. He had no family ancestry of nobility or lineage to knighthood. He never learned to fight or joust and could barely shoot a straight arrow. He had no skill for weaponry, although he did spend many hours in the great woods behind the abbey, practicing with a sword he had found when he was fourteen years old, one winter's day upon a solitary walk.

The tip of its silver blade glinted in a ray of light that suddenly struck through the towering pines and he pulled it up from a mound of melting snow. It was surprisingly heavy, rusted and ancient, and he guessed by the raw yet meticulous craftsmanship that it had probably been dropped in the forest by an Irish knight during the Norman invasion of the last century. Elan held the sword up in the quivering stripes of sunlight and for the first time in his life, felt alive, proud and something he never felt before, which he wanted to believe might be love.

He didn't dare bring the sword into the abbey, so he returned the following day with salt water and an oilcloth to clean off the tarnish. He measured it and sewed a sheath for it with the leather he'd gathered from the old shoes of several monks, too lofty to question his request. He made a home for it by placing a sheet of fleece in the hollow of a fallen tree, where he knew the good nixies often went to sleep, and each time he pulled it from its sheath, he could tell they had blessed it. In return for their confidence, he halved fallen walnuts and lined the shells with dandelion tufts, making beds for the invisible protectors of his sword, Elan's very own sword, which he finally named, after he had a dream about Ireland's legendary metalsmith, Goibniu.

On the night of the storm, he read on from *The Song of Roland* back in the kitchen:

"When I shall stand in this great clash of hosts
I'll strike a thousand and sev'n hundred strokes
Blood-red the steel of Durendal shall flow..."

The page fell into a shadow as the last blue lick of fire clinging to the logs in the hearth wiggled violently in another gust of rushing wind. He rose to take more firewood from the dwindling pile beside the kitchen door. Someone knocked. Elan stood with the kindling in his arms. It came again, a quick, furtive knock, light yet desperate and certainly not from the hands of man, nor a daemon or a ghoul, and yet too sturdy and large to be coming from the hands of a faerie. And ghosts don't knock; they just walk in, or rather, through. The knock came again and he heard a voice, muffled by the pounding hail and stormy rain.

Elan threw the sticks on the fire to light up the small kitchen and went to the door. The voice on the other side was crying. He lifted the latch. It was a girl around his age. Her red cloak, dripping wet, was pressed to the white dress beneath it and clung to her slender figure. Her long black hair hung icy and flat around her snow-white face. She rushed inside and he shut the door and led her to the hearth.

She began to undress.

He didn't protest.

"I'll be right back," he told her and ran to his tower cell to take the blankets off his bed.

She was hugging herself and shivering before the fire when he returned, completely naked save for a pink ribbon around her neck. He wrapped the blankets around her shoulders. After many long minutes of silence, the heat brought color to her cheeks and her hair began to dry in thick, bouncy curls.

"I'm not well, kind sir. I must sleep," she whispered.

"Come with me."

Elan took her to the tower where she lay upon his straw mattress, wrapped in the blankets, and closed her eyes.

He quietly dashed down the winding stair to put out the fire and gather the scrolls and her soaking wet clothes. He lit another fire in the tiny stove in his cell and hung her dress and cloak before it, then sat in his one chair and tried to read *The Tales of Fiorin and Fianna,* to keep himself awake during the night in order to care for her, but found that he didn't need to read nor had he the slightest urge to shut his eyes, for her sleeping beauty could have kept him awake for centuries. That night, Elan Fidhne O'Halloran fell in love for the second time in his life, and knew that this time it was for real.

The storm had abated when the girl awoke just before dawn. The rain and hail had stopped, yet the gusty wind trapped a fleet of autumn leaves to continually spiral around Elan's tower like a cyclone. The girl sat up in bed and watched them whirl past his window.

"Good morning," she said. Then somewhat oddly, but politely, she asked,

"May I have some milk?"

"Milk?"

She smiled. "Please?"

He went down to the kitchen where a few early risen monks had gathered for porridge and were just letting in the milkmaid who carried two full pails.

The monks rarely spoke and especially not to Elan, which was something he'd grown accustomed to during his years there. Save for the few orders his father used to give him for doing chores, the lullaby his mother once sang to him when he was a babe, the occasional friendly warnings given him by O'Maolin the fisherman and the grave questions put to him by Father Braonain, the girl, asking for milk, was the only other human soul that had ever addressed him in a direct and personal fashion.

May I have some milk? The voice fluttered in his head like a butterfly and he laughed, also another first, as he dipped the ladle into the bucket to fill a ceramic cup up to the brim.

When he returned to his room, he saw that she'd unwrapped herself from the blankets and put on her white dress.

"Is it dry?"

"It will do. Thank you."

He gave her the cup and she took little sips, one right after the other until the milk was gone.

"My name is Elan," he told her.

"Isabelle, from Meath."

"Meath? Why, that's a far journey."

"Oh, not really. When one is determined…Where am I now anyway?"

"You don't know?"

"I remember the storm."

"You're in Clonbur, in a monastery."

She looked him up and down, at his dull white habit and black cowl, then stared into his eyes.

Her eyes were so green, almost yellow.

Suddenly, the loud iron knocker of the front door of the abbey banged once, twice, thrice. Again and again, brutally. Elan heard the monks shuffling into the front hall and then an aggressive, gruff voice resounded up the stairwell.

"Oh, no," the girl said.

Elan hurried downstairs and when he reached the bottom, he was obnoxiously pushed aside by a huge, evil ogre swinging a club.

"Where is she? You monks can't fool me! I know she's here...Isabelle! Isabelle!" The ogre started up the stairwell. The great mass of his body barely fit in the narrow passage way and his legs thudded like tree stumps as he forced his way and weight up to the tower.

Most of the monks ran into the chapel to kneel fervently in prayer while the remaining few nervously set the icons in the foyer that the ogre had toppled over with his club, upright again.

Elan followed the hideous being, ridiculously trying to slip through his legs and move ahead of him to his room, to save the girl, but the monster's bulk prevented him.

"Isabelle! I know you're here! I can smell you!" The ogre reached the small tower cell and ripped the door off its hinges. Elan raced up and stood behind him.

The boisterous intruder roared, turned around, barged back downstairs, raided the meager pantry in the kitchen and stormed out the back door.

Elan stood in the doorway, astonished. The girl was gone. Instead, on his bed, atop a red cloth, sitting peacefully with its paws curled beneath its belly, was a fluffy white cat.

He went to it and scratched its chin. "Isabelle? Is that you?"

The cat opened its green-yellow eyes and purred, yet didn't respond, which was highly unusual, for as we know by now, Elan was gifted with the ability to speak to animals.

He stood and picked the ceramic cup up off the floor. "I'll get you some more milk, little kitty, would you like that?"

The cat closed its eyes, purring.

He went into the kitchen only to discover that the insane ogre had drunk down both buckets of milk, and when he returned the cat was gone. He searched the corners of his room and then the entire abbey for her without success. When he finally came back to his room, he noticed a pink ribbon on his bed where the cat had sat and the girl had slept. He tied it around his wrist and looked out the window. The drop down was deadly and he feared he might see a clump of white fur in a rain puddle but saw only clumps of wet autumn leaves. He looked beyond into the forest and did see something, a red and white shadow seemingly running through the trees.

A witch or a faerie she must be, he thought, but a good one for sure. She had to be good because...because he'd fallen in love with her. Alas, she had disappeared! All the chivalrous romantic poems he'd been reading whirled in his heart and at that moment, as the bells of the chapel were calling him to prayer, Elan left the monastery as fast as he could and ran straight into the woodland to the spot where he'd hidden Goibniu. He tucked the sword securely into his belt and ran through the forest in search of his lost love.

"Excuse me, kind sir, have you by chance seen a beautiful young maiden in a red cloak pass by?" he asked a chipmunk, who pointed to the other side of a great ravine.

Elan stood at the edge of the wide, abysmal gorge as a wave of hopelessness overcame him. It would be impossible to cross. But suddenly he heard a series of creaking noises and stepped back as the roots of a tall, ancient oak tree tore free from the soil beneath it and the oak toppled over in one fell swoop, creating a bridge across the divide.

He got to the other side and ran and searched and put the same question to a woodpecker, a squirrel, a rabbit and a snake, darting through the forest, turning this way and that until he found himself in the deepest, darkest center of the woodland, long ago having trodden off the path. The last rays of sunlight subtly faded from the towering black branches of ponderous trees as Elan finally sat on a moss-covered rock and felt the cold dampness of the twilight seeping through the woolen cloth of his habit.

In his life, the boy had never wept. But there, in the heart of the savage forest, as the rich smells of decay and rebirth rose from the earth, his eyes swelled up and a flood of tears flowed down his flushing cheeks. He opened his lips, pink as when he was a child, to taste them.

"Who...who...who..."

Elan looked up in the direction of the call until his moist eyes adjusted to the blackness surrounding him. In a single stripe of moonlight, he saw the silver feathers of an orange-eyed owl.

Before the boy could speak, the owl said, "You must be lost, my child."

"I am, sir."

"But why have you ventured so far into the woodland?"

Elan told the owl his whole story and found comfort from his wounded heart by doing so.

The wise owl listened attentively and when the boy had finished, he said, "She is not a witch, your Isabelle. She is a princess, daughter of the queen who lives in the Caislean na Circe."

"Have you seen her? Did she come this way?"

"No, no. She has been out of the forest since noon, after all, how could she have come this far? You are the only human to ever cross the great ravine."

"Then she must have returned to the castle."

"Who...who...who..." The owl couldn't help but hoot occasionally. "Perhaps, but it would be risky. You see, Isabelle is a princess but also part faerie."

"A faerie princess?"

"Well, of a sort. Queen Tristina Agnette of Dunadhaigh, her mother, is a faerie that married a mortal, King Clonricarde de Bougos. It was the life she chose *a cause de l'amour*" (It is a well-known fact that owls often have the habit of speaking alternatively in French).

"Alas, King Clonricarde, who at first appeared to be a charming man, turned out to be a greedy miser and when his only daughter turned fifteen, one year ago, he made a deal with an evil ogre who agreed to pay the king a boatload of gold for betrothal to Isabelle. Queen Tristina Agnette wouldn't have it, she loved her daughter so, but upon the request of the king, as she had given up her faerie powers during their wedding vows, the poor woman could find no recourse to the terrible ordeal.

"Soon, the boat arrived on the island. The ogre stepped ashore and after the king had seen all the gold, the unfortunate wedding ceremony was performed on the spot, the ogre drooling as Isabelle and the queen clung to each other in tears. The ogre had a second boat docked at the island to carry away his bride, but just before they got in, the ogre went to the boat filled with gold with an auger in his giant hand and punctured its bottom in several places with holes.

"King Clonricarde de Bougos, eager for his riches, barely hugged the princess good-bye before he was in the boat, filling sack after sack with gold coins and carrying them onto the shore. He had only just started when he noticed that the vessel was surely sinking. He called to his knights, servants and vassals to help him unload the cargo yet they were all so drunk from the wedding feast, as the ogre had provided his own blend of strong mead, that the few who did come to his aide were of little assistance. Down, down, down the boat went as the king continued to fill up his satchels and toss them onto shore. Finally, just as the shimmer of gold was leaving the surface of the water, King Clonricarde's cloth sack got caught on an oar hook. The king pulled and tugged but could not get it loose, nor could he give up that last sack of gold. Alas, as the moon rose in the heavens, the boat sank to the bottom of the lake with the greedy king attached.

"The next morning, Queen Agnette, who had locked herself in her quarters to mourn and fast, did not hear the commotion that was taking place on her island. The knights, servants and vassals awoke from their drunken slumbers to find an island littered with a hundred sacks of gold. They each grabbed one, piled into all the boats belonging to the king's fleet and sailed to the mainland to start life anew.

"The queen has been alone in the castle ever since, probably drowning herself, metaphorically, in tears."

Elan shuddered at the thought of Isabelle wed to the awful ogre and prayed that the beast had not yet found her.

"Thank you, sir," he said. "May I rest here for the night?"

The owl blinked its orange eyes. "Who…who…who…"

Elan draped his cowl over his head, wrapped his habit tightly around him to keep warm and lay down on a mossy patch of earth to finally sleep, knowing what he must do.

He awoke at the brink of dawn and moved on, following the directions the owl had given him. He found a little stream and hurried along beside it until it widened and broke off into a tiny waterfall. There he met some beavers and asked them to help him build a minimal raft whilst he wound brambles around the tips of broken branches to use as oars. By noon, he reached the isle of the Caislean na Circe, or, as the beavers called it, Cushlaun na-ker-ka.

He walked through the vacant courtyard where knights had once stood on guard and straight up to the castle's impressive door. He knocked and waited. Of course, if the princess had in fact returned, the lonely queen wouldn't answer, fearing it might be the ogre. Elan saw a little purple hummingbird drinking nectar from a honeysuckle vine. He asked it to fly round to all the castle windows and if it saw a beautiful young girl, "then give this to her." He took the ribbon from his wrist and the hummingbird held it in his beak.

The bird returned shortly and the ribbon was gone. He knocked again and the princess opened the door. "You've come!" she said.

"Yes. I've come to save you."

She let him inside.

"But Isabelle, this is the first place the ogre will look for you."

"I know, I know. I've only been here for an hour and must leave quickly. After a year in that beast's paws, I desperately needed to see my mother."

The purple hummingbird re-appeared at a windowsill and told Elan that a ship was approaching the island.

"He's coming!" Isabelle grabbed her red cloak and took Elan's hand. "We must go. We must hurry!"

"And the queen?"

"He doesn't want the queen, he wants me."

"But can't you just turn into a cat or disappear or something?"

"You don't understand, but there's no time now to explain. Take me to your ship please."

He brought her to his tiny, makeshift raft.

"That's it?"

He shrugged.

They climbed on. Elan grabbed the oars. The waves began to rise, troubled by the ogre's approaching galley ship. Elan rowed as hard as he could. Last night's storm had turned the lake over and a fast tide was moving southward to their advantage, but it wasn't enough.

"Have you no powers?" he asked.

"Since I was sold to that devil, no. My faerie powers have all been relinquished except for by chance, upon a night when a full moon shines brightly through a storm. Hence, the night before last, after twelve months in agony, I was able to set myself free. I changed into a tiny faerie and was traveling east from Meath on the back of a magpie when it began to hail over Lake Corrib. Alas, the moon was hidden and I fell from the back of the magpie and landed in the forest near your abbey as a mortal. Now he shall surely get me!"

The raft rose and dived over the roaring waves and the spray soaked them. "We can't make it like this, we need help." Elan searched the sky but didn't see one hawk or seagull and looked down at the water but all the fish had fled to the depths of the great lake.

"Look!" Isabelle pointed to a slippery, dark shape moving beside them.

"It's a seal!" Elan said happily.

"Not just a seal," the princess cried with hope. "I believe it's a *selkie*!"

The seal came close to the raft and Elan spoke to it. Within minutes a dozen selkies surrounded their feeble vessel and carried it smoothly along, far away from the Caislean ne Circe, past Inchagoill and the Carrahmore shore, and finally into calm waters where, with half the raft torn in pieces, Isabelle clung to Elan as he rowed forth, bravely into the bay of Galway.

They made it to the shore and collapsed on the small, pebbled beach, entwined in each other's arms. Elan had not slept properly in days and was exhausted, yet refused to rest until he was sure his love was safe from harm.

"Where are we?" she asked.

"Galway," he answered. "The place where I was born." He rose and took her hand. "Come, I have a plan."

They walked along the shore, as the dense clouds in the sky grew darker.

"It looks like another storm is coming," she said. "Yet the moon is no longer full. We must find shelter."

"Ah! That is my plan dear lady, or shall I say princess, or faerie?"

"I am nothing as long as the ogre is alive."

Elan stopped in his tracks and turned to her defiantly. "And I intend to change that, Isabelle."

She moved her face close to his, so close that their tender lips were less than an inch apart. She was about to speak when he put his finger softly to her parting pink lips and said, "Shh. Listen."

"As I walked by the dockside one evening so fair
To view the salt water and take the sea air
I heard an old fisherman singing a song
Won't ya take me away, boys, me time is not long
Wrap me up in me oil-skin and jumper
No more on the docks I'll be seen
Just tell me ol' shipmates, I'm taking a trip mates
And I'll see you some day in the Fiddler's Green…"

The merry melody and lyrics sailed on the breeze. Elan laughed. "Why of course! It's perfect. I know that voice." He took her hand again and they ran around the bend where a burly, dark bearded sailor was tying his boat to the docks, singing at the top of his lungs:

"Now Fiddler's Green is a place I heard tell
Where the fishermen go if they don't go to hell
Where skies are all clear and the dolphins do play
And the coast of cold Greenland is far, far away
Where the girls are all pretty and the beer it's all free
And there's bottles of rum growin' from every tree!"

The couple ran up to the boat and Elan shouted, "Corcoran O'Maolin!"

The fisherman turned. In ten years, he hadn't changed except for a few extra lines at the corners of his sparkling, sea blue eyes. "And who might ya be, young lad and lovely lassie?"

"'Tis I, Elan Fidhne O'Halloran. Do you remember?"

O'Maolin opened his strong arms. "Ah, little Elan, I was wondrin' what'd 'appened to ya! Come here and give old Corcoran a hug, would ya?"

Another first in the boy's isolated life: a hug.

"Now, who's this pretty girl ya got wit' ya?"

Elan told the fisherman that she was a princess being hunted by an evil ogre.

"Eh? Dat true, eh?" He peered into Isabelle's emerald green eyes.

"Yes," she answered. "Your friend Elan saved my life."

"Did he now?"

"I suppose I did." Elan proudly put a protective arm around the faerie princess. "But we need to find shelter as soon as possible so I'm taking her to my parents' place."

O'Maolin frowned and his bright eyes dimmed. "Ah, Mr. and Mrs. O'Halloran have gone to the other side. Just a few years back t'was. I'm sorry, son."

"And my brothers and sisters?"

"Grown as ya are now and out on their own. Gone south into Leinster where they heard of work on some fancy lord's farm, a descendent of the great King Anguish, father of the fair Iseult. 'Tis what they're sayin' in the pubs," Corcoran said with a wink. "Ah, I am sorry boy, I truly, truly am."

Elan felt another tear rising from the depths of his soul. He hadn't really even thought about his family in ten years, yet they *were* his family.

"Oh, don't ya get all glum on me now, O'Halloran! Look at ya! What a fine young man ya've grown into. Listen, why don't I take the two of yas home to meet the Missus?" He slung a large salmon over his shoulder. "Wait 'til ya see what a meal she'll turn this into!"

They followed the fisherman as he walked toward town, rambling on. "She still thinks I'm in my twenties, that Katie O'Maolin does, and makes me a supper fit for a king even though I keeps telling her dat I can't eat like I used to, ya know? Oh, my Katie's a peach, always has been she 'as, but believe me...after all these years of cookin', now she's round as one, too!" He roared with laughter and his companions giggled also.

He continued, "Dat's right, laugh along. They sure like that one in the pubs, they do!" And he began to sing a new song, his accent even stronger:

"Now whin Oi wuz a little boy an' so me mudder told me,
That if Oi didn't kiss the gals me lips would grow all mouldy!
An' so Oi sailed the seas for many a year not knowin' what I was missin'
Then Oi sets me sails afore the gales and started in a-kissin!
Oi got meself an Oirish gal, like a rose her lips so red…
She stole me boots, she stole me clothes and put me in her bed!"

That evening, Katie O'Maolin made a wonderful supper and afterwards, as Isabelle helped her make up two beds before the hearth, Elan stepped outside of the hut where Corcoran sat on a tree stump with a goblet of sweet wine, savoring the misty moonlight. He offered Elan a sip and the boy's blood warmed. After some minutes of silence, they both witnessed a leprechaun who was scurrying toward his little burrow yonder, trip and do somersaults. They laughed and Elan asked the jolly sailor, "Do you see many faeries out here, Mr. O'Maolin?"

"I often do. 'Tis why I'm sittin' 'ere."

They waited and watched, passing the goblet between them, yet nothing luminous appeared. Finally, Elan said, "I need to kill an ogre."

"Ya do, eh?"

He explained his love for Isabelle and the events of the past day, and related the tale the owl had told him.

When he finished, Corcoran sat staring into the darkness for some time. "From Meath, did ya say? Oh my, now it's much easier to kill an ogre from Ulster or Mayo ya know…but from Meath!"

"Well, can you help me?" Elan's fatigue turned into courage.

"The only way I knows to kill an ogre from Meath is to poison 'im wit' the blood of the tongue of the red dragon who lives in the caves near Druim Snamha."

"Oh." Elan's eyes lowered with instant defeat.

"Here, let me see dat sword ya got in yer belt."

Corcoran examined it carefully. "A wee bit old fashioned but it's a fine ol' weapon indeed. Tomorrow I'll sharpen the blade for ya."

"So I must slay a dragon?" Elan asked as he placed Goibniu back in its sheath.

Corcoran laughed. "Oh no! Ya just got to cut off its tongue!"

"Right." Elan rose and went back into the hut, once again feeling worn and weary and now heated by wine.

In the bright light of morning, after a sound sleep beside Isabelle on the kitchen floor before the glowing red embers in the hearth, the unfeasibility of saving his love no longer seemed impossible. Together with Corcoran, they made ready his sword and summoned the leprechaun from its burrow to draw a map that led the way to the caves of Druim Snamha. Of course the leprechaun charged two bits of gold for his cartography services but O'Maolin didn't mind giving it to him. "My wife will just have to go without her Sunday pie this week, I imagine!" He laughed.

So Elan set out on his journey, leaving Isabelle behind in the O'Maolin's little cabin, in tears at his bravery and sacrifice for her happiness, although she had begged him to take her along.

"You know it's far too dangerous."

"Then why don't we stay together here, picking raspberries and elderberries during the day and sleeping beside each other on the kitchen floor at night? Perhaps a storm may come again when there's a full moon and I'll have my powers and…"

"You know as well as I that your dreadful husband will certainly find you soon. We can't take chances. Oh, Princess! I may be a dreamer, a peasant's son, a romantic and a fool, but I've become a learned man. If anything, all those lonely, dreary years at the abbey have made me a sensible, practical fellow."

"Huh!" She grew angry. "Leprechauns, selkies and talking owls…how very practical you are, O'Halloran!" She turned to walk off in a huff but he grabbed her arm, turned her around, pressed her to his chest and kissed her pink lips with great passion.

Then, off our valiant hero went to cut out the tongue from the red dragon of Druim Snamha and murder the terrible Ogre of Meath.

Isabelle waited impatiently in the fisherman's cabin with no word from her lover for three and a half weeks. Corcoran told her there was hearsay neither at the harbor nor in the pubs and Katie said she hadn't heard a single rumor about a tongue-less dragon nor a dead ogre in the nearby village or the fields.

Alas, thirty days after she'd first taken shelter in the abbey, Isabelle walked back to the O'Maolin's hut with a basket on her arm filled with gooseberries beneath a late afternoon sky rapidly turning dark with stormy clouds.

She passed by O'Maolin, who was sitting on his tree stump with his flask of sweet wine starring up at the sky.

"What are looking at?" she asked.

"The moon, dear maiden; the round, full, bright shining moon."

She stopped to gaze at it beside him. Her basket became heavier. It was filling up with rain. Fat drops of stormy rain!

They both ran into the cabin.

"Now where's that darling princess?" asked Katie O'Maolin.

"Why, she's right here behind me," Corcoran answered, but when he turned round he saw only a basket filled with berries on the floor.

"How much of that wine 'av you been sipping, Mister?" Katie took the flask away from him.

"But I swear she was wit' me, looking at the full moon."

Suddenly a tiny, sparkling white halo of light began flying around the cozy room. The O'Maolins watched in awe.

"'Tis Isabelle, I believe!" Corcoran laughed. "She's turned into a faerie!"

The little light bounced up and down, letting the sailor know what he said was true then out the window she flew.

Isabelle reached Meath where the moon was still shining through the rain. As she approached the ogre's castle she noticed a giant body floating in the mote. It was the hideous ogre, dead. And there in the muddy grass, another body laid flat, Elan's body. She swooped down and landed directly on his heart. It had stopped. She didn't have time to weep. His blood had just begun to grow cold. The moon began to wobble in the liquid sky.

She'd never before performed such magic but knew it could be done: by kissing the lips of a mortal who had just died, a faerie could bring him back to life, but only as another faerie. It was her only hope, his only hope. She kissed him.

The rain grew fierce and hid the moon but the ogre was certainly dead. Her powers were back for good.

Elan, more beautiful than ever, rose from the ground. His hair was full and wavy and long, his pallid monk's complexion changed to a healthy glow, his sweet eyes bright as dark jewels and his habit turned into a suit made of the finest gold thread, the suit of a a faerie prince.

"How…? What has happened?" he asked, embracing Isabelle who looked more radiant than ever in an emerald green silk gown that made her beautiful eyes sparkle.

"I had no choice my love, but to make you immortal."

"I remember dying…I remember saying your name with my last breath."

"Yet you live, and shall live, here in the faerie world. I'm sorry, but I took the liberty to make you a prince."

"Then, dear Isabelle, I shall make you my princess!"

And the two flew back to the Caislean na Circe, where they summoned all the faeries from the shores of the Atlantic Ocean to the Celtic Sea and had the grandest wedding that Ireland has ever seen.

"Ah, you're pullin' our legs now, O'Maolin," said the sailor Dermot Donaghue.

"You want us te believe dat you and your Katie just came back from a faerie wedding in a castle on an island in the Lough Corrib?" mocked the sailor Timothy MacGowan.

"He's been drinking the sweet wine again, I say," laughed the sailor named Ffyn O'Flanegan.

"Believe whats ya wants ta!" Corcoran winked at his friends, lifted a net full of trout from the water and began to sing the new song he'd learned from his dear, newly wed friends, Prince Elan and Princess Isabelle of the Lough Corrib faeries.

Elizabeth McKague

VII

Malta, Italy
Present

Marianne stormed, or rather silently stormed—that is, a storm was brewing within her as she crossed the threshold from the fake marbled hallway of the Hotel Pheonicia into their fourth story suite. She tossed her bag on the sofa and stood in the open doorway to the *salle de bain*, where Claude was sunk, pleasantly mindless in the whirlpool bath.

He blinked in her direction to see that the salt and pepper had been erased and that her long, wavy, brittle hair was now as red as Persephone's. "Did you have a nice time in the underworld then, my dear?"

"A nice time? This place is crawling with tourists and there is not one thing or person around here that appears to be real!"

"It is called the *Realm of Shades*, after all."

"What the hell are you talking about?"

"Your head is on fire, love…come, why don't you join me in the bath?"

She touched her locks. "It will fade."

"Love fades. The Inferno…not so sure about that one." He lifted his shoulders and sat upright in the tub. "Come along, the temperature right now is perfect and check this out…" He pushed a button setting the jets on full force, making the water around him suddenly erupt like a foamy white volcano.

"I'm not getting in there."

"Why not?"

"Obviously, I just had my hair done!"

Claude calmed the jets. "What happened, Marianne?"

She closed the toilet seat and sat down, then began to cry.

"Sweetheart, what is it?" Claude stepped out of the tub and wrapped a towel around his waist. "My God, what…you haven't acted like this since you went through menopause."

"Shut up. I hate it here, I want to go home."

He went to her and was about to place his wet hand on her hair but she pushed it away.

"Listen, one more night and then we'll go back to Gozo in the morning," he said. "I actually like it here. It's luxurious."

"Of course you like it here. You're French!"

"Okay. Okay, now…"

"And I don't mean Gozo, I mean home. Home!"

"Paris? You want to go back to Paris?"

She shook her head, whimpering.

"England? Seriously, England?"

Her newly dyed hair rustled like autumn leaves. "No, no. Not Gozo, not Paris and not bloody England…just home!"

Claude took another towel, (there were at least six neatly rolled on a rack) to dry himself off. "Alright, alright now. Let's go into the bedroom and talk about this."

"I can't believe you. *That* won't help!"

"No, I mean, there's weird echoes in here and I have to take a leak."

"Oh, sorry." She unraveled a wad of tissue paper to blow her nose and moved into the grand bedroom where she stood before the sliding glass door of a small balcony that overlooked the astonishingly large hotel pool, surrounded by lounge chairs into which beauties and beasts appeared to be melting. One person, one person only, was swimming.

Claude came up behind her. "Marianne?"

"I'm old, Clues."

"I'm older."

"You're a man."

"I understand." He put his arms around her. She turned and placed her head against his shoulder and squeezed him tight like a sad little girl who believes her teddy bear is real.

"You okay now?" he asked after some time.

She pulled back and opened the glass door. The air was hot but had salt in it and there was a cool, bluish glint rising up from the pool.

"I miss the kids," she finally said. "I feel so wretchedly old without them. Used up. Torn in half."

"Ah, that's home. I get it. So, we'll have Esmond take the tube from Oxford and visit them in Paris."

"People *leave* Paris in August; they don't go there."

"Then we'll buy them tickets to come here."

"But it's impractical. Besides, I'm sure they have plans with friends or girlfriends."

"Then they bring their girlfriends."

"Another toe, two toes…"

"Alas, my pretty bather is already on crutches, baby, it doesn't matter."

"But it does matter. What about the book? What if it doesn't sell? What if it's a bunch of rubbish?"

"It is a bunch of rubbish."

"It is?"

"Maybe, maybe not. Maybe it's a monument to beauty, but nobody reads anymore so who cares anyway? Art has two lives."

She smiled, not "the smile," but a kind of smile that knew, a human smile of knowledge trapped in the silence of eternal recognition.

"Hey, I'll get dressed and we'll go out before dinner for a drink somewhere nice and shady."

Marianne nodded and went out onto the balcony. The lone swimmer climbed out of the pool and shook his head of dark curls. He was wearing Hawaiian bathing trunks. She quickly grabbed Claude's new eyeglasses from their case on the nightstand and put them on then went back out onto the balcony.

It was Dave.

Although the sun was sloping toward a suddenly intimate horizon, the air continued to sizzle with heat. Outside the resort hotel, the medieval streets appeared as a viscous river of tourists in white cotton shorts and tank tops, glued to their languid torsos. Between the beads of sweat on their tanned foreheads and the threads of sweat trickling down their red necks, shaded eyes cast down upon the glossy, pastel paper shopping bags locked in the clasp of elastic-looking knuckles.

Claude had put on a pair of taupe linen trousers and a white muslin shirt with the sleeves rolled up to his elbows and the top three buttons undone to expose the slight gray hairs on his chest. Marianne wore a strapless, turquoise dress that seemed, in her husband's clandestine opinion, as if it had been designed to glow in the moonlight like plankton or some other kind of phosphorescent underwater algae. They'd stopped in the air conditioned lobby of the Hotel Phoenicia and were staring out of the 360 degree array of tinted windows at the scintillating, slow motion scene on the street.

"Flotsam and jetsam." Claude's lips curled to one side. "I don't want to go out in *that*, do you?"

"No." Marianne frowned.

"Let's just have a drink on the terrace here."

"Which terrace? This place has six bars."

"Come along." He offered her his arm, turned her around and directed her to a display of brochures near the reception counter. "Here, you pick."

Marianne held the glossy quarto before her nose and read aloud, "The Helmsman's Room, The Sandpiper Cafe, Bliss Bar, Clamshell Cocktail Lounge, Honeymoon Haven and The Everlasting Nipple of the Bathing Woman in the Half Devoured Painting of Monsieur Renoir."

"It doesn't say that!" He snatched the flimsy brochure from her hand. "They're all in Italian."

"*Ma certamente.*"

"Okay, let's just go to whatever bar is on the top floor."

"Sound's risky."

They walked to the elevator. "You're having fun again, aren't you?" He tickled her waistline thanking the lord she still had one.

"*Again?*"

Luckily, it was early enough that they were seated at the last available table at the edge of the terrace, with a phenomenally dramatic view of the Mediterranean Sea.

"I'll have a glass of the Laurenti Viognier," Marianne told the pretty, slim-nosed waitress and Claude ordered the 1565 Victory Lager.

"Beer?" Marianne squealed as Claude watched the waitress's behind. "You haven't drunk a beer in ten years!"

"It's cold and I'm hot." His eyes left the disappearing wide bottom of the thin-nosed girl and twinkled upon his wife's surprised expression. "And I'll have you know that this particular beer has a historical context as it happens to be named after the Maltese victory over the Ottoman Empire in the great siege of 1565."

"How do you know that?"

"Well, it's the only logical conclusion for its name."

"But…beer?"

"And I think I'll have steak for dinner."

"To each his own," she huffed, "said the woman as she kissed the cow."

"My, we are clever tonight, aren't we?"

"You are. But I, my dear, am feeble, misguided, bereaved by age, cursed by womanhood and abandoned by all save my beer-drinking, meat-eating muse."

"I love you, too."

No smile. She sat back. The moon rose. Her dress illumined.

For a moment Claude gazed out over the sea as if it was something new and amazing, something he'd never seen before, although he'd been gazing at the same sea for half a year now, day after day, night after night, only from a different angle.

The wide-bottomed waitress brought their drinks. He looked at his wife and told her, "Your hair looks very nice tonight."

"It'll fade." She drank silently.

Her dress was quite the glimmering sponge now in the moonlight and he imagined starfish and seahorses buoyantly bouncing around in it, feeling as he suddenly did, like the man in that story by Octavio Paz, who falls in love with a wave.

"Tomorrow," Marianne whispered, although Claude knew not why, "Let's stop by the post in Xaghra when we get off the ferry."

"Yeah. Okay."

That deceptive pearl, the August moon, rose into the glass of the balcony doors of their suite at the Hotel Phoenicia at midnight. Claude awoke in the gossamer light from the lamps along the harbor filtering through half drawn white curtains to find himself utterly alone in the humongous, 400 euro a night bed. He turned on the lamp. He rose, went into the bathroom and pissed in the dark, then turned on the light, but no one was there. Half asleep, he returned to the suite and opened the wardrobe…but why would she be in there? He stepped out onto the vacant balcony. The night air was warm. The empty pool, lit from below the taciturn blue surface, was so still it looked like a photograph.

He could have called out her name, quietly into the soft, stationary air, but did not. Deep down, he felt troubled and aware.

He returned to the room, turned off the lamp and lay on the bed but did not pull the white moonlit sheet over him. He was naked. After dinner he had made love to his wife for six, maybe eight minutes before they both, hot and light yet heavy at the same time, drifted breezily into a deep sleep.

Claude lay still and waited. Perhaps forty-five minutes passed before he turned his back to the door when he heard her trying twice with the electronic key. From the husband's knowledgeable eyes in the back of his head, he watched her sea green dress fall to the floor then felt her breasts pressing against his back and her right arm wrapping round his shoulder.

Marianne pulled the strewn sheet neatly over their naked limbs. It seemed, in the interval she'd been away, to be freshly washed in moonlight.

As they sat in white plastic chairs at the half round table on the balcony the next morning, he asked, "Are you going to eat your croissant?"

She lifted the pastry up then let it fall back upon her little white plate. "This is not a croissant."

"Regardless, are you going to eat it?"

Marianne slid the plate towards him, sipped black coffee and set her eyes away from him, downwards upon the glassy blue of the cool pool.

Claude chewed and spoke at once, "Where did you go last night?"

Marianne didn't answer.

Claude swallowed and began to repeat the question but she answered directly without diverting her gaze.

"The bar."

"Which bar?"

"In the hotel."

"Which hotel bar?"

"The big one. The one off the main lobby."

He ate in silence and poured himself another glass of orange juice. "Do you want…?"

"Just coffee for me this morning, Clues, thanks."

"Why?" he asked.

"Hmm?"

"Why did you go to the bar?"

"I don't know."

"To have a drink perhaps?"

"Yeah, to have a drink."

Claude sat back in the white chair and looked down at the pool. They both watched two little boys do cannonballs straight into the still water, making pretty splashes as their sedate and beautiful Italian mother lay back in a lounge chair.

"What did you drink?"

"Hmm?"

"Last night…at the hotel bar off the main lobby…what did you drink?"

"Water."

"Marianne…"

"I don't know. I don't know! I felt anxious up here in the room and the moon…I…" She finally turned to look at him. "The American was there."

"The American?"

"You know, the surfer, the Californian."

"Dave?"

"Yeah."

"Really?"

"It seems he and his wife followed us here." She laughed.

"They followed us here?"

"I'm kidding. It was coincidental."

"So, how is she?"

"Who?"

"The wife."

"Not sure. She was sleeping."

"At the bar?"

"No! In their hotel room."

"Oh." Claude crumpled a paper napkin. "Those croissants were terrible."

"Told you."

"What did he say, the American?"

"Not much. In a form of complete sentences, anyway." She chuckled.

Claude did not. "But why, Marianne?"

"I don't know! I told you…I'm old and I want to go home."

He stood. "Okay. Okay."

Her eyes as she glared up at him were filled with love and fear. "Let's catch the early ferry, shall we, so we can make it to the post?"

"Of course."

As they waited on the docks, they listened to a street musician playing Arcangelo Corelli's violin concerto, opus six, number four in D major flat.

VIII

The Red Velvet Lining
St. Petersburg, Russia, December in the year 1800

Valentin Vasil'ev Antonoff wrapped his red wool scarf around his neck up to his ears and turned his back on the Winter Palace that appeared to be floating upon a glass plate of green grime. In the distance, the spindly, black wooden mast poles of ships anchored in the harbor of the River Neva, appeared like the spokes of a giant iron fence piercing through the icy sky. He was hurrying. He was hungry and wanted to reach home before the unpredictable descending of ominous fog. It was nearly two o'clock. Night would begin at three and if the shadows came, he'd be lost.

He crossed a wide bridge over the Moika canal and entered the fervent activity of the Sennaya Ploschad, a large market nicknamed the Hay Square, where, at that hour, all of St. Petersburg—peasants, merchants, gentry and aristocracy—seemed to be gathered. Valentin discreetly eyed the women of nobility in their long fur coats, buying flowers or muffs, thinking what a life they must lead. He was secretly fascinated as well by the occasional military man whose dappled horse would slosh through the wet, snowy lot, his green Prussian-styled uniform a reminder of the so-called Mad Tsar, Paul I, and this new, supposed "City of Order."

Perhaps it was a confused period in Russian history, but Valentin, as most in his status, cared little for politics. He was a starving musician and had two projects at the forefront of his mind: composition and survival. Sometimes the instinct for female company preoccupied his thoughts but he was intelligent enough to decipher the difference between need and desire, and so, unlike his closest friend Rastislav, who was always broke by either gambling or the brothels, had the discipline to shake it off.

With freezing bare hands, he opened his empty violin case and neatly filled it with the carrots, onions and potatoes he'd just bought. The district where he resided, southeast of the Hay Square, was a dubious, poverty-stricken den of hardship and crime and Valentin had learned that the alley orphans would sooner steal a man's sack of potatoes than a handcrafted violin worth a thousand rubles.

Just as he was finally crossing the Kameny Bridge over the Griboedov Canal, it came. That's how it happened, in an instant the clear air would be flooded with fog so thick that if you put your hand before your face and moved it out an arm's length, it would disappear. People got lost in it always, for it cloaked all signals: monuments, street signs, storefronts, and even the bluish lights of the oil bulbs in the lampposts were smothered. People lost things in it, lost people in it. Children would be separated from their parents and lovers from their beloveds. And as with the blindness, so it was for sound. A voice calling out for a disappeared companion traveled only an arm's length into the thick, gray robes of impenetrable mist before it was drowned.

Only through sheer habit was Valentin able to find his house on Gorokhovaya Ulitsa where he rented a small flat on the first floor. When he entered the building, he saw Rastislav in the cold foyer, seated atop a short stack of dry fire logs, sipping from a bottle of vodka, just opened, and smoking a cigar.

"I won at roulette." His friend grinned.

Valentin smiled and shook his head, contradicted by disapproval and envy. He unlocked the door to his tiny two rooms and lit the lamp as Rastislav dragged in the woodpile, tied together with rope. "I'd never thought I'd see the day when I'd be buying firewood! Back in the Ukraine it was unthinkable. You cut your own trees, shot your own bird for the table, skinned your own rabbits to make a coat. That's how I grew up. Oh, you know this city is killing me, Val."

The violinist had heard the story often enough before, yet played along. "Then why don't you go back to the farm?"

Rastislav took a swig from the bottle. "The farm? Aren't no cards or whores on the farm!"

They lit a fire in the hearth and Valentin put the vegetables in a pot to make a stew then poured a glass of vodka and picked up his violin as his friend tuned his own viola. Despite the man's debauchery, the tall, robust Ukrainian never ceased to play like the devil. Valentin seriously wondered sometimes if what Rasti (as the loose ladies called him) often said might possibly be true: "Sold my soul, I did…sold my very soul."

The violinist sighed when he woke in the morning to see the empty vodka bottle, the empty pot of stew and the blankets tossed over the armchair where Rasti had slept the night before. He'd obviously left earlier as the gambling houses opened at eight. Val tidied his room, made tea, washed up and was about to shave when there was a knock on the door. It was just past nine and his first student for the day was not due until ten. He answered the door in his shirtsleeves with his jaw covered in lather and a towel around his neck, thinking Rastislav had probably forgotten something.

The woman on the other side, a beautiful, lavishly dressed woman in a green velvet dress with a minx shall falling off her shoulders, looked at him for a few seconds before she burst out laughing.

Val stood, self-conscious and somewhat stunned by her presence for her type was rarely seen this side of the Griboedov Canal. "May I help you, Madame?"

She stopped laughing though her fresh, rosy complexion was still lit with tenderness and joy. "Yes. I apologize…You are Valentin Vasil'ev Antonoff?"

He nodded.

"Oh good. I've finally found you."

A woman like this, looking for him, must be *his* lucky day, he thought, and he invited her in out of the cold foyer. The heat from the fire last night still warmed his rooms. He excused himself to wash off the lather and put on his waistcoat.

"Can I offer you some tea?" He placed a cup and his one saucer on the little table beside the armchair where she'd seated herself.

"No, thank you. I've come for lessons, Monsieur."

He cleared his throat. He'd never given lessons to a woman before. "Of course. So, are you a beginner or have you been playing long?"

She laughed genially, heartily. That laugh of hers, already it had become infectious to him.

"Goodness, gracious, no, no, they are not for me. I don't have a musical bone in my body, but it appears I do in my blood. You see my twelve-year-old son, Mikhail Davidovich, is incredibly gifted. He's been studying under Yegor Borodin Duskin since he was six, but alas, as you may have heard…"

"Yes, I read it in the papers. A sad loss indeed, Duskin was one of the greatest violinists in St. Petersburg! Ah, well, a full and prosperous life did he lead."

The woman made the sign of the cross with her delicate white hand over her lovely bosom and Val stood for a moment in silence to honor the old genius, then had to ask, "But Madame...your son—that is quite impressive. Why me?"

She carefully took a letter out of her purse and handed it to him. It read:

My dear Ayola Proniakina zhena Davidovicha,

> *As you are aware, my days are numbered. Mikhail possesses an innate talent that must not go to waste and I implore you to continue his musical education in my absence. I suggest contacting one of the following violin teachers to take my place:Alexi Alekseev Berezowsky, Boris Gubinich Popov, Dmitry Ivanovich Kuznetsov, Yury Sviatoslavov Sokoloff or Valentin Vasil'ev Antonoff.*

Very truly yours,

Yegor Borodin Duskin

"I see." Valentin returned the letter, adding, "My name is the last on the list."

She shrugged. "I must admit, kind sir, that I have tried the others, yet without success. They either haven't the time or," she paused to glance around Val's small two rooms and lowered her pretty face a bit, "the financial need."

Valentin was not embarrassed; on the contrary, he was still recovering from the shock that Yegor Duskin even knew that he existed. Therefore, he accepted the position at once.

Aloya stood and handed him a card. "Here is my address. Are you able to come tomorrow to meet Mikhail?"

"Of course."

"At one o'clock?"

He nodded and thanked her as he opened the door then went to his one tiny window, clouded with frost, and watched her carriage drive away.

His ten o'clock student arrived directly. He had two more lessons that day, at twelve and at four, yet did not receive any pay. The boys were from the neighborhood and although their families were caring and decent, they were also very poor. Yet they gave their word, and considering that it was close to Christmas, Val knew from experience that they wouldn't go back on it. He'd burned Rasti's single remaining log in the hearth to keep his flat warm throughout the day, but by the end of his final student's session, his rooms were freezing and he cut the lesson short for fear that the poor boy's fingers might become frostbitten.

The bells of St. Isaac's cathedral rang out through the fog at six o'clock and the sound of the chimes dimly melted against his windowpane like snowflakes. He peeked outside. It was in fact snowing and, as usually happened at that hour, an overwhelming sensation streamed through his red and blue veins and purple arteries, weakened his mind and defenselessly crashed through the mirror of his soul and sent him falling, falling into an abyss of utter loneliness. It happened at six a.m. too, as he lay in his little bed beneath a moth-eaten quilt, the agonizing sensation pulsated in his limbs, ached in his muscles and seemed to shatter his bones. Loneliness. Each day, twice a day, Valentin not only experienced but succumbed to this terror of knowledge that he was alone in the world, that in the morning in his bed, he had no one to hold onto and that no one was there to hold onto him. And when the bells of St. Isaac's chimed in the evening, it conquered him, the despair that there was no one in the coming of night who was waiting for him.

Val let himself suffer and shivered with cold. He wrapped his red scarf around his shoulders and rosined his bow but his own fingers grew numb and he was forced to place his violin back in its red velvet lined case. His stomach rumbled, his head ached and he wondered if perhaps this gloom of loneliness was nothing more than low blood sugar. He had to get out but had no money. He put on his shabby wool coat and paced his room for warmth in vain. He thought of Aloya Davidovicha, her laughter, her thick black hair, her sparkling blue eyes, ruby lips, green dress, minx stole and white fur cape. He glanced at the address on her card. He knew the area, on the embankment of the Fontanka canal, north of the Mikhailovsky Castle, across from the Summer Gardens. Tomorrow, he decided, he would definitely ask for payment upfront from the Davidovichs. He paced some more before the ash in the hearth. The armchair! Valentin quickly searched under the cushion, hoping to find a few kopecks that may have fallen out of Rasti's pockets the night before. Ah ha! Five coins of 50 kopecks each and four rubles. In minutes he was out on the street, joyous at the ticklish wet snow falling lightly on his cheeks. It was a bit of a walk but he knew of a clean tavern with an inexpensive menu near Sadovaja Square.

The tavern was animated, filled with wintry bodies in wool and furs, and the minute he entered he felt that there couldn't possibly be a warmer place that night in all of Petersburg. He found a seat at a long wooden table and ordered a steaming bowl of *shchi* topped with *smetana*, and a bottle of *Meddovukha.*

"Cabbage soup garnished with a spoonful of sour cream, a crust of rye bread and a bottle of mead..." he heard a voice next to him say. "Can't get more Russian than that!"

Val turned and said, "Why, it's my dear friend *'khokhol'*..." using the somewhat derogatory term for identifying a Ukrainian.

Rastislav slapped the violinist's back. "Eh...don't start with that, now, I'm not in as good a mood as yesterday. Lost half on Red 29 and tucked the other half away under Vasilia Laikina's skirt! But alas, it wasn't for safekeeping!"

Val slid two rubles toward Rasti on the table. "Get yourself a vodka, friend...it's your coin anyway, I found it in my armchair."

And so the two stayed in the cheerful, cozy tavern until midnight when Vasilia Laikina appeared and sat on Rasti's lap, at which point Valentin rose, went home, and went to sleep, fearing six the next morning when that great, vast, sweeping sensation of isolation and desolation would bury his expansive soul as if beneath a cold, snowy, Siberian plain.

The daily cannon shot from the Peter and Paul Fortress boomed across the grey-green Neva River and resounded throughout the Nevsky Prospeck at noon. Anxious to be timely, Val had left his flat early and found himself crossing before a large pink house, numbered 104, on the Pestelya Ulitsa half an hour before the scheduled appointment. He kept up his brisk pace as his long, thin legs charged forward through the pale blue smoke of his own breath in the chilly air, and was soon backtracking his way along the back yard gate of the Mikhailovsky Castle, a newly constructed haven to house Paul I, the Mad Tsar. By mere chance, he caught sight of the Tsar himself, leading his generals in a horseback riding party about the frosted yard. The brown and black horses were of course no different from any other horses, yet there was something about their balance and stride, so stiff and fierce, that seemed to set them apart from the rest of their species. Beyond the glistening white yard loomed the glistening yellowish-orange palace, an architectural wonder, so bizarre and occult, it appeared ominous, mystical almost.

Val crossed a wooden bridge over the Fontanka canal where chunks of ice bobbed in the fast-moving current like ancient princely ruins floating in the death of the aristocracy. He entered the Summer Gardens.

For a moment, a golden ray of sunlight shot through the overcast sky, and the silent black and gray trunks of birch trees and elms turned crimson as if on fire. For a moment, only. He was the only person in the Gardens. The benches were covered with hats made of snow and on the path, side by side footprints belonging perhaps to lovers who had danced out together in the early morning after a delicious night of lovemaking, were now damp and filled with slush.

He passed by the ever-radiant statues of Alexander the Great, Marcus Aurelius, Queen Christina of Sweden and an array of allegorical figures from classical myths, then finally reached the Neva embankment where he leaned on the wrought iron railing adorned with gilded rosettes spanning between pink granite columns.

Valentin stared across the river at the distant marshes and the blurry outlines of the islands. It was where he grew up, where the peasants lived, where the level of poverty for most was far, far below the level he was at now. His mother died giving birth and his father, a simple, caring individual, raised him alone. Vasil Antonoff died when Val was fifteen years of age and upon his deathbed, said to his only son, "Look under the bed."

Valentin did so and found, inside a dusty leather case with red velvet lining, a violin, handcrafted by his mother's father in the age of Peter the Great. Now a penniless orphan, stuck on Vasily Island, Valentin Vasil'ev Antonoff knew not what to do except learn to play the instrument. A considerate neighbor left potatoes and goats' milk each morning on the front step of his father's house and so the boy survived for another year, until he believed he had found his purpose for existence. Then, upon review of the fact that no one would notice his absence (except perhaps the neighbor with the goat), he sprightly took a barge across the Neva into Petersburg as a musician one fine springtime day.

That was ten years ago. He was now 26, paid rent for two tolerable rooms of his own, had been recognized by the master Duskin and was on his way to a noblewoman's home to...the appointment! He turned, ran through the Gardens and was climbing the marble stairs of the large pink house on Pestelya Ulitsa at exactly one o'clock.

The door was opened by a butler who asked to take his somewhat threadbare wool coat, frayed red scarf and torn suede gloves, then asked for the young man's card. Val didn't have a card, so simply whispered his own name into the butler's rather large left ear, and henceforth, was properly announced. The violinist crossed the threshold from the tidy foyer into the parlor where Madame Davidovicha sat prettily in a baroque-styled chair upholstered in ivory colored satin. The room was so warm, so warm he thought that until this moment he had never known warmth before. A grand fire blazed in the hearth and shadows flickered on the walls that were covered in baby blue fabric. Sweeping, golden velvet drapes hung along the sides of two tall windows clouded by a thin white gloss created by the contrast on either side of the glass panes by heat and frost. Val felt the tiny icicles melt from the tips of his wavy, shoulder length, flaxen blond hair and drip quietly into the pink carpet, so plush it laid like a bed over the parquet. And at the far end of the room he noticed a yet to be decorated, freshly cut Christmas tree.

"Mr. Antonoff, so pleased." Aloya waved for him to take a seat and continued, "I'm so sorry my husband can't be here to meet you but he has work. Fedorov is an architect." She said with pride, "He helped design the Tsar's new castle, you know."

"I didn't know. But I passed by it on my way here. Quite a unique mix of styles."

"Yes, Fedorov worked under the famous architect Bazhenov, a friend of the Tsar's who shares His Majesty's odd interest in Martinism."

"Martinism?"

"Oh, some sort of ritualistic, esoteric form of Christianity that preaches the fall of man, deprivation of a divine source, mystical processes of return and illumination."

"And are you and Monsieur Davidovich practitioners of this organization?"

"Oh, heavens no! Fedorov doesn't care much for religion and me...well, I go to mass on Sunday like everyone else and forget about it for the rest of the week!" She laughed. "Will you have some tea?" She called for her maid to bring in the tea then went on in a lively manner, "Mikhail is upstairs, I'll take you up soon, but I thought perhaps we should have a bit of a chat first. Yesterday, I realize, we didn't discuss the particulars."

"Particulars?"

"Yes, you know, the money."

Val nodded, so overcome by the coziness of the room, her beauty, the butler and the crisp, festive scent of the fir tree that he subconsciously wiped his plan to ask for an advance clean off his slate.

The maid came in with a tray and Val watched Aloya professionally pour the tea out of a pot into two cups made of fine, thin porcelain, with a silver lining along the rim and painted with miniature pink roses. As she handed him his cup, he thought that he'd never seen anything so lovely and fragile in his life, as that teacup.

Madame Davidovicha went on, "Mikhail will need two hours instruction per session and the going rate, I've heard, is ten rubles an hour."

"Very well. Twenty rubles a week."

"Oh, no! I meant two hours *per day*, Mister Antonoff." She crinkled her brow to do the math. "Six days per week, Sunday, of course is excluded, so that will be…one hundred and twenty rubles per week."

Val, who had just sipped his tea, reached over to set the darling teacup in its saucer on a side table and, stunned by her proposal, accidentally set it too close to the edge. It fell onto the hard wood parquet floor at the border of the pink carpet and broke. He shuddered and stared at the shattered pink roses and silver lining as if the thin porcelain cup had just died. He stood and began to gather up the pieces. "I'm so sorry, Madame. Oh, I am terribly sorry!"

"Please, Monsieur Antonoff, do sit down. Boris will do that."

In came Boris, the butler, with a broom and dustpan.

"Please, forgive me." Val felt he would cry. "You may take it out of my salary. I'm so sorry."

"Take what out of your salary? What are you talking about?"

"The cost of the teacup."

Aloya Proniakina zhena Davidovicha laughed and laughed and laughed that infectious laugh of hers. "Why, dear sir, it's only a cup. I have twenty more like them and three more sets at that." She stood. "So it's agreed. One hundred and twenty rubles a week and here…" She handed him an envelope that she took out of a red lacquered box that was set atop an end table. "My husband insisted that I pay you half upfront."

He quietly put the envelope in his pocket and followed her past the newly cut pine tree, through a lavish dining room where the table itself was nearly half the size of his little flat, up a flight of stairs, down a hallway strewn with Persian rugs and into a three room suite where the twelve-year-old Mikhail Davidovich welcomed his new teacher with a bout of scrutiny that eased in a manner of seconds into genuine benevolence and affection after they picked up their violins.

After the lesson, as Valentin walked along the Gribeodova Canal, the chilled, dusty, dense late afternoon fog that depressed all of Petersburg seemed to move out of his way as if he were walking through a white light tunnel, made especially for him because he had sixty rubles in his pocket. The thought of returning to his cold little flat made him shudder so he stopped in at the tavern in Sardovaja Square where, not so surprisingly, he found Rastislav sitting in the exact spot as the night before, with Vasilia Laikina still cooing in his ear, her red skirt bobbing over his knees.

Val bought them a round of beer and offered to take the funny couple onto Nevsky Ulitsa for a proper meal at a decent restaurant.

The bells of St. Isaac's chimed six times as they entered the restaurant but Val felt only a wave of energy and hope propelling out of his heart into his red and blue veins and purple arteries, not because he had money, but because he was in love with Aloya Proniakina zhena Davidovicha.

The party ordered *baklazhanovaya ikra, pelmeni, draniki, golubtsy, borscht* and a bottle of vodka, and toasted to their health.

The next day he arrived at the pink house a bit early, hoping to find the Madame in her parlor, but Boris told him she had gone out and somberly led Val upstairs to Mikhail's quarters.

When the lesson was finished, Mikhail followed his teacher downstairs where they found his mother before the naked tree, opening a wooden crate of ornaments.

"Oh, can Monsieur Antonoff help us? Please, please mother?"

Aloya hugged her son warmly. "I'm sure he has better things to do this afternoon, dear."

Mikhail raised his big, blue eyes up at his teacher.

Val smiled. "What could possibly be better than decorating a Christmas tree?"

Alas, how his blood pulsed as she passed to him the gold, silver and red little trinkets, their fingers touching again and again!

When Mikhail busied himself at the opposite side of the enormous tree, Val whispered, "I came early today, supposing we might chat over tea."

She blushed and this time, took his hand and, opening it gently, placed an ornate glass angel in his palm. "This one is my favorite. Be careful."

He hung it on a high branch attentively then stepped back to gaze at it beside her. "So, you don't have three more sets just like it then?" he teased.

She nudged his shoulder. He closed his eyes and felt as if he could fall. She laughed that laugh that ached in his soul and said, "Come early tomorrow, Monsieur Antonoff…for tea."

That evening as he lingered on the embankment of the canal, glaring at a rose petal sunset extending in a pearly atmosphere across the expanse of the city from the Cathedral of St. Nicolas to the Smolny Convent he asked himself, could it be? Did she reciprocate his feelings?

Although he still had 40 rubles, he decided to forego the tavern and stopped at the Hay Square where he ordered firewood to be delivered and bought his usual vegetables to make a stew. Val laughed at the irony that in fact tonight he wished to be alone, more than anything else, to welcome the six o'clock daemon in order to mock it malevolently.

Val was amazed to see a blue sky as he walked past the gates of the Mikhailovsky Castle the next day and took it as a good omen. There was a Swiss clock on the mantelpiece in the Davidovich's salon. As Val sat nervously across from Aloya, who was wearing red...of all colors red, all the things he'd planned to say to her became absorbed in the methodical tick-tocks that seemed to synchronize with the beads of moisture forming on the windowpanes.

"How is Mikhail progressing?" Aloya handed him a cup full of tea that he dared to take regardless of his trembling hands.

"He is gifted beyond doubt, Madame."

"There are no problems with his behavior, then? Duskin would sometimes complain of obstinacy and irritability."

"I have not encountered such as yet, but you can be assured that my threshold for reactions of that sort is very high. I myself am frustrated beyond..." He stopped for an instant, then continued, "The artistic temperament is an un-tameable beast. Alas, in time, one learns to lay down with it peacefully, like the lion and the lamb."

He searched in her Mediterranean blue eyes for some kind of recognition, creative kinship, for a slice of sympathy but his compassionate gaze was returned only with a vague, vacuous shine. I am the Black Sea, he thought, and she is the White Sea. Alas, we live on the opposite sides of this great mass of land and yet sit here together, all warm and rosy.

"Tell me, Monsieur Antonoff..."

"Please call me Valentin."

"Tell me, Valentin, what is it that makes you frustrated?"

"Pardon?"

"Musically..."

"Oh, oh." He loosened up. Her lovely hands that knew not of artistic passion suddenly appeared as foreign; yet so white they were like porcelain, and he feared that if he ever touched them again as he had yesterday, he would break them. He wanted to say, "Ah, Madame Davidovicha, your house is filled with heat but the fire in me is made of labor. I am a peasant by stock and I cut down my own trees." Instead, he answered, "Pietro Locatelli's violin concerto opus three. The capricci with their high registers, double-stops and arpeggios that overextend the left hand through passages that demand such wide fingering it drives me mad! Each time I reach the second movement I either freeze or fumble."

She sipped her tea and her lips curled up.

Don't laugh, oh, please don't laugh, he begged, wordlessly.

She only smiled. "And what happens in the third movement?"

Now he laughed. "Ah! If I can in fact make it to the third movement, I'm complete perfection and I play like a true virtuoso!"

"Well, that is good to know, Valentin."

He crinkled his brow.

"For future reference," she added.

Their eyes met with intensity. In his imagination, the clock stopped ticking and he laid her down upon the plush pink carpet and…and…

"I believe it's time for Mikhail's lesson." She rose. "You can show yourself upstairs?"

He nodded, picked up his violin case and as he passed her she whispered, "Until tomorrow, for tea."

He arrived the following day at twelve-thirty. Boris took his shabby coat, scarf and gloves. Although he still had 35 rubles, his tormented mind or heart (he had yet to understand which), occupied all his time outside of the pink house and he hadn't the reserve to shop. His name was announced with a rather dreary, curt manner by the sterile butler but Valentin was not piqued for he assumed all butlers were, by nature, reserved and void of character.

Aloya was seated in the ivory upholstered chair, her white hands resting daintily on its birch wood arms, carved at the ends with rosebuds rubbed with a gold gilt sheen. He had the impulse to rush up and bend before her upon one knee but there were two other women present in the drawing room. He merely glanced at them and sighed with a dreamy gaze into Aloya's blue eyes.

"Monsieur Antonoff, I present to you Inessa Nikitichna Babinskina."

Val bowed before a girl of perhaps twenty years of age whose complexion was the color of fresh milk and whose thick golden hair had the look and texture of a lion's mane. She was no doubt seductively attractive, yet he sincerely showed absolutely no interest in her ravishing youth, and the corners of his lips tightened almost with disdain.

Inessa did not notice this and stretched out the back of her hand flirtatiously for him to kiss.

Aloya proceeded to introduce Tatyana Alekseeva zhena Kanadtseva, a lady obviously closer to his own age but also ten years younger than her hostess. She was also rather stunning, especially because she had green eyes and a very slim waist, yet Val kissed her hand with a posture of neutrality and artificial deference, much like the perpetual mask worn by Boris.

Aloya had obviously invited the two women to test him. He sat with them, drank tea from the delicate teacup, ate a few tiny cucumber sandwiches off the silver platter, answered their questions about his music, laughed at the infantile jokes of the naive girl with the lion's mane and pretended to be enlightened by Tatyana Alekseeva zhena Kanadtseva's banal philosophical insights, all the while sharing his entire heart, his entire being with Aloya alone through the soft expression in his eyes and lips, and fiery cheeks.

At last, after a relative amount of coaxing, Valentin consented to play for the ladies before heading upstairs to the lesson. He chose *The Devil's Trill*, by Guseppe Tartini; a composition so radically impassioned by fury that when he left the parlor, Aloya's guests were blushing.

The next day was Sunday. He practiced all day.

On Monday, he was unsure whether or not he should arrive early, as on Saturday they had been prevented a private conversation by her company. He decided against it and was passing the tall iron gates surrounding the yard of Mikhailovsky Castle at five minutes to one when he saw Aloya rushing toward him, her white fur cape striking the wind. He had noticed the sky on his walk there, strangely translucent with crinkled strings of powdery blue, orange, yellow, and green tangled inside it like the dome of an opal. She ran to him and nearly fell at his feet, pushed by the heavy, abrasive wind. He caught her in his arms.

"Why didn't you come? I was waiting."

The desperation in her voice frightened him.

"I wasn't sure. I didn't know..."

"How can you not know? Oh, Valentin!" Aloya cried, pressing her face in his hands.

He pressed her against the wrought iron spokes of the castle gate and kissed her lips vehemently with ardent lust.

But no, that's not how it happened.

As Valentin was passing the tall iron gates surrounding the backyard of Mikhailovsky Castle at five minutes to one, he saw Aloya Davidovicha walking casually toward him, her white fur cape flying in the wind. He had noticed the sky on his walk there, it was strangely translucent with veins of powdery blue, orange, yellow, and green tangled inside it like the dome of an opal. As their paths crossed, she stopped tactfully on the icy sidewalk and uttered in a demure overtone, "You didn't come. I waited."

"I wasn't sure. I didn't know if...Shall I come tomorrow?"

She adjusted her minx wrap about her shoulders. "If you like."

Their eyes met.

She walked on. "Excuse me. I have an appointment at the apothecary."

For the next three days they met for tea. On Wednesday, she had more friends over but the other times they were alone. He never saw Master Davidovich at all. Once she merely mentioned, "He's a very busy man," and Val asked no more questions. Of course, each day was at once a torment and a joy for him and each time she laughed, which she often did, his soul burst out of his body and circled the wintry ether.

On Thursday, before he went up to Master Mikhail's quarters, he knelt to kiss her hand, which had become their little custom, and whispered, "Until tomorrow."

"Oh, Valentin, but tomorrow is New Year's Eve, then Christmas a week away. You see, I discussed Mikhail's schedule with my husband and we are giving him a two-week holiday from all his lessons. So, I...I won't be seeing you until the ninth of January."

He lowered his eyes. She could see how painful the news was for him and added, "Nevertheless, you'll receive half your normal wages, as a Christmas present."

He stood. "It's not about the money, Madame." And he climbed the stairs quietly.

On New Year's Eve, Val went with Rastislav to several decadent, embellished parties made up mostly of gamblers and loose women. His spirits were low indeed. Yet after a few glasses of vodka, the absurd merriment surrounding him raised his self-confidence and he ended up dancing and drinking and flirting with random prostitutes simply because he sought pleasure.

In the morning, Val woke with a headache. He looked out his little window and saw snow, fat, fluffy snowflakes falling in layer upon layer. It was beautiful. He lit a fire and decided to spend the holiday alone in his room, composing a concerto for her. He lost himself in the music that poured forth from the imagery in his mind of making love to her. At about four o'clock there was a knock on the door, so lost in his music was he that he opened the door truly expecting to see her there, her white arms reaching out of her white fur cape for an embrace.

Alas, it was one of his students from the neighborhood whose parents owed him a significant amount of rubles. The boy held out a tray of *bobal'ki*. "For you, sir. Happy New Year."

Valentin Vasil'ev Antonoff stared at the small plate of biscuits glazed with honey and poppy seeds and felt that he would weep with gratitude. "Thank you, Pasha. Happy New Year."

He closed the door, set the sweet breads on the table and did weep, with his bow stroking the strings of his violin on the first day of the year 1801.

The Hay Square was swarming with activity on the 2nd of January. Val crossed the canals with his empty violin case, smiling at smoking chimneystacks capped with freshly fallen snow, budding out from the rooftops of houses. Everyone seemed to be out for a drive in their *likhachs*, the wheels and horse hoof prints crushing to black, the powdery white roads. He stocked up on vegetables and grains as he intended to lock himself in his little flat for the week and finish the concerto he had begun, entitled, "Aloya."

He worked for two days in peace (save the six o'clock tremors), burning logs in the hearth and making oatmeal and stews. The solitude and the work loved each other perfectly, and the romance of his own music, enticed by his longing and fervor, became more real to him than the aching silence he was forced to endure without her.

He hoped Vasilia Laikina's skirts would keep Rastislav entertained for he didn't desire interruptions. Nevertheless, on Tuesday night at ten minutes to six, the *khokhol* was at his doorstep, a leg of mutton and a bottle of vodka in hand.

Val let him in. "Roulette?" he guessed.

"*Sem' odinnadtstat*. Dice, can you believe it? I never win at dice!" Rasti threw the lamb on the fire. "Do you have any rosemary or thyme? It's good with rosemary."

Val poured two glasses. "I have salt and pepper, my friend."

The smell of the roast filled his two rooms the following morning. Rasti made coffee then took his leave to only the devil knows where. Val tidied up, washed, shaved and returned to his composition. The chromatics in the second movement were too bold for the grave tempo, and the harmonics in the *allegro maestro* passages at the end with its double stop thirds...no, no, no, the harmonics were all wrong and he must find space to add some *pizzicato*. He sat plucking the strings with his fingers.

There was a knock at his door. Val sighed, probably Rasti or perhaps another plate of *bobal'ki* from a neighbor.

It was she.

He was stunned.

"May I come in?"

"Yes, of course."

She entered and stood blankly for a moment then took off her white fur. "My, it's rather toasty in here."

He took her cape and with great care, draped it over the armchair. "Would you like some pastry?" He quickly grabbed the plate of biscuits and held it out to her. "Or I can make coffee." He took the kettle from the hook by the hearth.

"Nothing. Thank you."

"Madame."

"Valentin."

"I'm glad to see you, Madame."

"And I, you."

They stood silently embarrassed for some time. The shattered bits of burning wood in the fireplace crackled, gleaming red. They both began to speak at once but stopped and finally, the awkward tension in that hot, small room with its triple shaded, soft green wallpapered walls of green birds on darker green branches, ceased when their eyes met, moistened by desire.

"I couldn't live..." she began.

"Nor I."

She went to stand before the slow fire and spoke with her back turned to him. "Through all the holiday parties and dinners, family and friends, all I could think of, all I wanted..."

Valentin went to her and the instant she turned her face to him he kissed the tears streaming down her flushed cheeks. Then her lips, as if in a dream, his lips to hers ardently.

She undressed, let down her long, wavy black hair, and lay on his bed. For the time of a single, ringing endnote he just looked at her. For the time of the silence before the applause he stood astonished at the genius of the beauty he saw.

"You are a work of art, Aloya," he whispered.

Her blue eyes smiled and he went to her as he'd never gone anywhere ever before.

The bells of St. Isaac's chimed the sixth hour as he lay on his back, naked beside her, breathing deep, blissful breaths and he told her, "You are the angel who has chased away my daemons."

She kissed his shoulder, her long hair tickling his bare chest. "An artist without daemons, whoever heard of such a thing?"

"Well," he sighed. "For the time being. For this hour, anyway, I am merely, wholly, just a man."

Her lips met his and he pulled her close again. *Adagietto, Allegretto, Vivacissimo!*

She cried out and then, afterwards, laughed. "Well, you certainly were right!"

Her laughter piercing his soul, he rose and poured two glasses of vodka. "About what?"

"By the time you make it to the third movement, Valentin Vasil'ev Antonoff plays like a true virtuoso!"

He laughed also and they drank.

She dressed. "I must go."

"I understand." He handed her the white fur. "I wish I could say... tomorrow."

"It's impossible." She kissed him again. "I'll write to you." Her blue eyes twinkled and she left. He went to the window and watched her carriage drive away.

The next morning as Val lay awake in his bed, unable to abandon the lingering lilac scent of her eau de cologne, the image of her long hair on his pillow, her hands stroking his flaxen blond hair, her perfect breasts and dark nipples and the feeling of the moment she spread her legs and let him in. There was a knock at his door. He leapt from beneath the moth-eaten blankets and put on a robe. The wooden floorboards were so cold he thought his bare feet would stick to them. It is she! It must be she!

He opened the door. It was a messenger who politely handed Val a letter.

But it wasn't a letter. It was an invitation.

Dear Valentin Vasil'ev Antonoff,

    You are cordially invited to our holiday feast at 104 Pestelya Ulitsa, at 5 p.m. on Christmas Eve.

Merry Wishes,

Monsieur and Madame Fedorov Malinin Davidovich

At first he was disappointed, but on second thought, he felt inspired. It was ideal; he'd finish the concerto and play it before everyone, even her husband, as a gift. No one need know it had been written especially for Aloya and no one would know, except her. Only she would understand the arrangement: *Adagietto, Allegretto, Vivacissimo!*

He gave his reply to the messenger then and there and returned to his concerto.

The rest of the week flew by and he arrived at the pink house promptly. When Boris balefully took Valentin's new, secondhand suede coat lined with fluffy black wool, his brand new leather gloves and tattered red scarf that Val had become too fond of to replace, the butler smiled somewhat sinisterly.

"Thank you, Boris," he said.

"You're very welcome, sir."

He entered the parlor. Tiny candles illuminated the enormous fir tree. Parties of about a dozen or so personages were mingling in small groups with tall fluted glasses filled with a pale gold liquid in their hands.

Mikhail rather magically appeared directly before him. "Monsieur Antonoff! Monsieur Antonoff, come and see what Grandfather Frost has given me as a present!" The boy excitedly grabbed his teacher's hand and pulled him to the far side of the room, weaving through the gathering like a jackrabbit being chased through a bush by a fox. From beneath the Christmas tree, Mikhail retrieved a modern violin, handcrafted in Italy.

Val examined it. "Why, it is superb, Mikhail. You are very lucky and with your talent, you certainly deserve such a treasure."

The boy's shoulders buckled with pride and glee. "Shall we play? After the dinner, shall we play a duet?"

"Yes, yes of course, if you wish." Val turned towards the guests. He noticed Inessa and Tatyana, who obviously had been watching him intently, and excused himself from the excited, joyous lad to greet them.

They blushed consecutively at his approach and lifted their tall glasses to their glossy lips.

"I say, what is that you are drinking?" he asked.

"Champagne!" blurted Inessa.

"Davidovich had it shipped in from France," explained Tatyana, with an elitist-intellectual air.

"Oh, it's so lively, so bubbly!" Inessa giggled.

A lackey came by with a serving tray and Val took a glass. "Mmm, it's very nice indeed."

"Have you ever tasted anything so lovely?" A rosy glow concentrically spread on each side of Inessa's fresh complexion, from her nose to her lion's mane.

He took another sip and couldn't help but remark, with a wide, sensuous grin, "But once, dear ladies, I did taste something lovelier."

He drank and conversed with the two prettiest girls at the party and although he did not see Aloya, he knew that eventually she would come to him.

And sooner than later, spurred on by jealousy, she appeared before him in a black velvet gown trimmed with gold lace and sparkling, silver buttons. Her blue eyes shone like the sapphire stars of another world that had suddenly been revealed above winter's dark palette of Russian sky.

"Mister Antonoff." With one look she sucked him up into her own, lofty, sapphire ether. "So glad you could come."

He bowed and kissed the back of her hand, while playfully and discreetly, tugging at her wedding ring as if to pull it off.

An older couple, Mr. and Mrs. something "-anoff", or "-ovich", or "-enlin", joined their little group. Minutes passed and he knew not of what he spoke or listened to, for all he could say in his mind were words of passion for Aloya and all he could hear was the repetition of an accelerating, climaxing tempo. The champagne plunged into his heart. The parlor with its pink carpet and gold drapes that he'd known with such intimacy became as absurd as a circus tent and finally, after Mikhail announced that the first star had appeared in the black night sky, Boris loudly proclaimed those propitious words, "Dinner is served, Madame."

They entered the elegant dining room where small bundles of hay had been swept symbolically into the corners. Val was seated on the right side of Mikhail at whose left side sat Fedorov, at the head of the long table covered with the traditional white cloth. He was embarrassed. As was customary, Aloya must have arranged the seating and he wondered, why such a scheme to place him in such high regard? He recalled a frequent saying of Rasti's, "A woman speaks two languages, one of which is verbal."

Regardless, for the first time Val got to get a good look at her husband. He was 40 or a bit older and a few inches taller than the violinist who stood just below six feet. He had broad shoulders and a fine build for a man who indubitably never missed a meal. His slightly balding head of finely combed hair was the same color as Val's, except for the silver speckles in his long sideburns and the white streaks in his meticulously trimmed moustache and beard. His face was unquestionably handsome yet his eyes lacked imagination and his brow and nose lacked character. His lips were tight as two taut ropes, browned by years and years of seriousness or possibly, languid prayer.

Because he had already chosen to do so, Valentin disliked the man before he was even introduced, but as they all sat down to dinner, the way Fedorov Malinin Davidovich looked into his dear son's eyes, with such paternal love and sincere care that showed a kind of closeness Val had never known with his own father, the violinist dared to be prudent with his heart and put away the inevitable predisposition of a secret lover's envy.

Then, as Fedorov stood to say the Lord's Prayer, Val became so touched by the meaning of the season that he almost felt genuine affection for his host and rival. Perhaps, he thought, not unlike Mikhail's conversion from defensive scrutiny into pure acceptance when he first met his new music teacher. Aloya was seated at the other end of the candlelit table and it was impossible to even slightly turn his head to look at her beyond the other six guests lined up at his elbow. But after the prayer, he had the chance to as she stood and went round, drawing the sign of the cross on each person's forehead with a finger dipped in honey. When she drew Val's cross, she cleverly and oh so swiftly let her fingertip slip down to his lips that he dared to pucker up as if for a kiss.

The *kutya* was served and eleven dishes followed to represent the twelve apostles: mushroom soup, pickled cucumbers, black caviar, kidney beans, fried salmon, *pirozhki* stuffed with cabbage and egg, potato pancakes, lentin bread dipped in honey and chopped garlic, beet salad, dried fruits and for desert, *bobal'ki*, which Val passed on, as he'd been so wrapped up in his composition he'd forgotten to make his stews for the past few days and had nibbled away at the kind neighbor's gift. Yet he did accept a glass of cognac that he raised with the others when Fedorov stood and pronounced, "*S Rozhdestrom!*" And as he did so, at last turned to the other end of the table to meet the direct, merry gaze of his lover's twilight blue eyes.

Fedorov patted his son's shoulder. "And now for the entertainment."

"Can Monsieur Antonoff join me in a duet, father?" the boy whispered as the party began to move back into the parlor.

"That is an excellent idea. I do think I should hear this young man play, after all, he is your teacher."

Mikhail and Valentin quickly discussed what piece to play and decided on Antonin Vranicky's *Variations, Opus 7*.

Valentin was lifting his own violin out of the red velvet lining when Mikhail appeared before him holding his old violin.

"What about your new Italian beauty?" Val asked.

The boy shrugged timidly. "I'm not used to it yet."

"Ah, I see. Do you mind if I play it?"

"Oh, please do. I'd be honored." Mikhail gave it to him.

He tuned it in D minor and they practiced for a few minutes in the hall that led to the stair, then returned to the parlor and stood proudly erect before the audience.

The performance was flawless and above the thunderous clapping, Val heard Fedorov yell, "Bravo! Bravo!"

It gave him courage to make his request. "Monsieur Davidovich, if you'll allow it, I have composed a new piece of my own that I'd like to play for your family and friends on this gracious day as my gift."

"By all means, Maestro. How very kind."

Val half-bowed, lifted his bow and played *Aloya*, already nearly as much in love with the Italian instrument as he was with the namesake of his composition. He did not look at her once, nor at anyone in the room, for when his eyes were not focused on the strings, they were lifted up towards the heavens. Yet he knew she was watching him and that the single tear that fell from her lovesick blue eyes during the first movement turned into four during the second, and by the time he was playing "like a virtuoso", her cheeks were as salty and red as the leftover beet salad.

As the last note echoed through the silence, in that moment of suspension before the applause, he thought, a man has two languages, one of which is eternal.

The night sky was clear as he walked home, his limbs warm in his new coat, his stomach filled by good food, his brain heated by cognac and his artistic temperament fired up with pride.

Pride. *Pride.* He woke the next morning in a sweat. Pride that would soon become hubris! What was he doing? How could he? Fedorov was a good father and Mikhail an angel with such talent! No, no, it must end. How could *he*, a poor peasant from the islands, disrupt the unity of such a decent family? He would end it, he would tell her tomorrow at tea before the lesson.

Alas, that very night at ten to six, there was a knock on his door.

She was wearing the same green dress she had on the day he first met her. Aloya wafted through the door like a breeze and threw her white fur and minx stole on the armchair. "I told Fedorov I was going to visit my aunt in the Ligovskij Prospeck, at the other end of the city, so I have hours."

"Madame..."

She wrapped her arms around his neck. "I loved your piece. Oh, how I loved it! To me...it was to me, wasn't it?"

"Yes, it was. But I've been thinking and..."

She kissed him and put those lovely white fingers of hers through his messy locks. "Oh, you mustn't do *that*. No thinking. No, no, no, just loving and lovemaking."

Her face, her body, her open affection and her green dress falling over her hips erased whatever thoughts he did in fact have and he couldn't refuse. The crisis of her presence and bounty overwhelmed his sense of morality and he ravished her right there, before the last log burning in the hearth, atop her white fur cloak that, with one quick movement, he tossed down upon the cold, hard wood floor.

"Tea at half past noon!" Her virulent laughter whirled spasmodically round and round as she put on her green dress, as if one of the little green birds on his wallpaper had sprung to life only to find itself trapped inside his two rooms.

He did not go to the frosted window to watch her *likhach* drive off. Instead, he sat naked on his bed before the red embers in the hearth and poured himself a glass of the cognac that had been delivered that afternoon as a present from Fedorov Malinin Davidovich.

The affair continued on: circumspect innuendos housed by the plushy carpeted parlor and tenuous teacups in the afternoons, and two or three times a week, a knock on his door in the evening hours.

"Oh, my poor aunt in the Ligovskij Prospeck!" she'd dramatize as she whipped off her muff and minx to toss on the armchair. "My husband sends his well wishes."

Then the laugh and the intoxication of flesh against flesh throughout the inner space of frozen January and the dank, mutably gray tones of February. And so, the nights when Val wasn't burying his scruples in melancholy compositions or cognac, he buried his pride between her thighs.

Inevitably the day occurred when Rastislav's forceful knuckles rattled on Val's door just as Aloya was climbing her ecstatic heights. The knocking stopped abruptly but returned a half hour later. The *khokhol* was greeted by the blushing violinist and entered the steamy room to see the noble woman facing a small round mirror above the mantle to pin up the long, black ringlets of her hair. Rasti's smile spread from ear to ear as he set down the food and drink he'd brought.

Val introduced Madame Davidovicha and added, "Who was just leaving."

Rasti poured vodka into three glasses and unwrapped a roasted chicken as he said, "The more the merrier is always my motto," before he turned to Val and whispered, "Whist. Can you believe it? I never win at whist."

Aloya eyed the tall, dark Ukrainian up and down and back again. "Who said I was leaving? Yes, thank you, Rastislav Alekseev Slivka, I'll have a glass of that."

Perhaps she was bored. The pink house, the angelic son, respected husband, silly girlfriends, stanch butler and dutiful maid; perhaps she wanted something that moved beyond all that? Yet Valentin still could not see a kindred spirit in her jewel-like eyes. He often wondered if she were mocking him, but of course there was no reason to, and she may be bored but she certainly was not cruel. Maybe Fedorov had a problem, a male problem…but that didn't seem likely. Or maybe she preferred his youth and vigor, and he had to admit, his inexperience, yes. Her laughter pained him worst of all when she'd find it necessary to show or explain something to him during sex.

All these thoughts were clouding up his brain one day as he was putting vegetables in a pot to make a stew when the most absurd of all answers popped up before him…perhaps she loved him?

On March 12, Valentin arrived at the pink house and was let in by Aloya herself. Mikhail was unfortunately ill with a minor cold and Boris had gone out to get medicine. The maid was busy making soup in the kitchen and they found themselves completely alone together in the parlor.

"Will you have a seat, Mister Antonoff? Shall I ring for tea?" she spoke provocatively, licentiously.

The privacy and the plush pink carpet aroused him. Her white hands trembled. He took her in his arms, pushed back a lock of black hair that had fallen over her face and kissed her. They heard the front door open, but before they could part, Davidovich was in the entranceway from the foyer to the parlor where he stopped, pale as a ghost, his broad shoulders slumped and his demeanor gaunt.

The lovers separated and looked at him, speechlessly.

"The Tsar is dead," he said quietly. "The Tsar has been assassinated, murdered in his own bed."

Valentin grabbed his violin and dared not look Aloya in the eye as he swept past her husband and out the door. Fedorov had certainly seen them. It was over.

The violinist did not return to 104 Pestelya Ulitsa and when he dreamt, which he often did, of the days lost when he'd hurry to get there at twelve-thirty, he saw himself passing the back yard of the Mikhailovsky Castle where the shiny new black iron gates were covered in rust. And when he dreamt of her green dress draped over his armchair, it turned into a pool of water and then into a pool of blood.

He took on the neighborhood students again, composed, drank with Rasti, cooked vegetables and, like everyone else in Petersburg, awaited the coming of spring. When it did come, Valentin taught the neighborhood students, composed, drank with Rasti, cooked vegetables and stayed clear of the Pestelya Ulitsa, the Mikhailovsky Castle and the Summer Gardens. Paul the First's son, Alexander, took the throne and a sweeter *zeitgeist* filled the air. Val soon found that he missed the devoted musician's soul of the sensitive, 12-year-old Mikhail more than the bewitching, supernatural laughter of the child's stone blue-eyed mother. She hadn't loved him. She had used him. And now, he was free.

At the end of May, on the first aurora of the first day of *Beliye Nochi*, Valentin Vasil'ev Antonoff woke at six on a park bench in the Summer Gardens. Along with the entire population of St. Petersburg, he had gone out with Rasti the night before to celebrate the onset of the White Nights of summer, a period of ceaseless light that would last until mid-July, in which dusk meets dawn at midnight. They caroused in the streets, a bottle each in hand, cheering at the acrobats and jugglers parading in their costumes, and laughing at the sudden influx of a thousand stray cats that had been hiding in the jackets of the alley orphans all winter and finally been set free to prowl the streets.

They drank with strangers under the rising pearl moon that hung in the hot air against a backdrop of butterscotch, peach and violet clouds that held the refection of the disappearing sun like a perpetual mirror of light. Drunk, they rested against monuments and statues, and became—like the spires, bridges, figures and sails—silhouettes all against the stars blinking through the lustrous blue-silver glow of the shades of non-existent night. And finally, having traversed Nevsky Prospeck, they walked, or rather stumbled, north along the Fontanka Canal, sighing at the romance of splendidly dressed men in white linen suits and beautiful women in flowing, gossamer yellow or black silk gowns who had spent the entire white night, arm in arm, strolling the embankments of the latticework of tributaries streaming through the city in glistening, opalesque luminosity toward the Baltic Sea.

Val sat up and inhaled the scent of lilac. The sky was dusted with pink. He watched a squirrel scamper up a tree. The gates to the park had not yet opened. He must have jumped them in the early hours of morning with Rastislav. He looked around but his friend was nowhere to be found. The vodka still burned in his red and blue veins and his purple arteries felt swollen in a haze. He smoothed his wrinkled jacket, knocked the dirt off his shoes with a stick and walked in post-drunken mechanical strides toward the southern gate where a guard, who appeared non-regretfully foggy-headed as well, let him through.

And there he was, on the Pestelya Ulitsa, for the first time since the day the Mad Tsar had died. He moved slowly. The sky was growing brighter. He felt symmetry with the world, so he stopped before the pink house, number 104, and looked up to see her sitting in the frame of a second story window. Her long black hair was web-like and tousled. Her white hands, white as a ghost's, rattled on the pane and her blue eyes...he searched her eyes for some sign of recognition, some mnemonic recollection of the bed they had shared, for a slice of sympathy even, but his compassionate gaze was returned only with a foreign, vacuous glare as if he had asked the time of day from an animal. She stared straight at him yet her face, much thinner and darker, was void of emotion and her dimmed blue eyes, once as luminous as a white night sky, sank in deep, depressing sockets of fear.

Val stood, watching, waiting, in quiet tears. At last a nurse appeared in the window and benignly took the trembling resemblance of Aloya Proniakina zhena Davidovicha away.

The sky, now languidly smudged with tangerine ink, hovered above him and seemed to drag behind him as he turned the corner and began his way back to Gorokhovaya Ulitsa. He stopped in at the tavern near Sadovaja Square and said farewell to Rastislav then returned to his two small rooms, packed up the few items of clothing and worth that he owned, and with his violin in hand, went to Moscow as he'd never gone anywhere before. Yes, on that day, Valentin Vasil'ev Antonoff went to Moscow, a place where wind and light reverse, a re-invented man.

IX

Gozo, Italy

Present

Claude came down the stairs dressed in black linen trousers and his pale green, silk, short-sleeved shirt. Marianne was lying on the sofa in the living room reading an Italian art magazine, still in the blue jeans and grey cotton tank top she'd worn all day.

"You're not ready." He kissed the big toe on her bare left foot.

"For what?" She didn't look up as she turned the glossy page with a feline-like paw.

"Gianni's, baby! It's the last day of July."

"Is it? Hmm. I don't know. I really don't feel like it."

Since the writing began, they'd made a ritual of going to Xaghra's finest restaurant at the end of each month to spice things up, but Marianne had been sullen since the last story. In silence, she turned another page.

"*Risotto al salmon selvatico…Acciughe in salsa verde e rossa…Pasta con Gorgonzola cipolla…*" Claude named a few of her favorite dishes from Gianni's menu. "*Mousse di cioccolato fondente!*"

She finally raised her eyes, taking in his appearance. "Well, just look at *you!*"

He posed, copying the position of the male fashion model in an Amaretto advertisement on the back cover of her magazine. "You like?"

"You're a fool."

"Let's go!"

She tossed the magazine to the floor. "I don't know what to wear."

"The iris dress."

"I don't have an iris dress."

"The puce one."

"No."

"The wave dress."

"What wave?"

"The turquois one."

She shook her head.

"I don't care what you wear, only, not that pumpkin thing."

"I don't have a pumpkin thing. You're weird, Clues."

"I'm hungry and…" He tugged at the end of his neatly ironed shirt. "Let's go! Get up. Get up, get up! Giddy up, old horse!" He laughed.

She got off the sofa. "You better pour yourself a glass of scotch old man, this is going to take me awhile."

Claude was sipping his scotch on the rocks and singing a 70's song by Serge Gainsborough, apparently to his bougainvillea, an hour later, when she came out onto the front porch wearing a stylish black dress that flattered her figure, somewhat beyond his disbelief.

He stopped singing. "Wow."

"They're Italian flowers, Clues, you shouldn't serenade them in French."

"Is that new?"

"I bought it in Valleta after I got my hair done. But I couldn't fit into it until now."

"Why do women do that? Buy clothes they don't fit into?"

"Because they want to fit into them. It's a kind of aspiration."

He looked at her again. Yes, she'd lost weight, maybe three or four kilos. "Well, you look beautiful."

She laughed.

"What's funny?"

"You haven't said that to me in years."

"I told you that three nights ago."

"Yeah, well, it seems like three years."

"Marianne, where have you been?"

"I'm here, I'm right here. It's just that I miss the boys."

"I know." He came to her on the porch and kissed her painted lips, the way he learned how to so as not to smear her lipstick. "Listen, we'll finish the book…"

"I don't want to talk about the book."

"Neither do I. Listen, I'll buy their tickets, we'll have them come out in a few weeks if you want."

"Really? But what if they…"

"They'll come. Believe me."

"Okay. I believe you."

Claude continued to sing Gainsborough songs in the car as they drove into Xaghra and sooner than later, his wife, her mood elevating, joined in.

Unusually, Gianni's was packed for a Tuesday and they had to take a seat at the bar to wait for a table.

"What's going on?" Claude asked the bartender.

"Family gathering, over there." The striking young man pointed to a group of several tables surrounded by Italians ranging from ages five to ninety-five.

Marianne glowered at the party.

"Do you want to leave?" Claude asked her.

"No." She looked at the wine list then ordered a glass of Frascati. Claude ordered Barolo. He felt good. He'd ridden his bike around the island that morning, went for a long swim, wrote four pages that he was sure were genius and above all, made love to his wife the way he used to when he was young at the crack of dawn. The laughter and loud voices of the party swelled and subsided throughout the restaurant like a fast-forwarded film version of an ebbing and flowing tide-scape for an entire century.

Marianne remained pensive.

"We can go to Ta Frenc," Claude offered.

"No, look, they're serving dessert. Oh! It's the old man's birthday."

They both studied the crowded tables to see a still handsome and very charismatic elderly man looking much like Marcello Mastroianni in *A Fine Romance*, stand to blow out a birthday candle. The entire restaurant clapped and Marianne, charmed by the grace of it all, let go her solitary regrets and smiled.

"Seems like it's all happening at Gianni's tonight, babe," Claude said.

"Not yet." Marianne sipped her wine. "That woman over there has been staring at you since we got here."

"What woman?"

"There, behind you."

Claude was about to turn his head but Marianne grabbed his arm. "Well, don't look!"

"Then how do I know who she is and why she's staring?"

"Maybe she thinks you're cute."

"Cute?"

The woman at the far end of the bar behind Claude's back would not keep her eyes off him and Marianne grew tense. "Okay, look, but do it discreetly."

He did so then turned back to his wife with an alarming expression on his face.

"Clues, you look like you saw a ghost."

"I did."

"What's going on?"

"It's Genevieve."

"*The* Genevieve?"

He nodded.

"Oh, God."

Genevieve Desmarais was the woman Claude loved before he met Marianne.

At that time, he felt he loved her. So much so that he believed he neither could nor would ever love anyone in the same way, with his absolute being, again. Yet in the quite infrequent reminiscences over the past three decades when he by chance thought of Genevieve, he understood now that what he had then felt as real love was, in retrospect, infatuation.

She was 29. He was 26, and although he was an adroit businessman, his bookshop had only been open for a year and he was far from being financially stable. Yet at this time Claude Renoir, and this is true, was far more emotionally, intellectually and spiritually mature than other men his age.

She sang at a cave bar, *La Caveau de la Huchette* in the Latin Quarter on Thursday nights at nine. She had a trounced, insouciant, Edith Piaf-like voice, and a face and figure, or so he imagined in his bubble of obsession back then, not unlike Brigit Bardot. Tall, sexy, blond and pouty with the most strikingly beautiful hands he, to this day, had ever seen. The rest of her emanated a severe erotic vibe but her hands—how virginal, graceful, and when she moved them it was as if every gesture was illuminated by pity. Yes, he remembered likening her hands to the virgin's in the astounding *Pieta* by Michelangelo and how afraid he had been that first time to touch them lest he taint them forever. Yet he did touch them. He touched her everywhere…

"Clues, she's still staring."

He glanced back and sighed. In 34 years, her face had aged appropriately and her tall, 5' 9" frame was perhaps 10 kilos heavier, yet she was still a knockout.

"I suppose I have to talk to her."

"You don't *have* to."

"I do."

Marianne turned to watch the birthday party and Claude stood and went to the end of the bar.

"*Bonsoir,* Genevieve."

"*Bonsoir*, Renoir! I thought that was you!"

They kissed each other's cheeks.

"You look the same except for the white hair." She actually reached out for a minute as if to touch it. Her hands, he saw, were still pure.

"So do you," he lied. "Except obviously your hair is still blond, shorter, a different hair cut..." He stuttered and turned his head just enough to see if his wife was watching him. She was watching the ado over Mastroianni.

"Are you here alone?" he asked her.

"Heavens, no. My...my date stepped out to take a phone call. It's so noisy in here!"

"There's a party it seems. But what are you doing in Gozo?"

"I was on tour in Italy but I needed to get away from the big cities. No one knows who I am on this little island. I love it!"

Claude remembered a day, maybe ten years after he'd been a married man, Etienne and Esmond were nine and seven, when he went into Virgin Records on the Champs Elysées and saw a display of her CDs beneath a grand poster. He gazed at her picture for a long while but didn't buy any of her music. He bought Henryk Mikolaj Gorecki's *Symphony #3* instead.

"Your date? You're on a date?"

She laughed. "*Oui*, Renoir, even at my age, people do date. So, who is the lovely lady you are with tonight?"

"My wife," he answered immediately. "For twenty-seven years."

"Impressive."

He raised his grey-white eyebrows.

"Kids?" she asked.

"Two boys. In college now."

"Ah." Genevieve took a sip of her wine, Orvieto he guessed, by the color and the shape of the glass.

"Come, let me introduce you to Marianne."

"Of course. Yes, that would be nice."

The second Marianne kissed the singer's cheeks, Claude could tell she was jealous. Not Marianne, but Genevieve.

"I remember listening to your songs on the radio in Paris; they seemed to be all the rave back in the nineties," Marianne said.

She had to do that. Okay, thought Claude, go for it babes, not a big deal.

Genevieve winced. "Two boys, how wonderful for you."

"Yeah, they're great kids. Oxford and La Sorbonne. Do you have any children?"

"A daughter. I had a daughter. Her name was Beatrice. She was beautiful. She danced. I taught her to play the piano. She danced like the wind!"

The Renoirs were quiet.

Genevieve sipped her wine. Her handsome face became tight and scornful. "She died of leukemia on her seventh birthday."

The Renoirs remained respectfully silent.

The Mastroianni party began to gradually break up. The cute bartender came to take their empty glasses and Claude ordered another round. Genevieve's date appeared and put his arm around the singer.

"Ah, looks like we'll finally get a table." He was introduced as Ricardo.

The Renoirs refrained from giving each other knowing glances. Ricardo was tall, tan, svelte and sexy as a Roman god in his tailored white suit, but not a day over thirty. Marianne knew at once that he was a hired man.

Her date, thought Claude. It made him sad.

A hostess came to the bar and told the singer and her young Adonis, who apparently had been waiting longer than the Renoirs, that "The table you requested by the window with a view is ready."

"*Grazie.*" Ricardo took his date's arm.

"Why don't you join us?" Genevieve suggested. "We have the best table in the house and that party will still linger for at least another hour."

"Yes, she's right," Ricardo added. "We Italians are like the French that way."

All had to laugh. Marianne accepted and Claude feigned appreciation.

The dinner went swimmingly although Claude was on edge. He didn't want to remember how she had been with the impression he had of her now. He never would have thought she'd resort to a hired escort, nor that she'd need to.

The next morning Marianne's mood elevated and she happily busied herself with domestic chores in preparation for the visit of her children. Yet Claude slunk into a stressful, melancholic torpor and didn't write a word for days.

On her way out to the post office in town, Marianne noticed his bleak expression when she passed him as he was watering the bougainvillea. She came back and put her arms around him from behind, hugging him tightly, so tightly it was as if they were fighting a great, gusty storm.

He released his hand from the spray lever on the hose.

"Clues, what's going on, darling?"

"Hell is empty and all the devils are here."

"Well, that certainly is morose!"

"It's a line from Shakespeare."

"I *know* that...*Macbeth*."

Claude pressed his thumb once again upon the spray lever, "Wrong. It's from *The Tempest*."

Elizabeth McKague

X

The Rose
London, England 1593

Inigo Gregory set down his quill, tilted his head and slanted his eyes up at the menacing, abstract figures on his wall that were being unveiled by the erratic flame thrashing upon the last quarter-inch of wick in his shade-less lantern. He'd broken the glass yesterday. It was an accident.

Yes, there, emerging in the shadows formed by dilapidated gray paint he saw a cat, a horse, a Japanese fan, a castle, a ship, a shoe, a mouse...no, the mouse was real.

Ah! These four walls!

It had been months since he was able to brave the London streets properly in an ordinary fashion. Just yesterday he risked his health to go out and buy ink. He tied his long, faded blue, velvet cape closely around his whole body and wrapped his black wool scarf up to his nose where he tucked a cloth scented by lavender in a tenacious attempt to ward off the stench of the outside world. With two pairs of stockings ineffectively protecting his feet against the vermin living in puddles upon puddles from creeping through the holes in the soles of his boots, the scarf up to his nose and his broad-rimmed felt hat hiding his face, only his soft, pensive eyes were exposed to the contaminated air. Thus he ran through Southwark to High Street. Thus he dashed into the print shop and tossed his two pence on the desk before the bewildered printer, a nearly dead man for sure, whose whole life had been devoted to the printing of words and now, but one word was written on that ghostly white face hovering over the counter: plague.

He quickly returned to his room thinking the printer would be lucky to survive the night.

Inigo wanted his life back. He wanted the stage.

His love dared to come in the beginning, months and months ago, before the quarantine. She came. His room was damp and dark and cold. In the occasional cords of crimson light crossing his window from the streaming sparks of bonfires annihilating dead things in the muddy street below, he saw her face, glowing with vitality and youth. O', how he kissed her! O', how it felt to be inside her!

The last letter he received, three weeks ago, said, "I am alive. Are you?"

He laughed, thinking about the irony of it, and continued to scribble as if it were the last of his days.

Inigo woke the next morning and moved the curtain to one side of his lonely window to see a plucky sun bulging out of a sheepish cloud.

There were echoes in the street. Human voices. More wails of disease...but no, wait! Exultant cries traveling in windswept refrain from Whitehall to Shoreditch, sailing over the Thames and stampeding across that iconoclastic sleeping dragon of a bridge to the Southwark slums. "No more quarantine! The plague is over! No more plague!"

He unlocked the iron frame of the windowpane and leaned out to look at the street below. People were running about in cheering droves chasing messenger boys carrying banners declaring the return of a less noxious season in London town. A herald ran past yelling, "The theaters are open! The Rose, The Curtain, Blackfriars and Bear Baiters! Theaters are open! Come one, come all!"

Inigo dressed and ran out into the yellowish-grey daylight feeling as if his life had changed simply because he was alive. He gaily breathed in the sooty air as he crossed his neighborhood and finally entered The Rose and stood in the center of its yard.

William Shakespeare, Augustine Phillips and Thomas Lodge were seated in the gallery tossing about a cornucopia of mellifluously honeyed lines such as, "There are no lyrics to the song of dream," or "We are the stuff that dreams are made of," and "Our little lives are surrounded by a sleep," while Christopher Marlowe and John Hemmings danced about play-fencing on the prop-less stage.

John theoretically sliced Marlowe's shoulder as Kit turned and shouted, "Look now who's not dead!"

"Gregory, you bastard!" Phillips yelled from the gallery.

"Lodge, old man!" Inigo shouted. "I thought you were in the Canary Islands?"

"I was," Thomas's bombastic growl rang out. "Until I heard there was plague in London and thought it best I didn't miss out!"

Marlowe jumped down from the stage and slapped Inigo's back. "Really though, glad to see you, friend."

"And I, too, am happy to be back amongst you clowns, shifters, scallywags and ruffians! What's the play?"

"*The Emperor of Constantinople,*" Shakespeare suggested.

"Who wrote it?" Inigo asked.

"Some new fellow. Peter Bell, Bellfy...oh, I don't know."

"Is it good?"

"No, it is not," Marlowe contested. "Which is why we shall be doing *your* history, *Henry the Fourth*."

"You mean *your Doctor Faustus*," Will sparked.

"Inigo, have you a play?"

"I do not," he lied. He had spent the quarantine writing, but none of it was fit for his fellows. Not yet.

Thomas Lodge shuffled through a stack of scripts. "Here's one: *Three Ladies from London*."

"Ridiculous," Shakespeare hissed.

"*The Fall of the Roman King*," Lodge read out.

"What king? Preposterous." Shakespeare laughed.

"*The Pilgrim and the Princess*."

All laughed.

"So, it's settled. *Faustus* it is."

All agreed.

"Kit, will you play Faustus, then?" Will asked.

"What about you, boss?" Marlowe suggested.

"And take direction from you?" Will sneered.

Marlowe once again put his arm around Inigo. "Alright, I shall be Faustus and Gregory, my Mephistopheles."

"Well, let's to the Tabard Inn then, troupe!" Hemmings jumped off the stage. "No more plague—the taverns are open!"

And so with Kit on one arm and John on the other, Inigo marched out of the straw-covered mud of the yard and into the labyrinthine dark alleys where the normalcy of wrestling pits, cockfighting tents, pickpockets, cozeners, prostitutes galore, drunkards and nips once again threw their lives into the yellow-grey light of day.

"*Totus mundis agit histronicum*," Shakespeare muttered as he walked beside the players.

"What's that now, Will?" Lodge, limping on his clubfoot, caught up with the group.

Inigo translated, "The whole world plays the actor."

The Tabard Inn was crowded and the malmsey wine was flowing. The players edged their way to a table in the back where the Burbage boys had hours ago stretched their long legs over a few wobbling chairs, reserving the troupe's usual corner and placing bets upon who would in fact show up, that is, who had not died of plague. As the players took their seats, John Burbage said to his brother, "Pay up! There he stands—Gregory!"

"Piss off." Don emptied his pockets and nudged Inigo. "I've lost the next round 'cause of you, ol' chap. Lend me a shilling then, won't you?"

"Me? You bet on me kicking the bucket, did you?"

"Weakest of the lot and all…you know how it goes."

In a flood of unexpected guilt for being alive, Inigo waved his arm to order a round and was ecstatic to see Beatrice waddle over with her black eyes and duck-like behind, and place two bottles on the table. "Two pounds, three pence."

Inigo grabbed her apron. "Have you seen her? Is she alright?"

"Two pounds, six pence, if you please."

"Have you heard from my Ilsa? Is she alive?"

"Two pounds, nine pence."

He put the coins in her chubby hand. "Beatrice?"

"Don't know. Haven't seen her." She turned to go back to the bar but he held on to her apron, ready to rip it off if he had to to get an answer. The players laughed.

"Looks like Gregory's given up acting…practicing now to bait the bears!" Hemmings joked.

The barmaid swatted John's jowl. "If I'm a bear then you're a dog! Dogs, all of you!"

"Beatrice!" Inigo pleaded.

"She's fine. Let go my skirt. Her brother's in here somewhere."

Inigo stood and searched the tawdry dim tavern and soon his wide, blue eyes spotted Niles. He downed a glass of much wanted wine and went to him.

"Ilsa is well, actually. Better than the rest of us," Niles told him. "Stayed at the Earl's mansion throughout quarantine."

"How kind of him to keep her safe."

"Kind? What *kind* of 'kind' d'ya think?" Niles laughed and returned to pawing the pretty young woman pressing up against him.

Inigo, relieved that his love was unharmed, went back to the table and drank with his friends until…

When he woke the next morning, the last thing he remembered was stumbling in slants of ghostly moonlight through the labyrinth, arm in arm with Kit.

The four gray walls he'd come to know so well seemed to mock him. He had to cross the Thames and go to the Earl of Southampton's mansion. He had to see her. He splashed cold water on his face and put on his boots and his cape. He'd slept in his clothes. His pockets were empty. He went to the theater, hoping to borrow boat fare from Kit, but William had already started the day's rehearsal and nobody argued with Shakespeare, it just wasn't allowed.

Inigo had met Ilsa just before the onset of plague. As a favor, he'd gone to the Southampton mansion to deliver a new sonnet by Will to the earl, who had commissioned a series by London's up and coming star playwright. Inigo was let in by a stuffy old steward and led into one of the many dens on the second floor where he found himself waiting for nearly an hour. He began to grow extremely agitated from boredom but had promised Shakespeare to hand over the single sheet of poetry in person. Soon, he was sure he'd been forgotten. Finally a young girl of about sixteen years of age came into the room wearing an apron and proceeded to wipe a cloth over the bookcases, the oil lamps, arms of chairs, tabletops and so forth. She did not look at Inigo once. After fifteen minutes of dusting, she left the room. He shifted in his chair. He'd already examined the books and found nothing of interest. He'd already memorized Will's lovely poem. The girl in the apron returned to place a decanter of brandy on a table covered with a lace doily. He watched her, as he had done during her oblivious dusting, intently. Suddenly she gasped, almost shrieked.

Inigo stood. "What is wrong?"

Her pretty face contorted and turned as white as if she'd seen a ghost. "Nothing."

He walked up to her. She backed away from the table, an object that seemed suddenly offensive to her. She turned and for the first time looked at Inigo, looked gently into his eyes then approached the table and with a violently shaking hand, lifted the decanter to expose a red stain on the white doily.

"I spilled some. It is ruined," she confessed.

"A simple mistake," he said in the calmest voice his actor's craft could muster.

"You don't understand. It's the second time I've mussed up today. The head maid has warned me. She hates me. I'm new here. Oh, how she hates me! And I believe she's a witch. I know she is. Last week I saw her making potions and now she's trying to get rid of me, something like this could…oh, what have I done? I can't lose this job!"

Inigo examined the stain. "Why, it's but a drop, half a drop. Here, simply turn the doily on its other side and place the decanter over the spot." He did so for her. "There. Done."

The girl pouted shyly. "Thank you, sir."

"Call me Inigo. And what are you called?"

"Ilsa."

"A beautiful name. Unusual. I think I'll put it in a play."

"Do you know about plays, sir?"

"Quite a bit, I'm afraid. I write them and act in them."

"Oh, how I've longed to go to the theater! My brother keeps promising he'll take me on a Saturday but always goes with another girl or leaves me at home while he goes out to get drunk."

"Doesn't sound like a very reliable fellow."

She shrugged. "Niles is alright. He's all I got."

"Your parents?"

"We're orphans since I can remember. Least we have a roof over our heads now that I got this job. So, you can see how much it means to me."

"Yes." Inigo smiled gently at her sparkling, river-gray eyes. "Well, I can take you to the theater if you'd like."

"You can?"

"Of course I can. I'll bring you with me before the doors open for the public, show you backstage, introduce you to the actors and give you one of the finest seats on the third tier…with a pillow!"

"But sir…"

"Inigo."

Ilsa blushed. They heard someone coming down the long hall. A shriveled old woman in a black dress and white bonnet crept into the room and glared fiercely at the poor young girl.

"What are you dawdling 'bout in here for?" barked the head maid.

Before she could answer, Inigo said, "I asked for a glass of brandy."

Ilsa, her hand still shaking, curtsied and poured him a glass. As she set down the decanter, she could not hold back a slight smile.

"Alright then. On with you!" The old bag roared as she turned back into the hall, waving her baggy arm for the young girl to follow.

As she scurried past Inigo, he whispered in her ear, "Saturday...where do you live?'

"Amster House, Ludgate Hill."

"Ah, that's right near Blackfriars."

Ilsa could only nod, as the Earl of Southampton appeared directly. "Ah, I see you've made yourself comfortable. Please excuse the wait. So, let's see this sonnet now, shall we?"

And so the love affair began but alas, was cut off after just a few months when the city, already diseased, was cursed by pandemic.

When Inigo arrived at the theater, not only had rehearsal begun, but as soon as Will saw him, he was roped onto the stage. Ilsa would have to wait.

"Downstage, Gregory! Where are you? Certainly not in this marvelous Hell we're trying to conjure!"

He followed Shakespeare's directions.

Starving, listless, distracted and wan, Inigo, in frame and countenance, made an ideal Mephistopheles. Henslow, the producer, stopped by that afternoon and was so impressed by the spectral, black-robed figure on stage that he sent an errand boy out to buy cold meats and beer to refresh the players.

The rehearsal continued toward evening and when it was time for Helen of Troy to appear, the troupe paused dumbly.

"So, where is our Helen?" Will, whom it had been decided should direct the play, with Kit as Doctor Faustus, scoured.

The actors' blank stares met each other.

"Yes? What?" Shakespeare crossed his arms over his chest. "Or shall we write her out?"

"We can't write her out!" Marlowe spoke with great conviction.

Shakespeare turned in a circle, rubbing the bald spot on his head in a methodical manner as if summoning demons. "Where's our lovely castrate Wiggins, hmm?"

Hemmings stepped forward. "Dead."

"Oh." Will sighed. "Marlowe, what about John Kyd?"

"Don't know his whereabouts, Will."

"But don't you room with him?"

"He left for the countryside just before the plague."

"I see." Shakespeare paced the yard, rubbing his head, summoning angels, then quickly jumped up onto the stage and approached Indigo. "That boy you were speaking to in the tavern last night…"

"Niles Broadstairs?"

"Whatever. But he was a pretty sort." He turned to the players. "Don't you agree?"

"Yes, yes, indeed," they all agreed.

"Get him."

"But he's not an actor," Inigo said. "He's a shoemaker."

"Shoemaker, glove-maker, doesn't much matter does it? All he has to do is walk across the stage wearing a dress, nothing to it, really."

"No, no. Nothing to it at all," the players echoed.

"Where does he live?"

"Near Blackfriars."

"Very well. Cross the river and bring him to us as quickly as possible, here…" Will took sixpence from his pocket and gave it to Inigo. "I don't care if we're here until midnight, my friends, I will have my Helen of Troy!"

Marlowe leaned to one side and whispered in Inigo's ear, "Now, *that's* a great line!"

Inigo smiled, took the coins and went to the Southwark docks but as it happened, Blackfriars playhouse was remarkably, considering the fact that all of London had just come back to life the day before, opening with a new play that very evening. Not a single ferry was free and he didn't wish to wait for those halfway across the river to return. He walked along the muddy embankment to the base of London Bridge. It was a wretched spot to catch a boat, most of them being depressed fishing boats or run-away villains and smugglers. Inigo gave a one-eyed fisherman two pence and in minutes was sailing on the heavy gray water beneath the first portico of the London Bridge above where he counted fourteen severed heads pierced by tall poles. Some were fresh, the blood still dripping all the way down into the river; others, black, skeletal, cold, but most were in that terrible in-between stage of sagging flesh and dead hair whipping violently in the wind to a background of thunderous clouds that had suddenly appeared in the dusky, brown sky. Inigo felt pity for the good souls of his town who were forced to witness such atrocities daily. It began to rain. The little fishing boat tossed on the Thames.

As usual, sets of round, hungry eyes in the flushed, dirty faces of children in rags, cowering together on the steps of Amster House, stared up at Inigo's approach, this time with more trepidation than ever before as he was still wearing his long, black Mephistophelian robe.

"Good evening." He spoke, to their ears, rather ominously.

"It's the devil!" The eldest child, a boy, stood to protect his sisters who slouched nonchalantly behind him, picking lice from each other's heads.

Inigo pulled down the Chiron-like hood of the costume. The lamplighter came by and lit the lamp at the base of the porch. Inigo's straw-colored hair, dewy with rain, gleamed in the torchlight.

"Now, now, son, it's just me. You remember me, don't you?"

The boy put his hands on his hips and pursed his lips. "Ilsa's friend." He stepped aside to let him pass. "She's upstairs."

"She is? But I thought…well, she is. Very good then." He bowed at the boy's feet theatrically. "Thank you, kind sir, and good evening to you!"

The boy asked for a penny.

The fat landlady, also the children's mother, answered the front door when he rapped. "Ah, me thought you dead, Gregory!" she said. "I lost me youngest, you know."

"I did not know. I'm sorry."

"A tragedy 'tis that. But me husband's made it through…a tragedy that, too!" She burst out laughing.

"I'm calling on Mister Broadstairs, is he in?"

"*M i s t e r* Broadstairs! Well, you're a fine one now, isn't ya? Yeah, yeah, they're both here. Sister is prettier than ever, stayed with the earl for quarantine, you know."

Inigo began to climb the winding, narrow stairwell.

"Drunk as a fish though, Niles is!" the fat lady called out. "Been drinking since freedom day, mind you!"

The Broadstairs rented a single room on the third floor. Besides the fat lady's family, the crumbling old building housed a pair of poverty-stricken newlyweds, an old man who was known to have been a court astronomer during the reign of Henry VIII, an emaciated musician in his thirties whose harpsichord echoed at all hours in the damp halls and a temporary lodger named Michael Drayton, whom Inigo learned was an enthusiastic young poet at that moment, for he almost collided with him on the dim winding stair.

Drayton gleamed at the actor saying, "I've got it! I've got it!"

"Got what?"

"A title for my sonnets."

"Yes?" Inigo smiled at the furling youth.

"Idea's Mirror," Drayton said with great dignity.

"Clever title." Inigo pressed himself against the wall and let the poet pass.

Ilsa, glowing with health, answered the door. Before Inigo could speak, she was in his arms weeping tears of joy.

"My love! My dearest! You've come, you're alive!"

It took all his actor's skill to hold back his own tears, but in his manhood he could not refrain from kissing her sweet pink lips fervently, feverishly, lustily.

"Three months," he whispered. "Yet here we are, my dove."

"Who's there?" Niles' sloppy, belligerent voice called out behind her.

"It is Gregory," Ilsa said calmly.

"That bastard. What does he want?" Niles blurted.

Inigo walked into the little room where two single mattresses were placed at opposite ends with a wobbly, badly carpentered table and two chairs set between them, one out of which Niles stumbled to accost the actor. "Did you bring any wine?"

"Not tonight. But I've got a part for you."

"A part?"

"A job…in a play. Shakespeare insisted. He's sent me to bring you to The Rose."

"I hate the theater." Niles fell back into the chair.

Ilsa frowned and leaned her head of long soft hair on her lover's shoulder.

"How much does it pay?" Niles grumbled after some moments of deep contemplation that seemed to have sobered him.

"Not much."

"Then fuck off!"

"But there is beer."

"Where?"

"Half a barrel left, I believe, at the theater."

Niles stood and took his cloak from the back of the chair. "Onward!"

"Come with us. You can stay at my place tonight," Inigo whispered to Ilsa as he squeezed her waist.

She nodded, followed, and locked the door to the dismal den she shared with her sordid brother behind them.

Doctor Faustus ran at The Rose six nights a week with a Saturday matinee for a fortnight. The party at the Tabard Inn after the final show was a tight one indeed. Inigo woke the following day bewildered at the non-descript images emerging through the peeling paint on his wall: a Japanese courtesan with a fan, a unicorn, severed heads on poles and even a contorted portrait of the Queen herself, all of which seemed to judge him. He sat up in bed. A lost sparrow or some type of little bird must have entered through his open window during the night and was flying about in a frantic, confused delirium.

He vaguely remembered saying farewell to Kit below the bridge in the early hours of morning as Marlowe, pissed out of his gourd, fell into the boat of a letter carrier heading toward the countryside.

"This time, Gregory my dove, I'm out of London for good!" Kit proclaimed as he tossed six pence into the oarsman's purse.

"But what about The Rose?" Inigo cried in a slur.

"I am the rose, sweet Gregory and you...a blue flower, the 'forget-me-not' of prose."

"I mean the theater. What about the stage?"

"Hah! Let those whores of spectacle and the bishops of said whores turn the pages of history without my natural artistry leading them from freedom into the abyss to find a trap door! A playwright is nothing more than a ploughman and an actor...ah! An actor is but a butcher of his own identity."

"Kit?" Inigo pleaded.

"My brother." Marlowe toppled onto his seat as the wooden rowboat left the lamp lit shore. "Please understand, I cannot allow myself to bake bread for the barters anymore!"

Gregory watched the vessel sift through the shifty moonlight tickling the wide river's ebb, then turned to let the subconscious soul of his drunken self guide his way home hearing Marlowe's last words echo under the bridge, "Alas! I cast away!"

Inigo rose from the lumpy mattress that made up his bed and poured the last bit of water from a clay pitcher into a cracked porcelain bowl to splash his face. He watched the trapped bird whiz about below the dull, black ceiling beams and sighed. It will tire soon, he supposed, thinking to himself, *It must rest somewhere, eventually*, and continued to visualize carefully taking the sparrow or nightingale or whatever it was, gently in his hands and setting it free out the window.

Why am I lacking in the art of nomenclature? he pondered. *How can I not know the types of birds, flowers or plants...other than the rose? I am a poet after all. I should know these things, the names of herbs and whatnot...like Shakespeare.*

He pulled on his pants and boots, thankful he'd remembered to remove them before sleep. It's what made Will such a great writer: his correct use of specifics in dialogue. He created imagery, added resonance; yes, Will's work was wrapped in tenderness and Marlowe's in wrathfulness and Inigo...caught in between, a non-descript flutter of wings!

The bird landed on the bedpost. Inigo could see its tiny heart beating in its breast. He reached out his hands but it flew off, only to repeat the same hypnotic dance in the dead air of the dilapidated room.

After several more failed attempts to help the poor creature when it landed time and again, Inigo reclined on his bed and gave up the prospect of setting free wings by concentrating on his own self-pity and artistic lamentations which soon enough faded into a daydream of Beatrice's fleshy arm slapping down before him a plate of bacon and eggs.

The bird flew out the window.

The thought of the waitress lead to thoughts of his lovely Ilsa, then to all the species of birds he wanted to learn, then to Nile's ridiculous portrayal of Helen of Troy and then eventually all led back to the idea of bacon and eggs.

He went to the Tabard Inn.

Shakespeare, Lodge, Augustine Phillips, Hemmings and Thomas Kyd, who had just returned to London, were unexpectedly seated in the dark, back part of the bar. Gregory approached their table happily, believing that, like him, all had desired a giant breakfast after last night's shindig. Yet there was no sign of food and each player sat with eyes lowered upon a barely sipped pint of bitters.

He sat with them. Beatrice waddled to the table and he ordered his meal. They all looked up at him for a second, then once again bowed their heads and hunched their shoulders beneath crimson, aquamarine and cadmium cloaks. Well, he knew the names of colors. "A rose by any other name would smell as sweet," he muttered, then said aloud, "Alas, I cast away!"

"What's that?" Phillips lifted his red eyes for a moment.

"Oh, nothing. A phrase Kit said last night down at the river. It just occurred to me for some reason."

"You were with Marlowe last night?" Will sat upright. "After we all left the tavern?"

Inigo ripped some crust from a half loaf of bread Beatrice, at that moment, tossed on to the table. "I saw him off in a boat beneath the bridge. He said he was headed southeast, I believe."

"Deptford," Kyd said quietly. "He went to Deptford."

"Really. Well, that's a nice spot. He seemed to be in need of a change of scenery."

The troupe sat silent for a moment, brooding. The scent of bacon frying in the kitchen wafted through the dark, empty tavern. Inigo ate some bread and sipped his pint of ale jovially, searching the sad faces of his friends for some sort of clue. "Is there something...have I offended...?"

Will stood and looked off into the distance at an angel or devil—with him, one never knew. "Christopher Marlowe is dead," he said, then walked out of the room.

"Killed in a knife fight in Deptford," Hemmings added and proceeded to fill Gregory in on all the details. "An argument with Ingram Frizer over the pub bill. Robert Poley was there, saw the whole thing. Kit was stabbed over his right eye..."

Beatrice slapped Inigo's breakfast before him. He watched her turn. Her huge hips seemed to fill the space of the tavern. He suddenly felt ill, trapped, his mind dizzy with a flurry like the sparrow. He got up quickly, the rubbery eggs and greasy bacon untouched on his plate, and ran in a panic out of the Tabard's dark atmosphere into the daylight. The morning's mist had cleared. Caterpillar clouds trailed the blue sky.

His play. He must finish his play in honor of Kit. Inigo walked in long, unsteady strides to High Street to buy paper and ink. He passed by The Rose. An audition announcement had been newly posted for Will's latest play, *Richard III*, to be held that very afternoon at four o'clock.

How can the man continue on like that? Does he not even take a day to mourn? He pounded his fist at the poster then walked on thinking, *Kit was never close to Will, really. But he was to me. I must finish my play.*

For the next two days and nights, Inigo sat at his desk. The nub of his quill had flattened, his fingertips black as Mephistopheles' robe, his face grimy with the smoke slithering in through his window from the street fires warming the vagabonds below, his white tunic plastered to his torso from sweat, his thick blond locks wilting over his shoulders and the standard three-day stubble usually on his chin, now lining his jaw with a full grown beard. He had not slept or eaten.

Because he came.

Marlowe's ghost.

The minute Gregory filled his ink well the scent of a rose filled the room. He dared not look around for he felt his dead friend standing there behind his chair and the next thing he knew Kit had taken his hand and began to move it over the blank parchment, inscribing word after word. The ghost was unceasingly assiduous and together they wrote, and wrote and wrote.

On the evening of the third day, there was a knock on his door. He looked up from his desk. The view in his window, a pale, ashen sky moistening the sinister silhouettes of chimney pots atop the slanting roofs of brick houses, remembered him to his self and to London. The knock came again and he heard Ilsa's shy voice calling out his name.

He stood and looked about his room. Marlowe's ghost instantly disappeared. He went to the washbasin and wet his face and hair.

"My love!" she cried, hearing movement within.

"Just a minute!" He took off his filthy, stinking shirt and threw on a clean white tunic then unlocked the chain.

Ilsa stepped nimbly over the threshold. She carried a basket on her arm. "What has happened to you? I brought you some things." She took bread, butter, green apples and a bottle of beer and set them out on his crumpled bedspread. "You look wretched. Are you ill?"

He said nothing, staring at her gifts.

She placed her palm on his forehead. "Why, you're feverish!"

Inigo took a knife from a drawer in his desk and cut into an apple. "I've been working rather hard, 'tis all. Thank you."

They sat on his bed together while he ate and drank.

Ilsa sighed. "I stopped by the theater first to see if you were there. Shakespeare told me that he hadn't seen you for days and that he was surprised you didn't show for the auditions."

"Surprised? Truly, for a man who writes with such insight into the heart of passion, of grief and despair, of death and deeds…and yet when it comes to fame he has no boundaries! Kit was right about the barters and baking bread." Inigo swigged from the bottle of warm beer. "Hah! Ah, well, my dear Ilsa, you shall see that your own honest Gregory shall not at any cost, sell his fine soul."

"I don't understand what you're saying, my love, you must be delirious. Shakespeare appeared quite sympathetic. After all, he is only doing his job."

Inigo laughed. "Theater is not a job, it's a realm of shades, a little world surrounded by a sleep, but a dream…alas my kitten." He squeezed her thigh. "We players and playwrights are but fools."

She sat looking prettily puzzled while he finished the much needed, though meager, meal. A breeze, carrying the scent of dusk, came through the window and tussled her hair. He was exhausted but took her in his arms and had her then as if he did not know her, as if she had no name other than "girl."

It had been over a week. He woke to a knock on his door. His room was chilly. Outside, it was drizzling. In that time, he had not seen Ilsa or anyone, save four individuals: the new printer on High Street; the child who stole cooling mincemeat pies from rich people's windowsills and sold them for two pence in a little park at the corner of Southwark Street and Blackfriars Road; the apothecary from whom he bought a pinch of opium; and Beatrice, who he gregariously enticed into "loaning" him a few bottles of wine.

Marlowe's ghost returned and the writing did not cease until last night, as he listened to the raindrops tapping on the edges, it seemed, of every object in London until he wrote the words, *The End*. Then the phantom let go his hand and Inigo Gregory, all alone, proudly lifted his pen and was about to sign his name, only to find the nib of his quill dry and not a drop of ink left in the inkwell.

The knock came again. It was hard, almost brutal, certainly not from the tender hand of his love. The minute Inigo opened the door, Niles stumbled in reeking of heavy drink and the mud of the streets.

"What is it? Is Ilsa alright?"

"Oh, she's just peachy, peach that she is." Niles sat at Gregory's desk and looked about in a stupor. "What a dump this place is." He gurgled and then to Inigo's disgust, touched the neatly completed manuscript on the desk. "What's this?"

"A play."

"You, *you* wrote a play?"

To save his integrity, Inigo dare not let a case like Niles know of his artistic pursuits. "No. Not I…it's by…by Christopher Marlowe."

"Really? Which one? *Tamberlaine the Great, The Jew of Malta, Massacre at Paris*?"

"Something else. It's never been staged."

"I thought Kit was dead."

"He is." Inigo quickly snatched up the manuscript and slipped it into the drawer in his desk then began to fill the washbasin on floor. "I have to bathe, Niles, do you mind?"

Niles stood. "Right. A bath, how nice for you."

"Why have you come here?"

"I was at the Tabard."

"And…"

"And I ran out of coins."

Inigo laughed. "I owe Beatrice nearly a quid myself. My pockets are empty."

"Yeah, yeah." Niles grumbled as he went to the door, "Well, I have other resources you know…"

Inigo shook his head and was glad to hear the man slam the door behind him but sad to understand that the other resource mentioned was sure to be his sister's little purse.

His tattered leather boots bludgeoning the mud-spattered roads, Niles ambled down High Street in a blurry haze. He went into a baker's shop and begged for a piece of bread and came out chewing day-old hard crust as he stood absently staring into the window of the printer's shop next door. A light went off in his head. The window displayed printed copies of the various works of Christopher Marlowe, which in itself was not peculiar, but the price tags attached to the sloppily stitched books were. Niles walked into the printer's, the bread still getting soft in his mouth and shouted, "Twenty bloody quid for a play by Kit Marlowe?"

The printer looked up from his type blocks. "A dead man gets a better price than a live one, my friend."

"Hmm." Niles went out and somehow found his way back to Amster House, where he slept all day and woke that evening to an ingenious, in his mind, idea just as Ilsa was returning from the Earl of Southampton's mansion.

"Ah, my dear sister, tell me, did you get paid today?"

"You know I did."

Niles smiled as he jumped out of his thin straw bed. "Well, you know I saw Inigo this morning and I must say he is not looking well, undernourished and overworked and in need of some good female company and a fine wine to drink."

"Oh!" Ilsa's innocent heart swooned with sympathy.

"But do not fear, dear girl, for I have an excellent idea. Now, give me a few pence to cross the river while you run to the market and buy what you need to make your friend a decent supper, and I'll go to his miserable flat and send him straight over to you."

"That is a good idea, brother! Yes, here you are..." She handed him two pence for ferry fare.

"Um...since I'll be on the south bank, well, I thought I might stop by the Tabard."

Ilsa handed him a few more coins. "But that's all, Niles. We already owe the land lady and the butcher and the milk man."

"Hah! Those days are over. Just you wait, sweet sister, just you wait!"

Ilsa put on her bonnet and followed him out the door where he left her at the market and ran down to the docks in a trance of evil plans.

Inigo answered the door cleanly shaven, in clean clothes and polished boots.

"Going somewhere special?" Niles pushed his way into the lonely, grey-walled room.

"Not really. I was thinking of visiting the boys at The Rose. I haven't been out much lately and thought..." Inigo stopped, indignant at himself for speaking so freely to such a scoundrel.

"But my good man, you see the players all the time. Now, I have a surprise for you. My dear sister is, as we speak, preparing a scrumptious feast for you to be held in our room at Amster House. I myself am on my way to the Inn so you two lovebirds will be quite alone."

"Oh, darling Ilsa! She truly is a kind soul, is she not?" Again, Inigo cowered inside for showing emotion to Niles.

"Yes, yes. Now, hurry along."

"Of course." Gregory opened the door and waited for Niles to walk out ahead of him, but Niles suddenly fell to his knees.

"Man, what is wrong with you?"

"I'm not sure. I'm quite dizzy. I feel that I must lie down."

"Well, there is the bed. Here, let me help you." Gregory sat at his desk and

161

sighed as Niles crossed his filthy boots at the end of the bed.

"But my friend, I must not keep you from your date. Ilsa would certainly be disappointed. Oh, I can see her weeping before a table set for a king right now! No, no, you must go along."

"But you…"

"Don't worry about me. This has happened before. I just need an hour's rest and I'll be fine."

"But I need to lock up."

"Oh, well, that's not an issue. Listen, I'm going to the Tabard as soon as I recover. Give me your key, I'll lock up for you and leave the key with Beatrice."

"I suppose it's a sound enough solution. Very well." Gregory placed the key on the desk and left the depressing room.

He arrived on the steps of Amster House feeling fresh and revived. The play was finished, his masterpiece complete. Yes, tomorrow he would show it to Shakespeare and the rest. Of course, Inigo himself would play the lead, Kyd would play the rival and the great and powerful Will would direct. The Rose would be sold out for weeks on end! And then, with all of London begging for further performances, *The Marriage of Count de Lampere* by Inigo Gregory, would move to Blackfriars and maybe even The Lord Chamberlain's Men, and ultimately go down in history as the longest running play in England!

The fat landlady's children were playing with a new litter of calico kittens on the mucky, brick steps.

"Now aren't they cute?" Inigo picked one up and held it in the air with one hand like an artisan checking for flaws of his craft in a shaft of direct sunlight.

"Three sous!" shouted the boy.

"You're selling the kittens?" Inigo laughed.

"Two sous!" pealed the little girl.

"But my dear children, there are kittens crawling about the streets of London town everywhere. Anyone can pick one up for free!"

"A penny? Just a penny?" The boy pouted with such humility that the happy playwright had to feel in his pocket for a single copper coin.

"A present for me lady." He winked at the kids as he went up the stairs.

The door ajar, he walked into Ilsa's tiny room with the kitten wriggling against his chest. She was setting the wobbly table, wearing a lavender dress with her long blond hair twisted atop her high forehead in a crown of delicate braids.

He gave her the kitten which she immediately cuddled with the sincere affection of a lonely little girl. Her emotion touched him so deeply he felt he could weep. Had anyone in his entire life ever thanked him for anything or appreciated his kindness? Was he, in fact, kind? He didn't know. Even in Shakespeare's plays, was kindness ever a major quality in a character? What were his own qualities, he wondered?

It was a different age. How far the stage had come from the old morality plays of the last century. Virtues were no longer abstractions in the character of a man or woman; they were now qualities. Vigilance, endurance, honor, courage and to a degree even etiquette—the noble traits that once belonged only to the aristocratic pride of dukes, lords and princes were now slowly filtering down into the very souls of the middle and lower classes...all because of plays! In essence, Inigo mused as Ilsa cradled her new kitten, such themes were the foundation of *The Marriage of Count de Lampere*. Gregory was suddenly struck with an interior epiphany, that he had, in his play, defined a new way of believing in one's self. He had opened the portal to a new way of being, a new era, and a new theater where justice and common courtesy prevail. He'd done so in collaboration with Marlowe's ghost and a melancholy wave of grief came over him for his dear, dead friend.

Ilsa set the kitten on the floor before a saucer of milk, "Inigo, are you alright?"

"Fine, my love, just a bit overworked, but this repast is perfect!"

The excited couple sat down on either side of the wobbly table to a peasant's feast of stewed turnips, pickled herring and a freshly baked tart stuffed with woodland strawberries.

Meanwhile, Niles swiped the manuscript from Gregory's desk, scribbled the initials CM at the end of it and took it to the printer's shop on High Street.

"I have here, good sir, the last written play of Christopher Marlowe," Niles told the acquisitive young businessman.

The printer thumbed through the handwritten manuscript and suspiciously eyed Niles.

"Two hundred pounds." Niles crossed his arms over his chest.

"Insane. Fifty quid or you take it across the river where they'll charge you 5 quid to print one copy of the bloody thing!"

Niles gladly accepted the offer and spent the rest of the week at the Tabard Inn.

Three days later, Inigo woke upon Ilsa's tiny little mattress, his arms around her breast and his skinny yet muscular bare legs entwined within the soft, snowy flesh of her thighs. He hadn't left her flat since their quaint and lovely supper and knew he was in love. He kissed her dearly, dressed and left her sweet maiden self to sleep. He passed by a barbershop on his way to the ferry and, feeling in tiptop shape, decided to treat himself to a grand shave.

After he got his keys from Beatrice, the four grey walls, hiding within themselves as he entered his room, seemed to open out upon an entirely changed universe like four mirrors reflecting the future and he said aloud, "Act. III, Scene VII...I must make a correction!"

He opened the drawer in his desk.

It was empty.

He panicked. He spun in circles and the grey walls reversed their reflective surfaces to mock him. He went to the window and looked out at the black, stinking chimneys and piles of bricks. In the street below, a prostitute cackled, a drunk man fell face forward into a puddle, a robust woman ran after a stray chicken, caught it and instantly snapped its neck, children covered in soot kicked the fallen drunkard, the prostitute cackled, the drunk man slipped while trying to scramble to his feet, the robust woman pulled the children by their hair...and Niles strode past along the scum-covered cobblestones wearing brand new clothes and boots and swinging a bottle in his hand.

"No, he couldn't possibly have...." Inigo's heart sank. "No. No!"

A herald boy jumped over the drunkard and followed the drops of chicken blood staining the street, calling out, "*The Marriage of Count de Lampere*, the very last play written by the acclaimed, deceased, revered, deceased, genius of the deceased Christopher Marlowe opens at The Rose Theater...tomorrow!"

The Marriage of Count de Lampere—the world, that is, all of England, knowing it to be written by Kit Marlowe—ran for six weeks at The Rose, moved to Blackfriars for a fortnight, then to The Lord Chamberlain's Men and ultimately was staged at White Palace before the Queen.

Inigo left the theater forever. He married Ilsa, moved into the countryside, became a cobbler like his father before him and produced five sons, one of which survived. His name was Christopher.

XI

Gozo, Italy

Present

"How's it going?" Marianne peeped into his study drying her hands on a dishtowel.

"The key is to re-create by the need." Claude deleted an entire paragraph without a second thought.

"Was that mine or yours?"

"Yours."

"A whole block...just like that?"

"You have a tendency for redundancy."

"I do not." She sighed as she read the last few lines on the screen. "Did you love her?"

"Ilsa?"

"Yeah."

"Of course. But you, *you*, to use a cliché, 'always had a very special place in my heart'."

"It was nice of you to name your son after me."

"What was nicer is that the dear boy survived." He turned round in his wooden armchair, lowered his new spectacles and squinted at her. She was wearing the pumpkin blouse again. "Are you going into town?"

"I just got back."

"And?"

She handed him the blank white envelope with the obscure stamp. He opened it immediately and sighed. "Serifos."

"Greece?"

"260…A.D."

"But that's so long ago! How are we supposed to remember?"

Claude shrugged and pushed his eyeglasses back over the bridge of his nose. "Do you remember when I decided to write my novel, my one and only novel, and I asked you, half-seriously, how does one write a novel, Marianne?"

Marianne shook her head. "I remember you asking but I don't remember what I said."

"You said, 'Clues, just write the same thing over and over again for at least three hundred pages until you get it right'."

"Literally? I said that?"

"Exact words."

"Well, I must have been teasing you or provoking you or trying to persuade you not to write a novel because…"

"Because?"

Sincerely, she answered, "Because I didn't want to see you get hurt."

He laughed. "My dear, how on earth does one get hurt by writing a novel?"

"Humph!" She turned in full circle and the orange peasant blouse billowed out like a parachute. "You, of all people on earth throughout history should know the answer to that one!"

She went back into the kitchen. He got out of his chair and followed her in there.

"It was a great novel."

"Is a great novel, a great work, Clues, truly."

"I wasn't hurt."

"I know."

"Were you?"

She continued drying the few dishes disdainfully. "Yes."

"I'm sorry."

Marianne looked in the refrigerator. "Perhaps I'll braise the tuna steaks I just bought in town with olive oil and cilantro. How does that sound for dinner?"

"How did it hurt you?"

"Your book? It hurt to see you put so much into it but at the same time remain distant from it. It hurt to see you not being hurt by writing it."

"I don't understand, Marianne. I have no idea what you're talking about."

"We never really talked about this before, have we?"

"So, let's talk about it now."

She hung the dishrag on a hook and looked out of the kitchen window at the slight view of the pink horizon far out upon the sea. "When I wrote my novels, I hurt. I mean it hurt me to write them. It hurt loving them then letting them go, you know?"

"I do not, love."

"Each character, each word is like a lost man trying to return home. And he, the story, comes to me as a kind of Odyssean nobody out of nowhere…comes to me—the navel of the sea—and I fall in love with him and want to keep him forever so I bewitch him until I realize he must go. No, that's not it. Until I realize that he must evolve. Alas, with tears I watch him set sail. In each book, in each story, I am the witch Calypso."

Claude leaned against the window, partially blocking her view. "I never knew your approach to writing was so romantic."

She smiled the smile. "Perhaps that's because my approach to marriage is not."

Elizabeth McKague

XII

Twilight in Serifos
Greece, 260 a.d.

"Maybe today, maybe tomorrow or the next day." Eudoxia's melancholy thoughts were dissolved by fresh hope as she sat on the window seat and gazed out beyond the acres, past the olive grove and golden stony cliffs at a horizon of purple ribbons bleeding into the deepest blue, it seemed, that the sea had ever been. Even now, toward dusk, the immobile heat made a constant buzzing sound in the air outside like a suffocating beehive. Her apartment was on the second story of the palace, and the palace rested atop the pinnacle of the highest mountain on the island. Two white butterflies rose up and played in the open window then floated back down.

Nemerte, her maidservant, came into the room for dinner instructions. A prosperous merchant from Naxos had arrived on the small island of Serifos and as queen she was obligated, even while her husband was away, to receive him, his wife, their five children and their servants for the length of his stay.

"I've no idea," Eudoxia told her. "Roast a lamb or something and mix the finest mead from the cellar. Great Poseidon! I wish Agapetos were here!"

"Any day now, I'm sure of it," Nemerte cooed.

"Are you? Why? Have you had a vision, have you seen a sign?"

The old maidservant nodded. "A flock of sparrow-hawks passed over our roofs at dawn and look there, on the shutters, two white butterflies."

"Ah, you are a good woman."

Nemerte spread the queen's indigo gown out upon her bed as Eudoxia turned back to the expansive view of her husband's kingdom and leaned her head against the turquoise shutter. "Tell cook to stuff it with figs and bay leaves...the lamb."

King Agapetos had left the island on the first evening of the new moon. He'd only sailed to Cypress to give and take treasure, and promised to be back before the moon began to wane, yet now it was but a sliver.

Eudoxia wasn't worried at all. The king was a brave sailor and a brilliant leader, and all those stories about Odysseus had no proven validity anyhow. The Aegean Sea of the Cyclades was filled with delicious fish and beautiful nereids. It was the Ionian depths that were filled with treacherous monsters and evil Sirens, as everyone knew. Alas, she was just restless. She missed him so and wanted to tell him of her own discovery while he'd been away. She had to tell him about the shepherd boy.

Chariton was his name. Each twilight as the queen sat upon her windowsill, reflecting upon her duties, her daughters, her dearly loved husband and her life, she'd watch the herd of fluffy sheep descend the pasture on the hill, clumsily yet rhythmically, as if the giant lips of Zeus had blown upon a bouquet of dead dandelions and sent the gray white tufts to roll down the slope on a sea breeze. Chariton followed, waving his carved branch of birch with his black sheepdog faithfully panting at his side.

The path he took fringed the periphery of the olive grove and curved round a small marble temple King Agapetos had built years ago. There, a select group of the wealthiest youths on the island would gather to honor Apollo in the setting sun and speak of lofty ideas, practicing an art of discourse, Eudoxia learned, called philosophy.

The queen had her doubts as to whether or not these sons of rich landlords were truly devoted to the love of wisdom or chose to visit the olive grove so they could catch a glimpse of one of her daughters, who at that hour decorated the first floor terrace, where they'd sit in fine garments, singing vows of chastity to Artemis before dinner time.

Iphianassa, Panope, Thaleia and Marpessa: four lovely girls born one after the other, but oh, how Agapetos longed for a son! Alas, after Marpessa, his queen could no longer produce children. The king blamed himself for spending so much time on his travels. Nemerte said that Aphrodite had put a curse on Eudoxia for giving birth to such an array of beauty. But the queen knew the truth; that her husband's name and their very kingdom on Serifos was destined to be forgotten in history.

Each evening, after Chariton guided his flock safely into their pen for the night, he'd follow the path his own sandaled feet had made over the years through the olive grove home. Where that home was, Eudoxia did not know. He'd walk slowly with a tired tranquility, and each and every evening, stop in a cluster of trees close enough to the assembly of young philosophical neophytes so that he could eavesdrop on their conversation yet remain secretly hidden.

The study session would often begin with Dareios unraveling a papyrus scroll and reading a passage by some obscure Neo-Platonist such as Demetrius of Amphipolis, Marinus of Neoplois, Eusebus of Myndus or his favorite, Ascelepiodotus of Alexandria. The boys would proceed to comment or question in turn, and a discussion would ensue upon the nature of *ethos, eros, sophos* or *pnuema*.

"It is a man's duty to measure his own values," wise Dareios began.

"Against what?" asked eager Basilius.

Sardonic Galenos quickly added, "The Olympians? Shall we cheat on our wives, eat the flesh of our relatives…take a giant piss on a virgin?"

The boys laughed and Iason passed around a flask of wine while Basilius spread a cloth on the dry ground and laid out flatbreads and mounds of goat cheese wrapped in basil leaves.

Timon, the eldest and most serious of them all spoke then. "The gods are immortal. Therefore, immorality is inconsequential. We, men, are mortal and so must, as Dareios stated, 'measure our values'."

"But against what?" Basilius pleaded.

Timon lit a pipe and passed it to Galenos. The strange, inky, sweet-smelling smoke traveled on the breeze and into Chariton's hiding spot. "Against the stars," he answered in a whisper to himself.

"Against the principles of the universe," Timon finally said.

Galenos, after swilling a large draught of wine from the flask, blurted out in a rage of mental anguish, "But what are those principles? How do we know them?"

"Through this, this moment, this study, this discourse…" Dareios calmly offered.

"Yet the moment flees," Iason argued.

"Does knowledge flee?"

"No!" they all answered.

Timon continued, "Ah! Have you not read your Plato carefully my friends? Today we know this; tomorrow it may change. 'All I know…'"

"'Is that I know nothing'." Together the boys finished the Socratic quote in a chant.

Basilius was not satisfied and continued to plead, "Then what do we rely upon? Where is the source of truth? Wherein lies the essence of knowledge upon which we can truly measure our values?"

The council grew silent. The silvery green olive leaves rustled in the salty air flowing inland from the sea and the dewy twilight became a darker mirror. Chariton rose from his position, crouching down with his back against the bark of a tree, and spoke aloud without realizing it, "The heart."

The boys, who were lying on their sides, leaned up on their elbows, widening their eyes and opening their ears. Dareios, who'd been sitting with his legs crossed before him, straightened his back then quickly jumped to his feet. "Who said that?" he called out.

The shepherd sunk back down behind the tree, afraid.

"Who is there? Show yourself!" demanded the leader.

Chariton kept as still and quiet as a sleeping sheep.

Galenos stood beside Dareios. "Shall I search the grove?"

Dareios thought for a moment, listening, then suddenly began to gather twigs. "Come, my friends, we must make a pyre as an offering."

And they all obeyed, for when the relentlessly inquisitive Basilius begged Dareios *who* had answered, "The heart", he was told that it must have been Apollo himself!

Eudoxia watched the smoke from the pyre spread out around the temple and saw the shepherd boy nimbly shielding his exit like Athena traveling in a mist. She laughed at the aristocratic boys burning their laurels in fear of and reverence to Apollo, and a second later, when searching the landscape for Chariton, saw that he had disappeared.

Nemerte came into the queen's chambers and instructed her to dress quickly as the merchant from Naxos and his tribe had been waiting impatiently for their host in the courtyard. "So, I sent the girls in to entertain him."

"Yes, yes." Eudoxia rose from her window seat and asked her maidservant as she arranged her dress over her shoulders, "Do you know anything about the shepherd boy? Who his parents are or where he resides?"

"Chariton, that's his name. He's an odd sort, a solitaire."

"I've been observing him these past few weeks; a loner perhaps, yet he seems happy."

"The poor child lost his parents three years ago when he was just fourteen.

One of Zeus' thunderbolts struck their home and they burned to a crisp. The boy was in the hills with his sheep, so saved. He has no siblings. He sleeps with his dog in the caves by the bay."

"But surely someone helped the child after the fire. A neighbor, friend or a relative?"

"Not a soul. Chariton has been rather alienated his whole life. You see, his mother…well, my queen, she was a witch."

"A witch! On my island?"

"She came from the shores of Syria you know, from a colony of Orphics."

Eudoxia pinned her dark, wavy ringlets on top of her head. Her face, so beautiful it was, glowed like an August moon. "Oh, nonsense! Those mystery cults are no more mysterious than rich boys burning laurel leaves in an olive grove. Really, Nemerte, the outrageous things men come up with simply to amuse themselves: secret societies, politics, war…when it's so easy to take pleasure in the delicate things right before their eyes. Why can't they be satisfied with the truth of two white butterflies landing on a shelf, or purple tassels of sky lowering into the deep blue sea?"

"I do not know, my queen."

"You're a good woman, Nemerte. Now, let us go downstairs and charm our anxious visitor from Naxos. What's he like?"

"As you surmised, dear Queen, he's a nervous, twitchy, devious sort of man."

"And his wife?"

"A miserable bore."

"And the children?"

"Full of themselves."

Eudoxia lifted her skirt and trailed out the door. "Good, then we have a delightful evening ahead of us."

Chariton and his sheepdog named Karpos, a loving animal that was more like a friend than a work dog, passed through the lands below the palace of King Agapetos and took their route toward the sea. The old Otonia, a fisherman's wife who took pity on the lad, was ready at her doorstep to give Chariton a loaf of black bread and throw some pork bones to the dog. At sunset, the two climbed down the rocky slopes to a slight sandy beach tracing the mouth of Livadiou Bay and took shelter for the night in a familiar cave.

The questions the aristocratic boys had asked that day were spinning in

Chariton's mind yet his weariness clouded any effort to discern their significance rationally. *Apollo! They believed he is a god! What fun*, the shepherd thought, planning to listen carefully to the symposium on the following day. He was genuinely curious about the lofty ideas those boys seemed so passionate about and also, the scrolls they opened with the complicated, tiny black pictures all lined up inside them. He knew it was writing but didn't understand how Dareios was able to look at it and speak of its meaning at the same time.

His mother had one book that she'd open under a full moon then repeat strange foreign phrases. As a child he was told never to go near this book, that it could be dangerous. Yet she taught him about the world, the stars and the sea, and his father taught him to carve wood and make a fine walking stick. Chariton curled up beside Karpos' black fluffy fur, missing his home with his parents, almost wishing to shed tears, but he was too old for that now. He had new curiosities as well, besides questions. He was curious about the girls who came out onto the terrace of the palace. They made him feel hungry, yet not in his stomach. He wanted to get close to one of them, just close enough to look into the eyes of such a lovely being.

Learning about ideas and looking at pretty girls became a kind of mission for Chariton. It was the first time in his young life that he began to feel as if he had a purpose for existing on such a beautiful island other than orchestrating a flock of sheep. Day after day, he hid in the cloister of trees in the olive grove to listen to the philosophy students and continued at random to vigilantly, half-audibly, blurt out simple, single syllable answers to their most perplexing questions. The rich boys' egos grew for they were sure Apollo was auditing their symposiums.

"We must tell no one on the island, not our fathers or brothers or even the king," Dareios warned the group.

"But this attention from a god is remarkable! Perhaps we are truly gifted beings, our fame should be known throughout the Cyclades," argued Galenos.

"You are drunk again, Galenos," wise Timon scolded. "Dareios is right. If others knew it would do us more harm than good. People would come from all corners of the world to hear Apollo. They would pollute our clean harbor with their ships, trample the olive grove and ruin Agapetos' dear little temple. Not only would the king ostracize us, but imagine what the god himself might do to us!"

"Our meetings here have become sacred. Apollo trusts us...how dare we forsake his trust!" Dareios lifted his eyes toward the treetops.

They agreed and made a solemn vow by burning the expensive incense Basilius had received from an uncle in the Orient upon a newly made pyre.

On the terrace at dusk, there was one princess in particular, slightly shorter, thinner and more delicate than the others, probably the youngest. Her long ebony locks hung loose beneath a headband made of ivory beads and when she turned in a circle, Chariton saw that her soft, lush hair reached below the waist of her saffron-dyed gown. From his position in the grove, at moments when the diminishing sun sent a few last dazzling rays upon the terrace, he could see her almond eyes sweetly longing. Once, it seemed she had looked at him directly, but of course, that was impossible. When he heard her sisters address her as *Marpessa*, he sang her name, over and over in his soul. He also noticed, while spying on the princesses of Serifos, that while the three older girls often cheated on their prayers to Artemis by letting their gazes drift toward the rich boys with their scrolls, that Marpessa kept her dreamy eyes transfixed upon the far off sea as if searching for someone. *Perhaps*, thought Chariton, *for me!*

"Basilius was staring up at you!" Iphianassa, the eldest, in a gown dyed crimson, teased her baby sister.

Panope, the second born, wearing a dress colored sky blue, nudged Iphianassa. "She doesn't care. Look at her! Lost again in her dreams."

"She never looks at the philosophers," Thaleia, in emerald green, told the other two.

"Then how does she expect to find a suitor?" Panope huffed as she waved her arm discreetly at the crowded temple in the olive grove below. "That is our lot—the richest boys on the island. And it's time to take your pick, girls! Except, of course, for Dareios!"

"Except for Iason." Iphianassa giggled.

"And Galenos," Thaleia chimed in.

"Galenos?" All of them, including Marpessa, reprimanded their sister in emerald.

"Why, he's a drunk!" Iphianassa scowled.

"And a fool!"

"Lazy, too. And that beard!"

The princesses burst into laughter.

"What you say may be true, but he's tall and well built. He has broad shoulders, a thin waist and adamantine thighs. You see, I plan on making at least ten children and I don't want to be unhappy when I do!" Thaleia protested.

Her sisters frowned and Marpessa returned to glaring sadly out at the horizon.

Iphianassa approached her. "Who is it you are looking for out there my darling? You can tell *me*."

The youngest sighed, her yellow dress illuminated by the very last light from the plummeting sun. "Father's ship. I miss him."

Chariton, who'd heard the entire dialogue carried out on a breeze, thought, *Oh! What a pure thing is she!*

At that very moment, the boys in the temple happened to be asking, "What is the purest thing that a man's eye can see?"

Instantly, the shepherd spoke aloud, "Marpessa!"

All heads turned toward the terrace, but the princesses had since retired.

At the north end of the palace on the second story, Chariton was not unaware of a shadowy figure, composed still as a swan and seated just inside a grand open window with turquoise shutters. He could tell it was a woman but never saw her face. Yet he wondered, from her position and angle, if he himself might be visible within her view.

Since the game of playing the role of Apollo began, the shepherd boy learned to leave Karpos in the sheep pen, lest a rabbit happened to hop through his cloister of trees. Alas, he dared not risk being found out because of a bark from his dear dog. For two weeks, the game continued. Then, on the final night of a waxing moon, the careless, vain Galenos, intoxicated by hubris, sent Basilius with a message that he was ill and unable to join the group. It was not true. That evening, while the philosophers practiced their discourse, Galenos stealthily crept through the olive grove, determined to get a look at the great Apollo.

Timon asked, "What is the greatest attribute of friendship?"

And Chariton answered with full force, "Loyalty," as Galenos was just passing the cloister of trees. He daringly rushed in, apathetic to his own fate if, in fact, he found himself face to face with a god! Alas, he found nothing but an impoverished shepherd boy, crouching on his knees. Galenos roared with laughter, grabbed the terrified youth and kept him held tightly by strapping the boy's arms behind his back.

"Ah, hah! I've got you now! Miscreant! Scoundrel! Imposter! Imposter!" Galenos' shouts rang through the grove and before the cicadas chirped again, the rich boys were surrounding Chariton.

"Here is your Apollo!" Galenos triumphed.

The dedicated lovers of wisdom, blasphemed at being fooled, could not contain their battered egos. Iason threw the first punch then Basilius joined in. The mild Dareios stood back in astonishment and by the time Timon was able to break up the fight, poor Chariton lay in the dry grass, his face bloody and swollen like a pomegranate, and his eyes like slits of little black pits. His chest caved in, he could barely breathe; they'd broken his ribs.

Upon witnessing the first blow to the handsome young shepherd's head, Eudoxia jumped off her window seat and ran through the palace summoning her guards.

The philosophers were immediately arrested and locked away in the palace dungeon, excepting Timon and Dareios who were summoned for questioning. The queen took her place on the throne and her daughters hastened to her side. After an elaborate examination, the two eldest and wisest of the olive grove boys were released and sent to carry the news to the landlords whose sons were guilty of the crime. The two innocents bowed before the throne and upon lifting his head, Dareios' eyes met those of the stately Panope, who daringly returned his ardent gaze. Eudoxia sent bread and water to the prison, dismissed the princesses to continue their prayers and hurried to one of the small guesthouses where her guards had brought Chariton. He lay barely conscious upon the grand bed. Nemerte was washing the blood from the poor boy's face and neck as Eudoxia entered the room, lit by a single torch in one corner with the bright, white weeping moonlight spilling through the shutters.

"He is alive?"

"Yes, my queen."

"Will he survive?"

"The gods will let us know. His chest is battered."

At that moment, Hypatos, the island surgeon, arrived, announcing, "Timon sent for me."

"Praise wise Timon!" cried the sympathetic queen.

Hypatos carefully wrapped the shepherd's ribs tightly in plasters and gave Nemerte a tincture to administer, "in small doses when needed."

"But how am I to know when he needs it?" asked the good maidservant.

"He will scream with pain," the surgeon said then left, but not before calling upon the great Asclepius for a blessing.

Eudoxia returned to her chambers but could not sleep. At dawn, she crossed the courtyard lined with lemon trees and opened the door of the little house where Chariton lay completely still. Yet unlike the night before, now his eyes were wide open and in them Eudoxia saw a trajectory of fear. She jostled her maidservant's shoulder. "Have you given the tincture?"

"But he has not yet screamed."

"Look at the boy! He is obviously in great pain and probably in shock as well." The queen poured a small amount of the medicine into a spoon. "Perhaps he doesn't know how to scream. After all, the poor child has been alone for years. Who is there to scream to?" And with that, she forced the liquid down Chariton's throat. He swallowed and coughed. The cough appeared to cause him great agony and he squealed in anguish.

"The medicine will work soon." Eudoxia wet a cloth to dampen the boy's feverish brow and released Nemerte so she could take the chair herself beside the sick bed. Both Chariton and the queen fell asleep but woke together as well when the sun reached the apex of the blue sky outside. A fragile light came through the shutters. Their eyes met.

"Your name is Chariton, is it not?"

He remained still and silent yet completely aware in a way that almost frightened the queen. So intense was his awareness, it was more like that of an animal than a human being.

"Do you remember what happened to you?"

He tried to speak but his jaw was swollen and his lips were too dry. Eudoxia patiently gave him spoons of water. "You are in my palace now. I will take care of you."

The fear in Chariton's eyes turned to horror. She administered the potion and gradually his bruised features became calm. Nemerte came in to take over and the queen went to bathe with her daughters in the lagoon.

The following morning, the local landowners were pounding on the palace doors. This the queen had foreseen and her soldiers forced them away.

"All will be settled when Agapetos returns," Eudoxia said as she joined Nemerte at the sick bed. "My daughters are begging to visit our poor victim, but I believe it is best to wait until he is more presentable."

"I agree." The loyal maid told her, "He is asking for bread. It is a good sign."

On the third day of his convalescence, Chariton collapsed into a coma and the surgeon was called in.

"He is dying, his composition is rather delicate due to the severity of his injuries. He is not as strong as the other boys on the island," Hypatos said. "Only a miracle can save him."

For three more days, the shepherd lay inert save his slow breath. Eudoxia dripped water on his lips from a wet cloth and constantly prayed at his side. "My son," she whispered. "My dear son. You are a strong boy, a fine boy."

That evening, as the sea raged with an approaching storm, a ship pulled into the harbor of Serifos. Marpessa saw it from the terrace and raced through the courtyard lined with lemon trees. She stopped at the door of the guesthouse and called out to her mother, "He is home! Father has returned!"

Eudoxia gave the damp cloth to Nemerte and followed her girls through the olive grove, over the golden stone cliffs and down to the shore. The powerful, courageous Agapetos stepped off his ship and embraced his family affectionately. A fluffy black sheep dog ran up to the happy family, apparently out of a nearby cave, and followed them home.

At dinner, Eudoxia told the king what had happened. Agapetos proclaimed that he would meet with the landowners the following day and suggested that the whole family should visit the guesthouse to pray for the poor boy.

Nemerte was filled with excitement when the royal family entered the room. "He has woken! Dear Lady, my blessed King, he is awake!"

Chariton's eyes moved across the shadows of so many in the room and stopped when he saw those lovely almond eyes and the saffron dress. Next he saw Karpos dash through the open door and almost smiled.

"Look, he is trying to speak!" Iphianassa cried.

The queen knelt by his side. "What is it? Dear boy, we are all here for you."

The shepherd did smile, enigmatically, and nearly half laughed. "I know now..." he whispered so softly only the queen and king could hear him properly.

"And what is it you know, my son?" Agapetos asked.

"The answer...to...to the greatest question of all."

"You do? And what is it?"

"First...the question. No, first...some water please."

"Of course. Nemerte!"

The maidservant put a cup to the boy's lips and he drank, thirstily.

"The question. The greatest question, of course, is: What is the purpose of human existence?"

"My, my." Agapetos said zealously yet with warmth, "Sophisticated talk from a shepherd boy! So tell us then, my child...what *is* the purpose of existence?"

Chariton took a deep, painful breath as his eyes tenderly met those of the gentle queen's.

"Kindness," he answered. "The answer is kindness."

XIII

Gozo, Italy

Present

Marianne came out of the ocean, threading through the foam of the waves. *But oh, how very unlike Aphrodite is my beautiful wife*, thought Claude.

She plopped down on the beach blanket beside him, the salty water glistening in her already fading, dyed-red hair. "Do you think they're enjoying themselves?"

Claude looked back down and turned the page of the novel he'd been reading, *The Beautiful and the Damned* by F. Scott Fitzgerald. It was the third time he'd read it in his life. Not that he loved it particularly, but as he'd read almost every book worth reading (and this was quite a lot) by the time he was 30, the only solution for appeasing his erudite appetite was to go back and read them all over again. Alas, this task, accomplished by the age of 50, set him on yet another cycle, (with the exception of Alessandro Baricco and Roberto Bolano, two new authors he found admirable), and promised himself that by the time he'd gotten through a third round of Proust, he'd be ready to die.

Absorbed in his book, Claude ignored her question.

"Well, just look at them!" She gazed out at the Mediterranean that was the backyard of the Villa Calypso, to see Esmond and Sally, the girl he'd brought. *Silly name. Ridiculous name*, she thought, watching them splashing each other playfully in the low tide whilst Etienne, always the solitaire, was swimming like Byron in the Hellespont and disappearing into the azure sea.

"He's going out so far!" she said.

"He's a fine swimmer, always has been."

At that comment or in spite of that comment, Marianne stood and waved

181

her arm in the blue air, signaling her younger son to come back to the shore.

"He can't see you," Claude muttered.

She turned in a sudden panic. "Well, then…go out and get him!"

Claude let out a deep breath and sipped from a bottle of water. "Good God, Marianne. He'll turn round when he's ready. He's perfectly fine."

She sat back down. "I just worry sometimes. Etienne is so interior and dramatic."

"Hence, his studies in philosophy."

"God, I know! But do you think…why didn't *he* bring a girl?"

Claude laughed. "Because he knows you. Are you even aware of the way you've been treating Sally?"

"What? I've been very cordial."

"Perhaps. But everyone can see that you're festering inside."

"She's not worthy of Esmond. You must agree."

"No, I do not. I think she's cute and sweet."

"C'mon, she's a bored, silly English girl who comes from a family of new wealth that tries to mimic the old aristocracy by owning an estate in Devonshire and a Queen Anne style townhouse in Hampstead."

"Really!" Claude interrupted but she continued to rattle on, more to herself and the invisible nereids that were at that moment guiding Etienne towards Poseidon's cave, than to her husband. "She probably goes to her brother's tennis club on Saturdays, has tea at the Palm Court with her appearance-obsessed mother on Tuesdays, and dines with her money-obsessed banker father at La Gavroche every third Wednesday."

"Ah ha, and what does she do on Thursdays?"

Marianne wound a lock of her hair around her finger. "She volunteers at an animal shelter and on Fridays she goes out with Esmond and gets plastered, and on Sunday, perhaps she's back at the tennis club if by chance she took a fancy to a new instructor the day before, and if not, she mopes about in her pseudo-bohemian flat in Notting Hill Gate until she *must* go shopping."

"And on Monday?"

"She meets her friends for lunch in Chelsea and complains about being bored."

Claude shifted his semi-slim torso onto his stomach, facing away from the sea, and turned the page in his book. "I see. Thank you for such an insightful elucidation on Sally Norwood's itinerary, my sweet. I can now see why our eldest boy is infatuated with her."

"You can?"

"Sure."

"Well?"

"She's a doll." He laughed. "Don't worry. It won't last long. I think she's polite and pretty."

She let out a *hmph*. "Esmond doesn't need that, he needs adventure and glamor."

"Hah! I think that's what you need!"

She slapped his bottom and nudged his hip with her own. "And so I married you!" She rose to go back into the water.

Claude looked up at her. "You're happy they're here, aren't you?"

"Happier than I've been all year," she told him in truth, then added, "He's coming back in now, Etienne is."

Claude nodded. He was happy, too.

That afternoon when Marianne and Esmond alone went into Xaghra to buy groceries for the evening meal, he spoke only of Oxford, his career goals, fencing and kayaking clubs and asked her advice about some minor problems he'd been having with his allergies but said not one word about his girlfriend and consequently, his mother calmed down.

Marianne made braised balsamic chicken breasts with mushroom risotto but like David's wife, Sally barely touched her plate—vegan, gluten-free, the whole shebang. Claude insisted that his wife whip up the tomato basil thing, but Sally wouldn't hear of it. Yet, unlike the American, Miss Norwood didn't touch a drop of alcohol. Claude drank more wine than usual and Etienne followed his father's predilection as if they were in some kind of competition. Esmond, in high spirits, ate and drank more than his mother had ever seen, but not out of the natural fortitude of his tall, lean physique.

When Sally also refused the rhubarb and strawberry pie that was served for dessert, Marianne gave herself a second serving and, with great vulgarity and tactlessness, blurted, "Fine. More for me!"

To this, Etienne laughed out loud and his mother joined in, but no one else did.

That night in bed, Claude, still reading the Fitzgerald as Marianne curled on her side and pouted, said, "This can't go on all week. You'll ruin their vacation."

"I know. I've been a real bitch, haven't I?"

"Yep. You're jealous. That's what it is. Esmond has always been your favorite."

"I have no favorites! Now that was unfair of you, Clues. Anyway, we both know you've always been closer to Etienne."

"I had to. You were always fawning over Esmond."

"I didn't fawn! Perhaps there is a bit more…sentiment there, he is my first-born after all, but I never fawned. A mother can't help but love both her children equally."

"And no woman will ever be good enough for either of her sons."

"It's just that she's so English."

"What's wrong with that? You're English."

"Yes, but I'm different."

"How so?"

"Because I married a Parisian." She sat up and stared at him as if she would eat him. "And our boys grew up in France, thank God!"

"Esmond won't turn 'English' just because of a girl, babes. Listen, you didn't turn French because of me."

"Of course not, but I did adopt many French customs, attitudes, habits…"

"Still, you've remained a slapdash ol' bird nevertheless."

She punched the pillow that was propped up behind his head and laughed. "Oh, I have, haven't I?"

"C'mon. I'm joking. We are who we are, with or without country."

She settled back down under the sheets and laid her head on his stomach. "I suppose as writers we are forever, in one way or another, in a perpetual exile."

"Correct." He turned a page. "So please, loosen up my dear, not just about Esmond but about everything: the postcards, the next story, the future and the past…sometimes I fear you'll drive me to be a drinker like our chum Scottie here and you, you'll end up like Zelda!"

"Won't happen."

"Hope not."

"Never."

"How can you be so sure?"

"Because you're too vain to abandon your brain to alcohol and I'm much too clever to go insane."

"This is true." Claude continued to finish the chapter as she slid her hand down to rub his cock.

Claude, amazed, put the book down.

Marianne showed a significant improvement in benevolence the following day and the Renoir family, including Sally, felt more at ease. They all went into Xaghra, Etienne driving the Fiat and Claude on his bicycle, where bicycles were rented for all so they could ride out to the orange sand beach of Ramla Bay. Marianne had packed a vegetarian lunch. That morning, as she was preparing the tomato basil thing, Sally came into the kitchen and asked to help. Immediately, Marianne accidentally cut her finger deeply. Blood dripped all over the sliced tomatoes that lay on the cutting board. Sally nervously helped her clean and bandage the wound, and then they stood back to blankly stare at the ruined ingredients of the salad.

"I keep telling Claude we should plant tomatoes. I don't know what to do now. That's all we've got."

"Wash them off," Sally suggested. "It's only blood. No one will know after you drench them in olive oil."

Marianne looked at her quizzically.

"I won't tell." The girl shrugged.

Marianne burst into laughter. And so, when the picnic was spread out upon a blanket upon the literally very orange sand before the sparkling blue sea, the two females had a secret and smiled at each other. A smile that no one noticed, except, of course for Claude.

"I think the kids are becoming restless on this tiny island." Marianne rubbed a glob of anti-aging face cream onto her face.

Claude was already in bed, finishing the Fitzgerald. "Mm hmm. Not much to do here but ride bikes, swim, eat and drink. I mean it's not like they're going to write novels!" He laughed.

"Perhaps we should all go to Sicily for a few days."

"Well, that'll cost a butt cheek."

"Clues…for my boys!"

"Yeah, yeah, I know. I'm loving us being all together, too. I'll look for a villa to rent tomorrow."

"But in Palermo or Cefalu. I think they need a big city with night life and festivities."

"Dimple and all." Claude went back to reading and by the time his wife had turned her face into a kaleidoscopic universe of milky green, white and blue tints from a variety of anti-aging creams, braided her wiry red hair and slipped into the sheets beside him, he closed the book and was staring straight ahead, the yellow light from the lamp beside the bed yellowing his own face in contrast to hers.

"Finished it?" she asked.

"Fuck, baby. That is the most wonderfully depressing piece of literature I think I've ever read three times in my life."

The next morning over coffee and omelets on the veranda, Marianne proudly presented the idea of Sicily to her children, only to be ridiculed by her own audacity.

"Nightlife?" Esmond giggled.

"Discos?" Etienne roared.

"But I thought…?" Their mother frowned.

"Mama, mama." Esmond sympathetically continued, "We came here to see you, to spend time with you and dad."

"Honestly." Etienne philosophically absorbed his brother's sentiment. "We have enough clubs and cafés in Paris and London. I thought this was about an island vacation, a family vacation."

Mrs. Renoir's eyes, wet with tears, twinkled as if the sea itself, brimming over with love, had entered into them as she kissed her boys' foreheads and cleared away the breakfast plates.

Claude sighed with relief, reflecting on the image of *The Woman in the Bath*'s generous bottom intact.

When the kids went into town at noon, Claude passed by his wife as she was folding laundry. "It's you who's restless, my dear, am I right?"

"I'm not. It's just…we should be working."

"We will. After the family holiday."

"Is that what this is? I thought it was real life."

"It is. What more do you want?"

She placed a stack of freshly laundered towels in the linen closet. "I'm afraid I'm a lost cause."

"No, no."

She sighed and turned to look him in the eyes. Her eyes were moist and filled with more sincerity than he'd seen in them since they moved to the Maltese Archipelago.

"Esmond, Etienne, you and the work are enough for me. It always has been."

Claude was impressed. He didn't expect that from her, *he* came before the work and the work came last.

Nine days later, Claude drove the kids to the ferry. His wife, having melted on the porch beneath the burgeoning bougainvillea after kissing them goodbye, knew it was best to stay behind. He had a new postcard with him when he came back.

Elizabeth McKague

XIV

The Great Moment
Hoboken, New Jersey, 1918

Lollie listened to the radiator rattle and rumble, and the sound increased in her brain twice, thrice, a thousand times as she imagined the sound of the sky Michael was listening to at that very moment in Soissons, France.

His last letter arrived over a month ago. Whether his battalion had since moved she knew not, but on her Saturday off Lollie went to the public library and looked it up on a map. She needed to know where he was. She needed to know exactly. *Exactement.* She learned the word that day too, sitting for hours at a dark, heavy table, turning the pages of a French phrase book under a green shaded singular lamp. "She's a smart learner, that Charlotte Blaise," said the folks back home, adding, "Shoulda stayed in school."

Smart enough to leave Louisiana at sixteen and elope with Michael, Lollie mused. She was seventeen now and relieved because she felt all grown up.

The letter was dated July 16, 1918. It was September already. Autumn in Hoboken—yellowing leaves, brittle, slanted sunshine and the Hudson River, all sinewy and gray.

The radiator at St. Mary's Hospital rumbled and rattled and sent out oily mists of steam that mixed with the dry, searing steam of her iron. Press, stroke, slide, lift, lower, press, stroke, slide. Eight hours a day in the hospital's laundry room. Sheets, sheets, and more sheets. They'd go into the huge, tin bleach tubs blotted and streaked with blood and urine and come out cloud white, thin as paper because they were so worn. Lollie and the other girls hung them on the wires to dry, hung the weary ghosts to sigh.

Michael made her laugh. He made her tea, which she'd never before tasted.

He stirred in some honey and kissed her without waiting and without shame. He took her to New Orleans where they were married by a preacher who, ironically, had the same last name as Charlotte: Reverend Blaise. She took it as a good omen for, smart as she was, her superstitious upbringing in the marshland would forever cloud her mind. So many unexplained blank pages whispering the signals and symbols of real meaning, hidden behind this infectious world of dumb, white, sodium hypochlorite and boric acid veils.

It was more or less a fifteen-minute walk to St. Mary's from her room on River Street where she shared a flat with Rachael, a secretary for Shults Bread Company. Charlotte and Rachael were amiable yet their interests and lifestyles tended toward opposite extremes. Lollie's solemn and repetitive routine in the steamy hospital basement, ironing and folding while obsessively daydreaming of Michael, contrasted with Rachael's at a desk in a stuffy office downtown, where her high strung temper was suffocated by redundancy and ennui. Often, in the early evening as Lollie sat at the speckled, pink Formica table before the kitchen window, mechanically eating a solitary supper of steamed broccoli and rice, or an omelet, or a piece of rye bread spread with mustard and a slice of hard Swiss cheese, Rachael would burst breathlessly in through the cracked, black wooden door, snap off her heels and throw them against the wainscoting and start in the middle of a rampant monologue she'd begun internally on the bus ride to River Street from Washington Square. Lollie didn't listen and Rachael didn't care. She'd pour herself a glass of gin, sit at the table, light a cigarette and ramble on, her round black eyes wobbling into Lollie's vague stare. When she was done talking, she'd snub out her Camel and go to change out of her ankle-length, beige cotton dress.

"Listen, if your name is Charlotte, then shouldn't they call you Lottie?" Rachael called out from her bedroom into the kitchen.

"They did. But when my little sister couldn't pronounce the t's and began calling me Lollie, I guess it just stuck, ya know?"

"No." Rachael came out of her room in a pair of swank jupe culottes and a paisley patterned hip-length tunic. "So, you have a sister."

"Six sisters and five brothers. Used to be more but two died of scarlet fever and my oldest brother got killed in a knife fight."

Rachael placed a pine green, felt cloche hat over her bleached blond, bobbed hair. "I bet you miss them."

"Not really. I doubt if they even notice I'm gone."

Rachael screwed up her lips. "Hey, I'm going downstairs. Wanna come along?"

No. Always, no.

Downstairs meant the beer hall at the street corner of which Lollie knew nothing except for the brightly painted windows advertising Excelsior and Centennial beer.

"Oh, c'mon. Aren't you the least bit curious?"

"Curious, yes, I am," Lollie answered. "But not about beer."

"What about boys? Aren't you curious about boys?" Rachael smacked her red lips together and ran her pinky finger over them to smooth out her lipstick.

"I already know about boys."

"About one. One boy! One boy is not all boys."

"Well." Lollie picked up her porcelain plate and teacup and brought them to the sink. "That's what you say."

Rachael laughed and roared and mumbled to herself as her heels echoed all the way down the stairs and could still be heard out on the street three flights below, loudly mimicking, "That's what you say."

Lollie didn't have a stylish French hat, nor a bohemian outfit to change into. She wrapped a ruby-colored shawl she'd knitted herself around her shoulders and walked down to the docks to watch the sun fizzle out over the dusky river as the great ocean liners and steamers lay anchor along the piers. She wasn't alone. Many girls like her, in old clothes and handmade shawls, stood waiting for the ships to unload their men.

Of course they'd send a notice if he were coming home, but one never knew. And it became a kind of ritual for her. She felt almost like a good witch, standing there shivering in the cold night coming, pretending that a six-foot tall, broad-shouldered, handsome man on crutches, head bent with fever, was Michael. Or *that* one on the stretcher, bandaged to the chin yet still breathing, or that one, hairy and dark with wild blue eyes darting all around, looking for answers or shocked by all the questions, clean as a whistle, in perfect health but bewildered out of his mind, was him.

When all the ships had lay anchor and the docks finally emptied, most of the women would turn around with bitter expressions, weakened knees and bitten fingernails, and briskly, with a strange impulse of recovery, find their way, unaccompanied, home. Only the true believers would stay, waiting in shawls of vain hope.

On Tuesdays, Charlotte left the laundry room after lunch and wheeled the book cart through the hospital wards. The blood on the sheets in the tin wash tubs was just red marks. Here the blood was real, soaking through the bandages on their foreheads, noses, eyes, jaws, chests and stomachs. Distributing books was a tricky job. The beds, separated by hanging sheets like guardian spirits, were too close together to create an isle wide enough to move the book cart through. So she'd learned to pile a stack of books in her arms and try to keep her balance lest she stumble over a pair of crutches or the so many arms and legs frozen in casts, dangling in the thin waves of air between the beds like icebergs.

Once in a while a uniformed general or admiral would walk into the ward and stiffly make his way to a target bed to perform a two-minute speech composed with outlandish, heroic rhetoric then place a medal on the sheet covering a certain private, corporal, or lieutenant who, everybody in the wing would then understand, was soon a dead man. And sure enough, when the general left, a priest would arrive.

Lollie smiled softly as she passed out the books. A forced smile that appeared genuine because it was drowning in sympathy. She'd make a great actress, she thought. Well, that was the plan all along, the reason they hitched up north. When Michael returned, they would move to Manhattan and make their dreams come true. He would find a gig for some newspaper and work his way up until he became a reporter, writing for the *New York Times*. And Charlotte would be climbing the ladders on Broadway from Ziegfeld's *Follies* to one of the pretty maidens in *Florodora*, playing Ibsen's Camille or Shaw's Eliza Doolittle to Chekhov's Nina and Shakespeare's Juliet!

"I'm not dreamin' darling!" he told her as they jumped into the back of a truck heading out of Mississippi. "We have a future together, you and I: fame, fortune, glory and love. Lots and lots of love!"

River Street had the reputation of being a sinful den of sleazy dive bars and flophouse hotels frequented by horny drunken longshoremen and pirates from the Barbary Coast. But the rent was cheap and after the horrors Lollie witnessed on the docks and at the hospital each day, the rowdy atmosphere, the dirt and stench and grease that characterized her neighborhood didn't bother her. It was home.

Hoboken itself was densely populated first with Germans, and Italians off the boat came in second. As the war escalated, a curse of spy hysteria spilled over the port town. Mr. Becker became Mr. Baker; Miss Braun, Miss Brown, frankfurters were renamed hot dogs and sauerkraut became liberty cabbage.

Hoffmann and Goethe were removed from the book cart, and at the symphony, programs promising Wagner and Beethoven were replaced with Handel and Berlioz. Charlotte's father was Creole but her mother was Spanish and German. Alas, she made an effort everywhere she went to look, speak and act so as not to arouse suspicion. Rachael was Jewish and Michael was Canadian.

The beer halls on River Street were always packed with a mixture of doughboys on a bender the night before shipping out and those newly returned in a condition healthy enough to regenerate. As Lollie headed home from the docks, she passed by the bar at the base of the Columbia Hotel at the end of her block and could hear the crowd inside chanting in sing-song, "...*by Christmas you'll end up heaven, hell, or Hoboken!*"

She stopped for a moment at the window upon glimpsing a pine green cloche hat inside. Rachael, sandwiched between two tall, bright-faced, good-looking soldiers with considerably fine posture, saw her and waved her arm in the air dramatically, beckoning her to join them. Lollie shook her head and walked on with her eyes on the sidewalk. When she reached the brown brick steps at the front of her building, she looked up at the sunset. The sheet of sky beyond the chimneys and rooftops was like a soft, pink tulip with all its petals opening wide. It made her feel fragile; it made her feel that she needed to regain her own life. She turned back and entered the beer garden.

One of soldiers glued to Rachael, the dark haired one, bought Lollie a foaming glass of beer. She'd had it before. Sometimes Michael would come home from the grocer's with meat, bread, milk, potatoes, and a few green bottles. She liked to take sips from his glass simply because he let her, but she found the taste bitter. "I prefer tea with honey," she'd tell him, and he'd laugh.

Rachael was laughing, the soldiers were laughing, but Lollie didn't understand the joke, the foul language and sexual connotation. It had been many months since she'd truly laughed. Perhaps she'd forgotten how. In the bayou, every day was filled with laughter because her brothers and sisters were so silly. But that was gone and she was all grown up now. She realized then, tucked into the beer garden, sandwiched like a pickle, that she never once, throughout her entire childhood, ever saw her parents laugh. She took another sip of the drink and smiled her book cart smile, thinking about how Michael made her happy and started all his letters with, *Dear Honey.*

Michael leaned over the guardrail of the upper deck and lifted his freshly shaven chin to feel the salt spray on his neck. He couldn't remember himself anymore but knew that Charlotte would remember him and that he could return to being the man she had faith in. It wasn't a lie, yet neither was it true: *to go in a boy and come out a man.* It was more like a rotten bargain, an aphoristic subterfuge they used to get you to trade in your individual soul for some absurd fallacy of higher purpose, honor, identity.

"A bloody Faustian game of chess," Richard, the English soldier he befriended in the trenches at Ypres, used to say.

A battalion of men in wheelchairs suddenly whizzed 'round the stern of the ship and scurried toward the stem, racing. It was a calm afternoon with a sluggish, pastel blue sky over the Atlantic. In distant spots as big as whales, the water looked silver. A year ago, on the troopship overseas, the soldiers would have deck races using their strong legs, for show, for fun and for an attempt at glory. Now, the idea of glory made Michael despondent. He watched the squadron of wheelchair rabbits squealing by with his one good eye and tipped his hat to them. "*Go in boys,*" naive of suffering, "*and come out men,*" with one objective: pleasure.

One night, while hitching up to New York, as they lay on blankets in the storehouse of a kind tavern keeper in West Virginia, Lollie had asked him, "What part of my body do you like the most?"

He answered her immediately. "Your back."

"My back!" She giggled.

"Really, I'm serious. It's so beautiful, the slender, hourglass shape, the perfect curve of your spine, it's like a sculpture, a wave of art."

They snuggled closer together in the blue light of the lantern. "So, what about me?" he asked her. "What's the part you like best?"

"Your…"

He tickled her and kissed her, slightly embarrassed but moreso, proud.

"No. It's not *that*!" she whispered. "It's your eyes. Your bright blue eyes."

"Can you love one eye, my darling?" Michael asked the expansive ocean breeze. Then walking on, he thought, *Well, at least I still got* that, *and it's in fine shape, if I don't mind saying so.*

In the ship's dining room, which was but a fraction better than the mess tent at Chateau-Thierry, he continued to daydream of making love to Lollie as his fork touched his plate but not the inedible food upon it. Even something as simple as a potato became a kind of frothy green pudding slopped beside a cube of (presumably) boiled beef, glowing with pink. At least the meal was served with tolerably rancid port wine.

As night fell, he walked on the deck once more and looked up at the stars with his bright blue left eye. The Port of Liverpool and a personal history of hell were behind him. In twelve days he'd be in heaven, he'd be in Hoboken. Michael took the billet notice that was given to him as he boarded the gangway that morning and read:

Compartment 19, Hatch 4, Deck B.

He found his berthing place and climbed a ladder up to his cot that was more like a hammock, made of a strip of canvas stretched between iron pipes. There were two soldiers asleep on the cots beside him and three rows of cots below, holding men with their eyes shut or staring as if mesmerized into the darkness surrounding them. He felt lucky to be on the outside. A blanket was folded at the base of his slice of canvas and a lifejacket was placed at the head to use as a pillow. They slept in their uniforms. They had nothing else, no baggage save a battered photograph of their girl and a few letters in their pockets. Michael lay on his back, placed his hat on this stomach and folded his arms around it. The guy below was snoring loudly and the young lad beside him purred. He wished to be out in the air again on deck, winking back at the stars.

Lollie wanted to get a kitten. She wrote in her last letter, "When you come home we'll go to the shelter and pick one out, maybe a black kitten with white mittens and we'll name her…what should we name her?"

He pondered the question while his left eyelid grew heavier and responded in thought. No point deciding that now, honey, the name should depend upon the personality of the creature. Lollie, Lollie, my sweetheart! Sometimes he called her "Honey" and sometimes he called her "Doll."

All through the night, a ship of nightmares moved gradually forward from the history of hell behind them toward heaven, toward Hoboken.

Air raids, guns shots echoing, cannons rocketing, the sky exploding and the earth sinking, sinking, sinking. Cleaning rifles, draining ditches, piling up sandbags, guts on the floor of the front line, rats in the walls of the support line, vomit in the mud of the reserve line. Trench cycles, terror cycles. Listening to raindrops from inside a leaking tent. Seeing a full, yellow and silver moon while pissing on the snow. Barrage fire, the sky lit by white fire at midnight, the earth shaking, shells crashing, grenades pouring, machine guns crackling like rabid monster chickens, missiles hissing through the air like poisonous snakes tearing holes in space, in the ground, in men. Piling up corpses to create a wall. Tear gas, mustard gas, gas masks. Masks, masks, masks and holes, holes, holes. The ship was sinking. Each soldier wrapped in their blankets like forest animals in the shelter of their burrows, exhaustion sinking so deep into their limbs, if they had them, until it began to torture their souls.

When the bugle woke him the next morning, he thought it was a dream until he realized it was a memory. He and Richard were on sentry duty in the abandoned village of Guignicourt, less than 10 kilometers from the front lines at Riems. They found the tallest house, planning to keep watch from its attic. First they rummaged the cupboards and found stale crackers and dry salami that they ate like savages. Most of the furniture was blackened by fire but in the back room, a grand piano stood untarnished and intact. Despite Richard's warning of being discovered by the Huns, and after half a decanter of sherry, also taken from the cupboard, Michael played "Daisy Bell, I Wonder Who's Kissing Her Now" and "Roses of Picardy," and the two of them drank, sang, wept and laughed until midnight. The glass in the attic window was shattered and they spent the night watch huddled under blankets and batting off pigeons. In the morning, Michael found a bicycle in the shed and again, Richard pleaded caution, but Michael rode out in the dawn, following paths through the forest. He saw a deer—a lone doe nibbling on dry leaves. She looked at him, he at her, their eyes saying, *Even if I die, will you live for me, please?*

Richard was killed in the battle of Cambrai. He fell back into the trench with his brains blown out and landed at Michael's feet. It made Michael angry. His Patroclus was gone and for the first time since he'd been overseas, he saw the enemy in front of his eyes. He took risks, he took command; he thought, ate and slept in the center of violence. He forgot about his past, about his young wife and his dreams, and charged, slaughtering the enemy with the wrath of Achilles.

Michael's ship docked later than the rest, at 9 p.m. A half hour later, he set foot upon the continent of his birth. He moved with the swarm of soldiers crossing the wide pier. At its edge, a round-up of women in beaten, leather, Cromwell buckle shoes beneath pleated skirts with bleak hues, hugging themselves beneath green, blue or yellow knitted shawls, stood absolutely motionless excepting their searching eyes and gaping pink mouths. He knew the exact color of Charlotte's shawl for she'd sent him a rope of cherry red wool enclosed in one of her letters. He tied it like a bracelet around his wrist where it was still, weathered and faded. Surely she'd be there amongst the girls. They must have sent her a notice: it was standard procedure. A few captains he'd played chess with on the boat passed by and saluted him. He walked slowly toward the pen of women with dignity and composure. After the battle at Cambrai his rank was elevated to corporal, then sergeant and so on until here he was, a major. The men who weren't rushing into the arms of their girls and lifting them off their toes began to disperse down the avenues toward town. Michael moved in gallant, easy strides amidst the chaotic homecoming throng but did not see his Lollie. After nearly an hour, the few dozen lingering shawls finally turned their backs on the harbor in tears. Green, blue, yellow and red, but not ruby. Anyway, he'd have noticed her back, even if her face had become changed by fear and worry, he'd notice her back.

There was a slight fog fizzling out under the amber glow of the street lamps. His heart beat hard as he walked up River Street.

Mrs. Miller, previously Mrs. Muller, the landlady, made the sign of the cross over her enormous bosom and squeezed Michael dearly when he appeared at the top of the brown brick steps.

"But she's not home yet," Mrs. Miller told him. "Come on in for a cup of coffee, a drink. I've made a casserole. Yes, yes, you must."

Michael politely refused and the landlady gave him the key to their old flat. He went in. All was dark. He saw his and Lollie's books in alphabetical rows in a small bookcase in the bedroom they used to share. On the nightstand, a framed photo of their marriage and in the closet, her few nicer dresses and her starch white laundry aprons hanging beside his own two waistcoats, one black and one gray, his white linen shirts, black blazer and black cotton trousers. On the shelf above, his dear old apple cap and on the floor below, his brown leather Darby boots polished clean as a whistle.

The room that used to be their living room was closed off by a Japanese folding screen and now functioned as a second bedroom. He peeked in and saw a mess of brightly colored muslin tunics, hoop skirts, slinky lingère and high heeled shoes strewn all over the hardwood floor. The bed was unmade, magazines were scattered, vinyl records were tossed out of their jackets, ashtrays full, wine bottles empty and from the ceiling hung streamers of glittering tinsel. Oh, he knew about Rachael. Not personally, but most of Lollie's letters, after telling him how very, very, very much she missed him, ended with complaints regarding her roommate. He went into the bathroom to take a leak. Wet nylons hung dripping over the shower curtain rod. He went into the kitchen and opened the icebox: half a quart of stale milk, a wedge of hard cheese and a liverwurst sausage. His stomach growled and he realized he was starving.

Mrs. Miller served him a full plate of spaetzle and added water to his whiskey. She spoke to him of how sad and lonely Charlotte seemed but it was soon made clear that her own verbal appetite preferred the gossip of Rachael's wild, rampant ways. The meal and drink did his mind and body justice. He felt happy to be home, thanked the portly landlady, put his major's cap on his head of dark curls, walked out into the night and went straight to the beer garden on the corner.

It was steamy inside. Blue ribbons of tobacco smoke furled on the surface of a sea that was made up of olive drab military hats and speckled with drops of soft, female bob cuts or hot iron curls. Michael made his way to the far end of the bar where the light was neutral. His one eye was extremely sensitive. A pack of privates in a huddle separated to make way for him and one of them offered him his barstool. The honor astonished him for he'd not yet been in a public situation where the title displayed by his uniform elicited respect and attention. He ordered a pint of ale, wondering where she could be at this hour. Perhaps she'd taken a night shift at St. Mary's or he had missed her on the docks. Mrs. Miller's whiskey had awoken his spirit and the ale was making his blood warm. He felt human again and was nearly euphoric by the fact that he would hold her; make love to her, maybe even in an hour or at worst by tomorrow!

Somebody put coins in the player piano and "Pack Up Your Troubles" started tinkling into the scene. The boys all sang and Michael joined in. He was a fine tenor, very fine. He began a conversation, asking about life back home, with the private who'd given up his seat, a fellow named Johnny who returned unharmed a month ago. The piano continued to roll out cheerful songs and the boys took their girls in their arms and danced about in the center of the hall. With warm-blooded instinct, Michael's eye was drawn to a young blond woman wearing a fancy green hat, spinning about on the dance floor. So pretty, he thought, but what a tramp! Yet he watched her, flaunting her stuff before a tall handsome lieutenant who then shifted to one side. Behind him, flowing and free, swaying and twisting, was Lollie's back. She was holding hands with a tall, dark captain. The man put his hands on her hips and brought her closer, so close to him as she placed her delicate fingers, calloused with iron burns, on his shoulders. The man leaned forward and stealthily put his lips to hers. Michael's one eye shut tightly. When he opened it, painfully, a minute later, he saw the dark handsome captain standing dumbly alone with a fresh red streak blemishing his face. Lollie was nowhere to be seen. Michael rushed out of the bar and saw her running down the street. He could tell by the way she moved that she was probably crying. He ran up to her, grabbed her gently and turned her around. They sunk to the sidewalk for she'd pulled him down, crying and grasping his waist as if for life as he pressed his lips, tender as cherry blossoms drifting on a breeze, to her hair, her forehead, her eyelids and her feverishly wet, blushing cheeks.

Elizabeth McKague

XV

Gozo, Italy

Present

Aloysius Zaccagnino owned a yacht that he docked at the Mgarr-ix-Xini harbor, about six kilometers from the Villa Calypso.

Claude and Aloysius would serendipitously often find themselves on the same bike path into Xaghra and so began talking and became acquainted. At this point, after eight months on the island, they were gradually building a friendship, although Claude was sure to keep up his barriers for there was indubitably something shifty in Signore Zaccagnino's black almond eyes. The yacht owner was incontestably rich, perhaps a billionaire, at least a multi-millionaire, yet he never mentioned what business he was in or had been in, and appeared, like Claude himself, to be retired from a regular life of long working hours. He was not exactly bright but often witty and above all, at the age of 62, extremely fit and handsome. He lived on his yacht with his fourth wife, a 27-year-old, drop-dead gorgeous Polish girl named Kornelia Gronowska. His previous three marriages, Claude learned, were also to girls at least a decade his junior: Fabia Papageorgiou, a Greek goddess; Ana Luiza Da Cunha, a Brazilian horse rider; and Marghcrita Mastrogiacomo, a Venetian ballet dancer who he married when he was 28. Each of his marriages lasted exactly ten years.

"You don't waste time," Claude joked.

"I don't like to be alone," Aloysius confessed.

It was the only thing that he ever said that proved to Claude that his new friend had any emotional depth. Yet he liked him, and liked walking about the streets of Xaghra with him; two tall, trim, good-looking middle-aged men with white hair taking over Claude's blond curls and Aloysius' chestnut, widow's peaked waves.

Sometimes, they'd park their bikes in Mgarr-ix-Xini and drink anisette at Sicilia Bella, a restaurant overlooking the harbor, where Aloysius would point out his yacht, named *Sogni d'Oro* which translated into French as *Beaux Rêves* and in English, the unoriginal and quite banal, "Sweet Dreams." Yet he never even hinted that he might one day invite Claude to come aboard.

Then one Sunday as Marianne and Claude were shopping at the street market in Mgarr, they ran into the billionaire and his lovely Polish princess. The wives were introduced and immediately began speaking in Italian about the exquisite quality of the market's pomegranates, figs and plums as the men, feeling unexpectedly awkward, mumbled on about the weather. Within minutes, Kornelia announced to her husband that the Renoirs would be joining them on their yacht that very evening for dinner.

Claude suddenly became overly wary. "But darling, didn't you want to go over those pages tonight?"

"Pages?" Kornelia asked.

"We're writing a novel," Marianne explained.

"Together," Claude added.

"It's the reason we moved to Gozo."

"Oh, how wonderfully interesting! I'd love to hear all about it. Really, the cultural scene on this island is so limited. Please do come tonight, my chef is one of the best from Malta. I'll have him make us a delicious feast."

"Of course we'll come." Marianne smiled warmly at the girl. "Claude places far too much emphasis upon our writing."

Claude's forehead crinkled up at his wife's irony and Aloysius was delighted to notice in it more than a few wrinkles.

Kornelia literally jumped up and down. "Perfect! Seven?"

Aloysius, more pleased than embarrassed by his young wife's performance, smiled at Claude. "You know where it's docked."

"Yes, yes. Thank you."

"*Bongiorno.*"

"*Au revoir.*"

When the pretty, rich couple left, Marianne turned to the market vendor and asked for a dozen plums.

"What are you doing?" Claude grumbled.

"I'm going to make a tart to bring to the dinner party."

"She has a chef…it might appear as an insult."

"A dessert? Never. Two dozen, please."

"Marianne."

"I'm going to make a big tart for a big boat!" She started to cackle but stopped. "What was that nonsense about 'pages' anyway?"

"I don't really know Aloysius that well, that's all."

"What's there to know? He's attractive, tan, absolutely loaded and his wife is a supermodel."

"And you find that appealing?"

"Sure. You don't?"

"I don't know. It all seems a bit sinister to me."

"And that's what I find intriguing."

Claude put his arm around his wife's waist, twice the size of Kornelia's, as they walked back to the fiat, Marianne swinging the sack of plums at her side.

Sogni d'Oro was quite a Herculean sight as they walked up the pier, Claude in a dashing white dinner jacket over a black shirt and black trousers, and Marianne in a silk, blood red, knee-length dress but two shades darker than her hair, holding her enormous plum tart out before her with pride mixed with trepidation.

"Like Salome carrying the head of John the Baptist on a platter," Claude remarked dryly.

"Yes, for your Herod Antipas Aloysius!" She laughed.

"You're not going to be cynical tonight, are you?"

"I'm excited, Clues. I love yachts."

"When were you ever on a yacht?"

"It's my first time."

"I was on a yacht in Greece before I met you."

"You never told me that."

"It never came up."

"Why?"

"We don't usually talk about yachts."

"No, I mean, why were you on it, in Greece?"

"I met a guy, no, actually I met a girl and she knew a guy and…"

She frowned. "I don't want to hear anymore. Hello!" Marianne nodded to Kornelia who had just greeted them from the deck.

They climbed the stairs.

"What is that?" Kornelia, wearing a long, sea green gown, stared curiously at the powder puff pancake of tinfoil in Marianne's hands.

"I bought some of those luscious plums at the market and made us a dessert."

Kornelia laughed. "How thoughtful." A servant instantly appeared out of nowhere and took it away, then she continued. "Aloysius is in a conference call to Istanbul but he'll be with us shortly. Come, let me show you around."

They followed her across the vast, teak wooden deck that was polished like a basketball court and listened to her ramble on with pride.

"It was custom built in Spain in two thousand eight. She's forty-five meters in length, eight meters in beam with a draft of two-point-three meters. Her maximum speed is sixteen knots with a cruising speed of twelve to twelve-point-five knots. We have a four-person crew and, oh, here, I'll show you the flybridge helm."

She introduced them to Cristiano, the captain, who spoke nothing but Italian, then moved back onto the bridge deck where there was a butterfly-shaped swimming pool, then crossed the aft deck where lounge chairs and tables surrounded a Jacuzzi.

"Wow," Marianne stated.

"You like it?" Kornelia smiled.

"Very impressive," Claude added.

They went through sliding glass doors and entered the main salon where two sofa areas were divided by a long patina copper bar.

"The décor is spectacular," Marianne said.

"Oh, but you should have seen it before! Aloysius was with his last wife when he bought it and her taste was incredibly vulgar. Can you believe…she actually had a painting of a Toreador hanging over the bar! As you can see, I've replaced it with an…"

"Umberto Boccioni." Claude moved closer to examine the painting. "My, it is astounding. Well done, Kornelia."

"Do you know art?"

"He used to collect." Marianne stroked the white leather of one of the sofas.

Kornelia nodded absently, gesturing to the room. "And I had all the furniture re-designed, everything in the salon is by Matteo Nunziati and please, I must show you the master suite where my bed is custom-made by Nella Vetrina!"

They went down a spiral staircase to the master, "princess" suite with another Jacuzzi in the enormous marble bathroom, a walk-in closet and a separate sitting room and breakfast room.

"It's an entire apartment!" Claude whispered to his wife.

Kornelia then passed by a similar apartment with an interior in darker tones but didn't give them the full tour. "These are Aloysius' rooms and, while we're down here..." She followed the corridor to three further semi-suites. "Here are the guest rooms."

The Renoirs peeked into three separate studios, similar in shape and size, each like a grand hotel room yet with different themes of décor, based, ironically, on French impressionist painters.

Kornelia happily showed them. "The Monet suite, the Cezanne suite and at the end of the hall we have *La Chambre Renoir*."

Claude laughed. Marianne, by now, was overwhelmed and glad when they finally returned to the cocktail lounge where a different servant, an attractive young black man, was ready to pour drinks behind the bar.

Kornelia had a glass of Dom Perigon champagne, Marianne, a glass of Sancerre and Claude, Johnnie Walker Blue Label on the rocks.

"*Salute!*" they cheered.

"Please..." Kornelia sat on the white leather sofa. Claude followed, sitting in a wing-backed beige upholstered chair, but Marianne, at that moment preferring to stand, moved toward the wide window looking out over the deck at the twilight cradling the Madonna ta' Lourdes cathedral looming on top of the hill above the small port town.

"Please..." Kornelia insisted, patting the space on the sofa beside her.

Yet Marianne remained standing. "It's exquisite, this view."

Kornelia smiled in agreement, then the Polish princess, unperturbed, turned to the next best handsome man in the vicinity—the first being the bartender— and said to Claude, "Now tell me about your book."

"It's a novel," Marianne said from her post at the aft deck.

"We've never written a book together before," Claude added, drinking. "Marianne has had several novels published..."

"Claude had one published, too."

"But it wasn't well received," Claude grumbled.

"By the public!" Marianne came to sit beside Kornelia. "What do they know anyway? People have the minds of ferrets these days."

"Ferrets?" The Polish girl's Italian was still expanding.

"Like weasels," Claude tried.

Kornelia became unabashedly puzzled and waved to the sexy bartender to bring her another glass of champagne.

"What do you do?" Marianne asked their hostess.

She threw her arms in the air and replied, "This!"

Claude rocked the glass in his hand and the ice cubes double-clinked.

There was a clumsy pause. Marianne felt herself becoming tipsy already.

Kornelia turned. "Oh…here he is!"

The Italian walked into the salon wearing the same outfit as Claude yet reversed, white slacks and shirt, and a black dinner jacket. He had a taut look on his face that Claude intuited had to do with his conference call to Istanbul rather than the present company.

"Ah, a Scotch man like myself." He shook Claude's hand. "Glad you could make it." In the Italian hospitable tradition, he then kissed Marianne's cheeks. "You are lovely tonight, *Signora*."

Claude watched her blush, reveling in it.

"Your home is superb," she offered.

"Kornelia gave you the tour then? Good, good, very good."

The bartender poured Signore Zaccagnino the same drink as Claude and the man seemed to relax. Another servant, a pretty, dark Sicilian girl, brought in a tray of hors d'ouvres and named them as she set the decorative silver platter on a glass table before the sofa. "Here we have blue crab beignets and on this side, wild mushroom ragout on crispy polenta with comté cheese."

"Thank you, Maria." Kornelia picked up one of the "crab things" with a silver toothpick. "One of my chef's specialties, really delicious." The young wife then stood and moved to the bar, seeming to whisper something to her husband as she did so. Aloysius did not respond.

Marianne took a "crab thing," too, and ate it, whispering as well to Claude while she chewed. "These are good. She really does have exquisite taste, doesn't she?"

"Pardon?" Aloysius left the bar and sat on the sofa next to Mrs. Renoir.

"I was just commenting on your wife's fine taste in interior design, fashion, art, food…everything!"

"Ah, yes. You wouldn't think so from a Pole though, eh?" He chuckled, caring not if the remark embarrassed his wife or his guests.

"Do you ever take her out?" Claude clumsily tried to dismiss the comment. "Pardon?"

"Your yacht, *Sogni d'Oro*...has she sailed the seven seas?"

"That's how we ended up here, in Gozo, actually." Kornelia grinned clandestinely.

"And how is that?" Claude's upper lip curled as he drank and thought to himself, damn, this scotch is excellent.

"You see I am a great fan of Homer, the Greek poet..."

"Oh, yes, we know our Homer." Marianne was intrigued.

"A few years back I read a book, I forgot the title...anyway, it traced the route of Ulysses' travels and named, based on various nautical research, each of the places he encountered on our present day map. He met the Lotus Eaters for example when he landed in the Gulf of Gabes in Jerba, the Wind God was on the isle of Ustica, the monsters Charybdis and Scylla in the Strait of Messina, the Cyclops...oh, where was he, Kornelia?"

"The tiny island of Favignana," she answered soberly, although she was on her second glass of champagne.

"And the sirens sang from the Galli rocks in the Gulf of Salerno," Claude said. "I read the same book, years ago."

"Then you understand. I decided to make Gozo my permanent home here because I wanted to be hidden."

"Which is what the etymology of the Greek word 'Calypso' means," Claude added.

"Exactly. To hide here, on the ancient nymph's island, located, as the bard tells us, at the navel of the sea."

Marianne was impressed by the Italian's passion for Homer, and Claude, taking the last sip from his glass thought he might like this guy.

Hors d'ouvres munched on, another round of drinks on the upper deck to watch the sunset of interlaced ribbons of blood orange and rose, and with conversation flowing, the couples at last went into the dining room and sat down to a five-course gourmet meal of haute cuisine including

Artichoke Gratinata
Escarole and white bean salad with fennel and tarragon vinaigrette
Salmon with ginger sauce and cauliflower risotto
Lamb chops sautéed with rosemary and anchovies

But when the Sicilian girl brought the dessert to the table, white chocolate lavender *panna cotta* with Madeira rhubarb *pappardelle*, Kornelia became infuriated with her and demanded that she return the dish to the kitchen and bring out Marianne's plum tart.

Marianne protested profusely, not out of embarrassment, but because she really wanted to eat the white chocolate lavender *panna cotta* with Madeira rhubarb *pappardelle*.

As the two women continued to politely squabble, Aloysius rose and said, "I'm too full for dessert now anyway. Let's take coffee on the aft deck and put it off for a while."

Claude agreed and they went out into the salty, soft breezy air beneath a star dappled sky.

"I don't want it to end," Marianne found herself saying out loud.

"What?" Kornelia asked.

Modestly, she answered, "I've never experienced such a luxurious lifestyle."

The Polish girl smiled generously. "Yes, I like being rich. I was very poor when I met Aloysius. He changed my life." She paused and lowered her voice. "I'll never go back. Never."

Claude and Aloysius, drinking cognac rather than coffee, were deeply engaged in a regenerating dialogue about *The Odyssey*. Kornelia nudged Marianne. "Do you want to go in the Jacuzzi?"

"I don't have a bathing suit."

The young wife laughed. "Come on!" And proceeded to take off her sea green gown. Marianne, tipsy and progressive as she was, followed suit.

The two husbands, seated in lounge chairs, glanced over at the naked women. Claude saw Aloysius' tanned face glow with affection for Kornelia's beautiful, slender body but also noticed how he looked, it seemed, somewhat lustily at Marianne. Claude himself, at that moment, also felt little interest in the younger woman and was more turned on by his own wife's voluptuous form.

The sexy barman brought the girls a bottle of champagne and the night moved on under a rising tide and an enviable orange moon.

Marianne woke to see Claude washing his face in the *salle de bain* adjoining the room. She sat up in bed, confused. "Clues, where are we?"

"The Renoir suite," he told her calmly.

"I think I got drunk last night," she said.

"You did," he answered.

"Did I do anything stupid? Did I take my clothes off?"

"You sure did."

"I did?"

"So did Kornelia—to go in the whirlpool. You don't remember?"

"Sort of, yes, now I do. Oh, God! But did I do anything foolish in front of them?"

"I don't know and probably neither do they, we all got sloshed."

"Oh!" she cried in real anguish.

"Chill, babes, it happens sometimes." He came out of the bathroom in his black slacks with a fluffy white towel around his neck.

"Did we fuck here, in this bed?" she asked.

"I think we did. Actually, yes, we did."

"Was it good?"

"Hell if I know. I rang for coffee."

"Rang?"

He showed her a card that read "Room Service."

"It's like a hotel."

"It's a luxury liner."

They laughed. He kissed her.

"I had fun last night," he said.

"So did I."

"Aloysius is smarter than I thought."

"Rich men have to be smart, I imagine."

"But I still don't know if I completely trust him."

"Rich men must be untrustworthy, I believe."

"You seemed to hit it off with Kornelia."

"I like her. She's cultured and snobby in a good way about her tastes." Marianne got out of bed and went into the bathroom saying, "Perhaps we've made some friends on the island, Clues."

He nodded to himself. "Perhaps. It's about time, huh? I didn't realize how isolated we've been until just now. I haven't really missed our friends in Paris since we've been here. I suppose I do miss Cyril to a degree, and our bi-monthly dinners with Armand and Félicie."

She came into the room and began to get dressed. "Not me. I don't miss a soul."

There was a knock on the door. Room service.

Kornelia was sunbathing in her bikini on the foredeck by the swimming pool when the Renoirs finally climbed upstairs.

The sexy bartender was giving her a neck massage. "Good morning," she said and took a sip of a thick, green liquid out of a tall glass. "Great cure for a hangover. Help yourselves. It's on the table over there."

"Does it work?" Marianne went to the table.

"It's working for me."

Marianne poured herself a glass and looked at Claude, who refused. "We should be going," he stated adamantly to both women.

"Of course, you must write your novel."

"Wow. This works right away, doesn't it?" said Marianne, drinking the green stuff. "We had a splendid time."

"It was nice. We should get together again."

"Why don't you two come to the villa, maybe this weekend?"

"Where is Aloysius?" Claude asked. "I'd like to thank him."

"He left for Palermo early this morning. But yes, the weekend sounds lovely."

They said their good-byes and as the Renoirs climbed down the stairs to the pier, they heard a splash as Kornelia dived into the pool.

When they returned to the villa, Marianne picked up a fluffy orange cat that appeared to have been waiting on the front porch for their return. "Well, there you are! Did you miss me?"

"Who's that?" Claude asked.

"Our cat."

"Since when did we have a cat?"

"Since I started feeding him a week ago. I believe he's a stray—but not anymore, right little kitty?" She scratched the feline's chin affectionately.

"What's our cat's name?"

"Hmm. Haven't thought of that yet. How 'bout Maximilion?"

"Never. Uh, uh, impossible, no way."

"How about…Mister Kittens?"

"That's just silly"

"Schopenhauer?"

"Are you still drunk? That's ridiculous."

"Okay, you name him then."

Claude thought for a minute then proudly stated, "Byron."

"Byron the ginger cat...I like it."

Elizabeth McKague

XVI

Damascus

Dumascus, Syria 716 A.D.

There is a triangle.
It's called
The moon, the street
And the ginger cat.

Nadhir wanted two things, answers and money. Some years ago, in his youthful dreams, he envisaged the two things becoming one. Complete unity, like passion for God. Yet now, as he passed through the gate of the mosque with the moon above, the street ahead and the ginger cat with one ear on a prowl, he pitied himself and asked God for mercy. *Inshallah! Inshallah!* Alas, at the age of forty, the answers remained veiled and he could barely keep the stomachs of his two wives and nine offspring half-empty with flatbread and lentils.

A man driving a donkey cart through the straw-strewn street turned the corner. The cart carried a corpse. The man wore a turban. The wooden wheels of the cart rattled. The donkey was brown, the moon was golden and the stars in the night sky were grey.

Nadhir walked solemnly on and went into a café where he saw his friend seated alone at a table, cutting into a cooked silver fish with a knife and eating the white flesh with his fingers.

This friend's name was Abdul Lateef and they greeted each other warmly. One year his senior, Abdul Lateef had already achieved the things Nadhir longed for. Alas, they were disparate people with asymmetrical gifts and for Nadhir, like the night sky, life and God were all about symmetry.

Lateef was a wealthy merchant with four wives and only six sons. He owned four houses, five horses, and two camels, not to mention seventeen black and white speckled goats. Nadhir could hardly separate himself to love Aeesha and Shazmah equally and the only animals he could claim to possess were the spontaneous stray cats that found their way onto the steps of his second story flat. Tonight, he thought, I'll probably trip on them again, a usual occurrence that set off a chain reaction of feline howls followed by children crying and his wives bustling about between the four small rooms where his family of twelve members made their meager beds.

Nadhir's stomach growled as he watched Lateef finish perhaps his second or even third meal of the day. He ordered a water pipe to be brought to the table. It would cost two dinars but unfortunately he'd acquired the habit and treated himself to smoking once a day, usually at this time, in this café, directly after his work as an Imam at the Umayyad Mosque.

"Where did I go wrong?" he asked his friend who in turn sat back and licked the oil off his fingers before answering.

"You are a poet and a teacher," said Abdul Lateef. "And I sell carpets for a living. There is no wrong in either."

Nadhir sucked from the hookah and savored the sweet taste on his tongue. "Sometimes I become so lost in myself, in my worries…that I scare my wives."

Lateef laughed out loud, a powerful, full belly laugh. "And so you should! A wife should be scared of her husband, always. So, it seems you're doing a good job and there's no wrong in that."

"I cannot agree with you on that, my friend. I respect my wives and love Aeesha truly and Shazmah, perhaps even a bit more."

Lateef shook his head as Nadhir handed him the pipe. "You…" He stopped to take a big toke. "Your actions are a man's actions but your heart is a woman's soul."

The great cloud of smoke streaming from his friend's mouth suddenly blurred Nadhir's vision. "And you, what about you?"

"Me? Hah! My heart is a man's heart, that is sure. But my actions, as my name dictates, my actions are those of God's slave."

"So this must be why you have all the answers."

"Answers to what? There is only one question."

"Which is?"

"God is great."

"That's not a question."

"Hmm. Think about that. Think about that every day, every minute, my friend, and soon, *inshallah*, your worries will be erased." Abdul Lateef stood and tossed a single coin on the table. "I must go. Use this to pay for the fish and the pipe, give the old man a dinar and please, to ease your troubled spirit, keep the change."

Nadhir thanked him, "You are a good man, Abdul."

"Maybe you are right about that. But only God is great."

The shadow of Lateef's large frame loomed like a tent over a Bedouin upon Nadhir's tall, thin posture while he stayed seated on the carpet. "Come to my house in three days. Come alone."

"I will." Nadhir smoked but quickly remembered and called out as Lateef moved through the wooden posts of the café door. "Which house?"

Without turning, he answered, "The one on the Baruda Canal."

Nadhir used the weighty coin as he was instructed and stepped out into the tepid night air. The scrutinizing crescent moon hung on an invisible string in the blackest part of the sky to the north and the myriad stars dimly rocked in their vacant cradles. He followed a series of narrow passageways out onto a wide street where a few vendors at the *souk al haimidiyeh* had not yet packed up their wares at that late hour. He bought a sack of flour, poppy seeds and as a surprise for his children, a small bag of pecans, using up every last dinar in the change.

His home was not far from the market and although the accommodation itself was by no means lavish, the street where he lived was quite nice. Tussles of overgrown ivy clung to the flat, bleached stone facades of the houses and at the end of the lane there was a small courtyard where his children often played, he had to admit, happily, beneath a blossoming orange tree.

He was careful not to step on the cats. His children were already crowded beside each other in their beds and although, upon reflection, he realized that in fact he did love Shazmah more, he decided, because of his apprehensive mood, to sleep with Aeesha that night, instead.

Abdul Lateef's first house, (that is, the one he had the longest) on the Baruda Canal, had a yellow door. His goats and camels were at his second house, a low, flat construct with acres of grasslands in front and desert in the back, located on the outskirts of Damascus. His horses were kept in a stable on the property of his third house, a large, stony villa near the Bab al-Saghir, the smallest gate on the southern side of the city's surrounding wall. His fourth house, where he'd recently transferred his first wife, was just across from the

Umayyad Mosque in the heart of the Muslim quarter.

As Nadhir approached the yellow door that was framed by flowering pink jasmine, the ginger cat with one ear skirted out of an upturned wheel barrel and made a close circle around his sandaled ankles. He leaned over and petted the creature. "My," he whispered, "You do get around, don't you?"

The cat purred. He picked it up and knocked on the door.

Lateef's third wife, Jana, the youngest and prettiest of them all, answered. "No! No cats. They make my eyes water."

He set the cat down and it ran off. He followed Jana through a series of nicely decorated rooms exhibiting a variety of beautifully woven carpets to a deck overlooking the canal at the back of the house. She then left him alone with her husband who immediately set down the Qur'an and stood to greet his guest with a single tear in his eye.

"Chapter fifty-five, *Al-Arahman*, on the divine beneficence, the judgment of the guilty and the benefit of righteousness…it always gets to me."

Nadhir nodded. "I wrote a poem based on that chapter. Do you remember?"

"No. But I'm glad you did so. It's all poetry, the whole thing…" he said, and lifted the exquisitely leather bound gold leafed edition, "is poetry."

Nadhir sat on a pillow and crossed his legs. "Are we going to discuss the law of God today, my friend?"

Lateef sat likewise on the other side of a low table. "Something else, and it's not poetic."

They grew silent as Jana brought a tea tray out onto the deck. The two men watched her pour the tea and directly retreat into the villa. There were jasmine vines on a trellis over the deck as well. The flowery scent, the strong almond tea and the damp, humid smell of the canal combined gave Nadhir the strange sense that he was no longer in Damascus but in an unknown place very different from the Levant and the Mediterranean Sea.

"I have a proposal for you, my friend." Abdul Lateef smiled.

"Yes?"

"One year ago, the sultan of Aleppo ordered twelve carpets from me. We made one per month and are now finished with the order."

"That is very good."

"But I cannot deliver them myself as I must remain in the city to oversee my business."

"That is too bad."

Lateef pinched some cayenne pepper from a tiny bowl on the tea tray and sprinkled it into his teacup. "Ramadan begins tomorrow."

"That is correct."

"And your students have no lessons for one month, no?"

"You are correct again, wise Abdul Lateef."

"Ah. So, my proposal..."

"Would you like me to drive the carpets to the sultan?"

"I would. Of course I will pay you handsomely. You will take my cart and horses and follow the Silk Road."

"But..."

"I will take care of your family while you are on the journey. Jana has already spoken with Aeesha and Shazmah. Together they will bake flat bread and make lentils for your children at my expense."

"Oh, Abdul!"

"Now, here's the crux, as they say...do you know how to use a saber?"

"As I'm sure you did as well my friend, I learned at the age of nine or ten."

"I will also give you a saber."

"I don't understand."

Lateef rose and took a saber that was hanging on the wall, pulled the shining metal blade out of its sheaf and jabbed the sharp point at Nadhir, stopping just half an inch beneath his chin. "Bandits!" he said, then laughed his full belly laugh.

The beating yellow sun was just rising above the horizon when Lateef's sturdy cart, layered in the back with twelve of the finest carpets he'd ever made, crossed through the Bab al-Salama with Nadhir on the single box seat in front, valiantly holding the reins. The Arabian horses took to the savanna ahead with a fire as intense as the crowning sun and the majestic purple peaks of Mount Hermon in the distance seemed to cool the Orontes Valley air like an invisible shadow.

There is an octagon.
It's called

The seven gates behind me.

Plus one door
Named Honor.

Nadhir felt proud and as he turned east to follow the Euphrates River, a new sensation opened out within his soul, a foreign feeling, yet he was able to name it at once. Freedom. Hawks circled above in the white sky. A few caravans passed him by and his own cart rolled past several enduring travelers making their way from the desert into Damascus on foot. Madinat al-Yasmin, it was called, The City of Jasmine. And such an old city it was. Legend says that Shem, the eldest son of Noah, chose to live there after the flood. Less than one hundred years ago, Arabs conquered the city and just one year ago, right before the death of the great Caliph al-Walid, they finally finished building the exquisite Umayyad Mosque upon the site of an earlier Christian Cathedral where they found the head of Yahya ibn Zakariya, John the Baptist himself, buried under a pillar! Nadhir had never known any other city than thus, known in the whole of the Levant as the Ghoula Oasis.

He drove on toward Mount Hermon where he intended to cross the steppes and then continue north until he reached a village where he could find an inn for the night. He stopped to water the horses in a mountain stream at noon and rested himself beneath a cypress tree to eat an orange. The journey continued pleasantly and although he did come to several villages, they were not large enough to contain an inn and so he went on, thinking that if anything, he could always spend the night in a tent with a random group of Bedouins.

As fate would have it, the latter was the scenario in which he found a bed.

Nadhir made his tent over the cart where he knew he would sleep well upon the twelve carpets with the saber at his side. The Bedouins invited him to partake of their supper of eggplant and onion kebabs. He praised Allah and ate heartily, better actually than he ever did in his own home.

"Where are you going with your carpets?" asked Kisan, a newly wed husband of one wife with newborn twins.

"Aleppo," he answered, and although his religion forbade it, accepted a small cup of sweet wine for the first time in his forty years of life. Why? *Because*, he rationalized, *I am a poet and I am free.*

"We are coming from Aleppo," said Safia, the young wife with ebony eyes as she took one infant off of her breast and placed him in a basket from which she then lifted up his sister and brought her to the opposite teat. "I didn't like it there," she added.

"No?" Nadhir felt the wine begin to tickle his senses. "I've never been."

"It is filled with thieves," Safia muttered, her eyes lowering onto her babe.

"Bah!" Kasim drank his wine with great thirst. "And you didn't like Babylon because it was filled with whores!" he roared.

"We are now going to Damascus," she mentioned soberly.

"That is where I am from. This is the first time I've ventured beyond its walls. You will like it there, dear lady, for it is filled with jasmine!"

Safia smiled, Kasim drank, and Nadhir stayed silent as the North Star pierced through the black curtain of night.

When he woke at dawn the Bedouins had already packed up their camp and taken to the road. Nadhir drank water from his flask and let the horses follow their scent to a watering hole then turned back on route. He reached Aleppo at the twilight hour to discover an abundance of inns and chose one that appeared proper enough, paid for a room and a stall for his horses, then drove the carpets to the Sultan's palace.

Sultan Ahim spent some time examining each carpet. He walked barefoot on each one then did so wearing his pointed, gold, satin slippers. He lay on his back and his side, then upon his round stomach. He sat cross-legged then knelt then prostrated himself as if in prayer. He ordered a harem of dancing girls to dance on each carpet, called for an acrobat to do cartwheels upon them, pushed his servants into the center of each one for a wrestling match and finally decided to keep all of them except one. Alas, he was so pleased with his eleven carpets that he invited Nadir to his dinner table that evening.

Again, our Damascusene praised Mohamed and partook of a feast as he'd never even dreamed, decidedly a feast fit only for a king. *Fette magdous*, kebab *kashkhash*, *kibbeh* with cherry sauce, *halva* and *babousa*, and again, because he was a poet and he was free, he drank a small glass of spirits called *arak*.

"Your carpet maker will be paid well," said Ahim. "But you must not keep a bag of gold with you at the inn tonight. I must confess, although I try my best to rule the region honorably, Aleppo is filled with thieves."

"So I have heard, your Grace," answered Nadhir, his brain giddy from the liquor and his body, although he'd eaten so well, feeling light from the long drive.

"Then you must come back in the morning to collect Lateef's payment and..." Ahim winked. "I have an extra present for the artisan that I wish you to also carry back with you."

Nadhir obliged and slept better than the night before, better even than he ever did in his own home, that night at the inn upon a downy cot with his saber at his side.

He was not surprised to see two bags of gold, each the size and weight of one of Safia's twins, but he was indeed shocked when Ahim presented him with Lateef's gift, for it was a woman.

The Sultan grinned. "For your carpet-maker, a wife!"

Nadhir was going to comment that his friend's harem was already sufficient enough in his mind, but realized it wasn't his place to judge and the woman before him was in fact quite a jewel. Her eyes dazzled his spirit in a way he never before felt. It was as if, with her gaze, she were sucking his very spirit out of his bones and giving it flesh of its own, as if to make it apart from him as another entity, alive.

"And that is why," Ahim continued, his grin spreading from ear to pointed ear, "you are traveling back to Damascus with one carpet so that Gazala," he paused and waved at the beauty with bewitching eyes, "Shall have a comfortable place to sit."

The Sultan laughed but Nadhir and Gazala did not.

She sat like a statue on the single carpet in the back of the cart while Nadhir sat on the wooden box in front with the bags of gold tied to his waist and the saber at his side. He held the reins steadily yet the Arabian horses were beyond his control and galloped through the streets of Aleppo as if haunted by the stealthy air of the city and only relaxed once the wagon was out upon the open plains.

For the entire day, Gazala remained silent, answering Nadhir but once with her extraordinary eyes when he offered her some apricots around noontime. Toward dusk, he left the Silk Road and returned to the place in the desert where he'd camped with the Bedouins, yet the desert was vacant of life and the two travelers were alone. As before, he made a tent over the cart for his companion, planning to sleep in his cloak on the sand, saber and gold attached. He had been so bewildered by the horses' earlier disobedience, by the sensations whirling in his soul because of the compelling presence of the mysterious woman and by the flaming sun beating down upon his brow for hours, that he'd forgotten to stop in any village or farm they'd driven through to buy provisions for the evening.

Yet as he was making a spark with his stick of flint, Gazala, like magic, opened her traveling sack and produced a large paper satchel of smoked catfish, an entire loaf of black bread, a mound of soft goat cheese and a half bottle of *arak*. She spread her shawl upon the sand before Nadhir's skillful campfire and arranged the dinner there as if she were setting the table of Sultan Ahim. He thanked her. After they prayed together, he began to eat ravenously while she merely nibbled on some bread and cheese. But the *arak*, which he refused, she sacrilegiously drank profusely.

"I've never seen the gentler sex drink like that before," he muttered.

For the first time since the Sultan introduced her, she spoke. "Then perhaps, Nadhir Muftah Ghuzi, my sex is not so gentle."

"How do you know my full name?" He was greatly taken aback.

"I know things." She drank some more, directly from the brown glass bottle like a drunk in the street.

"Such as?"

"That you are a poet."

His initial surprise at her witch-like behavior turned into complete astonishment. He'd never shown his poetry to anyone except Abdul Lateef, not even to his own wives. For a brief moment he felt frightened and then felt ashamed of being frightened by a woman.

"That is incredible! How...?"

She laughed, took another un-ladylike swig from the bottle and withdrew from a pocket in her skirt, a piece of parchment branded by the characteristically broken lines of his elegant calligraphy.

"I found it between the boards of the cart."

It explained all, for he had inscribed it to Abdul Lateef and signed his full name. His good friend must have lost it or perhaps on the day it was given, a gust of wind must have tossed it into the back of the cart as he was driving away.

"Will you read it to me?" she asked, her voice now so sincere as compared to what he earlier thought of as menacing, that he accepted her request obligingly.

My soul flies from the fountain
To the cupola
It feels like the end of summer.
The light is changing from white to gold.
A baby screams from across the road.
Does it know?

Gazala smiled, the intimidating, seductive twist returning to her lips. "Do you believe in fate?" she asked.

"I believe in the Qur'an," he answered.

"The End of Days?"

"Yes, when Isa will judge all men, accompanied by Mahdi who will come upon a white stallion and rid the world of evil and assist Isa to triumph over the false messiah, Mesih ad-Dajjai."

"Really? And when will such an apocalypse occur?"

"No one knows."

"Tomorrow?"

"No, no. In the future."

"Ohhhhh." Her lips twisted downward.

Nadhir felt that she mocked him and wished to speak with her no more. "Come," he said, rising from his place on her shawl. "It is time for sleep. We ride at dawn."

She cleared the dinner items and crawled up into the caravan while Nadhir, as he'd planned, crept beneath the cart to sleep wrapped in his cloak between the wheels. An hour passed and the moon was high in the purple sky when the horses began neighing, trying to free themselves from their ropes, and woke him from a deep sleep.

First he heard it, a hissing sound moving in from the East. Rapidly, it grew louder and louder like an army of poltergeists charging toward the sea. Closer and closer it came in a flurry and at once he felt it, a thousand million pinpricks striking the vast empire of desert, riding on a current of wind the size and scope of a tsunami and instantly Nadhir, the horses and the caravan were in the midst of a sand storm.

He thought first of the horses; if he set them free they'd possibly be able to outrun it. But no, he surmised, peeking through the *keffiyeh* that he'd swiftly wrapped around his face, they'd more likely be capsized like ships. If he kept them tied to the sturdy acacia tree that had obviously survived storms in its past, they'd be buried, but depending on the length of the storm, perhaps only up to their haunches or their necks. He left them as they were and upon realizing that his own ankles were already sinking as if in a quicksand, rolled out from beneath the cart, grabbed onto a wooden wheel for support then lifted himself up and climbed into the tent where he secured the whipping flaps tightly shut by weighing them down with the two bags of gold.

Although he could barely see her in the pitch blackness surrounding them, he could sense that Gazala was frightened and found strength in the idea that a witch's tricks were no match for those of Nature's and God's.

"What is happening?" she whispered.

He told her.

"Are we safe?"

"I don't know."

They listened, sitting upright with their arms locked around their knees. The caravan began to rock in the ferocious wind. The hissing became so loud Nadhir could no longer hear the horses cry. Gazala remained silent.

He prayed.

And prayed.

The cart stopped rocking as its wheels were now buried in sand.

Nadhir continued to pray. He heard Gazala moving about then heard her uncork the bottle of *arak*.

"Here." She found his hand reaching out in the dark.

He drank. The sheets of the tent that had been fluttering wildly in the wind became taut, trapped by the rising mountain of sand.

There was nothing but silence and blackness for some time and then she cried, "We are going to die!"

Nadhir prayed. He prayed aloud.

"Stop! Stop you fool! Do you really think God can hear you?"

He continued to pray, chanting until he felt dizzy, lost and miserable.

The stifling air in the tent smelled of goat cheese and booze. There is nothing, he thought, nothing left but the blackness and our breath. The breath of a man and a woman and the dark.

The whirling sand outside slapped against the tent like a thousand whips and they both thought they could hear demons screaming in the brutal winds. Nadhir wished he could see her eyes. Suddenly she grabbed onto him and put her lips to his. Once again, there was movement and in seconds they were naked, clinging to each other in fear and desire. Clinging to each other for life and sex.

There is a box.
Its coordinates are
North, South, East and West.
There is a cross. It is measured
By Heaven,
> Hell, woman and man.

Nadhir opened his eyes in a calm ray of sunlight coming through the open flaps of the tent. He was naked and cursed himself. Gazala was not inside, neither were the bags of gold. He threw on his cloak and jumped, or rolled rather, out of the caravan onto a mound of sand. She was nowhere in sight. The horses were writhing, kicking their way free in a cloud of desert dust that spiraled around the acacia tree like a genie escaped from a bottle, as if Gazala herself had been released from inside the *arak* bottle and now flew about in a golden whirl to mock him.

His throat was parched. The jug of water in the front of the cart had sand in it but was drinkable. He gave what he could to the horses. A steady breeze was traveling westward, carrying off the sand in a slow but continual stream. Nadhir searched for Gazala and the gold in vain. He'd been had.

By evening, the wheels of the cart were rolling and the horses' strong hooves galloping. He traveled all night and reached Damascus at dawn.

He drove directly to the house with the yellow door. Jana answered his knock.

"He is not here, Nadhir Muftah Ghuzi," she said. "He is at his first wife's house on the outskirts of town."

Nadhir thanked her, but before leaving, as he was starving and dying of thirst, asked for water and some bread.

"Of course! Come in, come in!" She escorted him to the terrace where he sat upon some pillows in a near swoon.

"I shall leave the cart here," he told Jana, then added, "Please have your servant water and feed the horses for they are in need after our journey, as I am. I shall take one of them with me to find your husband."

"Of course, our dear friend. Rest first and I'll bring you food and drink." Her eyes smiled with genuine care and commitment to servitude.

Yes, Jana's eyes were truly beautiful, mesmerizing almost but in a different way than Gazala's. For true beauty is shy, he philosophized, and that is why it appears mysterious. Evil is ultimately obvious—which makes it banal. Yet pure beauty hides behind a veil. "I'll put these thoughts in a poem," he mumbled to himself and would have lost consciousness if Jana did not set a plate of boiled eggs, figs and fried bread instantly before him.

He reached the low, flat house where the seventeen goats lazily grazed on the brittle leaves of scattered emu bushes by mid-morning, only to be told by Lateef's first wife that the carpet-maker was at his fourth wife's house near the

Bab al-Saghir. Nadhir thanked her and rode back through the city to the stony villa on the south side of town to discover that his friend was in fact at the house he bought for his second wife, in the center of the Muslim Quarter.

The noon sun high in the sky, Lateef's second wife told him, "He is across the street at the mosque."

Nadhir left the horse with her servant and entered the sacred place. The minute he crossed through the courtyard he began to feel like his true self again. Who had he been upon the journey? Drinking with the Bedouins, exhibiting gluttony at the Sultan's and interminably painful, the lust he had unleashed during the sandstorm, with a witch, no less! Ah! Who was that man?

And the minute he left his sandals at the great door and the bare soles of his feet touched the many carpets on the men's side of the mosque, his mind turned to the Qur'an and he was proud to once again become a slave of God. He saw Abdul Lateef from a distance and approached his friend without a sound. He knelt beside him and facing Mecca, prostrated himself in prayer. They neither spoke nor looked at each other but Lateef knew Nadhir was there. After a quarter of an hour, the two men walked out of the mosque and were about to go through the gate when Lateef stopped. "Pardon me, my friend, I forgot something inside."

Nadhir nodded and leaned against a column decorated with a gold plated design, glad of the delay, for he so feared the imminent truth he must tell about his journey. With his hand, he shaded his eyes from the sun and looked about. People appeared solemn and good. In the street, women carried baskets of almonds and fruit. Children played in their own shadows and the ginger cat with one ear crossed the threshold of it all then disappeared.

There is a hexagon.
It has a crown of thorns.
How is it…
That the Bedouin's drum in the desert
Echoes in the courtyard?

"So," Lateef said when he returned. "We shall go to the café. My baked fish should be prepared just about now."

For several blocks they walked in silence then out of the blue, Lateef smiled. "Paprika," he said. "Jamal, the cook at the café, bakes it in a paprika sauce, I recently discovered." He laughed. "That is the secret! Now I want paprika with everything I eat. I've ordered four sacks of this spice to be sent to each of my wives."

Nadhir tried to smile politely. He was at a loss for words. His shame, embarrassment and most of all, absolute sense of failure, tore at his soul.

When they were seated in the café, Lateef asked casually, "So tell me, how did it go?"

"The sultan took eleven carpets, my friend, and paid you with two bags of gold."

"Ah! Wonderful. It is exactly as I expected."

"He also sent you a present."

"A present?" Lateef's fish was served and the merchant began to eat with a terrific relish. "What sort of present?"

Nadhir sighed and painfully told him the whole story. The fish was pushed aside at the first mention of Gazala and her bewitching beauty. When the story ended, Lateef sat back and stared at the dead eye embossed in the silver scales for some time.

"I…" Nadhir tried to apologize but the carpet-maker waved his hand in the air to stop him. A water pipe was brought to the table and they smoked.

Finally, Abdul Lateef puckered up his lips in heavy disdain and muttered, "It appears that like ninety percent of the city of Aleppo, the sultan is also a thief."

"I am so sorry," Nadhir whispered.

"Yes." Lateef rose. "I know."

"You are not upset, Abdul?"

The merchant sighed. "It is unfortunate but there is at this point, nothing you or I can do. That bastard Ahim will get what he deserves at the End of Days and you and I will watch him rot in Hell. Until then, there are many sultans in Syria and many more carpets for me to make."

He threw some coins, the exact price of the meal, upon the table.

"Oh, I almost forgot!" Nadhir took the saber from his belt.

"That? Bah! Keep it, I have many more in my many homes." And with that, the rectangular silhouette of Abdul Lateef's backside disappeared into the buzzing blaze of the street outside.

Nadhir finished the fish, eating slowly with his fingers then went with humility to the *souk al-hamidiyeh* where, after bargaining rather unambitiously, he sold the saber for 50 dinars.

He tripped over two cats, consecutively, in the dim stairwell of his house. His wives and children greeted him affectionately and were overjoyed when he set two sacks of flour, a large jar of olives, four blocks of cheese, a chicken in a cage and the surprise bag of pistachios upon the table.

His one journey out of Damascus was over and he was glad to be home. He watched his wives prepare the food, thinking it was right that women should stay where life stays, indoors.

After a feast (far better, because of the company, than the sultan's), Nadhir Muftah Ghuzi's children went to bed healthy and blessed, and he slept with Shazmah. At midnight he woke as if stunned in his dreams by the very real silver moonlight swelling in the open window. He went to close the shutter but first turned to see his lovely Shazmah sleeping peacefully in the glowing nebula and avowed to himself and God that he would learn to love both of his wives equally. The scent of jasmine tickled his soul and he decided to leave the shutter as it was.

There is a circle.
Beauty is everywhere
But evil

        still exists.

Elizabeth McKague

XVII

Gozo, Italy

Present

Marianne was sautéing garlic when Claude retuned from Xaghra. He came into the kitchen in a strange, semi-somnambular state. She turned to see him standing there frozen and empty-handed.

"Where are the groceries? Did you get tomatoes?"

He shook his head.

"Now, how am I supposed to make a sauce? I guess we'll just have garlic over pasta for dinner. Why didn't we plant tomatoes in the garden? Well, I can pick some fresh basil and just add more olive oil…"

"Marianne?"

"What's wrong with you?"

He took a deep breath. "It's the last one."

"What are you…"

Claude tossed a crumpled white envelope into the trash can and took a post card from his shirt pocket and gave it to her. It was a simple, bluish card with no picture. The address on one side read:

Sophie Volland

39 rue de Richelieu

Paris, France

And the other side consisted solely of a slanting, delicate handwriting that at times rose above a straight line, and in other places, the letters were jammed a bit too close together or were spaced too far apart. Marianne read:

J'écris sans voir. Je suis venu. Je voulais kiss votre main…C'set la
première fois que j'ai jamais écrit dans le sombre, ne sachant pas si

*je suis en effet formant des lettres. Là où il n'y aura rien, lisez que je
t'aime.*
Denis Diderot, 10 June 1759

She immediately dropped the card and Claude thought she might drop to
the floor herself. He took her hands in his. They steadied each other. She looked
into his eyes. The garlic was burning to a crisp. He stretched his arm around her
and turned off the stove.

"But how…?"

"It's the last one, Marianne…the last story."

"Oh God!"

"We must."

She buried her head on his shoulder for some time and he thought perhaps
she was weeping but when she lifted her face to kiss him, she was smiling. It was
an innocent smile and that moment, oh, he thought, how she looked so young!

XVIII

The Postcard
Paris, France, 1987

Claude Renoir owned an antiquarian bookshop in Paris, France, on the rue Malebranche, a small bending street nestled between the monumental Pantheon, the green serenity of the Jardin du Luxembourg and the flux of La Sorbonne. After graduating from university with a degree in philosophy and spending three rousing years traveling the world, he felt, at the age of 25, that the only way he could live back in Paris was to hide amongst the dead and so, he opened his bookshop. It was called (somewhat pretentiously, yet we must remember, he was just 25), Anamnesis, Les Livres Rare et Ancienne—Recollections: Rare and Ancient Books.

He came from a bourgeois family who supported the venture and valued Claude's taste and erudition. In fact, he was such a careful and assiduous book buyer that within five years, Anamnesis became known as one of the most esteemed antiquarian bookshops in all of Western Europe. During those five years Claude had numerous love affairs. He was tall and lean with a strikingly attractive, Etruscan-like profile emphasizing a full head of wispy, golden curls (like Shelley, he proudly told himself). He was usually drawn to older women as he found their confidence and sophistication more appealing to his romantic alter ego but also because, he soon realized, that women his own age often bored him to tears. Yet he was a man, and often couldn't resist the naiveté of those perky, chirpy, Sorbonne girls that came into his shop, mispronouncing the names of foreign authors such as Goethe, Ibsen, Ariosto and even Edgar Allan Poe. With these girls he took on the role of a kind of Henry Higgins and, with Voltaire-esque nonchalance, was determined to "cultivate their gardens." There was one pretty little thing named Sabine with whom he became especially fond, or more particularly, obsessed. Oh, the nights he'd spent longing for the following day when he might touch her long, soft hair and swan-like neck, even while he was dining with a forty-something divorcee at the Ritz (on her credit card) or discussing the sensual perversity of Charles Baudelaire or Georges Bataille with an elegant female professor over coffee at Les Deux Magots. And then, the next day, when Sabine came into the shop, oh, how he adored the way she'd tease him with her passive-aggressive play! Yes, in his nineteenth century romantic syllabus, Sabine was for him like Proust's Albertine and for a time, our healthy, handsome Claude Renoir became physically and mentally sick with love for her.

Marianne set the manuscript pages down. "This is absurd!"

Claude pushed his eyeglasses, as they had slid down, back up upon the bridge of his nose. "A tinge quixotic, perhaps, yes, yet true."

"But it has no place in the story."

"Background."

"I'm not going into my background."

"You were too young to have one."

"Ridiculous!"

"Not like mine..."

"Oh, little do you know."

"I was just recollecting that's all."

"Monsieur Anamnesis."

"Clever."

"What happened with her anyway?"

"Sabine? I've told you a hundred times before."

"Yes, but I like hearing the end."

"That's because I look like a fool."

"Uh huh."

"She wouldn't let me fuck her."

"And?"

"One day her 'real' boyfriend came into the shop and slammed a box set of, appropriately, A la Recherche du Temps Perdu upside my head."

Marianne's naughty laughter quickly turned into a sympathetic pout and she went to cradle him and kiss his cheek. "Let's get to work. It's a beautiful story."

"Of course it is. It's our story."

Claude went back into his study but crossed the threshold once again into hers after a few minutes. "You should tell your background."

"Mine's not so interesting."

"But it shows your purity."

"That is what attracted you to me, wasn't it?"

He twisted his lips to one side. "Still is, baby."

"Go! Out! Rascal!"

That night, after a bottle of Feudo Maccari Nero d"Avola 2012, a lemon meringue sunset and the ceaseless lull of the cerulean sea, he made his wife very happy indeed.

The next day, they resumed writing…

Mais, bien sur, all of Claude's affairs were short-lived and ended, befitting his Romeo and Juliet, Tristan and Isolde-type of sensibility, tragically. Yet his thirty-year-old ego reigned over his heart and he persevered in the corporeal world as a reputable book dealer by secretly reveling in his imaginative universe as a sort of early 1980's "glam" chevalier.

Then, one frigid November morning, she came into Anamnesis and the moment their eyes met, he knew it was time to grow up.

"You can't write that!" Claude protested.

"Sure I can."

"Reason?"

"Truth."

"Truce?"

"I said, truth."

Claude's shoulders hunched up, his eyeglasses slid down over his Etruscan nose and he returned to his study, defeated.

Then, one frosty November morning, an English woman came into his shop and Claude Renoir, for some odd reason, became extremely self-conscious, almost to the point of timidity. It was a sensation he'd never quite experienced before. When he saw her, really saw her as if seeing into her core while she moved closer to the desk as he stood mulling over several high stacks of paperbacks, it seemed as if they were coming alive together in a painting of a man and woman meeting for the first time in a Parisian bookshop and agreeing, as Goethe said, to "make their own little world in the great world of all."

"Thank you. That's better."

"You're welcome. Shall we continue?"

"Bonjour." Her accent was atrocious.

He looked up at Marianne who had to agree, "Well, at that time it was. Shall we continue?"

"*Bonjour,*" the handsome book dealer said stately, stressing an effort to correct her pronunciation.

"Do you speak English?"

"Of course." He held out his hand. "Claude Renoir."

She shook it timidly. "Marianne Bardsley. I've come from London especially to visit your shop."

"Yes?"

She took a few books, three, to be exact, very fine books wrapped in a soft, baby blue cloth out of a common, canvas knapsack. "I work for Holmes & Co. on Bond Street, I'm not sure if you…"

"Oh, I know the place. A real gem in the business."

"Right. Well, Mr. Holmes sent me to you with these three jewels."

"Ah, I believe I did receive a letter from him the other day. He mentioned a first of Dickens…is it true?"

"Viola." She unwrapped the cloth and produced a first issue of *David Copperfield*, Bradbury & Evans, London, 1850.

Claude took a pair of thin white gloves and put them on to examine the treasure. Marianne's eyes widened as she watched him tenderly rub a finger along the spine and open the cover to trace an engraving on the second page. After no more than a minute, he spoke softly, more to himself than to her.

"The gilt edges are spectacular. The red boarding on the front and back are a bit worn, there is a half inch crack on the upper spine yet only in the leather, which is also quite worn and many of the plates are darkened on the edges but overall…" He set the book down upon the cloth she'd wrapped it in. "What does he want for it?" Claude looked at her with a superior eye but her own clandestine gaze made his ego fumble.

"Ego…fumble? Really?"

"I don't know, I thought like, alter his ultra ego, I wanted to lower his grandiose self-image, I mean, bring the whole damn French thing down a notch, ya know?"

"Hmm. Whatever. Let's move on."

"Ten thousand francs."

"Hah! With that tear in the leather? Preposterous!"

Marianne smiled and started to wrap the soft blue cloth over the precious edition.

"It's not worth more than six."

She did not look up at him.

"Alright, seven."

She continued to wrap up the book, carefully.

"Seven-five, but that's my final offer."

"I can't let it go for under nine, Monsieur."

"Eight five and that's my final..."

"Fine. Mr. Holmes was quite adamant about the price of that one but the other two are negotiable." She then unwrapped a very pretty edition of William Blake's *Heaven and Hell* with color engravings, dated 1792, and an English translation of Rousseau's *La Nouvelle Heloise*, dated as well in the year of that fateful day at Bastille.

"Lovely, really, these two. Unfortunately I believe Rousseau sells better in French, but the condition here is exquisite. Let's see..." Claude took off his eyeglasses and paced behind his desk as Marianne stood still as a statue, whether from nerves or reserve, he couldn't tell. He placed his gloved finger on the books.

"I'll give you three thousand francs for these two."

"The Blake alone is worth that."

"Ah, she knows her books, does she?"

"I was so insulted by that remark."

"I made your cheeks blush rose red."

"Really, you were so full of yourself!"

"Apologies, darling."

"Alright. Eleven thousand-and five hundred francs for all three." He smiled at her, knowing he could definitely have coaxed her into letting them go for at least 500 less but wanted her to feel successful because she was young and so pretty.

She crinkled her brow and pursed her lips in a pout.

"And..." He ruffled his thick, Shelley-esque curls. "I'll even throw in a gift for you. Any book you choose from that side of the shop."

"The less expensive side, I assume."

"Fifty francs max, but I do have some nice books here."

"Oh, I don't doubt that, Monsieur Renoir."

"Claude, please."

"You wanted to fuck me then, at that moment, didn't you?"

"Yup."

"Because I ripped you off or just because you wanted to fuck me?"

"A little of both."

"We have a deal." She shook his hand again, less sensually than the first time, and stood back as he took a checkbook out of his desk.

"To Holmes…is it?"

"Edward L. Holmes."

"What's the L. stand for?"

"Lawrence."

Claude smiled to himself, thinking, *Oh, how very English.*

Marianne loosened the plaid wool scarf around her neck and let it hang over her black suede blazer, which he somehow watched her unzip from beneath his lowered eyelids. She was wearing a white blouse and a short, pleated black skirt, looking much like a Catholic school dropout because of the 80's style, heavy black eyeliner and cruel, mascara-thick eyelashes. But she didn't wear lipstick. He liked that. He liked her bare knees and her white leather go-go boots. Her burgundy-colored hair was long, wavy and looked unkempt and he pictured her spending the first part of her morning drinking a café crème and eating a croissant at a lonely window table inside a brassiere, then walking briskly along the Seine to his shop in the cold, bright sun.

He suddenly asked, while signing the check with an unnecessary dramatic sweep, "Are you staying nearby?"

She thought it rather forward but answered unscathed, "Not really. My hotel is in the eleventh."

She turned before he could hand her the check and began to notice some titles on a shelf. "But I had a lovely walk here this morning. Unlike London, Paris is a city you can cross on foot, if you're game." She pulled out a fine edition of *Une Saison en Enfer* and held it up in the air. "Like Rimbaud."

Claude laughed. "That's right, he did walk from the Belgian border straight into Paris."

"And after the shooting incident—you know, with Verlaine and all that—he walked all over Europe and at one point, because he wasn't eating much I suppose, but remember this fact to be true, that he had to hospitalized because his own ribs cut into his stomach lining!" She grabbed her waist then, a petite one that Claude was happy to notice, and shuddered. "Poor guy."

She pulled out a 1948 edition of the poems of Rilke. "And then, after

Abyssinia with the whole gun exportation thing, he ended up back in Marseille with gangrene and had to have both his legs amputated!"

"And died." Claude neatly ripped the check out of the book along the perforated line.

"After a lifetime of walking." She moved briskly into another isle with the Rilke still in her hand. "Is it true then? That all poets live a life of irony?"

"Ivory?" Claude didn't quite hear her for a passing siren had muffled her voice.

She peeked out from behind a bookshelf. "Irony," she repeated loudly.

He folded his arms across his chest. He was wearing a sea green hand-woven sweater that he'd purchased on the isle of Rhodes six years ago. "I don't know, but they do seem to die for the life they have led. That is, they do seem to die, unlike most, as if life had meaning."

Marianne came out of the stacks and wavered before his desk before turning down another corridor. "Meaning as in purpose?"

"Actually," he said, and with intellectual delight he tightened his arms across his chest and proudly felt his biceps flex, "I'd like to say 'destiny' but I couldn't back it up whole heartedly. I'm an atheist."

"That was a fashionable word back then, wasn't it?" Claude put down the few pages he'd been reading and took an olive out of the bowl she set on the table. The evening air was moist and a copious sea mist began to spill into the veranda.

"So much so," she said as she sat across from him, "that by the time you said it in 1987, it had already become cliché."

"I sounded cliché that day?"

"In retrospect, maybe, but to me that day...you seemed..."

"Yes?"

Marianne batted her eyelashes as if bathing them in the pearly mist. "That day you sounded quite brilliant. Very impressive. I thought you were, well, simply majestic."

He laughed. "Really?"

"Of course! You were French, tall, reasonably attractive."

He raised his eyebrows.

"Okay. Great looking and smart...what did you think of me?"

"You know what."

"I don't."

"I was thirty, single and horny. That's what I remember."

"Please..."

"I know I liked you. I liked you second, but first, I thought you were sexy."

Marianne closed the folder containing her pages and rose from the table. *"The Viognier should be chilled by now."*

"Hey!" He called out after her, knowing he'd unintentionally said something wrong.

"Let's put it away for now. I want to start the tilapia."

At one point, after dinner or during dinner or the walk on the mist-stricken beach, Claude reflected and understood and told her at bedtime, "Babes, you're sexier to me now you know, more than ever."

"Mais bien sur." She didn't believe him.

Regardless, he felt a deep welt of loneliness as he rode his bike into Xaghra the next morning.

In the bookshop on the rue Malebranche, Marianne chose the Rilke, a decent cloth edition with just a tinge of foxing. Although he found her choice somewhat pretentious, he was more interested in getting to know her better than making impetuous judgments.

"Would you like a bag or do you want to wrap it up in your little blue cloth?"

"A bag. I like the feel of the waxy paper and the insignia of the shop."

He handed her the gift, slowly. "Perhaps...can I invite you for dinner *ce soir?*"

She didn't hesitate to answer. "Sure."

"There is a place nearby on the rue Saint Jacques. Can you meet me here at eight o'clock when I close the shop?"

"*Oui.*" She turned to go. "*Au revoir!*"

"*A toute a l'heure.*"

She arrived a quarter after eight wearing an ultramarine blue dress that accented her reddish hair and bold brown eyes. Claude was ready and they set off. The place he had in mind, the restaurant Perraudin, was luckily just around the corner as it began to rain just as he was locking the rustic door to Anamnesis behind him.

It was a soft rain.

Marianne liked it and wished they would have a bit of a stroll ahead of them. Regardless, she enjoyed walking into the dimly lit, authentic, classic

French bistro with a tall, handsome gentleman at her side. Claude ordered a bottle of Chateau Monbousquet St. Emillon and they spoke of Nerval, Zola, Giono and Flaubert during a first course of pot-au-feu pate with onion marmalade for him and a garden salad for her. The bottle nearly empty, they spoke of Lord Byron, D.H. Lawrence, Virginia Woolf and Anthony Powell as their entrées of roasted leg of lamb with potato gratin for he and salmon with sorrel sauce for she came to the table. At the end of the meal, he ordered coffee yet Marianne preferred another glass of wine.

"I'd offer to drive you to your hotel but I don't have a car," he said as he paid the bill.

"I can take a taxi." She paused as the waiter took the cash. "Do you live close by?"

He laughed. "Above the shop!"

"Well, that's convenient."

He walked her to the nearest taxi stand but it was a Saturday night and many people were waiting. It began to rain fast and hard. He took her hand and they ran back to the rue Malebranche where she followed him through the dark shop and up an extremely narrow back stairwell that twisted round and round until it stopped before his apartment door. She remained quiet as she entered. He turned on a few lamps. His flat looked like the bookshop with the addition of some fine Baroque chairs, a modern white fabric sofa and a petite kitchen, fully equipped with culinary necessities and hanging copper pans. There was a large archway that led to a darkened chamber, presumably to his bedroom.

"Would you like a glass of wine?"

"Yes. Thank you."

She sat on the sofa. He brought wine and they spoke of how he was learning to cook. Then they spoke of art and he turned the dimmer track lights on in his bedroom where she discovered a collection of Impressionist paintings, authentic paintings hanging on all four walls. He explained how he was trying to become a collector and then he kissed her and undressed her and took her to bed.

"Is that really the way it happened?"

"You don't remember?"

"Sort of, it was a long time ago, Clues, and I had quite a bit to drink that night."

"Oui, ma chéri, that is the way it happened."

Marianne woke to the subdued ringing of distant church bells. She'd always remember that detail. She was alone in the apartment and knew he was downstairs. Coffee, already made in the French-press on the kitchen stove. She dressed, washed her face and looked desperately for a hairbrush but to no avail.

When she came into the shop from the back stairwell she found Claude seated at his desk, leaning back in his wooden swivel chair as if some powerful, unseen force had literally thrown him there, with a look of utter enchantment mixed with unqualified shock on his face.

"What's going on?" she asked, wondering if she should be concerned and began to feel unwanted in the way that most Parisians make foreigners feel, which, she then realized, she had not felt from him at all until this moment.

He straightened his broad shoulders and looked at her in amazement.

"Claude? Should I go? I'll leave, I'm going now, thank you for every…"

"No. Don't go. Listen." He stretched his arm forward and picked up a powder blue postcard that he had gently set atop the copy of Rousseau she sold him yesterday. He had his white gloves on. "Did you know this was in here?"

"What?"

"Come here. Closer. Stand beside me and read it."

She did so but confessed, "My French isn't that good."

He translated: "I write without seeing. I came. I wanted to kiss your hand… This is the first time I have ever written in the dark, not knowing whether I am indeed forming letters. Wherever there will be nothing, read that I love you."

Marianne read the date aloud. "Ten June, seventeen fifty-nine. Is it for real?"

"I think so. I do think so. *C'est incroyable*, no?"

"My God. It's beautiful."

"An original letter from Denis Diderot to Sophie Volland, do you know what this means?"

"Maybe."

"It's worth a fortune, Miss Bardsley."

"And that was in my book?"

"My book."

"Holmes' book."

"My book."

"I suppose you're right." She sighed in resignation and admitted, "I am familiar with book dealing etiquette."

Claude retrieved a clear plastic envelope from a drawer in his desk and carefully set the postcard inside it. "I know a guy on the rue Bonaparte who can authenticate it. I'm going there directly. Would you like to join me?"

She was pleased he'd asked but refused. "I should get back to the hotel, shower, change…it's my last day in Paris."

"Oh."

"My train leaves at six this evening."

"Oh."

"Well." She put on her black suede blazer that she'd kept draped over her arm. "I had fun."

"*Moi aussi.*"

"Well.,,"

"Why don't I take care of this and meet you at your hotel at, say…around noon?"

"Why?"

He thought her question odd and somewhat snobbish.

"I'd like to spend the day with you."

"Oh. Alright."

And consequently, because it was what Marianne wished to do, they spent the early hours of the afternoon traipsing through the Cimetière du Père Lachaise, adoring the graves of the literary dead then had a late luncheon of champagne and oysters at Le Wepler Brasserie in Le Place de Clichy, "where Guillaume Apollinaire once sank into reverie after a shoe shine," as Claude eloquently told her.

He accompanied her to the Gare du Nord and kissed her ardently on the platform before she boarded her car. His eyes were moist. Hers were tired. He'd been offered more than he expected for the postcard from the guy on the rue Bonaparte and did not mention this fact to this girl from England with whom, the night before, he had terrifically wild sex.

She didn't ask about the postcard or show any signs of oxytocin-induced enthusiasm and assumed an air of insouciance. She imagined she'd never see him again. Little did she know that the acclaimed bibliophile Claude Renoir of Anamnesis bookshop located in the rue Malebranche, Paris, France, had in the past twenty-four hours, fallen head over heels in love with her.

"You did?"

"Of course."

"I didn't."

"I know."

"Let's continue."

The following weekend Claude walked into Holmes & Co. on Bond Street in London, England. Marianne, who worked six days a week, was stacking in the fiction section.

"Hello."

"Oh my! This is a surprise." She climbed down from a ladder. "You're in London?"

"Obvious, isn't it?"

"Of course. Are you here to see Edward? He's in the country this weekend but will be back on Tuesday."

"I came to see you."

She wiggled her hips slightly, nervously, and straightened out the pale, button down blouse she was wearing. "*Monsieur…*"

"Is there a problem?"

She became shy.

"Do you have a boyfriend?"

"I did. Not anymore." She lowered her eyes. "I found out he was sleeping with another woman, actually, the week right before I left for Paris."

"So it's all good!"

"*Mais Monsieur…*"

"I came because I want to get to know you more. You intrigue me."

Marianne blushed. In fact, despite her rational indifference to the fantastic night they'd spent together, she had found herself thinking about Claude every day, almost every minute of every day, since her return.

"We can have dinner tonight. What time do you close shop?"

"My replacement comes in at four this afternoon but I can't…I have another job. I work from five until ten at Barry's Restaurant in Wandsworth."

"I'm not familiar with it.'

"It just opened."

"You're a waitress?"

Marianne hunched her shoulders, embarrassed for two reasons. Secondly, because she was, in fact, a waitress, but first and foremost because she was secretly infatuated with the chef at Barry's, a culinary genius named Maximilion Knight who was very close at the ripe age of 27 (two years her senior), to winning his first Michelin star. She thought he was enormously delicious! His tall, slim figure, his dark, medusa-like curls, his prominent chin that appeared to have an unfailing three-day stubble and his soft, pink lips, clear, deep brown eyes with lashes like a girl and especially, the large bulge in the jogging trousers he'd wear to work that she once noticed as he changed into his white shirt and striped apron. They had only a professional exchange as she worked front of the house and he spent most of his time bullocking the line cooks in the back. He was an aggressive artist and was focused to such an extreme on the food that she wondered whether or not he was aware of her at all, even when he did talk to her, or more often, scream at her as she took the dishes at the pass.

"Where have you been? This fucking chicken is cold!"

"Table six wants fucking salt? Tell them to get out!"

"Do you think the fucking pig's trotter is going to walk to the table on its own, then, my dear?"

"Marianne, Marianne, Goddamn, Goddamn!"

Yet most of the time he was right, for she couldn't help standing secretly to one side of the pass between orders, watching him in a daze as he diced onions like a speed demon, painted the dishes with garnishes and sauce or molded a terrine like a sculptor. And oh! Just the thought of him with his knives made her swoon! And his resolute expression, so serious, so lonely, she thought, a loneliness that could only be alleviated by coupling with each particular ingredient.

"Marianne, the *tagliatelle* is up, Marianne!"

He didn't say "fucking" *tagliatelle*. That had been two weeks ago. Then toward the end of her shift, as she brought the cheese trolley through the passé, he'd winked at her. That night as she was on her way out the door, Maximilion swept up beside her and opened the door for her. She stepped outside with him and several line cooks followed.

"We're off to Knightsbridge for a bit-a-fun, will you join us?"

She pretended to hesitate yet quickly stepped along with the boys happily. They went into a bar, at that time on the cutting edge of London's trendy scene. Chef Knight drank one beer and then a coke. Marianne drank three glasses of wine. He gradually began to ignore his pals and focused on her as if she were a fresh oyster. He listened to her and somewhat non-discreetly looked at her lips and boobs like a natural bloke, and she started to tell him how she felt with the words, "Do you want to…"

"Want to shag you? Yes, I do."

They went to her place, a courageous little pad on Lowndes Square, just one block from Barry's restaurant. The sex was spectacular, brilliant, tremendous, fucking exceptionally gorgeous! She wanted to marry him and move in to a cottage in Surrey with wisteria hanging off a classic thatched roof and have children, two boys and a girl and live forever in a fantasy of lovemaking and *filet de sole amandine!*

They slept in an embrace for four hours, then had sex again at five o'clock the next morning before he left, explaining that he had to be at the restaurant to receive a shipment of caged snails that had been sent over night directly from Bourgogne.

He didn't wink at her as she came and went at the pass the next night, nor the night after that. His usual temper and stoicism played steadily and she soon learned from the sous chef that Maximilion was engaged to a minister's daughter, "Rich, with silky blond hair and a wildly cute ass."

The following day, Holmes sent her to Paris. Maximilion Knight never was her boyfriend. She'd lied to Claude. She lied because the Master Chef was, and would remain the best fuck of her life. What she felt with Claude in Paris was real and it frightened her because the moon plays the same tricks everywhere you in the world and she understood, that morning when she woke above his bookshop to the pacified ringing of the bells of L'église St. Jacques du Haut Pas, that Monsieur Renoir was going to be her husband.

"You can't say this!" Claude protested.

"We have to write the truth."

"But it's not true...you're woolgathering."

Marianne batted her eyelashes and refilled her glass of Viognier. "I have to turn the oven down, people should never over cook things, especially fish, that's what Chef Knight used to say."

"How can you write this? It's our story!"

"I'm sorry, Clues, it adds gravity, controversy, mystery."

"The fuckin' mystery of Maximilion Knight?"

"Well, obviously there's no mystery there," she said cynically.

When Marianne brought the dinner plates out onto the veranda, her husband, the bibliophile, Claude Renoir, was gone.

She spent the next two hours alone at the Villa Calypso, finishing the bottle of wine and picking at the baked tilapia with dill sauce while gazing in ultra-conscious reminiscence at the consoling dance of the non-reflective sea.

Claude came home on his bicycle, drunk, and went to bed.

Thirty-year-old Claude considered his options. "Would you be uncomfortable if I dined at Barry's tonight, then?" he asked.

"Of course not." She shelved a copy of Chateaubriand's *Memoirs of an Egoist* a few shelves above Collette's *Cheri* and added, "I'd be honored."

He entered the restaurant at eight-thirty and had a leisurely meal of lobster ravioli with a glass of Bordeaux followed by a lemon tart and two cups of café crème. He walked her the one block to her plucky little flat in Lowndes Square. She invited him in. They drank cheap Chablis that she had in her refrigerator and made love on her bed, a rather worn down mattress that covered most of studio's hard wood floor.

Claude spent the next two days smartly buying books in Mayfair and Piccadilly and was pleased to find some precious rare editions in a boutique in the West End, all of which he brought to show her during her afternoon shift at Holmes & Co. In the evening he'd try another fabulous entrée from the menu at Barry's and insisted, after eating the pig's trotter with morels, on complimenting the chef.

Maximilion came out of the kitchen with his three-day stubble, tempestuously twisting curls and dark eyes ablaze.

"You know," Claude told him in English with an exaggerated French accent, "I have dined all over the world, but must say this was the best meal I've ever had in my life."

"*Merci, monsieur.*" The chef shook his hand then quickly strode back into the kitchen to yell, for a variety of reasons, at the dishwasher.

Those sixty seconds encompassed the only time that the two men who ruled the imaginative life of Marianne Suzette Bardsley, ever met.

Marianne had been up for two hours when she went into the kitchen from her study to make a fresh pot of coffee. Claude had just come downstairs and was standing at the counter in a cream-toned tank top and black underwear, doing just that. His curly, whitish hair was windswept and slept on, and she thought he looked sexy.

"Where did you go last night?" she demurely asked.

"Town."

"To a bar?"

"The fisherman's bar."

"What was that like?"

"Smelled like fish and beer."
"Did you eat?"
"I don't think I did. No."
"I can make some eggs."
"That would be nice, babes."
"Are you hung over?"
"I don't think so. No."
"You drank beer?"
"Scotch."
"It's unlike you to..."
"Drop it."

She took three eggs from a basket beside the stove and gently, smoothly, the way she used to watch Maximilion do it the few times he made breakfast for the line cooks, cracked them open and set them in a buttered frying pan. "Are you going to write today?'

"I plan to go for a swim."
"I'll come along."
"If you wish."
"Clues..."

"Let's move on with the story. Get out of fucking London. It's time now, don't you think?"

"I've been working all morning and, coincidentally, am at that point just now."

Claude stared at the coffee maker percolating while she stared at the eggs slowly sizzling in the pan.

"Do you want toast?" she asked.
"Yes."
"Do you want to make love?"
"Maybe later."
Then he smiled at her and they both laughed.

Claude the bookseller returned to Paris and immediately started writing love letters to Marianne. She received one almost every day for the following month and although she did not respond as often as he would have liked, the few letters she did send him were highly engaging, genuinely rather romantic and at times, it seemed to him, unless he was reading too much into them, almost erotic.

He asked her to come to Paris but she could not leave either of her jobs, so he hired a trustworthy employee to take over Anamnesis for a week and made the jaunt back to London town. Expecting him, Marianne found time to tidy up her shoddy little flat, buy a few bottles of not so cheap Chablis and put fresh flowers, a pathetic arrangement of daisies and snapdragons that she picked up from a vendor at the tube station, in a barely cracked vase that she picked out of the trash bin behind Barry's restaurant. He was impressed and this made her very pleased indeed. She had missed him. She had grown to love him during their separation and her feelings for Claude rose up to the forefront of her consciousness, replacing the ache that her short-lived affair with Maximilion had made her suffer deep down inside.

She began to see bridges. Each time he entered her, she saw a bridge. Specific bridges, famous bridges—behind her closed eyes, because she kept her eyes closed throughout. And during the act she would, she felt, become that bridge. It would start in her imagination and gradually move through her whole body. Her neck, shoulders, belly, cunt, ass, limbs, feet and hands seemed to morph into the parts of each bridge until her back arched when she came and the bridge was completed, finished, sturdy and standing opaque in history.

The first bridge she saw, the first time he made love to her in his apartment above the bookshop as velvety rain creamed the tall windowpanes facing the night, was the Ponte dei Sospiri, the Bridge of Sighs, built in 1600 in Venice, Italy and celebrated in the poem by Lord Byron.

The next time, the very next morning in the hazel lavender tones of an ambiguous, gauzy dawn, she was surprised to envision and simultaneously become the Chengyang, Wind and River Bridge over the Linxi River in Sanjiang County, China, built in 1916.

Later that afternoon, after the cemetery and lunch at Le Wepler, when they returned to her hotel to gather her things to take to the station, she saw Le Pont Mirabeau.

Two weeks later when Claude made love to her in her tiny, slipshod flat on Lowndes Square, she saw nothing, but felt everything. The further, multiple times they fucked during his foray to London, it was the same behind her closed eyes, the same mixture of darkness and light but no bridges in sight.

Yet when she next traveled to France and they did it on his bed again and again, surrounded by all the art, she saw Les Ponts de Paris *seulement*: Le Pont Grand Palais, Pont Alexander, Pont ou Change, Pont St. Michel, Pont Marie, Pont de Bir-Hakeim, Pont des Invalades, Pont de Ile St-Louis and at last, in the morning before he would take her to the Gare du Nord, she became the lovers' bridge, Le Pont Neuf in all its mocking majesty!

But it didn't stop there. The following month when she met him in Normandy for a mini-break, she became the Ponte Vecchio and the Rialto Bridge at once. Their sex was wild, and one stormy night, as her body tightened and twisted and seemed to wind around him, she was the Carrick-a-Rede Rope Bridge in County Antrim in Northern Ireland.

For the next few months, it continued whether she went to see him in Paris or he came to London: the Charles Bridge in Prague, The Tower Bridge in London, the Chapel Bridge over the Reves river in Switzerland, the Brooklyn Bridge, the Stari-Most Bridge over the river Neretva in Sarajevo, in what was then called Yugoslavia and finally, randomly, the last bridge she saw was the Alcantara Bridge over the Tangus river in Spain, built by the ancient Romans in the quiet year of 104 A.D.

All those bridges, in the beginning, in the beginning of love, and yet, in their 29 years together, she'd never told him about any of them.

Edward Lawrence Holmes was sad to see his most trustworthy employee, Marianne Suzette Bardsley, leave his bookshop and to her surprise, Maximilion Knight also appeared rather moved to see her go. He hugged her kindly, wished her luck and even gave her a small tin of Russian caviar for the road.

Six months had passed since she walked into Anamnesis one cold, bright November morning with a few books to sell and now she was moving into the flat above the shop, engaged to the incontrovertibly successful book dealer, Monsieur Claude Albert Guillaume Renoir.

After reading a few of her short stories and poems, her fiancé assured her that business was booming and that there was no need for her to wait tables at Le Relais Louis XIII where she was sure to be hired, as Maximilion, having just won his first Michelin star, had given her a letter of high recommendation. Claude went on to suggest, one afternoon as she came into the shop with a bouquet of irises and a sack of fresh produce, smoked salmon and camembert from the Wednesday street market in St. Germain, that she spend her time and energy redecorating their rooms upstairs and attempting to write a novel.

"A novel? You must be joking!"

"Why not? You went to university, you studied literature, you're far more erudite than any of these Creative Writing Sorbonne twats that come in here and in my opinion, your work is quite admirable my dear."

"Claude, please, I can't write a novel."

"'Course you can."

She laughed. He took the sack of groceries and followed her to the back where she finally turned, irises in hand, upon the landing stair. "What's this all about, anyway?"

"Nothing. I'm dead serious. Tell me to my face that you actually enjoy being a waitress."

She shook her head.

"Wouldn't you be happier here, doing something you're good at?"

"What, decorating?"

"Writing." Claude passed her and they climbed the stairs in silence and entered the flat.

"You can do it. You should do it," he continued as they went into the tiny cuisine where Marianne immediately dumped a bunch of dried out daisies down the garbage shoot and poured water from the tap into a slender, Venetian glass vase.

"My mother gave me that vase," he said, watching her.

"It's a nice vase."

"Yeah."

"Claude, baby, I like working, I want to work. Le Relais Louis XIII is one of the best restaurants in Paris."

"But you're not the chef, darling, you're a waitress. It's not a career."

"Listen…"

"I mean, what's the point? We don't need extra money…the long hours, I'll miss you terribly at night and I mean…what's it all for? Oh, God…this isn't about Maximilion, is it?"

She began to place the irises, one by one, strategically in the vase. "Maximilion? What does he have to do with it?"

"I don't know. It's as if you want to impress him or something. After all, he's become such a celebrity lately. I've seen his television show."

"He has a T.V. show?" Her feigned ignorance was obvious.

"Fuck, babes, are you in love with him?"

"I'm engaged. Shut up."

"You love me."

"You know I do."

Claude sighed.

"Jesus! What the hell would I write a novel about anyway? I don't know about anything except for books and fine dining."

"You know yourself." Claude looked down onto the black and white tiles of the kitchen floor. "And you know about working for Maximilion. Write about that, about working in a restaurant under a wild and crazy master chef." He threw his arms in the air. "Why, it's brilliant! Hey, something like that would surely sell!"

"You think so?"

"Listen, I'm going to go downstairs and lock the door. Stay here, will you?"

"Where the fuck would I go, big boy? Jump out the window?"

She tried to see a bridge that Wednesday afternoon. She really wanted to, a bridge that could tell her what to do, but all she saw, in the last few moments before climax, was the bouquet of blue irises in the red glass vase for, as he'd turned her around and bent her over the kitchen table, for the first time in their six month history of lovemaking, she spontaneously decided to open her eyes.

XIX

Gozo, Italy

Present

Claude leaned his bicycle against the steps of the porch and walked through the house and out onto the veranda. Marianne was hanging laundered sheets on the line at the far end of the wooden deck. Besides his treasured bougainvillea, he loved that most about living at the Villa Calypso, how their bedsheets persistently carried the deep scent of the sea. She was wearing an angel-sleeved, white linen dress that wafted around her figure as the sheets sailed behind her in a mild breeze. For a moment, he saw her as a beautiful ghost.

"What took you so long? Did you get the wine?" she barked without turning.

"I put it in the refrigerator. You wanted white, right?" He sat at the table where she had set a pitcher of freshly made lemonade. "I stopped by Pagola's villa. We had a chat."

"He's back from Naples? How's his mother?"

"Dead."

She clipped up the last pillowcase. "How tragic. Is he okay?"

"He's fine. The woman was like a hundred and twelve or something."

Marianne turned to face him. "Honestly? Good God! Why on earth would someone want to live so long?"

"I guess that if you don't die when it's time to die, you just go on living." He poured himself a glass of lemonade.

She came to the table and sat diagonally across from him. "Did you go to the post?"

"Babes, c'mon. It's over. You know that. That was the last one."

"But seriously, Clues, is that how it ends…'she opened her eyes'…is that how it ends?"

"Apparently."

"Are you sure?"

"I like it."

"You would, you're French."

"What does that have to do with anything?"

"The French are big on *métaphore*." Marianne sighed and looked out upon the coast below. The beach was empty. Surfing season had been over for weeks. Soon the rains would come and then the short months of winter. That would be nice, she thought, to be inside and make fires at night, and cook wintry meals.

Claude drank some lemonade. "Did you put sugar in this?"

"I never put sugar, you know that." She sat back. "What I don't get, what I can't understand, is how Lautremont found that Diderot postcard."

"Lautremont? Our agent?"

"Sweetheart, wake up. You knew all along, as well as I, that he was the one sending them."

"No, I didn't. I never thought that."

"Come on, what did you think, they we're sent by some mystical muse or something?"

He shook his head. His eyes seemed distant. "I don't know."

"I still can't understand how he found it, or where he found it. I suppose he must have purchased it from whoever bought it from that guy you knew on the Rue Bonaparte. I can't believe I never asked you this, but, how much did you get for it anyway?"

Claude took a deep breath and leaned forward, placing his chin in his hand over the table. "It was so long ago, what does it matter now?"

"I'm curious. Tell me. As you said, it doesn't matter now, but I'm curious."

"I never sold it, Marianne."

"What?"

"That day, after we…well, I did go to the Rue Bonaparte immediately and was offered twenty thousand francs but the eager businessman I was back then thought I might get a higher offer elsewhere. I then went back to the shop and put the postcard in a book in my own collection upstairs, I remember perfectly, I put it in my own French copy of *La Nouvelle Heloise*, planning to try and sell it later. That day, I was so enamored with you, darling, so excited to meet you at your hotel."

"Yeah?"

"Yeah! And the following weeks, all I could think of was coming to London to see you. Which I then did, and again, and again."

"So you never tried to sell the postcard?"

He half-laughed. "See, this is the weird thing. So, during those next few months as we were falling in love, what with all the trips between Paris and London and my bourgeoning success in the book business...I somehow forgot about it. But then, and this is the weirder thing, upon deciding to propose to you, I remembered it, as well as that it was worth a small fortune. I remember the day exactly! It was the morning before I was to take an evening train to the ferry to cross the channel to get down on my knees. I was stoked, babes! I went into my private library, pulled *La Nouvelle Heloise* off the shelf and opened it only to discover to my horror that it wasn't there. I searched my desk, other books, everywhere, frantically all afternoon. I remember the sky growing charcoal colored, I had to pack quickly and make it to the station. I told myself it had to be somewhere and that it was obviously not stolen, and didn't disappear on its own. Whatever, I forgot about it again. You said 'yes' and came to Paris."

"And you never found it?"

"I never saw it since that first day I put it in the Rousseau."

"Hmm."

Claude continued, "I did look for it a few more times though. Before our wedding and again, when you were pregnant with Esmond and luckily, the Chinese people moved out of the third floor apartment and we were able to take it over and combine the two stories to make room for our family. You brought your books from London and remember...? We created a whole new library. I looked for it then. That was the last time. Then, of course, came Etienne and we were so busy and life was so beautiful and ultimately, when my cousin died and I inherited the painting...well, I just didn't give a fuck about that postcard anymore."

They both looked out at the horizon. It wasn't going to be another spectacular sunset yet there were a few weak streaks of gold and cranberry spindling out of the dark part of the sea.

"What's for dinner?" he asked.

"Sole *meuniere* with peas and rice pilaf."

"It doesn't make sense."

"What? It's a classic."

"No, the Diderot card. Where the fuck did it come from?"

"I thought it was Lautremont, but now…"

"No. How would he even know about it? I never told anyone but you. Unless you told him."

"I didn't."

"God, what a mystery!"

"Whatever. It's over."

"Are you sad?" he asked.

"Melancholy."

"Me, too."

They sat in silence. Twilight.

"Clues?"

"Yeah?"

"You didn't put the Diderot card in *Le Nouvelle Heloise*."

"Yes, I did."

"No, you didn't."

"Of course I did! I remember perfectly."

"You remember incorrectly."

"What are you talking about?"

"You beautiful old fool, you romantic old son of a bitch, I love you!"

"Marianne, what the fuck…"

"That day, after the Rue Bonaparte, obviously, thinking of me, you put the postcard in your own copy of the same edition of Rilke poems that I had taken from the shop the day before. We've always kept two exact copies of the same book, except the binding on yours isn't as tight as mine."

"Now there's something that makes sense, but…"

She sighed. "I found it when we first moved here and our books arrived."

"The Diderot card?"

She nodded. "In your Rilke, where you first hid it thirty years ago, dreaming of me."

He rubbed the bridge of his nose. "My God! You're right. I did put it there. You're right. But then…so you…?"

"When I found it I knew I wanted to write a book about us, about falling in love but it wasn't enough. Then I thought about all the other times we've fallen in love in history, you know, all those bedtime stories we used to tell each other and so I...well, the whole postcard thing came to me."

Claude sat back. One star, Venus, rose in the sky. Then he laughed and laughed and finally stood.

"Where are you going?"

"To get the wine."

When he came back to the table they drank for a moment in silence then Marianne said, "So, what are we going to do...now that it's over?"

"To begin with, plant tomatoes, I suppose."

And she smiled the smile.

Elizabeth McKague

About the Author

Elizabeth McKague is a college professor and the author of six further novels, twelve chapbooks of poetry and one screenplay. As a single parent, she worked hard to provide a loving and artistic home for her son and daughter who, adults now, are beautiful and incredibly talented musicians. She collects fine and rare books, has traveled often to Paris and permanently resides in San Francisco.

Visit her author's website at http://www.lizmckague.com/

Elizabeth McKague

Navel of the Sea

Chimney Bluffs by David B. Seaburn
The Loons by Sue Dolleris
Light Surfer by David Allan Williams
The Judas List by A. G. Hayes
Path of the Templar—Book 2 of The Jumper Chronicles by W. C. Peever
The Desperate Cycle by Tony Tame
Shutterbug by Buz Sawyer
Blessed are the Peacekeepers by Tom Donnelly and Mike Munger
The Bellwether Messages edited by D. S. Janik
The Turtle Dances by Daniel S. Janik
The Lazarus Conspiracies by Richard Rose
Purple Haze by George B. Hudson
Imminent Danger by A. G. Hayes
Lullaby Moon (CD) by Malia Elliott of Leon & Malia
Volutions edited by Suzanne Langford
In the Eyes of the Son by Hans Brinckmann
The Hanging of Dr. Hanson by Bentley Gates
Flight of Destiny by Francis Powell
Elaine of Corbenic by Tima Z. Newman
Ballerina Birdies by Marina Yamamoto
More More Time by David B. Seabird
Crazy Like Me by Erin Lee
Cleopatra Unconquered by Helen R. Davis
Valedictory by Daniel Scott
The Chemical Factor by A. G. Hayes
Quantum Death by A. G. Hayes and Raymond Gaynor
Big Heaven by Charlotte Hebert
Captain Riddle's Treasure by GV Rama Rao
All Things Await by Seth Clabough
Tsunami Libido by Cate Burns
Finding Kate by A. G. Hayes
The Adventures of Purple Head, Buddha Monkey and Sticky Feet by Erik and Forest Bracht
In the Shadows of My Mind by Andrew Massie
The Gumshoe by Richard Rose
In Search of Somatic Therapy by Setsuko Tsuchiya
Cereus by Z. Roux
The Solar Triangle by A. G. Hayes
Shadow and Light edited by Helen R. Davis
A Real Daughter by Lynne McKelvey
StoryTeller by Nicholas Bylotas
Bo Henry at Three Forks by Daniel Bradford
One Night in Bangkok by Keith Rees
Kindred edited by Doc Krinberg
Cleopatra Victorious by Helen R. Davis

Coming Soon:
Talking Story: Storytelling Meets Phenomenology by Jamie Dela Cruz
68 Via Condotti: Book One - Eternity Ltd. by A. G. Hayes

Elizabeth McKague

Navel of the Sea